A FANTASY ADVENTURE
IN THE DAYS OF NOAH

SON
OF THE
DOOMSDAY
PROPHET

STEVEN J. BYERS

This is a work of fiction. Any resemblance to actual persons, living or dead, events, or locales is entirely coincidental.

All rights reserved. No part of this book may be reproduced in any form or by any electronic or mechanical means, including information storage and retrieval systems, without permission in writing from the publisher and copyright holder, except in the case of brief quotations in critical articles and reviews.

Independently published by Steven J. Byers.
www.StevenJByers.com
Copyright © 2023 Steven J. Byers.

Editing & Proofreading by Alyssa Cederman.

Cover Design by Jeff Brown.

Interior Design by Lorna Reid.

Map by Nathan Hansen.

Marketing Consultation by Rodney Hatfield.

ISBN: 979-8-9885457-1-2
eISBN: 979-8-9885457-0-5

THE ANCIENT WORLD BEFORE THE FLOOD

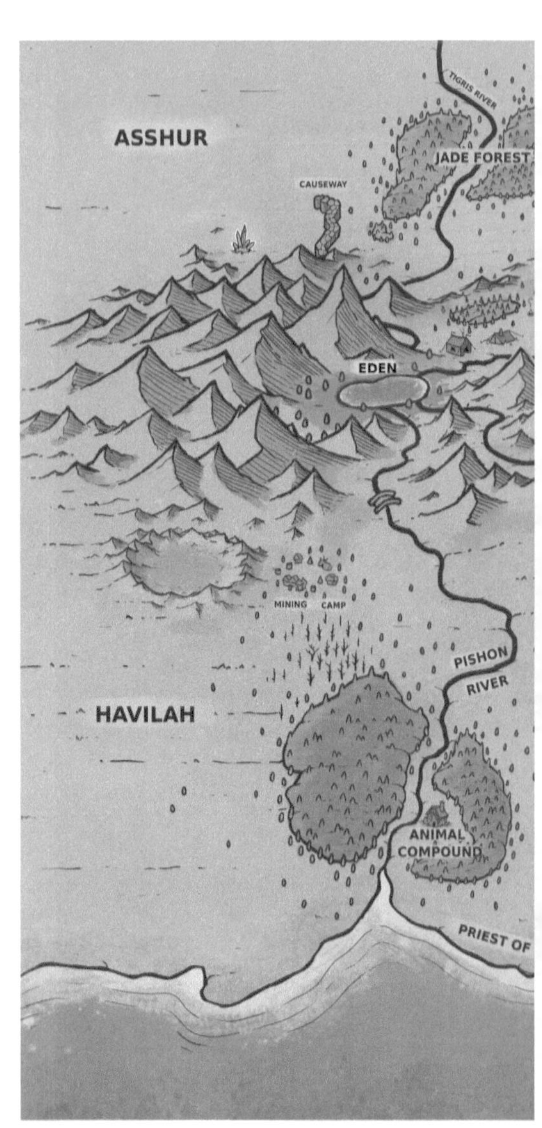

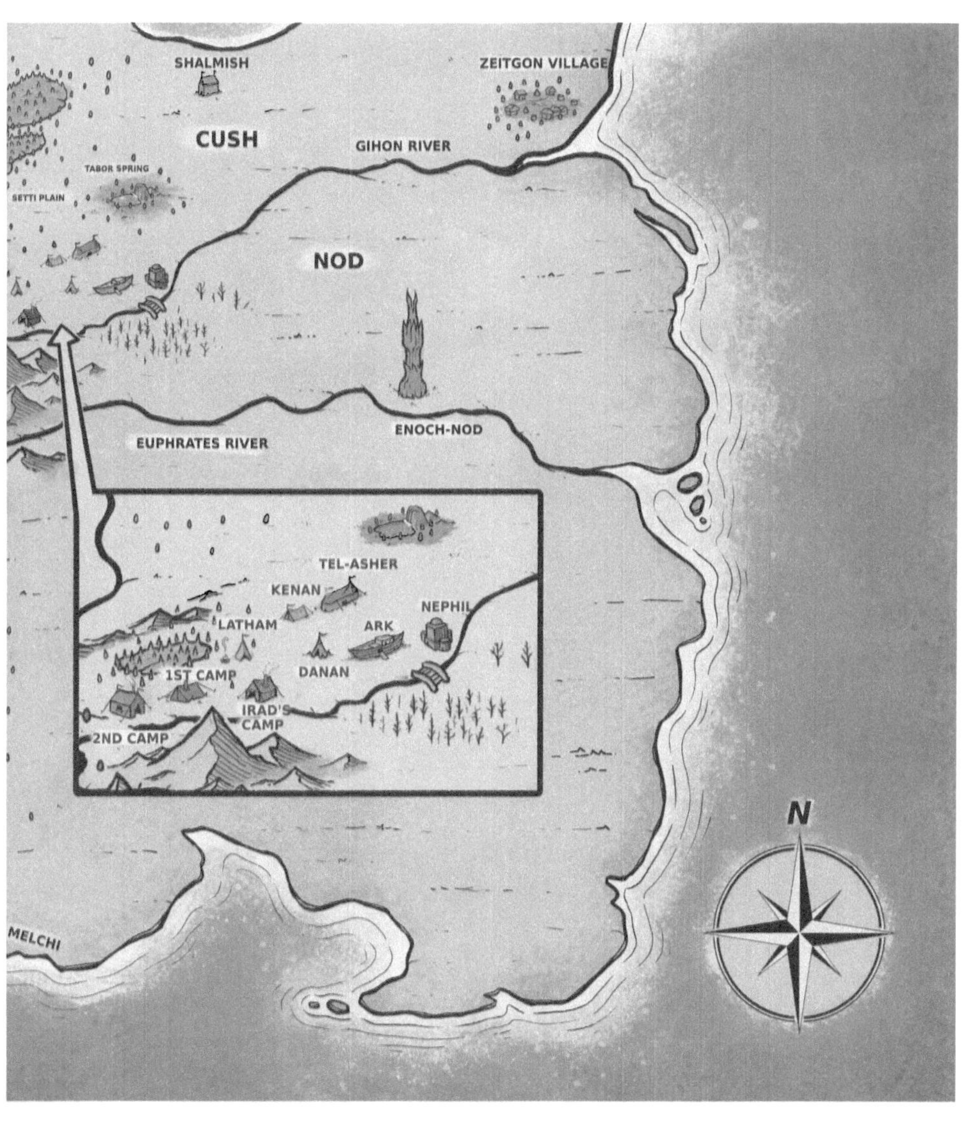

SHALMISH
ZEITGON VILLAGE
CUSH
GIHON RIVER
TABOR SPRING
SETTI PLAIN
NOD
EUPHRATES RIVER
ENOCH-NOD
TEL-ASHER
KENAN
NEPHIL
LATHAM
ARK
DANAN
1ST CAMP
IRAD'S CAMP
2ND CAMP
MELCHI
N

PART I:
THE PROPHECY OF DOOM

PROLOGUE

I, Jayfeth, was born in the five hundredth year of my father Noah, the prophet of the ancient world's doom. Sadly, all of his warnings went unheeded and those who did not listen paid with their lives. Only the few who sought refuge in the ark survived the cataclysm. Now, a new generation has arisen that does not remember the tragic lessons of the Flood, dismissing everything that happened as a myth. They forget the past at their peril.

Of the wisdom which came down to us from the elder days, all that remains are the writings of my brother Shem. But Shem, like our father, possessed the vision of a prophet, recording the revelations he received directly from God. Because I am not a prophet, I set forth my hand to write an account of the events I witnessed in those days so the history will not fade into legend. Because I am now the sole survivor of the ancient world, I alone know what was lost.

ONE

L ooking up, Father leaned his axe against the tree he was felling and said, "What brings you all the way up here, Brother?"

"I heard a report and decided to investigate it for myself," said Irad as he stepped into the clearing.

"I suspected it wasn't a social visit," said Father, wiping the sweat from his brow. "But first, rest yourself for a bit. You must be weary after a long journey. Jayfeth, fetch a cup of water from the spring for your uncle while I get the bread and cheese."

Irad was taller than Father and lean—built more like my Grandfather Lamech. While Irad ate, Father told him news of the nearby families. He also instructed me to go home and inform Mother that we would have a guest that evening, probably as much to spare me from what followed as it was for the sake of the preparations. But I was anxious to hear what Uncle Irad had to say, so I lingered behind a brush pile to eavesdrop. Their sharp disagreement is one of my earliest memories.

When Irad had finished eating and drinking, he pointed to the lumber with a sweep of his hand and said, "Now tell me about this."

"Ah, I knew you'd get around to that," said Father. "The Lord has commanded me to build a great project."

"What is it?"

"An ark."

Irad pondered this for a moment. "You mean a boat? Some of our young men hollow out trees to make canoes and float them in the Gihon for sport. But you have felled enough trees for our entire clan."

"No, Brother. This is not for many canoes, but for one large boat."

"Only one!"

"And this is only a small part of that which is needed."

"You must be joking," said Irad, bristling. "A gigantic boat a mile from the river?"

"I am not joking," said Father. "This is what the Lord told me to do."

"And why, pray tell, did he say to do this?"

"To be a witness to the people that an awful disaster is coming," said Father.

"Disaster?" said Irad. "Why do you say such things? The Creator would never allow it."

"You were there when the Ancient One spoke the prophecy."

"He is an old man in his dotage. No one took him seriously—except for you."

"I know it's hard to believe," said Father. "But God says something terrible is going to happen. And you can't deny that evil is growing in the world."

"Among the Cainites, perhaps," said Irad. "Why don't you build this thing in Nod where it might do some good? Building it among your own tribe will make us a laughingstock."

"That's what this is really all about, isn't it?"

"Is the disgrace of our family a trivial matter? It's bad enough to have one brother who is accursed without the other one being thought a fool."

"Gomer is *not* accursed," Father countered.

"That's your opinion," said Irad. "But bad luck has followed him since the day he was born."

"I don't care what other people think—"

"No, you don't—and that's the problem," said Irad. "But I do care. Our clan used to be the most respected of the entire Sethite tribe. And now look at us."

"You worry too much about your prestige," said Father.

"I will not sit here and be insulted," said Irad, rising to leave. "You used to be a sensible man. I do not know what has happened to make you such a fool. The clan will not be pleased with my report. For your sake, I hope you come to your senses soon before you end up being shunned by the whole tribe."

Father shook his head as Irad strode away in a huff. Then I remembered what he had instructed me to do and started to sneak off.

"Jayfeth," he called. "Come here."

"How did you know I was still here?" I said, expecting a scolding.

His answer, though, was gentle—maybe even a bit sad. "I may be a fool, but I am not yet so dull as to believe a pile of brush could make that much noise by itself. At least we didn't get your mother all in a state preparing a meal for a guest who wasn't staying."

Curious about their conversation, I asked, "Papa, what is a prophecy?"

"It's a message from God," Father began. "A long time ago, the Lord told your great-great grandfather Enoch to name his newborn son Methuselah. It was a strange name, but Enoch obeyed even though he didn't understand. Centuries passed and still no one knew the meaning. Then, not many years ago, when the tribe was gathered at Tel-Asher for the high festival, the mystery was revealed. The time for speeches came and each of the elders spoke in turn. Being eldest among them, Methuselah spoke last. When he rose, the Spirit of God came upon him and he prophesied:

'I am grieved that humankind is turning away from me. Before the evil that is rising in the land reaches its full measure, a day of disaster has been appointed. You are Methuselah, which means When Your Time Comes, It Will Come.'"

"I don't understand," I said.

"Neither did most of the people at the time," said Father. "Or maybe I should say they didn't want to understand. There was much arguing over it. But it's clear to me that your great-grandfather's name is a prophecy—one that is bound up with his very life. If the evil foretold goes unchecked in the lifetime of the Ancient One, the earth will be destroyed."

Father must have seen a look of alarm on my face because he added, "This is why I haven't told you before because I didn't want to frighten you. But that day is still a long time from now—if nothing alters the course of future events. I have hope that this great ark the Lord has instructed me to build will be a witness to the people that they need to turn away from evil. Then perhaps the doom can be averted."

I pondered this for a few moments, but I also had another question on my mind. I asked, "Who are the Cainites that Uncle Irad spoke of?"

"They are descendants of Cain," said Father. "Long ago, he killed his brother Abel and was exiled from this land, while the Sethites remained here in Cush. The breech between our peoples is nearly as old as the world itself, occurring generations before even the Ancient One was born. Ever since then, we have lived such separate lives that the Cainites have practically passed into legend."

Little did I know at the time that the Cainites were about to step out of the legend and upend our lives.

TWO

ot long afterward, my mother Mara gave birth to my brother
Shem. She was a warmhearted soul and as devoted a wife and
mother as there ever was. The years had been kind to her face,
though I have little doubt that she had fretted much over not being able to
give my father children for so many years. And when at last she did, it was
little wonder that she doted on us who were born to her in her old age.

Many of our clan came to celebrate Shem's birth in the following weeks.
We were unaccustomed to so many visitors, even though the clans and
families were not widely dispersed in those days. You could not go more than
a mile or two down the Gihon River without encountering another family
or village, and there were regular comings and goings between the camps in
my early childhood. On festival days, our gathering numbered in the
thousands.

Not all the Sethites lived near the river; the greater number lived on the
Setti Plain where springs and streams abounded. Of all the families, though,
we lived farthest upstream toward the headwaters, which put us at the
westernmost edge of the Sethite territories. As a consequence, I began my life
more isolated than most children before my brothers were born. So I spent
much time with the creatures of the forest and meadow to such an extent
that I could understand and make myself understood with many different
kinds. I did not comprehend at the time that communicating with animals
was in any way unusual because it seemed perfectly natural to me. Lest you
think more highly of me than you ought, I should note that the creatures of
that age seemed more highly sentient than they afterward became. I was
unaware of any special gift I possessed and, as far as I know, it was merely a
matter of devoting the time and effort. I was surprised as I grew older that it
wasn't more widely practiced.

While our relatives carefully avoided the uncomfortable subject of the ark, they were abuzz with rumors about strange visitors from the lands beyond the Gihon. It was even said that there were hunters among them, which I found disturbing because of my love for animals. We never ate meat.

These fragments of stories I heard about Cainite sightings fired my imagination and kindled all sorts of wild thoughts about what they might be like. Father, of course, took a far more serious view of these reports. He suspected that the return of the Cainites to the Gihon Valley at that time was no coincidence, but rather must be directly connected to his revelation.

I had not given much thought to what would happen after Shem was born and was surprised by the changes. The biggest, of course, was that I did not receive nearly as much attention from my parents as before. I was also confined to camp for several weeks to help Mother and it seemed a very great hardship to be doing what I considered women's work. I am ashamed to report that I felt very resentful about it all.

When I was not helping Mother, I spent much time with my animal friends, especially our little burro Naysa. He was my first friend among the many animal companions I loved. Back then, we had no need of large herds—a few sheep and goats for milk and wool; a yoke of oxen for labor; and Naysa for a light pack animal.

I often wandered down to the riverside, the most interesting place within hearing of the camp. From its source in the Eden Plateau, the Gihon ran swiftly past our home and eventually to the Great Sea. Sometimes, I would drop leaves and sticks into the water and watch them float downstream. I imagined them drifting down through the land of Cush all the way to the Cainite territory and being discovered by some savage there.

The reason that nobody lived farther upstream was that no one dared to go closer to the forbidden land—the Garden from which the Father and Mother of All had been banished. It was said that an otherworldly being who wielded a flaming sword guarded it and that any who passed too close would be struck down.

The only time anyone ventured farther upstream than our home was for the annual sacrifice. Once a year on the prescribed day, the elders of each clan would make a pilgrimage to a hilltop only a few miles from where the Gate to the Garden was said to be. The somber procession would traverse in silence to the top of a bald hill and sacrifice a lamb on the altar constructed there.

When I was old enough to understand this, I was appalled at the taking of the lamb's life. I protested with an indignation that I later came to learn was not uncommon in my extended family since we ended up being the object of much of it. Father patiently explained that the sacrifice was required to atone for the sins of men.

"Why not kill the man for his own sins!" I raged.

Father looked behind him at the growing pile of lumber for the ark and then back at me. "You'd better have a care about what you say," he admonished. "Some day your own words could come back to haunt you."

The days of confinement were soon ended, but I began to sense a special bond forming between Father and Shem. Since I was the firstborn, that the birthright was mine was never in question. But there was a blessing of another kind that passed from Father to Shem that I did not understand—except for the feeling that I was left out of it.

When Shem was old enough to begin toddling around the camp, I took it upon myself to introduce him to all my animal friends. Though he showed interest at first, he did not share the same empathy for them that I did—to my great disappointment. Whenever I was not specifically calling his attention to them, his thoughts quickly returned to his first love which was learning. In those days, not many written records existed because people lived long enough to personally experience everything they might need to know. Since writing was so easily lost or destroyed, important matters were committed to memory for safekeeping and were not quickly forgotten as they are now. Often the stories of our people were put into song or verse as an aid to remembering. Those like my father who were exceptionally skilled were highly esteemed.

A notable exception to this was a written account passed down to Father from his father Lamech and so on all the way back to the Father of All. It was the account of the Creation and the Curse, with each successive generation adding its own new part to the story. The fact that our family was the keeper of this record had always been considered a very great honor among our people—at least until other matters brought us into disrepute. This record was related to the blessing that passed by me to my brother. And I would be less than honest if I didn't admit that I resented being left out.

The futility of my jealousy should have been evident, however, because this was a pursuit for which Shem was perfectly suited. He learned to read and write almost before I did. And whenever the elders would gather, he would sit at their feet for hours and listen as they recounted the sayings of God and his dealings with men, committing it all to memory. His devotion was remarkable, even at the tenderest of ages.

Following the annual sacrifice that year, all the families of our tribe gathered to celebrate the largest festival of the year at Tel-Asher, the place where it is said that the Father and Mother of All settled after they left Eden. I had always remembered Father being accorded a place of high honor in the assembly, but it was obvious that the attitude of the people toward him was no longer what it used to be. Several men took Father aside and spoke with him privately. I could not hear them, but it was not hard to guess what they were saying.

On the high festival day, the elders among our people would always select some of the best men to speak, sing or tell stories while many thousands sat and listened on the hillside. To be chosen was a mark of distinction in the tribe—one which Father had received for many years, for he was an eloquent speaker. That year, though, he was overlooked for the first time in memory. I considered it an insult to our family. But if it bothered him, he did not show it.

I fared even worse at the festival. Although I had looked forward eagerly to playing with my many cousins, they wanted nothing to do with me. My favorite among them, Uncle Irad's son Fehud, hardly spoke to me. I was sitting alone and forlorn among the tents when my uncle Gomer approached and said, "It can't be that bad."

"What can't be that bad?" I asked.

"Whatever it is that's troubling you," he said.

"None of the other children will play with me," I said.

"That is a shame indeed. And a misfortune with which I myself am not unacquainted."

The general sentiment in our clan was that Gomer was cursed because my grandmother had died while giving birth to him. Death was a rare occurrence in those days and considered a bad omen. His brother Irad had never forgiven him for it. Although to my young eyes Gomer had long crossed that gulf that separates boys from men, he was far closer to my generation than my father's. But I was too childish and preoccupied with my own problems to offer him much sympathy for his plight. However, his understanding established a kind of kinship of misfits between us—a resonance of emotions out of all proportion, it seemed, to our actual interaction, which was infrequent.

"So what do you do?" I asked.

"I meet it head on, of course," said Gomer. "Don't wait for them to come to you. Take the initiative."

"Do you think that will work?"

"There's only one way to find out. Anyway, even if it doesn't, it's better than just sitting around the tents feeling sorry for yourself." He slapped me amiably on the back and said, "Now I'm off to see if I have been selected to speak this year."

I wished him good luck, although even then, I knew he had no chance. He'd never had any standing in the tribe since the day he was born—and never would. His advice, however, persuaded me to act, though my wounded pride didn't need much coaxing to provoke a confrontation. I soon found Fehud and said, "What's wrong with you? You act like you don't even know me."

To my surprise, Fehud agreed with me. "You're right. But I'll make it up to you. Do you remember the spring we found last year? We'll go see it again—just the two of us. I'll tell the others I'm leaving."

Fehud conferred with the other children for a few moments and then rejoined me. As we took off over the rise north of the camp and left the tents behind, I was in high spirits. The spring was about three miles from Tel-Asher across the gently rolling grassland and hidden among willow trees— the kind of secret and separate place that boys delight in. The willows that ringed the spring formed a canopy of green overhead—a pleasant contrast to the sky that was always bluest blue.

Spying a lone cougar resting near the water's edge, I told Fehud to watch and see if I could crawl close enough to touch him without being noticed. When I was only a few feet from the cougar, his ears perked up. I lay as still as I could and held my breath. When the cougar settled again, I exhaled slowly and closed the gap. Reaching out my hand, I touched him lightly on the side. With a sort of detached curiosity, he turned his head and looked at me sprawled out beside him. I plucked a foxtail and tickled his twitching ear. He yawned lazily and stretched. I turned and called to Fehud, "I doubt if you could creep up on a cougar like that!" Hearing no answer, I turned to look. But Fehud was not there. I yelled louder, "Fehud?"

The cougar, seeing that he would get no more rest while I was around, got up and sauntered off. Perplexed, I made my way back to the place I had last seen Fehud. Suddenly, Fehud jumped out from behind a bush and wrestled me to the ground. Older and bigger, with the advantage of surprise, he had no difficulty overpowering me. With my face pinned to the ground, I heard the laughter of other children. Fehud had only been pretending to be my friend and had been conspiring with the others all along.

"So you think you're clever, sneaking up on a dumb animal," said Fehud. "That's the problem with your family—you think you're better than everyone else. Well, I sneaked up on you, so who's the cleverer?"

"Let me up," I said weakly.

"Now he wants to tell us what to do," said Fehud. "Well, see here. We're not going to do what you say. Did you bring the rope like I told you, boys?"

My hands were soon tied behind my back and my feet as well. Then Fehud said, "Let's see if he's clever enough to get out of that!"

Laughing and carrying on, they left me there, three miles from camp with no hope of being found anytime soon. Greatly humiliated, I lay there with my face in the grass and started to cry.

A few moments later, I heard a little girl say, "Don't cry, boy."

"My name is Jayfeth."

"Don't cry, Jayfeth."

"Who are you?" I asked, for I could not see her and I did not recognize her voice.

"Re-Aylah."

"Go away!" I said, because that was Fehud's baby sister and I had no desire to be made further sport of by her family.

"I'm here to help you," she said.

"I don't need your help."

"Then how are you going to get free of those ropes?"

There was nothing to be gained by being intransigent in the light of such an indisputable point. I muttered, "I suppose you could untie them."

"Yes, but first you have to promise not to tell my brothers that I let you go."

"I promise."

"You must also promise not to tell the adults, so my brothers will not get in trouble."

That demand was harder to concede because I was consoling myself with the thought of Fehud being punished severely. But I was hardly in a position to argue, so I reluctantly said, "Agreed."

"You must act as if this never happened," said Re-Aylah.

"All right, all right," I said. "Just set me loose."

As little Re-Aylah bent down over me, I looked up to see her golden hair against the willows and saw that she was exceedingly fair of face. She wrinkled her nose and said, "Don't look at me!"

I turned my head the other direction while she worked. She was not that much older than Shem and I feared that Fehud's knot-tying might be too much for her. But her fingers proved remarkably nimble for her age and soon I felt the rope loosen. I was free.

I sat up and rubbed my wrists. "I can untie my feet myself," I said.

"You're looking at me again," she said.

"Sorry," I said and began freeing my legs.

"Wait until I'm out of sight before you start back."

I was so humiliated that I didn't even thank her.

THREE

Mother was expecting again, and not long after the festival at Tel-Asher that year, she gave birth to Ham. The shock of a second brother was not nearly as great as the first. Even though he became the center of attention for awhile, I was better prepared for it. *At least it wasn't a girl,* I thought, and I held out hope that he would be a good playmate, since our kinsmen were no longer having much to do with us. In this, I was not disappointed because, unlike Shem, Ham proved to be quite a willing accomplice to all the mischief I could think of and soon came to be very resourceful in dreaming up his own.

When Ham was four, we heard a rumor that Cainites were in the area. Seeing one sounded like a great adventure, so Ham and I stole away secretly one Sabbath after our morning devotions and headed for Latham. The village was located some seven miles away through a pass in the hills that led to the edge of the Setti Plain, so we had to run all the way to make it in good time.

We reached Latham shortly after midday and were stunned by our first glimpse of the strange people who were there. They were extremely tall—the shortest at least a foot taller than the tallest among our kinsmen. Some were more than eight feet in height. The men wore headdresses and richly ornamented robes belted at the waist. The cloth was of a kind I had not seen before. Shiny thread that dazzled the eye was skillfully woven into the fabric. (I later learned that the thread was spun gold!) Bolts of this cloth were spread out in the market, causing quite a stir among the people.

So, these were the murderous Cainites, I thought. But they did not look like the savages I imagined. I wanted to get a closer look, but saw several familiar faces from our clan congregated near the main entrance to the market. Since I was anxious to avoid being recognized, I led Ham behind the Tent of Meeting and between the living tents, with the intent of coming in the back way undetected and blending with the crowd. This was working as planned until, as we passed one of the tents, we were recognized by Baldag, a cousin of my Mother, who happened to be coming out of one at just the wrong moment. Startled to see us, he asked gruffly, "Where is your mother?"

Ham, who was always quick-witted at such moments, called back over his shoulder, "She is well!" and kept going. I did not, at the time, regard this deliberate misunderstanding and evasion a lie. In fact, I was so busy congratulating Ham on his cleverness that I didn't think to question what Baldag was doing in someones else's tent at that time of day.

We inched up as close as we could to the Cainites in the marketplace without being obvious. A bronze-skinned man who seemed to be their chieftan, was saying, "No, my friends, we are not here today to sell these goods to you. We give them to you as gifts. Our peoples have been estranged for too long. It is time we had better relations."

This met with general approval among those who were gathered around. Keriath, chief elder of Latham, replied, "What you are saying is good, Ben-Tubal. We are honored by your gifts and agree that our peoples should be reunited. Moreover, I appoint Baldag as our emissary, since he was the one who first made your intentions known to us. Where is Baldag?"

"Here I am," said Baldag, who had just joined the gathering. Ham and I shrank back further into the crowd to avoid his gaze. "If it pleases Keriath, I will do all that you say. I will show them our land and introduce them to our people. Then I will return with them to Nephil for a time and learn their ways."

At Keriath's right hand, a young, handsome man nodded to the chief in approval. I noted that he wore the emblems of the next chief.

"Excellent," said Ben-Tubal. "Now, we should be off at once, for this land is wide and my people are not expecting me to be gone many weeks."

Ham and I started to back away, when I spotted Shaalah, another of my mother's cousins, coming straight for us. Just in time, we ducked behind several large water urns. To our dismay, though, she stopped right in front of us and spoke to another woman standing nearby. "Did you see that cloth, Faldimah?"

"What I wouldn't give for a bolt of that!" said Faldimah.

"And did you ever see such handsome men?" said Shaalah.

"You think all men are handsome," said a third woman joining the conversation.

"Can't say I think it of my husband anymore, Milcah," said Shaalah in a mock whisper, which brought cackles all around.

"Speaking of handsome men, too bad that Baldag is going away," said Faldimah. "He's the most eligible man in Latham."

"It might be just as well," said Shaalah. "I've been hearing things."

"I know what you're thinking," said Milcah. "But she is Keriath's daughter."

"And Giblith's wife," said Faldimah.

Then there was a fourth woman, who said, "You don't mean Minnah!"

"Shhh, Amraitha," said Shaalah. "Here she comes now."

I didn't really understand what they were talking about, but between the urns, I could see the person who was apparently the object of the discussion approaching. She was much younger and thinner than her matronly detractors, with hair the color of chestnuts and a face that could hardly help but inspire either adoration or jealousy. Although the chattering ceased, the silence that followed was as convicting as the accusations. It could not have been hard for Minnah to guess that they were talking about her.

I made a face and motioned to Ham to get down, but Minnah saw us anyway and I thought we were certain to get in trouble. But all she did was wink at us—a wink that was forever to alter my feelings toward her.

Realizing that the silence was too obvious, the women had begun prattling about some other topic as Minnah filled her water pot. But the moment she was out of earshot—if indeed she really was—they resumed their gossip with renewed fervor.

"She wouldn't even look us in the eye," said Shaalah.

"She's guilty, I say," said Faldimah.

"I don't believe it—of either of them," said Amraithah.

"You should see the way he looks at her," said Faldimah.

"I've heard Baldag holds a grudge against Keriath for picking Giblith over him to be the next chief," said Shaalah.

"So you've concocted this sordid tale?" said Amraithah. "Really, girls, you ought to be ashamed of yourselves. I'll hear no more of it."

I wished Shaalah had been the one to leave because the other women wouldn't have recognized me so easily and we might have slipped away right then. But the way Shaalah's tongue wagged, Mother was sure to hear of it if she saw me. So we held our ground and waited her out, though the conversation seemed unending. All we could do was wait and eat the loaves we had each tucked into the pockets of our tunics.

When, at last, the women moved on, Ham and I slipped out from behind the pots. It was well past the time that we needed to leave in order to make it back before dark, so we didn't have to tell each other that we needed to make haste. As soon as we were outside the camp, we broke into a hard run for home.

Not quite an hour later, we reached the top of a hill overlooking a narrow, wooded valley at the edge of the hill country. From that vantage point, I saw that we might be able to save some time and distance to the Latham Pass by cutting through the woods rather than going around by the road which skirted its furthest edge. Ham, like Father, was built for strength rather than speed and was tiring quickly. Since the shortcut seemed like our best chance to make it home without being late, I decided to try it.

The way was easy at first because the trees were sparse and we were generally moving downhill. However, I had not taken into consideration that the denser parts near the middle would slow our progress. We were soon picking through tangles and leaping streamlets, but we pushed on as fast as we could even when we could see only a few feet in front of us.

When we reached the main stream in the valley, I said, "Follow me," dashing across on stones that were just barely covered by the shallow water. But the mossy rocks were slippery under my bare feet. I lost my footing and fell in full length.

Ham howled with laughter and said, "If it's all the same to you, Jay, I'll find my own way across."

I picked myself up and tried to look as dignified as a soaking wet boy can look, ignoring the painful scrape on my ankle. "Come on," I said. "We're wasting time."

The way was mostly uphill after that and even more rugged. My shortcut had proved not to be so short after all. We were so intent on avoiding obstacles and making up time that we reached the road at the far edge of the woods before we even realized it. We topped a rise and suddenly found ourselves on top of the band of Cainites!

"Well, what have we here?" said Ben-Tubal. Standing right in front of him, I observed that he seemed even larger than I had first thought. I was too terrified to speak and even Ham was at a rare loss for words. Among them, we noticed a boy who looked to be about my age, although already much taller. He eyed me curiously, for I was still dripping wet, and said, "What a strange custom you Sethites have. We remove our clothes before we wash them."

Ben-Tubal and all his men laughed at the jest and even Ham snickered.

"We see there is much to learn about these people, Merib," said Ben-Tubal. "But they must find our ways just as strange."

"Hold on there," said a voice I recognized. "I know these boys." It was Baldag, but I didn't know whether to be relieved at that prospect or even more frightened. "These are the sons of my cousin. What do you think you're doing sneaking around without your parents?"

"What Baldag means to say," said Ben-Tubal, "is that we are concerned for your safety. We have heard reports of wild beasts attacking young children."

"Not in these parts," I said, remembering that there were said to be hunters among them and finally finding my tongue. "Maybe the creatures in *your* land attack people. Or maybe they're only defending themselves."

"I see," said Ben-Tubal. "So you can talk. Perhaps you can teach us about the animals of your land since you seem so well informed. We want to find out all we can about Cush."

"We would surely like to teach you, sir," Ham chimed in. "But we haven't the time now. Papa will be expecting us soon."

"How about if we escort you home?" said the boy Merib.

"Thank you," said Ham. "But that won't be necessary. We know the way from here and I am sure that such distinguished visitors as yourselves must have far more important matters requiring your attention."

"Yes," I said. "We really should be going."

"Our path lies in a different direction, Ben-Tubal," said Baldag. "His family lives on the upper reaches of the Gihon and we will soon be turning northward. Our time will be more profitably spent visiting the people of the plains."

"As you say, Baldag," said Ben-Tubal. "Farewell, young masters. Perhaps our paths will cross again."

"And don't worry," Baldag called after us. "Your secret is safe with me."

Somehow, I found little comfort in those words. And I came away from the encounter with two distinct impressions—that I liked the Cainites more than I had expected and that I distrusted my kinsman more than I had ever thought possible.

We made slower time after that because Ham couldn't hold much of a pace. We walked the last couple of miles as I was beginning to tire myself, though I told Ham that it was to cool down and catch our breaths so we would not look as if we had just made a long journey. Exhausted and more or less dry by then, we arrived home just as the sun was setting. I kept my injured ankle hidden to avoid awkward questions, but they never came. If Father suspected anything, he did not let on. As I lay down to sleep that night, I congratulated myself that we had gotten away with it.

The news that the Cainites were in our land had a disquieting effect on Father and he decided to seek out their delegation himself. Ham and I argued about whether we should ask to go with him. Ham wanted to go, but I was concerned that our previous escapade would surely be made known as a result. Over my objections, Ham begged Father to allow us to go with him, and to my dismay, he agreed.

Father's spirits brightened as we walked along the open road, which was good to see. He was an outgoing man and prone to brood when isolated for long periods of time. The trail of the Cainites was not difficult to trace because the whole land was buzzing with tales of the strange visitors. We caught up to them at the village of Kenan. Five weeks had elapsed since I had last seen them. In that time, they had cut a wide circle through the southern plain and now were on the last leg of their journey before heading back toward their home.

Ben-Tubal and his men greeted Father cordially. Ham and I held back as much as we could without being obvious, but I could tell that Ben-Tubal remembered us. To our great relief, however, he did not betray our previous acquaintance. And I was excited to see that the boy Merib still traveled with them as I was quite fascinated at the possibility of getting to know him.

"Esteemed Ben-Tubal," said Father. "You have traveled widely in our land and have distinguished yourself as an ambassador—an excellent beginning in healing the estrangement of our peoples. I see that one of my kinsmen even travels with you. Greetings, Baldag."

"What brings you down out of the hills?" asked Baldag, noticeably skipping the customary greeting.

"I would speak a word with Ben-Tubal, if he would," said Father.

"We're really in quite a hurry," said Baldag. "Ben-Tubal has important business to attend to and then is anxious to return to his people."

"I'm sure I can spare a few minutes, Baldag, and doubly so now that I know he is your kinsman."

"You might not want to hear what he has to say," muttered Baldag.

Ben-Tubal did not hear that remark or pretended not to. He said, "You have me at a disadvantage, friend. You know my name, but I do not know yours."

"Forgive me, sir," Father said. "I am Noah, son of Lamech. And these are my sons: Jayfeth, Shem and Ham."

Ben-Tubal's eyes widened, "I have heard your name and I am glad you have sought me out. I have desired to meet you, for you have the reputation of being a great prophet. Come, the elders of Kenan have offered me the use of their Tent of Meeting. We may talk there. And these sons of yours, have them come in, too. They look like fine lads." He winked at me as he said it.

Being invited to the Tent of Meeting was an honor for my brothers and me, because children were not usually admitted. Inside, we sat down in a circle on woven rugs. Unlike the living tents, the walls of the Tent of Meeting were unadorned in the custom that considered what transpired inside of far greater importance than the setting. At the top was a large round opening that admitted light by day and allowed smoke from the fire to escape when meetings were held there at night.

"I understand that you have come to our land to establish better relations between our peoples," Father began. "This pleases me because I have been grieved by the breech that began in the time of our distant forefathers. I praise the wisdom of your elders that they have made this first move and sent such a gracious ambassador to represent your people."

"You are too kind," said Ben-Tubal. "It was our ancestor who alienated himself from your people. We should have sought to re-establish ties generations ago."

"That is very conciliatory of you to say. But I'm curious—if I may be so bold—as to why you have chosen this particular time." The question prompted glares from the Kenan elders, but neither Father nor Ben-Tubal flinched.

"Hasn't our exile lasted long enough?" asked Ben-Tubal.

"Centuries too long. That's not what I meant at all. But as you noted, I am a prophet of the Lord and he has given me a dire warning. I am only trying to discern if the timing of your overture is related to this prophecy in any way."

All eyes turned to Ben-Tubal to see what his reaction would be. But he seemed to be the only one who was not uncomfortable with the frankness of Father's questions. He said, "And if it were related, would you view it as good or bad?"

"I wouldn't deem it necessarily good or bad—just useful to know."

"Then if it will be useful for you, I will tell you that I am making this journey at my own initiative," said Ben-Tubal. "As for whether the timing relates to your prophecy, I cannot say. But if you wish to know more, why don't you come for an extended visit to our land? We have diviners among us who can inquire for you. Our people shall be as your people and our dwellings shall be as your dwellings."

"I am honored by your offer of hospitality," said Father. "But first, I must inquire of the Lord. I am building a great project at his command and do not know if I may take time away from it."

"And this great building project that your god commanded of you, what does it signify?" asked Ben-Tubal.

"That God is calling people everywhere to turn to him or a terrible disaster will destroy the world."

Baldag leaned over to the Cainite sitting next to him and said, "I told him not to waste his time on this nonsense."

But Ben-Tubal, apparently unperturbed, said, "Then you had best be about your work. However, the offer to visit is an open invitation and I hope that your god will allow you to accept someday soon. Bring your sons and they can spend time with my son Merib. And now, I must be going, because I, too, am engaged in a great building project—Nephil on the Gihon, Gateway to the Land of Nod. I daresay none of you has ever seen anything like it!"

Father and Ben-Tubal took leave of each other, each promising to visit the other if time and circumstances allowed. For my part I was ready to leave and go with them right then. Looking back, I am astonished that my mind had changed about the Cainites so quickly after meeting them.

Since no one in Kenan offered us hospitality for the night, we set out for home. As we walked along, I said, "Papa, don't you think Ben-Tubal is a good man?"

"Almost too good," he said, but did not elaborate. And from that day on, he fretted more than ever.

FOUR

During the years that followed, our work on the ark seemed interminable. I was by then old enough to handle a small flint hatchet. But though I hacked away at the smaller branches, the gopherwood contemptuously resisted my puny swings. The effort we put forth was, by my reckoning, out of all proportion to the discouraging rate of progress. I began to lose heart.

Although Father and Shem seemed impervious to the frustration, Ham and I freely commiserated during our precious hours of idleness, which were probably not quite so rare as I believed them to be at the time. As we grew, so did our discontent over toiling our lives away on a project that had no discernable end, because Father seemed intent on clearing the entire forest. One day, Ham couldn't take it any longer and said, "Father, why do we wear ourselves out this way?"

"The Lord has commanded me—" Father began with his standard reply.

"Yes, you have told us many times," Ham interrupted. "But why must we use these crude tools that make the work harder than it needs to be?"

"What's wrong with these tools?" asked Father indignantly. "I have used them all my life. And my fathers before me. They have served us well."

"They say the Cainites have tools of forged metal that are far superior to flint," said Ham.

"We are *not* Cainites," said Father.

"That is true. But they have better tools."

Father frowned. "There's more to consider than just the quality of the tools."

"If they're better, what's to consider?" said Ham.

"If we adopt the Cainite ways, we could be corrupted by them," said Father.

"But the work on the ark would go faster," countered Ham. Wouldn't that be pleasing in the Lord's sight?"

"Not if we ruined our own testimony in the process."

"How would swinging a metal axehead instead of flint ruin our testimony?"

"You are full of words," mumbled Father, which meant that Ham had successfully argued his point. This was no easy feat because Father could be as immovable as the hills when he made up his mind about something. But one of the things I admired about him was that he thoughtfully considered the evidence in all matters before making judgments and didn't cling blindly to his positions.

"So, does that mean we can go to Nephil?" I asked enthusiastically. That we should do so made perfect sense to me, though I'm sure that my curiosity was a far great factor than logic. I was beside myself to see those strange people again, especially Merib—not to mention the fact that Nephil was a long distance from that stand of timber.

"I will consider Ham's counsel," said Father. "For now, though, get back to work before you wear out my patience."

I think it was not Ham's argument alone, however, that ultimately led to Father's decision to visit the Cainites. He had wanted to go ever since he met Ben-Tubal, but something he would not disclose made him hesitate. In light of all that was to transpire later, I see that his decision was not as easy as it seemed to me. I had been so sheltered in the Highlands that I had little regard for the possible corrupting influence of interaction with the Cainites or even the outright danger that could befall us in a strange land. What eventually tipped the balance—whether revelation or simple curiosity—I do not know, but Father finally resolved to take up Ben-Tubal on his offer. When all necessary preparations had been made, we set out for Nephil. Mother rode on Naysa's back with Father at her side. My brothers and I alternated between running ahead to see what was around the next bend and lagging behind whenever we found something that caught our interest.

The Gihon Road, which closely followed the course of the river, would have been the most direct route. However, it was also more heavily populated, so making good time would have been difficult if we had to stop every few miles to visit with our kinsmen. Father, however, seemed anxious to avoid contact with our people and I think that's why he also chose not to go the Latham route across the Setti Plain. It was a longer road but straighter.

You could travel fast on it (as I knew from experience), but again, several fair-size villages lay along it and I think Father didn't want people making our visit a topic of gossip. Thus on the second day, just beyond where we left Mother at her sister Libnah's, we took a divergence called the Upper Path, which veered to the left and up from the main road. It was little used, even in those days, and took us on a meandering journey on a ridge through the wooded uplands of the Gihon Valley. With my head full of exotic notions about our destination, I might have preferred a more direct route. I didn't complain, though, because anything seemed better than cutting trees.

I must explain here that up until that time, I had assumed that Nephil was merely another village, not unlike those of our tribe. We had small villages that were made up of several extended families and large villages that consisted of several hundred souls. But all of them, even the larger ones such as Latham and Kenan, had that familiar sense of "villageness" about them. The common areas—such as the tent of meeting and the marketplace, the private areas of the living tents, and the watering spots and the grazing pastures—all had a familiar look and smell and feel about them that you could recognize at once. I was totally unprepared, then, for what I saw as we topped the crest of the last hill and stared down into the valley. Nephil on the Gihon was not a village at all, but a true city—the first I had seen in my life.

Even though it was still far from completed, Nephil was already larger than anything I had ever imagined. But size alone was not the half of it—it was magnificent! The buildings were constructed with dressed blocks of white marble, perfectly fitted so that the seams were practically invisible. The layout of the city could be easily discerned as we made our way down into the valley. It was arranged in a semi-circle facing the plain on an elevation adjacent to the River Gihon. Overlooking the river stood the largest and most impressive of all the buildings—Ben-Tubal's domed palace, from which three expansive boulevards ran to the gates that were under construction in the city wall. As the sun gleamed off the buildings below and hundreds of workers scurried about their labors, it was the most impressive sight I had ever beheld. I wondered how I could have been so wrong about those people.

Father had sent word several days ahead of us by runner, so we were expected when we arrived at the main gate. An attendant named Bairn led us to an anteroom where we washed and changed our clothes. I was relieved to see that he was of normal stature (by Sethite standards) and that the whole city was not going to be full of giants. When Bairn brought us drinks, I watched

Father carefully as he took a sip. When he nodded to us in approval, we followed his lead. It tasted of lightly fermented apricots. After our long journey, it was quite refreshing and I started to ask for more, but the look on Father's face restrained me. He had instructed us to be on our best manners, to accept graciously what hospitality was offered and not to risk insulting our hosts either by refusing anything unforbidden or by over-indulging in any respect.

Before we were finished, a man named Takek joined us. He was one of Ben-Tubal's high-ranking officials and had come to escort us to the palace. Like Ben-Tubal, Takek was nearly eight feet tall. As he stood next to Bairn, who was shorter than Father, it was obvious that the Cainites were not all of one stock.

Noting my anxiety about leaving Naysa behind, Bairn went to make sure that my burro was being cared for in the stables that were located just inside the wall near the southern gate. Meanwhile, Takek led us down the main promenade of Nephil. It wasn't his size alone that impressed me, but the stately air of confidence with which he carried himself. These were not the wild-eyed barbarians that I had expected. Their culture was advanced beyond anything I had ever conceived and I began to feel very insignificant in my own eyes.

The avenue, paved with speckled granite, opened into an expansive courtyard that gave a breathtaking view of Ben-Tubal's magnificent palace. The great central dome was flanked by lesser domes all capped with gold. Around the domes were gold-plated spires that thrust their way gracefully skyward. Nothing like it had ever been built nor was likely to be ever again. I was embarrassed that I had thought Ben-Tubal was merely a local tribal chieftain. Obviously, he was the ruler of the greatest city on the face of the earth.

As we entered, Takek said, "Governor Ben-Tubal is expecting you," with a subtle emphasis on "governor" that suggested that this would be the proper way to address him. Takek ushered us into Ben-Tubal's court, a large, splendidly furnished hall under the central dome. The floor was an intricate mosaic of garnet, lapis lazuli, malachite and many other colorful stones set in an interlocking pattern of diamonds, circles and various shapes. These smaller shapes combined to form larger ones so that the patterns were repeated on different scales. A dozen finely-woven tapestries of shimmering silk depicting the signs of the heavens lined the walls. Light was admitted through a ring of narrow windows encircling the dome, dividing the sunshine into a series of dramatic shafts.

Ben-Tubal, a cloth of deep violet open at the front draped over his white robe, sat on a dais at the far end of the room. With more formality than at our initial meeting, he rose and said, "Hail Noah, son of Lamech the Far-Seeing and Methuselah the Ancient One."

"Hail to you, Governor Ben-Tubal," said Father. "How happy your people must be to live in this fair place with such a wise and discerning leader to judge them."

Ben-Tubal nodded politely at the compliment. Then, turning to my brothers and me, he said, "Greetings to you Jayfeth, loremaster of animals." It was a greatly exaggerated title I well knew, but when he said it, I suddenly felt very important. I bowed in respect as Father had taught me, though I'm sure it came off as a rather clumsy gesture.

"And welcome to you, Shem, who are said to be a seer as your fathers before you," Ben-Tubal continued. "And let us not forget the eloquent Ham, a craftsman of no small repute, I understand. Now, how may I be of service to you?"

"We are most grateful to you for receiving us," said Father. "As I mentioned to you when we first met, I am building a great project at the command of the Lord. I am told that your people are able to make tools of excellent quality out of forged metal. I have come to see if I might procure some of these to expedite our labor."

"Ah, you have indeed come to the right place then," said Ben-Tubal. "My ancestor Tubal-Cain was the one who first perfected the fiery arts. And the generations who came after him have not been idle. You will find no finer tools anywhere, I assure you."

"Your family's story is undoubtedly a fascinating one," said Father. "I would be honored to hear it told in more detail."

"Then you shall. We should have plenty of time to discuss such matters as it will take several weeks to outfit many hundreds. We do not actually make the tools here in Nephil."

"There are not many hundreds," said Father. "Only the four of us."

"And you do all the work yourselves?" said Ben-Tubal, but it was hard to tell if he was genuinely surprised.

"You can see why my sons think themselves ill used," said Father, with a sidewise glance our way. "Our implements are made of stone and the work is hard for so few. But we have hopes that more people will join us in our effort.

"If that's all you need, then I'm sure we can supply everything you want right here. Takek?"

Takek nodded and said, "Consider it done."

"Now, please allow me the pleasure of showing you my city," Ben-Tubal said to Father. Then he turned to us and added, "Don't be dismayed, boys. We don't mean to bore you all afternoon with the talk of old men. What you need is a better host. Takek, summon Merib."

Merib must have been listening because as soon as the words were spoken, the door opened and Ben-Tubal said, "Ah, there he is now." Merib had his father's straight, prominent nose and strong chin. I was surprised to see how tall he already was as he walked toward me at his deliberate, unhurried pace.

In my excitement, I ran and embraced him. He stiffened and glanced at his father. Ben-Tubal nodded and Merib awkwardly returned my embrace. I pulled away, concerned that I might have committed some social blunder.

"Welcome to Nephil, jewel of the Gihon and gateway to Nod," said Merib, a greeting that sounded overly decorous coming from one so young.

"Merib," said Ben-Tubal. "Will you and Jabib show our distinguished guests around the city? Go wherever you wish, but be back in time for dinner."

"Yes, sire," said Merib.

Outside the court, Merib relaxed a little, though like most Nephilim I have known, he was always a bit reserved by nature. He led us all around the city accompanied by Jabib, a dour-faced old man in a saffron robe who served as Merib's tutor and caretaker.

The three large boulevards extending from the palace courtyard to the gates divided the city into four wedge-shaped sections. The southernmost of these was given over entirely to a complex of buildings extending from the palace that housed dignitaries as well as containing the governor's private gardens. The middle two sections, beyond the spacious central courtyard, were larger and transitioned from public buildings to housing. Merib explained that the higher ranking officials had houses of their own, while others lived in apartments or dormitories. The idea of living in buildings seemed strange to me, but I did not say so. The northernmost section was a public garden and common area where many people congregated in groups passing their time in whatever way pleased them, whether arts, athletics, sciences or philosophies.

"So your people do this all day every day?" I asked. "How does any work get done?"

"We have servants, of course," replied Merib.

A servant class was a foreign concept to me. Because of the task of building the ark, my family was atypical among our people with respect to work. Most of the sons of Seth lived much more sedentary lives by comparison. Food was abundant throughout Cush, so gathering all that was needed required little time each day. The weather was never too hot nor too cold, so we had only the simplest requirements for clothing, and shelter was mostly for the sake of privacy. Neither did we need or make many things; the idea of possessions was something we gave little thought to in those days. However, even those few necessities of daily living required some time. The Nephilim, though, did not toil nor spin (except the artisans for their own good pleasure). Neither did they gather or cook. In fact, in all my days, I have never seen a people so entirely given over to the pursuit of leisure as the Nephilim. Their ability to do this, of course, depended upon having others accomplish those tasks for them.

Merib, sensing my puzzlement, "Hah, Jabib! We keep forgetting that they have only come down from the Highlands today and have little knowledge. The Nephilim are not the only sons of Cain. Have you not heard of the Enochites who live in the land of Nod?"

My recollection on this subject was dim and I found myself wishing I had studied my lessons harder. I was spared the embarrassment of admitting my ignorance because Shem had a keen memory for such matters. He said, "When Adam's son Cain became estranged from his family, he moved eastward to the land of Nod and founded the city of Enoch in honor of his son."

"Well said, Master Shem," said Jabib. These were very nearly the first words the taciturn man had spoken, though he had followed us around like a shadow all afternoon. His voice had an odd inflection, like the sounds were coming from far back in his throat and thicker somehow than any I had heard before. "These Enochites and others like them have increased greatly in numbers—beyond what the land can sustain. The Nephilim are undertaking to help them with employment and organizing food-gathering."

"Does that include hunting animals?" I asked. "We have heard disturbing reports."

"Unless you have known to what lengths gnawing hunger can drive you, I ask you not to judge my brothers too harshly," said Jabib.

I restrained myself from further comment, troubled that I knew so little about the world after all.

FIVE

Dinner at Ben-Tubal's palace that night was by far the most lavish affair I had ever seen. We sat in chairs carved of mahogany around a long table of the same. This seemed strange to us, accustomed as we were to taking our meals sitting on the ground. Neither were we familiar with using many utensils, for most of our fare was eaten with fingers or supped from bowls. I felt like a very crude lout amid such finery, but Ben-Tubal never raised an eyebrow. On the contrary, he went out of his way to make us feel welcome.

Ben-Tubal sat at the head of the table, with Merib on his right. I sat next to Merib, followed by his twin sisters Mashea and Pashea—who were about Shem's age. Father sat to Ben-Tubal's left. Then came Shem, Ham, and Jirah, Ben-Tubal's youngest daughter. It seemed like a small party for such a large table, because it would easily have accommodated five times that many. It also struck me as odd that I had seen no sign of Ben-Tubal's wife and the children's mother, so I made a mental note to ask Merib about it when I had a chance.

Father's eyes were constantly upon us, silently urging us not indulge beyond proper limits. Despite his warning looks, however, I could not help myself. I had never eaten such a rich feast—exotic fruits, vegetables, breads, cakes, and dishes I could only guess at. I ate every crumb set before me by the attendants and when they offered more, I greedily accepted until at last my stomach felt ready to split open.

As the final dish was being served, Father said, "Tell me, does my kinsman Baldag still dwell among you? I have not seen him here today."

"Yes, he has spent much time among us, though his duties as liaison between Nephil and Cush require him to be away frequently as he is today. There is none like him, wouldn't you agree?"

"And it's a good thing," I started to mutter under my breath.

But I stopped short of actually saying it, suddenly fascinated by the way Ben-Tubal's statement hung in the air, until I began to imagine that he might not have meant it as I thought he did. Father seemed to sense this as well and said, "As you say, there is no one like him."

The final dish was so extraordinary that Father inquired about it. Ben-Tubal summoned the chief baker, a short, round-faced man, who asked, "Does it meet with your approval?"

"My approval?" said Father. "Do not tell my wife, but I don't think I have ever tasted anything so delicious."

The chief baker bowed and said, "When I learned you were coming, I dispatched twenty-seven men—three for each of our guests tonight—to Cavah, two days journey down the river. The place is so named for the rare cavil tree that grows in that region alone. It bears fruit but once each ten years and each tree bears only one small fruit. The men searched for three days to find enough for one serving and they have only returned today. The outer rind is so tough that it had to be boiled for six hours before it could be peeled. We had to take great care, though, not to rupture the delicate membrane covering the inner fruit or else its sweetness would have been quickly lost. The shell it is served in is a glaze of baked honey. We use only honey from the meadows of the Mechpah region, although it is far distant from here. But its taste and consistency are unsurpassed. Once you have tasted it, nothing else will suffice."

At the time, I did not fully comprehend the significance of the baker's words, but Father was clearly shocked by such extravagance. All he could manage to say was, "My compliments."

"That will be all," said Ben-Tubal to the baker. Then, turning to Father, he said, "When we spoke earlier, you were telling me of the project that your god commanded you to build. I would like to know more about it."

"You refer to him as if he were mine alone," said Father. "But he is the great God over all and creator of the entire world."

"I meant no disrespect," said Ben-Tubal. "I dwelled long in the land beyond the river."

"May I assume, then, that the Lord is not worshipped in Nod?"

Ben-Tubal paused for a moment, then said, "They follow a different path."

"I suspected as much," said Father. "But when you say 'they,' do you exclude yourself?"

Ben-Tubal leaned close to Father and said quietly, "Ben-Tubal follows his own path."

They remained thus—their faces not much more than a foot apart—for a long moment while they studied each other. Finally, Father nodded and drew back. "I see. Well, you were inquiring about the word of the Lord?"

"Right," said Ben-Tubal. "Are you saying that the great God who created the world says it is going to be destroyed?"

"Yes."

"And everyone in it?"

"If they don't turn away from evil," said Father.

Ben-Tubal leaned back in thoughtful repose and then addressed his children. "Did you hear that, Little Ones? Take careful note of what is being said here tonight. Evil will not be tolerated in this house nor in any of the lands I govern." He turned to Father and said, "Tomorrow, I shall assemble all the people of the city and you shall speak to them. I want them to hear what you have to say."

This concluded the dinner. A servant led me to my room—my own room, something else to which I was not at all accustomed. It had been the most exciting day of my young life and I would have thought I'd be as happy as a person could be. But laying there in the darkness, all alone, a spirit of disquiet overtook me at the strangeness of it all. I soon found myself emptying the contents of my stomach into the chamber pot.

Breakfast was lighter fare—for which I was grateful—and served on a porch overlooking the courtyard in which people were already beginning to congregate. When I had finished my meal of diced fruit and a light, sweet bread, Ben-Tubal led us down a flight of steps and along a railed portico that separated us from the growing throng. Adjacent to the palace to the north was a temple with four massive columns of white alabaster and marble steps leading upward to the entrance. By the time we reached it, many thousands were gathered before us. It seemed the whole city had turned out for the occasion.

As Ben-Tubal stepped forward onto the temple platform, a hush fell over the crowd. "Citizens of Nephil, a mighty prophet has come to us to bring a message from his great god. Listen well, for he brings dire tidings."

Ben-Tubal motioned us to stand nearby and said quietly, "I want you boys to see this. You shall be witnesses to your father's triumph."

"People of Nephil, your esteemed Governor speaks truly," Father began. "God has given me a message. He is the maker of the world and all who dwell in it. We are the work of his hand and borrow the very breath of life from him. But we have turned our backs to him and disdained His ways. He is calling us back to his side. Will you heed his call? Because a day of doom and destruction has been appointed for all who will not. Seek his favor while it may be found—before it's too late!"

At that, Ben-Tubal stepped forward again. "You have heard the words of the prophet. What say you, citizens of Nephil? Will you heed?"

Great shouts arose spontaneously from the people, "Behold, the prophet! We will obey!"

I cannot begin to describe the look of amazement on Father's face. Tears filled his eyes, and though I couldn't hear him over the roar of the crowd, I saw him mouthing over and over, "Praise be to God."

The shouts went on until Ben-Tubal raised his hands to quiet them and said, "Since you have answered this way, I hereby decree that evil will not be tolerated in Nephil nor in any of the lands I govern. We will pursue only what is good. And the prophet Noah will intercede before his god on our behalf that we might be spared from this terrible fate."

Father reached into his pack and brought out an image of the great eagle that lived in our forest, which he had carved from black walnut. I had seen him working on it for many long hours by the light of our campfire and knew it was an exquisitely detailed likeness. The wings were outstretched and it seemed that if he let go of it, it might very well fly away. Father held it up and said, "As a testimony to your commitment this day, I give this gift to your governor. It will serve as a reminder that if you commit yourselves to God, he will bear up your souls like the wings of an eagle because his favor is incomparable."

Father gave the gift to Ben-Tubal and the crowd renewed their cheers. We then took our leave of him, much to my disappointment. Merib and I made many promises to each other, though neither of us had any way of knowing when we would see each other again.

As we made our way down the boulevard, the people parted to let us pass, pressing closely without touching us, and congratulating us with, "Well said! Hail to the prophet!" and many such sayings. Father did not know quite what to make of it all, but I enjoyed it immensely.

Naysa was waiting for us when we reached the gate of the city. The burro looked homely in my eyes after the finery of Nephil and I'm sure he was gladder to see me than I was him. But he had been well cared for and was now laden with the new implements that Ben-Tubal had given to Father.

Once we were outside the walls and heading up the Gihon, I said, "That was brilliant!"

"You really told them," said Ham.

"The glory is all God's," said Father, but it was plain to see he was almost as excited as we were.

"Before it's too late," I said. "That part really got to them."

"Hail to the prophet—that's what they shouted," added Ham.

"I think this is a sign," said Father. "We need to start taking this message to all the people. Now that you boys are getting older and can share more of the work, maybe we'll have time to start visiting the area villages. We can start with those along the river and then work our way out across the plain."

Getting caught up in Father's enthusiasm was easy with the applause of the Nephilim still ringing in our ears. He talked far into the evening around the campfire, sometimes to us and sometimes to himself, mapping routes and making lists of clans and villages he wanted to visit. Only Shem seemed to have reservations, so that I finally had to ask, "What are you so sour about?"

"Am I the only one who noticed that they are building Nephil on our side of the river?"

"So?" said Ham, who always felt it his duty to offer an opinion on every subject—whether he was supposed to be included in the conversation or not. "It's still a long way from the nearest Sethite village."

"Cush is a spacious land," I said. "Why should it bother you?"

"And how does he know so much about us?" said Shem. "And why should he care? Something just doesn't feel right."

"You worry too much," said Ham. "It would suit me fine if we moved there right now. We're heroes there."

"You're too easily impressed by the wrong things," said Shem.

"What's all that?" asked Father.

"Nothing," we all said at once.

"Hmmm, it sounded to me like you were arguing about something," said Father. "But if it was nothing, then you won't be missing out on anything by rolling out your mats and going to sleep. It's late and we have a long way to travel tomorrow."

We did as we were told and soon I was laying there on the crest of the ridge looking up at the moonless sky. I tried not to think about Shem's concerns, but without success. As the shadows undulated to the light of the dying fire, an owl hooted. It was a sound I had heard a thousand times in the Highlands, but it seemed unsettling so far from home. *That's a good question,* I thought. *Who, who, who are those people?*

After eight days journey back along the Upper Path, we reached the junction of the Gihon Road and the tents of Obed and Libnah.

"I'm sorry we can't stay, but we have to be getting back to work on the ark," Father had told his brother-in-law Obed. But he was only being polite. Obed had not asked us to stay and Father was only covering for his brother-in-law's breech of hospitality.

Father removed as many of the tools off Naysa's back as he thought he could carry (which was actually quite a lot) and handed a few more to my brothers and me. Then he gently lifted Mother onto Naysa's back so that she wouldn't have to walk. As we headed homeward along the Gihon Road, Father said, "What is it, Mara?"

"Oh, my sister," said Mother, waving her hand in exasperation.

"Not her too?"

"I'm afraid so. You'd think my own sister would feel some sense of loyalty to me. And that so-called husband of hers would hardly come within fifty feet of me. I never felt welcome for a moment the whole time I was there."

"Your sister and my brother—what a family we have!"

Mother managed a weak smile. "Well, I don't think I'll be visiting them again anytime soon. And they probably won't be around anyway."

"They're not planning to move because of their crazy brother-in-law, are they?" joked Father, trying to cheer her up.

"Better to be crazy than lazy," said Mother, reaching down from her perch and tapping him on the top of his head.

"Ho-ho!" Father laughed. "You weren't supposed to agree with me."

"I just wanted you to know that I made the right decision."

"Your reward for playing hard to get," said Father with an exaggerated bow.

"Obed doesn't like anything hard—that's for certain. He constantly complains that life on the river isn't what it used to be and that it's getting harder to find food. Of course, I never saw him lift a finger to help find any. Anyway, they're talking of moving back to Latham or maybe even to Nephil. By the way, how was Nephil?"

"You can't even imagine—"

"Father was brilliant!" I said.

"That's not what I meant—" said Father.

"They cheered us," Ham interrupted.

"Oh my!" said Mother, genuinely impressed, a reaction that came quite naturally to her whenever it came to her husband.

"Yes, we were well received," said Father modestly and a little embarrassed. He tried again to get the topic of the conversation off himself. "You've never seen anything like Nephil."

"It must be something," said Mother. "So many are going there and to the lands beyond, including Minnah, I hear."

"And not Giblith?" said Father.

"No, it's quite a scandal in Latham."

"That's a pity. Giblith is a good man and so is Minnah's father Keriath. I wonder what would make her do something like that?"

Ham and I exchanged a knowing look, but said nothing.

"So they cheered you in Nephil," said Mother. "My, my. It's good to know some people in this world still have a little sense." He laughed, but I knew she was as sincere as she could be.

By the morning of the second day following, we were approaching home. As we neared, though, the excitement we had felt ever since Nephil turned gradually to foreboding—a feeling so tangible that it seemed to hang in the very air. And then we realized something was in the air—smoke!

We burst upon our campsite, half expecting it to be ablaze. Finding it intact brought little relief, for from there we could clearly see where the smoke was coming from. Father staggered toward the clearing as if his feet were made of stone. The rest of us trailed along behind, but not too closely. Father stumbled around the still-smoldering embers looking for something to salvage. Nothing could be found. Fifteen years of toil—begun before the day I was born—had been reduced to ashes. Father fell to his knees, looked silently skyward for a moment and then hung his head.

SIX

After a few minutes, Father rose and mumbled something to Mother about needing to be alone. Slowly, he trudged up the hill and disappeared from sight, leaving the rest of us behind to rummage through our ransacked campsite. Our once tranquil meadow had turned into a forbidding place. A thin layer of soot defiled the whole area so that you could not even walk without kicking up gray dust. The stench of stale smoke fouled the air, clinging to our clothes, our tent, our food, and our very nostrils. In my mind, all this contrasted starkly with Nephil, the gleaming white city. We had been heroes there. But now, at home, we were like frightened mice whose nest has been disturbed.

As we waited anxiously for Father's return, Mother busied herself—and us—trying to hide her concern. (Ah, the wives of the prophets! Were there ever people who were less appreciated for the burdens they carry?) When some order had been restored to the campsite, Shem, Ham and I retreated a short distance while Mother began to prepare supper. Ham said quietly, "Where do you think he is?"

"I don't know," I said.

"You don't suppose something might have happened—" said Ham.

"Don't say things like that," said Shem.

"Somebody needs to say it," said Ham. "Whoever did this might still be around. Who knows what they might do to him if they catch him alone."

"I think it was just a message," I said. "If they wanted to harm us, they have had ample opportunity since we are so isolated here. And why would they go to the trouble of burning the lumber?"

"I'd like to get my hands on whoever did this," said Ham. "But who?"

"Well, I can guess," I said.

"You shouldn't say you know when you don't," said Shem.

"Don't you think it's suspicious that Baldag has been with the Nephilim for years, but happened to be absent at just the time when we were visiting there?" I said.

"Jay's right," said Ham. "He hasn't made any secret of his dislike for Father or this project."

"Just because you've never trusted him doesn't mean he's guilty," said Shem. "It's a very serious matter to make accusations like that without proof."

"All right," I said. "I'll keep my opinions to myself. But we should all be on our guard against him anyway. And whatever you do, don't let on like you're worried about Father in front of Mother. She has enough to worry about."

The sun was setting when we spotted Father coming down the hill. We ran to him and he scooped Shem and Ham up in his arms, while I climbed on his shoulders and he carried all three of us back to camp. Mother embraced him and laid her head on his chest, but said nothing. She, above all, knew how much he was suffering and her silence spoke more than anything that could possibly be said.

I, however, had not learned the wisdom of silence. Overcome by curiosity, I asked, "Did the Lord tell you who did this?"

"No."

"Why did he let it happen?" asked Ham.

"I don't know."

"Then what *did* he say?" I asked.

"He did not say anything," Father replied. He must have known what I was thinking because he added, "Just because I am his prophet doesn't mean he tells me everything. The last word I had from him about this was to build the ark. And until the day it is completed, that is what I intend to do. No matter how long it takes or whatever setbacks befall me. Now, start packing, because tomorrow we break camp. I know where there is more gopherwood."

Our new home was about a day's journey further up into the hills—even more remote from our kinsmen than our previous campsite. The spruce foliage there had just that hint of blue which gave me to know, even from a distance, that the scent would be a refreshing relief from the stale smoke we had escaped below. Cones were plentiful there, which made starting campfires easy. Nearby, a spring of water bubbled from the rocks and trickled a few feet into a small pool, where it lingered just long enough to offer itself for use before tumbling on down the slope. We washed ourselves, our clothes and all our belongings and were soon cleansed from the overpowering smell of smoke. We pitched our tent on a bed of needles and soon felt right at home.

As Father had said, the gopherwood was very plentiful there. A huge grove stood on a plateau not far from camp. All in all, it was an exceedingly pleasant place and I should have been well content to pass my youth there had it not been for this one thing. You see, I was not so quickly consoled as my Father concerning the fire. For while Father had poured far more of his effort into the project than I, he was already full of years. Proportionally speaking, it had occupied less of his life. I, on the other hand, knew practically nothing else except the ark. It was the reference point for my whole life and virtually every drop of sweat that had come out of my pores had been expended, so it seemed, in its furtherance. Therefore, once the camp had been established and the excitement of moving waned, it was with no trifling amount of bitterness that I resumed the work.

When a loud "crack" signaled the fall of the first tree, we watched it topple to the ground with a crash. "One miserable tree," Ham muttered.

"It's nothing but a stick of firewood for the cookpot compared to what we had before," I answered.

After surveying the fallen tree for a moment, Father let out a low whistle and exclaimed, "I have to hand it to you, Ham. These new tools are everything you said they'd be and more. I've never brought down a tree so fast. At this rate, we'll make up for what we lost in no time."

"If you call ten years 'no time'," said Ham.

"Ah, don't get discouraged, boys," said Father.

"Discouraged?" said Ham. "Just because we live twenty miles from nowhere. We have no friends. Even our own relatives despise us. And everything we have ever worked for just went up in flames. Why would we be discouraged?"

I thought Father would punish him for speaking that way, because none of us dared to talk to him like that. But Father only shook his head, walked back to the tree and began lopping off the branches.

"Why don't you quit thinking of yourself all the time," said Shem.

"Why don't you get off my back all the time," said Ham.

This was not the last of the outbursts by my youngest brother by far. Although he was naturally handy with the tools, his temperament was ill-suited to the isolation. And he didn't hesitate to give vent to his frustrations, which became a wedge between Father and him. Father took it as well as any man could and tried everything he could to encourage him, but to little avail.

Ham's complaints didn't help to soothe the resentment I was feeling. If not for the new tools that Ben-Tubal had provided to us, I might have been discouraged beyond measure. The metal was extremely hard and held a good edge, which proved to be very beneficial in working with the rock-like gopherwood. What also helped was that as we boys grew, we were able to do a real day's work, so the burden was not so heavy on Father. Thus within a few years, just as Father had predicted, we had as much lumber as we had before.

One significant difference in our routine that became apparent within days of our arrival was in food gathering. When we lived in the meadow near the Gihon, grains and vegetables and fruits grew in abundance all around us. All we needed for a day could be picked quickly with little effort. After we moved, though, the supplying of food had to be given more careful attention and required additional time. At first, I attributed this fact to the higher elevation. Looking back, though, I am convinced that food was already becoming scarcer all over southern Cush.

Once our new camp was well established and the lumber cutting was showing signs of progress, Father started making regular trips to the surrounding villages to proclaim the message God had given to him. We took turns accompanying him, so those remaining at home could continue the work and safeguard the lumber from another act of sabotage.

At first, Father had high hopes for an enthusiastic reception of his message as he had received from the Nephilim. He thought that if he could just talk directly to them and explain God's dire warning, they would listen. The initial optimism, however, soon gave way to disappointment. On his best outings, he was met with mere indifference, and it got worse from there. Returning home from one trip to the Lower Gihon Valley, we felt particularly dejected after visiting some of Father's cousins who lived there. Not only did they totally reject Father's message, they would have nothing to do with us whatsoever. We did not often travel at night, but the moon that evening was bright and we were anxious to get back to the amiable embrace of the Highlands. Neither of us was in the mood to talk, so we walked along keeping our own thoughts until distant voices from somewhere up the river broke the silence.

"That's odd," said Father. "No one lives on this stretch of the Gihon."

"Maybe it's just some late-night travelers like us," I said.

"You're probably right," said Father. "I doubt if it's anything to be concerned about."

Neither one of us had convinced the other, however. As we drew closer and could hear more clearly, we realized that the accents were strange to us. Father beckoned me to follow him off the road to our left toward the river. In the deep shadow afforded by the trees overhanging the riverbank, we approached quietly until we came upon about two dozen men. Even in the moonlight, it was easy to see that four of them were exceedingly tall—Nephilim. But the others were of a stock I did not immediately recognize. There were several boats on the near shore and the men were loading a great quantity of fruit and bushels of grain into them.

One of the men stumbled on a protruding root as he climbed the embankment. He lay on his hands and knees for a moment, sides heaving, apparently so weak that he had trouble standing up again. The Nephilite nearest him said, "Get up you lazy dog. We haven't got time for idlers." The Nephilite grabbed the back of the man's shirt, lifted him to his feet and gave him a rough shove forward.

When the boats were filled, all the men got in and paddled to the opposite shore. Father motioned me to follow him into breathtakingly cold water. It was only about chest deep there, but too swift to remain upright, so we half walked and half swam, trying to make as little noise as possible. The current carried us several yards downstream before we made it across. Although I had lived all my life within a short distance of the Gihon, that was the first time I had ever been on the other shore. The river formed a natural barrier that my people seldom crossed, because beyond it lay the land of Nod—and generations of enmity between the Sethites and the Cainites.

We made our way quietly back upstream, staying close to the cover of the bank until we neared a place where it sloped more gently. The men unloaded the boats and put the contents into two large boxes on wheels—the first carts I had ever seen. Our people did not make such things and I marveled at the clever design.

Just then, we saw one of the empty boats drifting toward us. "You idiot!" said the cruel Nephilite we had heard before. "Didn't I tell you to secure that boat?"

Then came the sickening *crack, crack, crack* of a limber rod on flesh and awful whelps of pain. The man jumped into the river, crying out again as the cold water stung his wounds, and splashed downstream as fast as he could to retrieve the errant boat. By the time we realized that he was heading straight toward us, it was too late to move. When he reached the boat and pulled it back to shore, he was only a few feet from us. We pressed against the shadow of the bank, hardly daring to breathe.

I could see him well in the moonlight. He was gaunt to the point that you could count his ribs by sight. His hair and beard were unkempt. But what I found most disturbing about him was his eyes—empty and vacant.

The man dragged the boat back along the shoreline by a rope and rejoined the band. By that time, the cargo was fully loaded into the carts which were hitched to teams of ponies. Two other Nephilim we had not yet seen drove these away toward the east. The remaining men, under the direction of the Nephilim, then portaged the boats away and quickly disappeared from view. Father and I stood there silently for a long time, deeply troubled. We crossed back to our own side of the river and walked along wet, cold and miserable.

"I should have done something," said Father at last. "I should have intervened. The Nephilite had no right to treat the man like that. Why didn't I do something? I had no reason to hide like someone who has committed a crime. I must be growing faint-hearted with old age."

"You are not faint-hearted, Father," I said.

"What's that?" he said and I realized that he had been speaking to himself.

"I was saying, who among all of our people is bolder in speaking out for what is right than you?"

"I didn't tonight," he said. "And I am ashamed. Being rejected by my own kinsmen has affected me more than I've shown—maybe even more than I have admitted to myself. But I will not be intimidated into silence. Lord, grant that your servant may speak the truth boldly!"

SEVEN

We arrived home late the following day. Though we were tired and weary of opposition, we did not rest long because Father had resolved to go to Nephil and would have no peace until he confronted Governor Ben-Tubal. Since I was an eyewitness to the offense, there was no question but that I would accompany him. Secretly, though, I feared that we might not be treated so well after Father met with Ben-Tubal.

Late that afternoon, Ham and I played not far from camp, while Shem sat nearby on an outcrop of rock studying his lessons and trying to ignore us.

"It's not fair that you get to go again, Jay," said Ham. "You just got back."

"I was there when it happened," I said. "Father might need me as a witness."

"He just doesn't want to take me," Ham said.

"That's not true," I said, though I wasn't completely convinced of my own words.

"Oh, then why do I always get the shortest trips?"

I started to tell him it was because he was the youngest, had the least stamina and complained constantly, but thought better of it. "It's probably because you're needed here," I said. "Father knows how good you are with your hands."

"Well, that is true," said Ham.

"I'm not missed as much because that kind of work doesn't come naturally to me. They say it's because I'm left-handed."

"I'd say you have *two* left hands."

"I'd say you have a big mouth for someone so short," I retorted with a laugh.

"Who are you calling short?" said Ham, lunging at me in a mock rage. We wrestled playfully on the ground as boys do. Despite the age difference, he was already almost as strong as I. But I still had the advantage of leverage and simply wrapped him up with my long arms and legs. I got him down first just to prove I still could (though I knew that probably wouldn't last many more years). Out of the corner of my eye, I saw Shem heading back toward camp and figured he was going to tell Father. Knowing we'd better quit before we got in trouble, I let Ham roll over on top of me to make him feel better.

"You've got me now," I said.

"That'll teach you," said Ham. "I'll let you up if you tell me about the wheels."

"All right," I said, sitting up. "But there's not much more I can tell you. They were spinning discs."

"What were they made of?" Ham quizzed. "And how were they attached?"

"I don't know. I didn't get a good look at them. It was dark."

"You were just scared."

"I was not."

"You know you're not supposed to lie."

"Well, maybe a little scared—but you would have been, too."

Father walked up in the middle of our discussion and could easily see that we had been at it. He shook his head and said, "Jayfeth, we've covered more than thirty miles in two days and we've hardly slept. How can you be up for horseplay?" He brushed pine needles out of our hair and said, "Go wash for supper. And don't tell your mother you've been wrestling. She doesn't understand about such things."

As we walked to the spring with our arms around each other, Ham said, "Wheels. Find out more about wheels."

We made quick preparations for our journey and set out with all haste. We took the Gihon Road, not stopping to visit anyone, and arrived at Nephil on the seventh morning following. Even from a distance, we could see that much progress had been made since we had last visited and the wall was nearly completed. The city buzzed with activity, including no small number of Sethite visitors. As we made our way through the courtyard, we saw that a pedestal had been erected upon which sat the carving of the eagle that Father had given to Ben-Tubal. He cringed when he saw people making offerings to it.

"This is a pleasant surprise," said Ben-Tubal cordially when we had gained admittance to the palace. "I am pleased to see you both."

This sentiment clearly was not shared by everyone, though. Baldag was there and made little effort to conceal his disdain. I couldn't help but notice that he had gained a considerable amount of weight since I had last seen him. Apparently, he had been taking full advantage of the rich palace fare.

"We are honored by your welcome, Governor," said Father. "I came to request a word with you—in private."

Ben-Tubal dismissed his attendants with a nod. Baldag, though, lingered, saying, "If this is a matter concerning the Sethites, perhaps I should stay, Governor. After all, I am the emissary of the Sethites."

"This doesn't concern the Sethites—or you, Baldag," said Father, uncharacteristically curt. "I wish to speak to the Governor alone."

"Thank you for your offer, Baldag," said Ben-Tubal, displaying no apparent discomfort in spite of the tension. "The delegation from Danan will be arriving this afternoon. I understand that their leader Hublis is expected to be the next chief elder of the Sethites. I would consider it a personal favor if you would go and see to the last-minute preparations. It's very important to me that our meeting with him go well."

"As you wish, Governor," said Baldag, but that didn't stop him from scowling at us as he passed by.

When the hall was cleared except for the three of us, Father began, "Governor Ben-Tubal, I am greatly distressed by something I witnessed last week. A band of men was gathering food near the river a day's journey from our camp. One of the leaders horribly mistreated one of the other men— beat him with a rod." Father paused for a moment before adding, "The man who did this appeared to be a Nephilite. That's why I wanted to discuss this confidentially."

Ben-Tubal sat silently for a moment before he answered. His countenance was inscrutable, so that I could not tell which way he was going to answer. "It is true that I have organized food-gathering parties. The land of Cush overflows with abundance, so it's probably difficult for you to comprehend the plight of the eastern peoples. The Nodites do not have enough to eat. And things are even worse in Havilah."

"Havilah?"

"The Sand-Land that lies west beyond the Pishon. It is a desolate place. Nothing grows there. Nothing."

"You are right," said Father. "That is difficult to imagine."

"Yes, but it is true," said Ben-Tubal. "If you ever go there, it is something you will not soon forget. We have taken pity on the people and are helping to supply them with food. But as for the mistreatment of any of the Nodites, Havilites, or any other peoples in my territories, though, I have no knowledge."

"But you would not condone such a thing."

"I am Ben-Tubal. Have I not given you my word that I would do only that which is right? I will make an investigation into this matter and will act accordingly."

"Thank you," said Father. "I could ask for nothing more."

Although Ben-Tubal urged us to stay for the night, Father declined his offer. Too much time had already been lost on our work, and he said that we needed to be returning to our own land. Father did agree, however, to stay long enough so that a light meal might be prepared for us.

While we were waiting, I had the opportunity that I had been looking forward to—seeing Merib. Takek took me to him in the Governor's private living quarters, but I did not find him as I expected. "What is the matter?" I asked.

"It is Jabib," said Merib. "He is very ill. I have overheard whispers in the court that he will not survive the week."

"Ill? How can this be?" I said, puzzled. Sickness was little known among our people and death came only to the most ancient, or in rare cases like my grandmother, to a woman giving birth. Jabib was neither.

Merib hesitated. When he spoke, he appeared to be choosing his words very carefully. "There are wasting diseases among the eastern peoples. And now they seem to be spreading—even to Nephil."

Merib crossed to the window and looked out across the river. When he spoke again, his voice seemed to be coming from far away. "The Nephilim are taken from their mothers at birth and reared by nursemaids and mentors. Jabib has been my mentor since I was an infant. We are very close."

"I don't know what to say. I'm truly sorry."

A long silence passed between us. Then Merib said, "What do you think happens when someone dies? You are in the line of seers. You should know."

"I am in the line of seers, that is true. But I do not have the sight." I could not recall a moment previously when I ever felt more shame about that fact. "Those among us who do know about such things say that the spirit departs and the body returns to the dust from which it was formed."

"And then?"

"They speak of a hope beyond the grave. But what that might be is shrouded in mystery. It seems to me, though, that it would be wasteful for the Creator to make living beings and then not preserve them somehow, somewhere."

"Officially, the Nephilim do not believe in an afterlife—at least not in the way you do."

"And unofficially?"

"Let's just say that we are not alone," Merib confided, lowering his voice almost to a whisper. "But as to what that portends for the afterlife, I do not know."

"What do you mean, 'we are not alone'?" I asked, intrigued. "And how do you know?"

"Jabib belongs to a sect—one of many in Enoch-Nod. I really shouldn't be telling you this, but he has had direct contact with them."

"Who?"

"The Others. The ones who come from—" Merib stopped in mid-sentence when a servant came in to summon us for lunch.

As we followed, I wondered why he was being so secretive and what other peoples there might be besides Sethites and Cainites. "I'd like to hear more about this sometime."

"Maybe it's best if you don't," said Merib. "At least not until we know what to do about it."

We returned home with all possible speed, as Father was anxious to resume work on the ark. I was tired that night after the long journey. Shem and Ham were already fast asleep after a hard day's labor and I was starting to drift off when I heard Mother say quietly to Father in their corner of the tent, "You can relax now. You're home."

"Relax?" said Father. "How can I relax when there is so much to be done?"

"So all this worrying is helping you to accomplish what the Lord wants you to do."

"Ah, I suppose you were appointed a prophetess while I was away and the Lord has given you this message to rebuke me."

"I wouldn't have to be a prophetess to see the strain on your face."

"You know me too well, Mara," said Father. "I fear that I am not up to the task."

"You mustn't be so hard on yourself," said Mother.

"When I am away, all I can think about is coming back home to work on the ark. And when I'm at home, I am consumed with thinking about all the people who need to be warned. It all seems so urgent. But I'm just one man."

"Yes, but you're the Lord's man and that makes all the difference."

"He keeps my spirit churning within me," said Father in an anguished tone. "I never have a moment's peace."

"Well, just lay your head on my shoulder and you will have peace," said Mother. "Tonight, at least, you will be *my* man."

A few days after we returned home, we looked up from working to see Baldag and a Nephilite approaching on horseback—fine, sleek horses far larger than any I had ever seen. Baldag's mount snorted at Naysa as they dismounted and approached and Naysa retreated. The Nephilite, carrying a basket in his arms, said to Father, "Ben-Tubal instructed me to tell you this. What you said concerning the mistreated Nodite was found to be true. The man who did it has been dealt with according to his misdeed, as Ben-Tubal promised."

"Tell the Governor that we appreciate seeing that justice was served," said Father.

"Justice?" Baldag sneered. "Here's your justice!"

He ripped the lid off the basket and I recoiled in horror at the sight. Inside, was the head of the Nephilite we had seen by the river.

"What!" exclaimed Father. "This is not what I—"

"Spare me your righteous indignation," said Baldag. "It has grown quite tedious."

"It's just that the punishment seems ... excessive."

"The eastern peoples have their own laws and customs. Or haven't you been able to 'divine' that, Prophet? They are so numerous that it takes strict enforcement to maintain order. Perhaps next time you will think twice before meddling in affairs you do not understand."

"And what is it that you do, if it's not meddling?" said Father sharply.

"The Governor has appointed me overseer of food collection in Cush," said Baldag. "What you don't understand is that we are trying to help the Nodites because they're too stupid and lazy to help themselves."

"It didn't look like 'help' to me," said Father. "It looked like slavery."

"Listen to me, Prophet. This man was a friend of mine. I came all the way up here for the satisfaction of seeing your face when you learned what you caused—and you have not disappointed me. I also wanted to give you a warning as your former kinsman. Do not interfere in matters that don't concern you. Or you can prophesy that something regrettable will happen to you and your family."

Baldag and the Nephilite turned and departed. We all stared silently after them for a long time, carefully averting our eyes from the basket they left behind. Finally, Father said, "Come, let us give this man a burial."

Father carried the basket down the hill until we found a pleasant meadow. We gathered many stones and piled them around and on top of the basket until we had erected a mound that was almost as tall as me. Father bowed his head and choked back tears, as I sat numbly staring at the gentian and columbine flowers blooming all around us.

Eight

In my twenty-seventh year, my beard began to grow—a sign boys of that day eagerly anticipated. It marked the age of attainment when a boy could be regarded as a man, gain admittance into the tent of meeting, and participate in tribal ceremonies. For me, though, it was a bittersweet milestone, knowing that many of these privileges would be denied to me. Shunned by the tribe, we were cut off from all such communal activities. Father was especially hurt by his exclusion from the annual sacrifice, the holiest day of the year for us, though he always set that day aside and kept it privately in his heart. Of all men alive, I am convinced that he best understood the meaning of the ceremony. Seeing it carried out by men who seemed to be performing an empty ritual grieved him deeply.

The custom of our people was that when a boy attained manhood, his father would take him on a pilgrimage to mark the passage. That, at least, would still be mine, so we made preparations and journeyed north. As we wound our way slowly through the foothills, Father seemed to be in no hurry and for this I was grateful. After working so hard for so many years, the leisurely pace was a luxurious relief.

Within two days we were in territory unfamiliar even to Father. The terrain sloped generally from our left to our right, falling away as it were from the Edenic plateau—the Forbidden Garden—that was the highest elevation in the land. Here and there, a break in the pines gave us a spectacular view of some scenic valley or lush meadow below. We talked at times, but were mostly content to simply enjoy each other's company. I could not help wondering, though, where our destination lay, so I finally asked him.

"I don't know," he said. "I have never been here myself."

"But how will we know when we get there?" I asked.

"Don't let your desire to reach your destination diminish the pleasure of your journey," said Father. "You may find that it was the journey that was the most important part of all."

At the time, I didn't understand that he was talking about life. Indeed, fully appreciating his wisdom in this has taken me a lifetime. Neither did I understand how he was applying it to himself, which was why he could take precious time from his monumental project to be alone with his son on that important occasion.

On the Sabbath, we camped at a place that marked a decision point for us. After six days of following the hills due north, they began to curve back toward the west. So, following the hills would require a change in direction and continuing in the same direction would mean venturing out of the hills.

For the meditation that day, Father recounted the story of Enoch, son of Jared. "Enoch was the greatest of the seers," he explained. "He walked with God and then he was no more, because the Lord took him."

"Where did God take Enoch?" I asked.

"To the place where he dwells, I presume."

"Doesn't God live everywhere?"

"Always so many questions," said Father, but with a smile. "God is everywhere, but I believe there is a place where he dwells in a special way."

The thought of Enoch being taken alive held great allure for me. Although death was rare among our people, and it had never come to anyone that I knew personally, I was aware that it was the inevitable fate of all living things because of the Curse. The mere knowledge of its existence created a place in my mind where I feared to go. I recalled the beheaded Nephilite. Fifteen years later, his grimace of death and his pale, lifeless eyes still disturbed me—not only because of the horrible way in which he died, but also because I knew I would share in that common fate. One day my eyes would be pale and lifeless like his. I asked, "Is it possible to escape death like Enoch?"

"Enoch was a holy man," said Father. "That is what his name means. But I do not see holy men among us today."

"What about you?" I said. "You're a holy man."

"Don't say that," said Father sternly. "I know you mean well, but you do not know what you are saying."

"Well, if you don't qualify, there's not much hope for the rest of us."

"Ah, but the hope we have lies in this very knowledge."

"I don't understand."

"It's simple," said Father. "The Lord is gracious and compassionate to the contrite of heart. Even though I try to be obedient, I know I am far from perfect. But the Lord is good to me anyway."

"If he is good to you anyway, why worry so much about trying to be obedient?" I asked.

"Because he opposes the proud and rebellious. Enoch prophesied that they will be punished when the Lord comes to earth accompanied by thousands of his holy ones."

"Holy ones?"

"The elders say they are spirit beings created by God before the foundation of the world," said Father.

"Spirit beings? You mean, they don't have bodies?"

"Not any form we would understand. But some of them rebelled and were cast out of God's presence. The serpent in the Garden was such a being."

"So where are these rebel spirits now?"

"I don't know for sure, but it is said that some of the Others roamed the earth in earlier days."

"Others!" I exclaimed as the realization unveiled itself to me. "Merib once mentioned that there were 'Others' living in Nod. I thought he meant other people—other descendants of Adam besides Sethites and Cainites. I didn't know he meant other *world!*"

"If that's true, it would be a very disturbing development," said Father. "But it might also explain some things ..."

"Like what?" I prompted.

"The plight of the Nodites for one. The Others have openly declared their rebellion against the Lord. Having them live among you would not be the way to secure God's blessing. But come now. We're supposed to be enjoying ourselves. Let us talk of happier things."

When morning came, we began to descend out of the hills, continuing on our northward path. We had not agreed to do this, nor even discussed it. But somehow we knew that was where we wanted to go. For my part, I was anxious to see what lay beyond the hill country. The early morning light reflecting off the land below shone a peculiar hue of green, different than any I recalled seeing. From that distance, I could not tell what it was, but the color was deeper than the grasslands of the Setti Plain visible in the distance to our right.

As we drew closer, I could see it was not the surface of a rolling grassland at all, but only the tops of some very strange trees that grew so closely together that they formed a dense green canopy over that entire region. They were smooth-barked and branchless, with serrated fronds at their tops splayed in all directions. As we entered the southern edge, I was quickly overwhelmed by the greenness of it all.

"This color reminds me of one of the jade figurines we saw in Ben-Tubal's palace," said Father.

"That's what we should call this—the Jade Forest," I said.

Practically no direct sunlight penetrated to the floor, but it glowed through the translucent leaves. Underneath grew an endless variety of ferns—short-leafed and long, coarse-bladed and intricate, and some gigantic in size. The moss of the forest floor was so thick and lush that it made walking difficult in places.

Rather abruptly, we stepped into an unexpected island of bright color in that sea of green, where orchids, hibiscus, poppies and other flowers grew to enormous size. Some blossoms measured a foot or more across and the dense foliage surrounding the area intensified their fragrance by confining it to the clearing. Delighted, we stepped carefully from flower to flower to examine them.

While we were thus engaged, I heard a whirring behind me and a dragonfly with a wingspan nearly as long as my arm passed by my head. He was soon joined by many other insects of various kinds, some of which, like the dragonfly, were unusually large. Apparently, they had been frightened off by our approach. But seeing that we meant no harm, they returned and filled the clearing with a loud hum.

Before long, Father grew tired and said, "This is a pleasant place. Let's rest here for awhile." He laid down and was soon fast asleep.

I didn't think too much about it at the time. After all, he was five hundred twenty-seven years old and could hardly be expected to match the energy of my youth. I was in no mood to rest, however. So I continued exploring the area while Father slept.

Just beyond the clearing, a streamlet ran toward the northeast, as nearly as I could reckon, and within a few hundred feet met up with a much larger stream. I turned back and retraced my path until I found a place where I could easily ford the smaller of the two and struck off in a more westerly direction. The further I went, the marshier the terrain became and the water-saturated moss squished between my toes (for I wore no shoes in those days). As I made my way along, the wildness of the place pressed in all around me.

Many days had passed since I had seen any human being other than my father or even any sign of human activity. I began to wonder why no men frequented that region.

Feeling disoriented, I turned myself completely around and realized that I did not know where I was or how to get back to Father. I tried to retrace my steps, but the springy moss did not show any footprints. I made my best guess and headed that direction with no landmarks or anything familiar to guide me through the jungle.

I heard something moving through the trees—something very large. I stood still, trying to get a fix on the sound because I could not see through the dense foliage. It was coming from my left. I could feel the sensation beneath my feet as well as hear it. I tried to get out of the way, but my strides were as nothing compared to my pursuer.

Over my shoulder, I caught a glimpse of the monster nearly upon me, his neck like a tree and every bit as tall. Expecting to be crushed at any moment, I screamed in terror.

As I did so, the monster suddenly whirled around, knocking down several trees with his gargantuan tail in the process. The last thing I remember was crying, "Father!" And then I knew no more.

Nine

I came around slowly with Father kneeling beside me and holding up my groggy head. I tried to move, but felt a sharp stab of pain in my left leg. My foot was pinned beneath an uprooted tree.

"Lay still," said Father. "I will try to free your foot."

Since the ground was soft there, digging underneath proved easier than trying to move the tree. Before long, Father's strong hands had cleared a small tunnel around my leg. Holding me under my arms and trying not to disturb my foot any more than he had to, he slid me gently backward until I was free of the tree. I tried my best not to cry out.

Once I was clear, Father examined the injury and said, "It is painful I'm sure, but the bone does not appear to be broken. The soft earth cushioned the blow and there is a small depression where you were laying that kept most of the weight of the tree off your leg. Otherwise, it could have been worse. We can thank the Lord for his kindness in that regard."

"You always speak of his kindness," I said through clenched teeth. "If he is so good, why would he create such a horrible monster?"

I was surprised that he did not rebuke me for such an impious statement, saying only, "You are delirious from pain."

"Let's leave this place," I moaned. "Before the monster returns to finish me off."

Father helped me up, but it hurt to put any weight on my foot. So he swept me up in his powerful arms and carried me. On what was to have been my passage to manhood, I was, instead, being carried by my Father like an infant. I felt humiliated.

When we had put some distance between that place and ourselves, we stopped to rest on a bed of moss underneath some overhanging ferns so that we were hidden from sight. The dimming light signaled the approach of nightfall as Father made a poultice of wet moss and applied it to my foot. It was painful at first, but seemed to draw out some of the swelling. A mixture of bitter herbs he carried in his pouch helped to dull the pain. Under other circumstances, these would have been boiled to make a tea. But since we had no fire, all I could do was chew them. They didn't taste good at all, but I did feel better afterward.

Father said he believed something in one type of the flowers we had seen in the clearing had made him sleep. When he awoke and discovered I wasn't there, he began searching for me, but found no trail. Then he heard a commotion in the distance and my voice crying out.

In turn, I recounted my story about the attack of the monster. I did not mention how frightened I was or that I had tried to flee in terror.

"You have seen a behemoth," said Father, obviously impressed. "I have heard the elders speak of such a beast. Judging from your description, it can be nothing else."

"Well, now that I've seen him, I'm ready to go home," I replied. "I have no wish to see him again."

"But you've always been such an adventuresome lad," said Father. "Where is your spirit now?"

"I seem to have gotten over it."

He laughed, but not mockingly, and I chuckled with him in spite of myself.

"You know now what you have to do," he said.

"No, I don't. And I don't think I want to."

"You must confront the behemoth. That is surely why we are here."

"Of all the things in all the world, that is the one I would least like to do!" I said emphatically.

"I have never shared this story before," said Father. "But when I was a youth of twenty-five and my beard first began to grow, your Grandfather Lamech took me on a journey of many days until we reached the Great Sea. We pitched our tent on the shore and waited, but I did not know for what. On the third morning, we saw far off in the horizon a plume of spray. As it drew closer, I realized it was a leviathan! This was not a torchlight tale, but a real beast, terrifying in appearance. About a hundred feet from shore, he leaped completely out of the water, propelled skyward by his powerful tail, silvery scales shining like jewels in the sunlight. He landed with a mighty splash and the waves nearly knocked me off my unsteady feet as we stood at the water's edge. Straight for us he headed. My knees quaked. My breath came in gasps. I started to run away, but my father told me to hold my ground. As he glided toward us, the leviathan's neck stuck above the water as tall as that sapling over there and more and more of his enormous body became visible above the water. He ran himself aground and extended his crested head toward us until I could almost touch his spiny beard, though I would never have dared. His nostrils steamed as he eyed us, and when he snorted, sparks flew from his mouth. My bowels quivered and I would have fallen backward had my father not steadied me. When he had regarded us to his satisfaction, he pushed himself backward off the sandy beach with his powerful flippers. He simply swam away without looking back, his wake glistening behind him.

"Neither of us spoke until the leviathan was far out of sight and my wits began to recover. Then your grandfather said to me, 'Today you have stood and faced the Prince of the Deep. And though you were afraid, you did not flee. Thus, you have proved your courage. Now I acknowledge you no longer as a boy, but as a man. But there is much more to being a man than courage. You also need wisdom, so heed my advice. When you saw the leviathan, you knew fear for the first time in your life. But I tell you now to consider the leviathan's Creator, the one who can lead this monster around like a pet. And God has made beings even more awesome than this—far beyond our ability to understand. Therefore, fear the Lord above all things. Then you will have taken the first step on the road to wisdom.'"

Father paused for a moment and added, "That was five hundred years ago and I still remember it like it was yesterday."

"That must have been terrifying!" I said. "I don't think I could have stood my ground."

"You have always had a special way with animals," said Father. "If you would conquer your fears, then face the behemoth."

As I have said before, Father was difficult to refute. In my heart, I knew he was right. But that did not make what I had to do any easier.

The night that enveloped us was blacker than any I had ever experienced. Neither stars nor moon were visible, and nothing combustible could be found to build a campfire. Sound did not carry well in that dense forest and those that I did hear were strange to my ears. Behind all the other night noises was the most peculiar of all, a soft but pervasive creaking. I laid awake much of the night trying not to think about the makers of those noises.

Morning dawned slowly as dim shadows emerged from the mist and gradually changed to green. With the new day came a fresh awareness of how stiff and sore I was—from swollen foot to tender ribs to bruised head. During the night, several pods had fallen to the ground nearby—presumably the source of the thuds I had heard—and I felt a little silly that such a benign thing had cost me sleep. Father cracked one open, and seeing they were good to eat, offered one to me. It had a chewy meat inside, sweet and satisfying. I ate another one and felt my strength returning.

"Are you well enough to stand up?" Father asked.

"I think so," I said as he helped me to my feet. I steadied myself against a tree, trying to shake off the dampness, while Father scouted around for a suitable walking stick. With it, I could walk putting minimal weight on my foot. Although it was painful at first, the discomfort subsided somewhat as we walked along.

We quickly picked up the behemoth's trail of destruction. With the new day, the encounter with the monster was starting to feel more like a bad dream. But I was glad that we could only travel slowly because of my foot and I secretly hoped that we would not find him again.

His path through toppled trees was obvious at first. But these soon grew fewer in number as the beast apparently began to pick his way more carefully. However, he could not avoid making tracks. Even where these were not visible due to the springy moss, we could feel the indentation as we walked.

Because we could see not far ahead, we came rather suddenly upon a great river. "It is the Tigris, I believe," said Father. "One of the four great rivers of the world. The elders say a spring flows from Eden and separates into the headwaters of the Pishon, the Gihon, the Tigris and the Euphrates."

"And what lies beyond the River Tigris?" I asked.

"That land is called Asshur, a wild, uninhabited place."

We sat and rested for some time staring away into the wilderness of Asshur. My mind was carried away by the idea of a place that was so disconnected from the world of men. It stirred something in my heart.

After awhile, Father pointed toward the near bank about half a mile downstream and said, "Does that not look like tracks?"

"Yes," I said. "And large ones."

My leg had stiffened even during that short break, but loosened up again by the time we reached the place Father had seen. The tracks indeed appeared to be the ones we had been seeking, so we we followed them back inland. At mid-afternoon we stopped for the day. My foot was swelling again and I was fatigued. I didn't know if we had gained on the monster, but I could go no further. I soaked my foot in a cool spring nearby, then wrapped another moss compress around it.

Since we had camped early, Father had time to gather some reasonably dry firewood, which was hard to find in that humid place. He also foraged around until he found enough vegetables to make a pot of soup. Famished as I was, that simple fare tasted as good as anything I could have asked for. And though the fire was rather smoky, I did not complain because it meant that I would not have to face the total blackness again that night. Exhausted from the day's walking, I slept soundly.

The next morning came like the previous, a misty change of color from black to gray to green. While I limbered my foot, Father picked some currants and soon we were on our way. Although I was not yet ready to discard my walking stick, I felt myself leaning less on it and we were able to make better time for awhile. The farther we moved away from the river, however, the more difficult the tracking became. The ground was not as soft there and did not take the same impression. Once, we lost the trail completely and had to retrace our steps until we found that the prints veered suddenly away to the left.

We smelled the flowers from a clearing ahead before we saw it. Father's previous experience with their intoxicating effect made him cautious, so we approached slowly. As we did so, we could hear the sound of air rushing in great pulses—the breathing of a great creature!

TEN

Father looked at me searchingly as I stood there motionless. I did not want to appear a coward in his eyes, so I mastered my panic as best I could and willed myself forward. We crawled for a way on our hands and knees, which was not easy to do with my sore foot. Then we dropped to our bellies and inched forward to the edge of the clearing.

There he was—behemoth! Like a hill sleeping in the middle of a plain, he was so large that my eye could scarcely take him all in at one glance. What these clearings were then became obvious—they were the places where the great creatures bedded. And since their stirrings kept any saplings from taking root, flowers grew in abundance. The tops of the surrounding trees were all nipped off (no need to wonder who had done that), allowing abundant light into the clearing.

The behemoth stirred and snorted, evidently catching our scent. I started to back away, but Father's hand on my shoulder stopped me and pushed me forward instead. As I rose to my feet, the beast opened his eyes and stared right at me. He rocked his body from back to front and stood up. I expected him to charge at any moment, but he didn't. Thus we regarded each other for a long time, neither of us advancing or retreating. As I studied him, I noted that his face and eyes were not as I expected them to be—not at all ferocious. I took this to heart and advanced timidly. To my surprise, the behemoth stepped back. I took two more steps forward and halted because the behemoth started to turn as if he might flee.

I suddenly felt ashamed at the realization of how badly I had misjudged him. He had not been pursuing me to destroy me in the jungle. Our encounter had been but chance and he must have been at least as frightened of me as I was of him when we had happened upon each other. I inched forward, not knowing how to speak to such a creature, but trying to soothe him with my voice. He did not flee, but began bleating quietly and rhythmically with each breath. I did not approach too closely because I did not want to frighten him by disappearing from his field of view. He slowly lowered his head, and when it was even with mine, I could see that his teeth were flat and worn from chewing on the vegetation that grew so abundantly in that place. His eyes were bigger around than my fists, though they still seemed disproportionately small for his great size. Gingerly, I reached out my hand and touched his mottled green skin. His nostrils flared for a moment, but he didn't shy away. His skin was not as clammy as its shiny appearance might have led me to believe, but was smooth and dry like polished pebbles.

He looked away from me and scanned the area as though he were trying to tell me something. "What is troubling you?" I asked.

He raised his head and gave a mighty trumpet—a plaintive, high-pitched sound so loud that I put my hands over my ears. It was a sad sound to hear, and though I did not understand what it meant, I could make a guess. I shouted up to him, "Have you become separated from your herd?" He lowered his head again and the look in his eyes led me to assume that I had guessed correctly. "Don't worry," I said. "We'll help you find the others."

I beckoned to Father and explained the situation to him. He readily agreed to do whatever we could to help him find his family. Since we had seen what appeared to be other tracks back by the river, we decided to begin looking there. The behemoth followed behind us, moving more gracefully than I might have imagined from his size. I soon realized why we had not seen the evidence of their presence in the forest. The supple trees of the jungle bent rather than broke as he passed, so that he was like an eel gliding through reeds.

Since my foot felt better and my walking stick made the behemoth uneasy, I discarded it and we made good time in arriving back at the river. Father and I split up—he went downstream and I went upstream with the behemoth loyally following me. Many tracks were evident on my search, but none looked fresh. When we met back where we had parted, however, Father was excited because he had found fresh tracks not more than a day old. By the time we reached the place, dusk was already falling. We camped there for the night, but did not build a campfire as we did not want to risk alarming the behemoth. We dined on the fruit that grew abundantly there while the behemoth grazed on the tops of the trees. I slept better that night than I had in some time.

I woke to the sound of the behemoth splashing happily in the river. When he began to honk, I knew he had spotted the tracks on the opposite bank. Since he seemed in no mood to wait patiently for us to eat our breakfast, Father and I quickly swam the river on our sides holding our packs in the air. The current was not strong there so we had no difficulty getting to the other side where the behemoth awaited us.

On the north side of the river, the undergrowth was even denser. In a short distance we lost the trail and did not know which way to turn. I said to the behemoth, "I don't know which way your herd has gone from here. Will you bear me on your neck so that I may get a better view?"

With some coaxing and gesturing I was able to make clear to him what I wanted him to do. He lowered his neck and allowed me to climb on. My arms could not completely encircle his neck because of its great girth, so I squeezed with my knees and clung on as best I could as he lifted me into the air. When his head reached the treetop canopy, I dared not let loose my grip to part the branches that scraped against my back for fear that I might slip off. I just held on and let him poke his head through. From that vantage point, I could see that the river made a great bend back to the north. Just west of there, I could see a hill that protruded above the forest. Reasoning that the behemoths probably never ventured too far from their great water supply, I decided to make our way to the hilltop in the hope that we would be able to see far up and down the Tigris. I indicated to the behemoth to let me down and sighed with relief when my feet were back on firm ground.

Although the hill seemed close when seen from above the tree line, it took most of the day to get there through the dense undergrowth. Since we were learning what to look for, we saw signs here and there that indicated that behemoths had once passed there, but none were recent. And those signs were few to be seen because the prodigious growth of the vegetation quickly healed any sign of broken branches or trampled moss. Indeed, I finally understood the soft creaking noise that had puzzled me since we entered the Jade Forest. You could actually hear the vegetation growing.

We did not reach the summit of the hill until mid-afternoon. No trees grew on the crest, but the flowers and ferns were plentiful and grew to waist deep in most places. Here and there, however, were patches that looked as if they had been recently shorn. I knelt down to examine one of these patches and grew excited because it appeared to have been recently grazed. One plant was still wet with sap.

"I think we're very close," I said. Once again I mounted the behemoth—

not as fearful as the first time, but by no means confident. I could see many miles from there, but did not need to look that far. To the east less than a mile away, two dozen behemoths were sunning themselves by the river. The behemoth spotted them at nearly the same moment I did. He let out a deafening trumpet and started galloping toward the herd. No amount of protesting on my part could persuade him to let me off and I clutched his neck for my life.

Their reunion was a happy one, though I have to confess that it took several minutes before I could appreciate that fact. While my ride on the galloping behemoth was an experience I would never forget, it was also one I would never willingly repeat—not for all the gold in Nephil.

The other behemoths were wary of me. By that time, though, I was more than happy to put some space between us while I recovered my wits. Clearly, they were herding animals. As I studied them together, I surmised that the females and young always tended to stay together. Apparently, though, adult males, like my friend, were a bit more solitary and sometimes spent time by themselves away from the herd. Thus, there had probably been no immediate alarm among them at the absence of their herd mate.

Father soon joined me and we watched them for some time. Seeing them all together was an awesome sight. But when the shadows began to lengthen, I realized it was time to go. I called to the behemoth, "Farewell, great one! We must be on our way."

He looked toward me and bleated, which I took as his way of saying goodbye. As we made our way from that place, Father put his arm around my shoulder and said, "Today, Jayfeth, you have proved your courage. You not only faced your fears, but in doing so, you have done this beast a good turn. From this day forward, I regard you no longer as a boy, but as a man."

It was the proudest moment of my life.

ELEVEN

Because Father wanted to visit my great-grandfather Methuselah, we did not plan to go straight home. We had not seen him for many years and Father wanted to take the opportunity to do so while we were in the north country. So, once we re-crossed the Tigris, we struck out toward the east and soon left the jungle behind. A spur of wooded hills that jutted northeast from the Edenic Plateau, generally following the path of the river, was traversed in a day, bringing us to the northwestern edge of the vast Setti Plain. Not many people lived that far to the north, but the elk and deer flourished there. We made good time crossing the gently rolling savanna and camped that night on a sweet-clover knoll. Since we stopped attending the annual festival on the plain, I had not seen stars stretching from horizon to horizon like that for a long time and the moonless night afforded a spectacular view. Father once told me that the stars sang while God created the world. And as I lay there looking up, I could almost hear them myself that night.

We set out early the next morning toward the rising sun. As we walked, I saw a shadow ahead that seemed to cover the whole land and I was greatly puzzled. When we drew closer, though, I realized that it was not a shadow at all, but a great herd of bison—a number beyond counting—extending as far as the eye could see. Father and I looked at each other and I nodded to him that I thought we should go straight through the herd. Going around, if that could be done, would cause us to lose time. And my experience with the behemoths had taught me that I should fear no creature (but not forget to give them the respect that was due them!).

A few of those closest to us would look up momentarily as we passed before going back to grazing. Most, though, took no notice of us at all. Picking our way through the herd made for slow going because we constantly had to zigzag. The herd was so intent on feeding that the animals did not even bother to move out of our way as we passed. I had seen bison before—small groups of stragglers that ventured near to some of the villages on the plain—but never that close. I hadn't realized before how large they really were. I had to look up to see the tops of their shoulders and their heads were like shaggy boulders, with beards that put my new growth to shame.

The morning was long spent when we began to see the far side of the herd. We did not stop to eat until we were safely past, for though the beasts seemed heedless of our presence, they could have easily stepped on us in their relentless foraging. Father baked bread over an open fire from the seeds of the grain that grew abundantly in that place. I would have liked it better with butter, but it was pleasing enough to taste and very filling.

The next day we began to bear more northeasterly and came upon a clan we did not recognize encamped near a small lake. Father warned them about the coming doom, but they responded with angry threats. Though I had begun to grow accustomed to indifference, open hostility still unsettled me. Father debated them until I feared that they might physically harm us before we moved on.

Two days later, we reached the home of the Ancient One. In a grotto by a spring that fed the River Tabor, we found him sitting cross-legged on a blanket, not far from the camp of his kinsmen.

"Greetings, Venerable One," said Father, as we sat down on the smooth limestone near him.

Methuselah did not answer. Though his eyes were open, they stared unfocused at the pool, and he gave no immediate indication that he had noticed us at all. He had been old—even by the standards of the day—ever since I had known him, so I could not tell that he had aged much since I last saw him. His eye perhaps was dimmer and his body a bit thinner. It was said that he hardly ate enough to sustain a bird.

Father waited patiently for him to reply. At long last, Methuselah said slowly, "Do you hear?"

Father tilted his head and listened intently for a moment, eyebrows raised.

"The earth groans," said the Ancient One. "When I was a youth, she whispered."

Father nodded in agreement. But I did not understand what he meant and strained my ears to hear what I was missing. Whatever it was that they shared escaped me. "I don't hear anything."

Great-grandfather had not yet acknowledged my presence. When he spoke, it was to Father. "He is not of the line of seers?"

"The Lord has blessed him in other ways," said Father. I tried to ignore the familiar burning sensation that rose in my cheeks despite the cool air of the cave.

"Come here, boy," said Methuselah.

Suppressing the urge to tell him that I was a man, not a boy, I knelt in front of him. His cheeks and eyes were sunken, and his white beard and hair, which hung nearly to the ground as he sat, had grown wispy. Given his overall appearance of frailty, I was surprised at the strength of his bony fingers when he gripped my shoulders and said, "Has your father not told you of the Curse, boy?"

"Why, yes," I answered.

"Do you think it just a fireside tale to amuse children?"

"No, Father Methuselah."

"Then how do you not hear the world groaning under its weight? You do not have to be a seer to know that evil is abroad. Every day the measure of judgment grows against the wicked."

I started to explain to him that I was actively engaged in helping Father try to set things right, but I could not find the words. His gaze penetrated my all-too-thin mantle of righteousness and seemed to look right into my heart. I felt, instead, like he was numbering me among the transgressors facing imminent destruction. I could not endure his stare and cast my eyes down to the ground.

The Ancient One let go of me and redirected his attention to Father. "This one doubts," he said, once again speaking as if I were not present. As soon as I was free, I backed away and tried not to look like I was sulking.

"He has a good heart," said Father. "There is hope for him."

"Perhaps," said Methuselah. "Or perhaps your discernment is clouded by your love for the boy."

"It wouldn't be the first time my discernment has been questioned," said Father wryly.

"No," said Methuselah, his tone softening a bit. "I'm afraid not."

"So, how do things go with the northern clans?"

"I think you know," said Methuselah. "A new generation has arisen. They do not respect the old ways."

"And what about you?" said Father.

"I am well cared for, if that's what you mean. They humor me, but I have little authority anymore. The clans look to new men with new ideas. And their hearts are turning ever eastward."

"Even this far north?" said Father, pausing for a moment to let this news register. "I would not add to your cares, but you should know that Jayfeth has heard that the Others are living among them."

The Ancient One didn't answer.

"Can you tell me what you know about them?" said Father.

Father Methuselah continued to remain silent for some time, having lapsed back into a trance-like state. I wondered what visions or memories were revealing themselves to his mind. When I was about to conclude that he wasn't going to answer, he spoke, quietly at first, but with growing intensity. "You have stirred recollections that have long been sleeping—and perhaps were better left undisturbed."

"Then the Others are more than just a myth," said Father.

"Oh, yes, though we knew them by a different name," said the Ancient One. "They are the Watchers—that is, they were the spirit beings who identified themselves as the Order of the Watch. I believe they were originally sent to earth in ages past to teach and to guide and to protect. But some of them became corrupt, following the example of the Serpent. In the days of my grandfather Jared, the Watchers declared open rebellion and were cast out of God's presence. When a cult of false worship began to form around them, my father, Enoch the Righteous, made a strong stand against them. I had always believed that he had driven them out, but perhaps he only drove them into hiding. If they have indeed found sanctuary among men, it would be an evil tiding. My father walks the earth no more. Who will stand against them now?"

"There is none like Enoch today," Father agreed. "The race of men is poorer without him."

"Still, there is a glimmer of hope," said Methuselah, looking right at Father. He leaned closer and added, "In spite of the fact that so few appreciate you."

"Now whose discernment is clouded by love?" said Father, and I thought his cheeks may have reddened slightly.

"I'm too old to waste words saying anything I don't believe to be true. And who knows? Even Jayfeth here might amount to something someday— if he can stay out of trouble long enough."

"Thanks," I said. "I think."

"You remind me of my own son Lamech when he was your age," said Methuselah. "And that's not half bad. You may turn out all right in the end."

TWELVE

S ince the rest of the clan seemed none too eager for us to stay, we left that same day. As soon as we were out of earshot, I asked, "Was Father Methuselah always like that?"

"Like what?" said Father.

"I don't know. He doesn't seem very ... tactful."

"He comes from an age where speaking the truth was more highly regarded than it is today," said Father. "Now, everyone always expects you to say what they want to hear—regardless if it's the truth. Actually, I find it refreshing to talk with someone who's not dissembling all the time. But I'm sure that it does come as a shock if you're not used to it. Don't be too hard on him, though. Remember he's carrying the accumulated heartaches of nine centuries. When you reach his age, we'll see how good your humor is."

At every tent and village we came to along the way, Father delivered his message with a fresh urgency. He shortened his speech, boiling it down to a few short sentences warning them of the coming doom and urging them to take refuge in the ark. If he was met with anger and opposition, he lingered long enough to debate the points. But if not, we did not tarry.

"Why do we stay longer where we are clearly not wanted," I asked him. "And move on quickly from where we are better received?"

"I have come to the conclusion that the worst possible response is indifference," said Father matter-of-factly. "This is not an easy message to hear. If it doesn't rankle them, they haven't really heard it."

"But how do you keep from getting discouraged in the face of such constant opposition?" I asked.

"Because I have hope that the message will prevail in the end," said Father. "I believe that many will ultimately turn their hearts back to God and be saved—perhaps enough to prevent the disaster."

Because of our frequent stops, it took nearly another month before we reached the Highlands. I was glad to have those familiar surroundings close in around me. The unrelenting rejection and bitterness we faced weighed ever more heavily upon me.

Instead of solace at home, though, we found strife. The moment we entered the camp, I could tell by the look on Mother's face that something was wrong.

"Ham has gone to Nephil," she said. "We told him not to, but he went anyway."

"For what purpose?" asked Father.

"He said we needed supplies. But Shem said that was only a pretense and they quarreled."

"How long ago did he leave?"

"More than three weeks. He should have been back by now."

"It's not just tools he seeks," said Shem. "He's up to something."

We were relieved when Ham returned the following day, but Father took him aside and rebuked him sharply. "What did you think you were doing going off to Nephil by yourself?"

"I had an idea for a device to make it easier to stack the lumber," he said. "But I needed parts to build it."

"You could have sent for them without going yourself."

"I had to show them what I wanted."

"Are you sure that was it?" said Father. "Or was it just an excuse to go back to Nephil? I always thought Jayfeth had an unhealthy fascination with those people, but you're worse than he ever was."

"Why shouldn't I admire them?" said Ham. "They're the most excellent people in the world. Next to them, we're backward."

"I'm not going to debate their merits with you," said Father. "The point is that there are people out there who are very hostile to our message."

"Our *own* people?"

"As I was saying, because of the hostility we are facing, we must stick together, two by two, whether we go out from here or stay in camp. It is not safe to be alone. And if you cannot agree with your mother and brothers concerning a matter, you must defer to them because they are older."

"So being older always makes them right?" said Ham.

"That's my final word on the subject. And if you don't like it … "

"If I don't like it, what?"

Father paused. "You'll just have to accept it anyway." I had the distinct impression he had changed his answer in mid-sentence.

Not many months later, Shem's beard began to grow and Father accompanied him on his rite of passage as he had done for me. Shem did not share many of the details with me because those journeys were considered private matters between fathers and sons. All I know is that their sojourn included a visit to the altar of the annual sacrifice. While they were there, Shem received a vision from the Lord, his first true prophetic experience.

"I saw the future," he told me excitedly. "Or more like several different futures all rolled into a single moment of time. Only there wasn't any time—at least I was not conscious of time. It's hard to explain. It was wonderful and frightening at once. I don't pretend to understand it all, but Father is going to help me sort it out."

"I'm happy for you," I said, but my tone must have betrayed me.

"I'm sorry," said Shem. "I wasn't trying to rub it in."

"It's all right," I said. "I'm glad that you've had a vision. I really am. It's just that … I haven't. Maybe there's something wrong with me. Or else God just doesn't feel the same toward me."

"I don't think that's it at all," said Shem sympathetically. "This is my destiny, Jay. I've always known it."

"But what's my destiny?"

"I'm not that good of a prophet. I'm afraid you'll have to find that answer on your own."

Ham's turn to go with Father came soon after Shem's. They, too, set out for the high country, but were not gone many days before they returned. It was clear that something was amiss. Father was angry—as angry as I had ever seen him. I took my brother aside and asked him what had happened.

"I did a foolish thing," said Ham, his eyes downcast. "We were encamped in the high hills, not far from the forbidden land. One night, an overwhelming urge came over me to go to the Gate of Eden to see if the tales about the Guardian of the Gate were true. So I stole away while Father was sleeping."

"You know you're not supposed to get that close to the Forbidden Land!" I said.

"Are you going to lecture me or do you want to hear the story?"

"Well, go on," I said. "What did you see?"

"That's what I thought," said Ham looking at me like a fellow conspirator. "You're as curious about such things as I am. Anyway, when I got within sight of the entrance, I could see what looked like a fire burning in the gate. And inside of the fire, I could see an awesome being like a … I don't know. I can't really describe it, except that there was definitely a mighty sword in his hand and he was swinging it back and forth." He demonstrated with a pretend sword.

"Yes, and then?"

"I left," said Ham.

"You left or ran away?"

"He wasn't the kind of creature you just walk up to and say, 'How do you do?' It was very unnerving. You wouldn't have done any better."

"No, probably not," I said. "How did Father find out?"

"I honestly don't know," said Ham. "It was still dark when I returned to camp, but somehow Father knew what I had been up to. He probably had a vision or something. It's an unfair advantage having knowledge like that. Whatever it was, he was furious and spoke harshly to me. I suppose I deserved it. But I wouldn't change what I did. I don't know if any man alive has seen what I saw!"

I let Ham's story sink in for a moment and reflected, "So, it's true then. The Others really are on the earth."

"Do you think that's good or bad?"

"I can't say for sure," I said. "Maybe both. But I'd say we're better off knowing about them."

Once all three of us were fully grown, the work of felling timber continued at a faster pace than ever before. Ham was always designing new devices to save time and labor. While I suspect that part of his motivation was just to get out of camp to go after parts, I have to admit that some of these were highly successful. The one I appreciated most was a system of pulleys within a frame. He had been fascinated with wheels ever since I had first described them to him and he had built several pushcarts that came in handy around the camp. The pulleys were an adaptation of this, transferring the work of the wheels to vertical lifting. It allowed us to stack the wood easier and higher than we ever had before, so we didn't have to drag the lumber as far or expend as much effort to lift it.

Thus, as the years went by, the stacked logs began to greatly outnumber the standing trees. I was beginning to wonder what we would do when all gopherwood in that stand was gone, but Father had always kept his own counsel about the matter. Then one day with no warning, he said, "This will be enough. When we finish this grove, we will have what we need. The Lord has provided well for us."

That was exciting news. Having spent nearly forty years of my life in hard labor at a task that seemed unending, I was relieved at the prospect of moving on to work that sounded less onerous.

When the stand was very nearly cleared, Father and Ham set out on another preaching circuit, leaving Shem and I to finish up the last few trees. It had been some time since Father had been abroad and he was anxious to see if his warnings had produced any effect. He planned to go to Nephil first and return by way of the Plain country. But they returned in less than three weeks, with Father looking more dejected than ever. "The Nephilim have lapsed back into the worship of false gods. The one place where I thought my warning had its greatest effect is worse off than before."

"Maybe you should make an extended visit there," I said. "Then you could teach them the ways of the Lord more adequately."

"But our work is here," he said, anguishing over the same old problem that had vexed him for many years. "My heart is torn between the two. What shall I do? I am deeply distressed."

Shoulders slumped, he trudged slowly up the hill to pray for guidance. I saw a tear form in Mother's eye as she watched him and I put my arm around her to comfort her. When she turned to go back to the tent, I returned to work. But my mind was elsewhere. How could the ark be a witness to the people when it was located so far from where anyone lived?

"Look out!" Ham yelled, disturbing me out of my rumination.

I had wandered into the path of a falling tree and scrambled out of the way just in time to avoid being crushed. It was close enough that I could feel the air it stirred as it crashed to the ground.

"What are you doing!" said Ham. "You've been around long enough to know that this is no place for daydreamers."

But I was not listening to his admonition. The crash of the tree had reminded me of something and had given me an idea. "I have to find Father," I said and walked away from the clearing, leaving an unhappy Ham yelling behind me.

Father had a favorite place at the top of the hill that he liked to go when he prayed. Sure enough, he was sitting there on a rock, head bowed. As I approached, I made as much noise I could, so that I would not startle him.

"Any messages from the Lord?" I asked as I sat down beside him.

"No."

"Then consider what I have to say. This is not the place to be a witness to the people. The place to build the ark is on the Plain of Nephil. All roads lead there these days. Then, everyone in that city and all who travel there will see it."

"But it would take a hundred years to move all this lumber to Nephil, even if we had a hundred men!" Father countered.

"We don't have a hundred men, that is true. But I know something that has the strength of a hundred—the behemoth."

"What do you mean?"

"If we could enlist the help of the behemoths, they could drag the logs to the river and then we could float them to Nephil."

Father thought it over for a moment and said, "Do you think they would do it?"

"I don't know," I said. "But what harm is there in trying?"

Father smiled slowly. "The people will say that Jayfeth is as crazy as his father."

"I won't take that as an insult," I said.

"All right then," said Father. "Make the necessary preparations. Ham can go with you. Perhaps it will satisfy his craving for adventure for awhile."

THIRTEEN

We set out within a few days and headed north along the path that Father and I had taken twelve years earlier. Ham had indeed been eager to come. Hearing about my encounter with the behemoth had made him envious, and I think part of the reason he ventured so close to Eden to see the Guardian of the Gate was to try and outdo me. But he had been in high spirits even before he knew he was going, so much so that I finally commented about it. "I don't understand it. You're the only one who hasn't been gloomy."

"Everyone's always telling me to cheer up," said Ham. "And when I do, they think it's strange. I can't win."

"I'm not complaining. Just curious."

"Can't a fellow be happy without having a reason?"

"Sure, it's just that you're usually not that kind of fellow."

"Watch yourself, Jay. You'll provoke me into being unhappy again."

"I wouldn't want to do that," I laughed. "We've got a long enough trip ahead of us without that. And speaking of trips, it just occurred to me that you've been like this ever since you got back from Nephil. What gives? Did they get in a new shipment of wheels or something exciting like that?"

"Oh, they've got wheels all right," said Ham. "And lots of other interesting sights. And not all of them are mechanical."

"All right, you're just toying with me now. Are you going to tell me or not?"

"I might. But how do I know if you're to be trusted?"

"If you can't trust me, who can you trust?"

"That's supposed to inspire confidence?"

"Just tell me, Ham."

"Well, you know how you're always going on about Merib," he said.

"You've always paid so much attention to him that you've hardly noticed he has sisters."

"I know he has sisters. So what?"

"Ah, but you haven't seen them lately and I have. They've grown up."

"Grown up?"

"I mean grown up into women," said Ham. "You know, girls do that."

"Of course I know that," I said. "But what's that to you?"

"I'm telling you that they've become really beautiful women—especially Jirah."

"Right."

"Don't be so thick, Jay. Do I have to draw you a picture?"

"No, I get the picture. It's simple enough. Jirah is pretty."

"I think she likes me."

This piece of news was so completely unexpected that it was practically incomprehensible. "Jirah, Ben-Tubal's daughter? And you?"

"Is that so far-fetched?"

"If you told me you sprouted wings and flew to the moon, that would be far-fetched," I said. "This is beyond far-fetched."

"Come on, now. Give me some credit."

"I'm not trying to insult you. I mean, I can certainly see how she would find it hard to resist your rugged good looks—"

"Careful," said Ham.

"It's just that it seems like a bit of a mismatch. After all, she lives in a palace of marble and gold and you ... What can I say? You live in a ragged old tent."

"You're missing the obvious point here. She has all that already. It doesn't matter that I don't."

"She's got to be a foot taller than you by now, Ham," I said. "Probably two!"

"That doesn't make any difference to Jirah. She knows a real man when she sees one."

"Sounds like you have it all figured out—except for the one obstacle you'll never get over. Father will never allow it."

"Well, aren't you the optimistic one," said Ham. "I'll make him listen to reason. We're moving to Nephil soon and it'll be easier then when Jirah and I can be together all the time. Father will see that it's meant to be."

"And if he doesn't?" I asked.

"I'm of age now," said Ham. "I can make my own decisions."

On the eve of the following Sabbath, we reached the place where the hills veered back away to the west and spent the night there. By early afternoon the next day, we were enveloped in the misty green hush of the Jade Forest.

I assumed that the most likely place to find the behemoths would be near the Tigris River, so I headed straight for it—or at least as straight as I could navigate in that place. But I must have strayed off course or circled back on myself, though, because we still hadn't reached the river by evening. We did, however, come to a place where the trees were much shorter and younger. I realized that this must have been one of the clearings formerly used by the behemoths. But it was long abandoned, and the new saplings showed several years' growth. The fact that it had obviously not been used for some time troubled me. Recalling how deep the darkness was in the midst of the forest, we decided to make camp there where at least some starlight would be visible.

We reached the river on the following morning and we were, indeed, some distance to the west of where Father and I had crossed the first time. We scouted around and were disappointed to find no fresh tracks. Indeed, those few we did find were very faint and hard to discern. Although much daylight still remained, we pitched camp there because I was at a loss to decide which way to turn—whether upstream or down or across the river. We spent the remainder of the day making a more thorough search of the near side of the river. Although we could have covered twice as much ground by splitting up, I had a growing sense of uneasiness that made me decide that we should stay together. Finding no signs, we passed the night on the bank of the river. I savored the light of the quarter moon and braced myself for the black nights I knew were soon coming.

Shortly after first light, we crossed the river, determined to make for the knoll where Father and I had seen the behemoths before. Since I had no behemoth to climb on, this proved difficult because I had to guess at the direction. And when I had long thought we should have reached the place where the clearing should be, I found only trees and more trees. On one hill, the trees appeared to be younger, but it was difficult to tell if it was the same clearing because of the way the vegetation grew so prolifically there. If that was the place or close to it, then I knew the river bent back in our direction and was only a mile or two away, so we made for it. As we went along, though, a feeling of foreboding grew within me. Something foul was in that place. Ham looked at me, sensing it too.

Suddenly, we were upon it—the rotted carcass of a behemoth.

At first I feared that it might be the one I had befriended. But upon closer inspection, the bone structure appeared to be that of a female—fully-grown, but not old. I wondered that a young, apparently healthy creature would have died for no reason. But Ham quickly discovered the cause. Between her ribs was a metal spear point larger than my hand.

"What are you doing?" I asked as I watched Ham remove the spear tip from its shaft and put it in his pack.

"I know what you're thinking," said Ham.

"Where else do you know of that metal implements can be obtained?"

"Let's not jump to conclusions. We don't know that the Nephilim had anything to do with this."

"This isn't the first time they've been accused of hunting animals for food," I said.

"I don't think it was for food," said Ham. "This animal rotted in its place."

"Then how do you explain what happened here?" I asked, but neither of us had an answer to that question.

A few minutes later, we reached the river and found what I was sure we would by then—nothing. I said, "If the behemoths are being hunted, they'll probably try to avoid the open areas along the river."

"Where do you think they'd go?"

"If it was me, I'd probably hide in the deepest part of the forest," I said. "I believe that's northwest of here."

"If I was that big, I'd stand my ground and fight," said Ham.

"You're not a behemoth."

"You're not mocking me about being short again, are you?"

"I wouldn't dream of it," I said. "If you're tall enough for Jirah, you're tall enough for me."

I quickly realized that I had previously penetrated only the outer fringes of the jungle. The tangle that enveloped us was even thicker than before, making it impossible to travel more than a few miles in a day. The visibility was so poor that we could have passed within a few feet of a behemoth and never even have known it. I began to despair that we would be able to find one.

The nights were worse. Since we could find very little wood that was dry enough to burn in that humid place, we built no fires. We passed many long nights surrounded by blackness such that we could hardly see each other. We lay side by side for fear of losing contact and were afraid to even venture far enough to relieve ourselves until morning came.

And when morning did come, it brought only murky green shadows. Our eyes became weary of it and we longed to see the sun and blue skies again. The longer we were there, the less we spoke. Our voices sounded strange in that place and we felt like intruders trying to avoid detection. I have to admit that this was a relief at first because my brother tended to talk incessantly. But a wild kind of loneliness descended upon us even though we were together. All that could be heard was the whispering of the growing vegetation and chirrups of insects that always seemed distant because they fell silent as we passed.

After several days of this, Ham finally said, "This is folly. We'll never find these beasts. I can hardly see the hand at the end of my arm. Let's leave this lonely place, Jay, and return to the land of people."

"I made a promise to Father ..." I began.

"You promised to try. We've tried, but the task before us was impossible. There's no shame in turning back now."

"Please, let's give it a little more time so that I can satisfy myself that we've done all we could."

"Satisfy yourself quickly then, because I'm heading home soon."

"You wouldn't leave without me?" I said.

Ham paused for a moment and then said, "No, but I will go—even if I have to bind you and carry you all the way to the Highlands on my back." I knew him better than to laugh that off as a joke.

FOURTEEN

The Sabbath came again and still we saw no sign of the behemoths. We lunched on the gourds that grew bountifully there, and found the light green ones were tart, while the darker green ones were sweeter. We discovered that by mixing the pulp of various gourds in combination that we could create delicacies that were pleasing to every part of the palate. After Ham had gorged himself, he lay down for a nap. While he was sleeping, I decided to explore the area around the camp, though I did not go very far. The last thing I wanted to do was to become separated as I had done with Father.

We had seen very few four-footed animals during all our time in the Jade Forest. They were no doubt there, just well warned by our bumbling through the thickets and easily concealed in the undergrowth. Insects and crawling things, however, teemed with abundance. I had not paid much attention to them before, but decided that studying them might be an interesting way to pass the afternoon. The first thing I noticed was a spider busying herself trying to free a fly that had accidentally become entangled in her web. I wanted to help, but the work was far too delicate for me to provide any assistance. The spider managed just fine without me and soon the fly flew off, apparently no worse for the experience.

I began looking on the underside of plant leaves and soon spotted a foot-long caterpillar with alternating bands of black and gold. She was munching away on the tender shoots of a fern, grasping the stalk of the plant she was eating with dozens of legs. I wondered what kind of butterfly she would become when she went through the change.

I continued poking around in the undergrowth to see what else could be found. Under one broad, flat leaf thousands of tiny eggs were attached, though I did not know what kind of insect might have laid them. I thought about how strange it was for them to abandon their eggs like that, in contrast to other animals that reared their young.

At that moment, the thought occurred to me that the behemoth might not have been killed for her meat, but for her eggs. Perhaps she had been nesting when the attackers came and she had died trying to protect her young. This realization, however, only led to a deeper mystery. I could not formulate any reason for the taking of her eggs, but I was certain that the purpose could only be evil. I did not tell Ham what I suspected. I had no proof and I did not think he would want to hear it anyway, for he was very sensitive about anything that might possibly malign the Nephilim.

As we continued on in the same general direction we had been heading, the elevation gradually rose and the ground became firmer underneath our feet. Emerging into a clearing, my heart raced to see that it had been recently used. I warned Ham again about the flowers as we explored the area, but that was probably a mistake. Every time he thought my back was turned, he leaned toward one flower or another and inhaled. Telling him not to do something only put ideas into his head.

Fresh signs were everywhere, (and fresh behemoth droppings are impossible to miss), so I knew the behemoths could not be far away. But the shadows were lengthening and we could pursue them no further that day. We camped there for the night at the edge of the clearing and seeing the light of the stars and moon again was like a gentle caress to my eyes.

At dawn we continued scouting the area. There were so many tracks coming and going that it was impossible to tell which might be the most recent. So instead of trying to track them and risk guessing wrong, we determined to wait there in the hope that they would return. We hid ourselves in the foliage at the edge of the clearing that had the fewest tracks, because the last place we wanted to be was right in the path of the returning behemoths. I could in no way imitate the trumpeting of the behemoths, but from time to time I made bleating sounds like the one that they made in the hope of calling them in. I do not know if this had any effect, but toward midday I thought I heard a distant reply. I called again. This time, the reply was unmistakable. The behemoths were coming.

I decided not to answer because I didn't know how convincing my call would be over a shorter distance. Since they seemed to be heading our way anyway, I didn't want to take a chance of scaring them. For some time, we could not hear their movements. I began to wonder if they had headed off in a different direction again. But I recalled that they could move with surprisingly little noise when they were not alarmed.

When at last we could hear them approaching—or feel them, I should say—it was only a matter of moments before they burst into the clearing. Ham's eyes widened with amazement. I put my hand on his shoulder to steady him or I think he would have fallen over backward. My own heart pounded within me as I marveled afresh at their enormous size.

There were only four in this herd—an adult male and female with two babies. As I looked more closely at the male, something about him looked familiar to me. Wonder of wonders, we had found the very behemoth that I had befriended!

Overjoyed, I stepped into the clearing, certain the behemoth would be glad to see me. To my dismay, he lunged several steps instead and put himself between his family and me, stamping and snorting as if he might charge at any moment.

"But I am your friend. Don't you remember me?" I said. The stamping and snorting quieted a bit. "We mean you no harm. Don't mistake us for the evil men who are hunting your kind."

Warily, the behemoth studied me for a long time. When he slowly lowered his head down to my level, I could tell that he finally remembered me.

"Allow me to present my brother Ham," I said as Ham stood up and emerged from the bushes. The behemoth readily accepted him, perhaps because he resembled Father. The behemoth grunted toward his family and they approached us, quickly overcoming their fears and allowing us to touch them without hesitation. The young ones were especially playful and wanted to roll around on the ground with us. We obliged them as best we could, but had to be careful. Even the younger ones could have crushed us if we would have borne their full weight with our bodies.

Explaining what we wanted them to do regarding the lumber was not easy. They were intelligent creatures, but I could never get them to understand more than a few simple words such as "come" and "help." As I spent more time with them, though, I learned that most of their communication was through touch, as they were exceptionally physical creatures. Their trumpets, bleats and grunts were only used when they were not in close proximity with each other. When they were together, they constantly huddled and nuzzled each other and I found them very responsive to my touch. I do not know how much of our request they understood. But when we set forth from the clearing they willingly accompanied us.

The following day I decided to see if the behemoths would let us ride them so that we could travel faster. I was going to ride Tor, as I began to call him because he was the size of a hill, while Ham rode the behemoth mother. Ham had taken to calling her Libby, an unflattering reference to the build of our Aunt Libnah. But Tor wouldn't allow Ham to mount Libby. Instead, he effortlessly bore both Ham and me on his back—we seemed but grasshoppers to him as he maneuvered nimbly through the dense forest. Ham and I had only to cling tightly and keep our heads down to avoid being struck by the passing branches. My arms and legs ached by the end of the day, but we had covered many miles.

In this way we reached the southern edge of the Jade Forest in only three days. There we faced a critical moment. I did not know if the behemoths would willingly accompany us out of their homeland. I also worried whether they would be able to find suitable food, so we spent most of the day cutting leaves out of the tops of the trees and binding them with twine—as much as we could pile onto their backs. I knew it would not last long because their appetites were enormous. But I hoped that if they could find nothing else suitable to eat, that food might allow them to get back to their homeland before they suffered any ill effects.

The next morning, we tried to set out, but the Tor and Libby were very reluctant. I spoke soothingly to them, stroked their necks and finally coaxed them out to the open. I suppose it was the first time in their lives they had ever stepped foot outside the Jade Forest.

I decided not to go straight through the hill country. The trees there were not as supple as those in the Tigris Valley and I did not wish to risk injuring the animals. Therefore, we bore to the east of the hills and took the longer route through the Setti Plain. I tried to avoid the inhabited areas as much as possible, but had to pass close by the village of Danan as we could not skirt it without going far out of our way. I can tell you that our procession caused no small commotion in the village as we passed. Ham and I laughed about the looks on their faces ever after.

When we reached the Tirnin River, we turned west. I had hoped that the valley of the shallow stream would afford us a relatively unobstructed passage up into the hills. I did not think about the rocks hurting the behemoths' feet. Although the stones in the stream were smooth, the behemoths were surprisingly tenderfooted. So we proceeded very slowly over the next four days until we finally reached home.

Before we could begin transporting the timber, we first had to clear a path from the hills to the river. While we were gone, Father and Shem had deliberated carefully about the route and decided that the straightest would not be the best. Instead, we made an arc that bore first to the east and gradually swung around to the south, intersecting with the Gihon at a point below where it emerged from the narrow passes of the high hills. From there, the channel deepened and ran straight for a distance. We found a place where the bank sloped gently and established our staging camp there in the hope that the river would be entirely navigable from that point forward.

Once we had selected the route, we set about clearing the path. For this, the behemoths proved invaluable, or else the road-building itself might have taken many years. We would indicate a tree we wanted to remove. Then Tor would set his shoulder against the tree, grasp it by twisting his neck and simply uproot it. We tried to salvage as much dirt as possible off the roots to fill the holes. First, the behemoths would shake them and then we would clean them as well as we could with our tools. The initial passes went a long way toward smoothing the path. In this way, we were able to complete our road in only four months.

The behemoths were willing workers and seemed very eager to please us. We were relieved that they could find sustenance in the hill country. They especially liked the grass that grew in the meadows, although they tired quickly of straining their necks to the ground. Ham fashioned a platform in the top of a tall tree on the lower end of the road that we kept stocked with acorns and apples for them.

Once the road was completed, we were ready to transport the lumber. My original plan had been to fashion a crude sled and simply drag the logs to the river. Ham, though, had an idea for attaching a series of wheels to the sled and kept badgering Father about it until he finally agreed to let him go to Nephil with Shem to get the necessary parts. I had my own reservations about this quite apart from Father's—based on what Ham had told me about Ben-Tubal's daughter—but I kept them to myself. Ham said his machine would make the work easier on the animals and that finally persuaded us. They returned without incident from Nephil inside of a month with enough parts to make two carts. Ham affixed the iron wheels to the runners and we stacked ten logs lengthwise in a pyramid on the cross members. The behemoths could have easily carried twice that much, but this number made for a stable load and we did not want to risk overburdening the animals. Mother braided a loop of thick cloth that fit around the behemoths' necks and across their backs. These we lined with wool to form a double layer of padding. Though the iron wheels made a deafening racket, our first haul around the hill to the river went smoothly and we congratulated ourselves heartily when we arrived.

"What did I tell you?" said Ham. "The wheels made all the difference."

"Yes, I must admit they worked brilliantly," said Father. "And let's not forget Jayfeth. All this was his idea to begin with."

"Well, it's one thing to have an idea," said Ham. "But another to carry it out."

"You've all worked together," said Mother. "That's why you were successful."

"Right as always, Mara," said Father. "Right as always."

On the second day we pushed hard and were able to make two round trips. However, Tor and Libby were footsore by the end of the day, so we determined to be content with one trip daily. As the months went by, the supply of lumber at the camp diminished while the stacks at the river grew. And when the better part of two years had passed, everything had been moved to the river.

We then began to prepare the lumber for transport down the Gihon. We tested its buoyancy, and to my surprise and relief, it floated reasonably well for its hardness. We experimented with several different designs for making crude rafts. The simplest method worked as well as any. So we bound together ten logs side-by-side, fastening them together with ropes, and were ready to head downstream.

Before we departed, though, it was time to return Tor and Libby home. Living together for two years and watching their young Teeny and Tiny grow up before our eyes, we had become quite fond of them all. They enjoyed our companionship as well and were quite affectionate toward us. But from time to time, I could sense that they longed to return to the Jade Forest and their own kind.

So Ham and I set out with the behemoths obediently following along behind. We did not hurry because my heart was heavy to come to the point of our parting. On the morning that we drew near to the Jade Forest, Tor and Libby's faces brightened. They ran ahead with Teeny and Tiny and disappeared from sight. We stood there for some time until they reappeared, perplexed as to why we had not followed. When at last I could make clear to them that we were to be parted, they whimpered loudly and urged us to stay with them. I fought back tears as I embraced each of them in turn.

"Come, Brother," Ham finally said, pulling me away. "It's time to go." He put a comforting arm around my shoulder as we set out for home.

FIFTEEN

Back at the river, we faced a dilemma that we had thus far avoided discussing. Upon our return, though, Shem broached the subject. "If no one else is going to say it, I will. There are only five of us. So in order to transport the lumber, we either have to leave it unguarded on one end or someone is going to be left alone."

While we were moving the lumber to the river, this had not been as much of a concern. The intimidating size of the behemoths tended to discourage the curious and would-be mischief-makers—not that we were attracting large crowds anyway. And we were traveling back and forth so regularly between the two sites that anything suspicious would have been quickly noticed. That was getting ready to change, though, with many miles and days separating us.

"I'd be worried sick about leaving someone by himself," said Mother.

"I don't want you to worry," I said. "But that seems preferable to leaving the lumber unguarded. I remember too well the fire that destroyed it during our last extended absence. None of us wants to risk that, especially now that we have many times as much to lose."

"I agree with your mother—leaving anyone alone for very long is risky," said Father. "There are people out there who are very hostile to us."

"We're grown men," said Ham. "We'll be fine on our own."

"I'm just not comfortable with the idea," said Father.

"You're the one who's always telling us that the Lord will protect us," said Ham.

"There's a switch—you telling me to have more faith," said Father. "I don't know whether to be comforted or even more worried. What about you, Shem? You have a good head on your shoulders. What do you think?"

"It pains me to say it, but I have to agree with Jay and Ham for once," said Shem.

"Not you too?" said Father. "I was hoping you'd be the voice of reason. But I can see I'm outnumbered here."

"Who's going to cook for these boys?" said Mother. "You know they won't eat right if I'm not there to cook for them."

I knew then we had won the debate and I remember hoping it was a good thing. "Ham's wasting away to nothing already," I said, patting his stomach. "Look at him."

"That's muscle," said Ham. "Well, mostly muscle."

"This is serious," said Father.

"I know it is," I said. "We'll be fine."

"Even if we agree to split up, we still have to decide who goes where," said Shem.

"The river is likely to be the most dangerous, quite apart from any outside interference we might face," I said. "Whoever is taking the logs downstream definitely should not be alone—in case the raft capsizes or something."

"Agreed," said Ham. "I think the safest place for the lone man to be is at the Nephil camp. The city will be right there and I'm sure Ben-Tubal would lend a hand if there was any trouble. In fact, I'll volunteer to stay there myself."

"What if the Governor is behind the trouble?" asked Shem.

"Don't start that again," said Ham.

"The Governor may have his own designs," said Father. "But you have to admit he has been nothing but helpful so far. I'm inclined to agree that Nephil would be the least dangerous place for the lone man. It would be harder for someone to do something there without witnesses."

"Then it's settled," said Ham. "I'll take Nephil."

"Not quite settled," said Father. "Shem will take Nephil—if he's willing."

"I'm willing," said Shem.

I looked at Father, wondering how much he knew or suspected about Ham and Jirah, but couldn't read anything from his expression.

"But why?" Ham protested.

"You and Jayfeth both said that the river would be the most dangerous," said Father. "You're the bravest among us, so you can transport the lumber down the river with Jayfeth. Unless you'd rather stay here and take care of your Mother ..."

A smile broke slowly across Ham's face, not only because Father had singled him out for bravery, but because he realized that all he had to do was say "yes" to ensure that he would be going to Nephil regularly. It was likely to be the best deal he was going to get. "I am the bravest," he said. "I guess you're right. The river is the place for me. Someone has to look out for the lubber."

"We'll see who ends up wet first," I said.

"All right then," said Father. "I still have misgivings about the plan. But if we're going to do it this way, the three of you might as well head downstream tomorrow."

With two long, slender poles, we steered the raft by pushing off from the bottom of the channel, which we could touch in most places. The raft was so heavy that it did not turn easily at first, and when it did, it had a tendency to spin. (Ham came up with the idea of a simple rudder to stabilize and steer the raft on subsequent trips.) As we grew more comfortable on the water, though, we began to enjoy it more and more. We soon learned to read the current and anticipate the maneuvers we would need to make to keep it in the main channel. That first trip traveling down the river with my brothers was among the happiest times we had shared since our boyhood.

Each night we camped on the shore, making sure that the raft was securely tied. Each morning, we set out at first light and thus made reasonably good time. Occasionally, we saw a kinsmen or a stranger staring at us from the bank, but no one offered us hospitality. They just shook their heads at what those strange sons of Noah were doing.

Even with two of us at a time poling hard, we could not affect our speed very much. Since it was tiring work, there seemed no point in wearing ourselves out for nothing. So we drifted along at the river's pace. While I had hoped that we could make the trip more quickly, it took two full weeks.

Finding a suitable location just upstream from Nephil, we winched the lumber from the river using one of Ham's pulley mechanisms that we had brought with us. We helped Shem establish a campsite, but when it came right down to it, I worried about leaving him there alone. He assured us, however, that the Lord would protect him.

Ham and I made our way back up the Gihon Road, stopping only at night. The return journey took seven more days, so that the round trip took three weeks. I looked at the massive pile of lumber and realized that moving it all was going to take a very long time.

Thus began a new cycle in our lives. Three-week intervals came and went uneventfully for awhile, interrupted only by a land trip where we drove our livestock—our burro Naysa, the oxen, and a few sheep and goats—down the Gihon Road because the pasture was better on the plain. We tried increasing the width of the raft and found that we could go as wide as twelve logs before the raft had difficulty managing some of the tighter turns in the river. For the longer logs intended for beams, the maximum width was four. We also tried towing a raft, but that proved so unwieldy that it hardly seemed worth the extra effort and risk. This did give us the idea of using one man per raft, though. I would not have attempted it at first. But with the addition of a rudder and the experience of a few trips, we became skillful at steering and familiar enough with the river that Ham and I could each handle a raft well alone. At that rate, I calculated that moving it all would take about twenty-five years.

After we had delivered our fifth load, Shem informed us that a delegation headed by Baldag had come to him from Nephil a week earlier.

"What did they want?" asked Ham anxiously.

"They wanted to know what our intentions were in bringing this lumber to the Plain," said Shem.

"What did you say?" I asked.

"I told them the truth," said Shem. "What else would I say?"

"I don't know if that was wise," said Ham. "We don't want to offend them."

"They will know soon enough anyway," said Shem. "Besides, we're building the ark here to be a witness. We cannot be witnesses by keeping silent—or by lying."

"Still, I think we should try to maintain good relations with them as long as possible," said Ham.

"For the Lord's sake or your own?"

"What's that supposed to mean?" Ham glanced sideways at me, questioning whether I had divulged his secret. I shook my head ever-so-slightly to indicate that I had not. If Shem had learned—or guessed—at Ham and Jirah's feelings toward each other, it was not from me.

"Easy, Ham," I said. "Shem's done what he thought best and it can't be undone. The important thing is what they will do about it now that they know."

"What they do makes no difference to me," said Shem. "I will do what I think is right regardless."

"You accuse me of looking out for my own interest," said Ham. "Aren't you saying the same thing?"

"Stop it, you two," I said. "Why worry about those who oppose us if we are divided among ourselves. We are defeated already."

"You're right about that, Jay," said Shem. "But it's difficult to be united when Ham takes issue with everything I say."

"You started it," said Ham.

I shook my head at them and said, "You were saying about Baldag ..."

"Yes," said Shem. "There is something else you should know. Baldag was dressed as a Nephilite."

"So?" said Ham.

"Because Baldag was supposed to be the Sethite ambassador to the Nephilim. Now it's like it's the other way around."

"He has spent much time among the Nephilim," I said.

"Too much time," said Shem.

"What's your point?" said Ham, impatiently.

"The point is this: I suspect that everything is not as it appears to be in Nephil—and that Baldag is at the heart of it."

"There you go again slandering the Nephilim," said Ham.

"Let Shem finish," I said. "I have detested Baldag ever since we were boys. And you have, too, Ham."

"To hear Baldag talk," Shem continued, "you would think that Nephil is all that matters and that our Council of Elders amounts to nothing. And I'm afraid there may be something to what he is saying. Why, in just these few months since I've been here, I have been amazed at the number of our brothers I have seen entering Nephil and passing to the lands beyond."

"Look at it. Cush has nothing to compare with that," said Ham, pointing to Nephil in the distance. "And Ben-Tubal is an excellent leader. I'm not surprised that he has won the hearts of our people as well as his own."

"Just because Ben-Tubal is an excellent man doesn't mean that Baldag is," I said.

"I agree with that," said Ham. "We've always suspected he was the one who burned the lumber. But just because he is a despicable schemer, that doesn't mean he is scheming with the Nephilim."

"Being suspicious is not the same thing as accusing," said Shem. "I'm only suggesting that we ought to be cautious. You both gave me the same warning about Baldag years ago. I'm just agreeing that you may have been right."

"That's a first," said Ham.

"If we're all in agreement that something is wrong here, I think you should tell Father about our concerns," said Shem.

"It will give him one more thing to worry about," said Ham.

"That's true," I said. "But he always knows what to do."

Late that afternoon, soon after Ham and I began our return trip, I saw a solitary figure watching us from partway up the ridge. I pointed and said to Ham, "It's Merib!"

"Quietly," said Merib as he made his way down to the road. "I do not want anyone to know I am here."

"What's the matter?" I asked.

"I have come to warn you," said Merib. "The palace is in great agitation over the report that you are moving your project to the Plain of Nephil. I have overheard some of the counsels and many are speaking against it." I was not surprised at this, but the expectation did not lessen my feelings of alarm.

"I urge you to stay in the Highlands," continued Merib. "I do not wish any trouble for you, so do not stir up any."

"Do you think it would come to trouble?" I asked.

"Why put it to the test?" said Merib.

"We're not afraid," said Ham, bristling for a moment before he thought better of it. "Besides, your father is friendly toward us and would not allow anything to happen."

"Ben-Tubal respects Noah," said Merib. "But Noah's words have disturbed some influential people. That is why he sent me to you secretly to warn you. If Noah persists, there are certain interests in the east ..." He broke off for a moment and softened his tone. "But there is a better way. Why don't you join us? Come and live with us in the palace. Ben-Tubal will not refuse you anything you ask. You can live in luxury, have many servants and choose any of our women who please you. You will never lack for anything."

"I don't lack for anything now," I said.

Ignoring that comment, Merib turned to my brother and said, "What about you, Ham? I know you have feelings for my sister Jirah. What prevents you from pursuing all that your heart desires with her?"

I don't recall any time in his life when Ham was at such a loss for words. He stammered and fumbled around until I was embarrassed for him. So I spoke up. "What you don't understand is that we don't have a choice in the matter."

"Is this your answer as well?" Merib said to Ham.

"I'm sorry," said Ham reluctantly.

"So am I," said Merib curtly. "But do not say you have not been counseled otherwise. All the same, the invitation remains open in case you change your minds. Just don't wait until it's too late."

With that, he slipped into the woods and we soon lost sight of him. Ham was sullen for the rest of the evening and hardly spoke. Merib's words had clearly hit the mark with him. Had I not been present, I fear that he might have gone over to the Nephilim that very night.

Neither were Merib's words without effect on me and I feared what might come in the days ahead. What especially haunted me, though, were my own words. Did we really have no choice? The question tormented me long into the night.

Sixteen

When Ham and I arrived back up river a week later, Father was quite concerned to hear about Baldag and the trouble simmering in Nephil. "I've been away from Nephil too long," he said when we had finished. "I will go and relieve your brother so that I can see things for myself and be a witness to the people there. I've been thinking that we should also make plans to venture into the interior of Nod so that those living there can hear our message too."

The next day Father set out down the river with Ham, while I remained behind with Mother. About a week later a group of men surprised us at our campsite. There were ten of them—four Nephilim and six Sethites—led by Baldag, looking pompous dressed as a Nephilite with an ornamented robe and gold jewelry. Though he had once been considered handsome, shaving his face only accentuated his swelling jowls, giving him a piggish appearance.

"We're concerned for your safety," Baldag was saying. "This is a dangerous undertaking and there are many perils. We would not want anything to *happen* to you, so we urge you to desist."

"Thank you for your concern," I said, alarmed by the way he emphasized "happen," which made it sound like something unfortunate was very likely to befall us—and not necessarily by accident. That, no doubt, was his intention—to intimidate us. "We will do our best to be careful."

Baldag called me closer and spoke in low tones so that Mother would not hear. "You seem like a reasonable man. Surely you don't believe in all this business about visions and the end of the world."

"My father received this word directly from God," I recited.

"So he says. But doesn't it strike you as odd that this message came only to him? More than forty years have passed since he supposedly received this warning. Still, everything goes on as it did before."

These words hit me harder than I let on, giving expression to secret doubts that I dared not admit even to myself. But I tried not to show it and replied, "The time has not yet come. But Father says it will."

"Be reasonable, man," said Baldag, no longer trying to keep his voice down. "Your father has lost his mind and everyone knows it. The people are deeply offended by his rantings. Some are angry enough that they might do something to silence him. You would do him a kindness by restraining his madness."

"That's no way to talk about my Noah!" said Mother, rising from her seat. I had never seen her so angry before. "Respect your elder, cousin!"

"Now, Mara, I'm not being disrespectful," said Baldag in his most patronizing tone. "Only honest. All this talk of giant boats and doomsday is sheer folly."

By then, I was also seething with anger. "One who visits the tents of other men's wives has little room to lecture about folly!"

Baldag must have been under strict orders not to lay a hand on us, or I'm sure he would have struck me down right there. He got right up in my face and growled, "You are badly mistaken, boy. The folly belongs to one who pries into other men's affairs. Mark my words, you will come to regret your impudence."

Baldag left in a rage along with his men. Mother was very upset by it all. I tried to console her, but to little avail. I wished Father were there so that we could both draw from his strength. It was not the last time that thought crossed my mind.

The next two weeks passed very slowly. Although no further incidents occurred, I found it very unsettling not to know where Baldag and his men were or what they were doing. The dread of what might happen weighed heavily on my mind. When Shem and Ham returned on schedule, I was very glad to see them.

After the confrontation with Baldag, I was more reluctant than ever to leave Shem behind by himself. He continued to assure us that the Lord was with him. I had little choice but to accept that and go on. So Mother, Ham and I left the following morning with two new rafts.

Three days later, we were traveling along and making good time. I was on the lead raft with Mother, while Ham followed along just behind us. As we rounded a tight bend in the river, we were dismayed to see several large trees fallen from the bank and laying in the water directly in our path. I leaped to the right side of the raft and poled as hard as I could. Every muscle in my body strained to steer us away from the fallen trees. But the channel there was narrow and the current swift. Try as I might, I could not avoid the collision.

The right front corner of the raft ran up onto a fallen tree, tilting the front end out of the water. The force of the impact threw me overboard while Mother, who had been sitting in the middle, managed to hold on.

But right behind her came Ham. His raft struck the back corner of ours and capsized it. As it tilted, Mother disappeared under the water. Holding my breath, I searched for her beneath the raft. Fortunately, she had found the small pocket of air between the raft and the fallen tree. I took her by the hand and we eased our way over to the edge of the raft. We pulled ourselves along the fallen trees hand over hand to the bank.

Then I saw Ham clinging to a large branch of one of the fallen trees. Blood streamed down his face and his eyes appeared dazed. I dove into the water and swam as fast as I could, reaching him just as he lost consciousness and slipped into the water. I grabbed his arm and pulled myself up onto the main trunk, dragging him behind me.

Ham was so heavy and the current was so swift that I did not think I could bear him to shore by swimming. Our situation was very precarious and I was at a loss to know what to do. Just then, the tree on which we were perched broke free of whatever was holding it. I knew we could not maintain our balance while floating down the stream, so I pushed Ham into the water on one side of the trunk and I slid onto the other side while grasping both of his arms. I was thankful to see that the base of the tree was secured firmly to the bank. When the tree pivoted, it began to carry us toward the shore. In a few moments, I could feel the bottom with my feet. I climbed over the top and pulled Ham to shore.

Ham soon came around, complaining mostly of a headache. But other than the gash on the top of his head, he had suffered no other injuries. Mother cradled his head in her arms and applied pressure to the wound to stop the bleeding.

Since we clearly would not be traveling any farther that day, I took the opportunity to scout around the area. To my dismay, I discovered that the trees had been cut by human hands. I could think of no purpose other than to cause us mayhem, but I found no trace of who the culprit might be.

About half a mile downstream, I spotted the box in which we kept our supplies spinning slowly in an eddy. Father had wisely constructed it so that it would float in case it ended up in the water. I carried the box back to where

Mother and Ham were. We dabbed his wound with a bit of wine and gave him some to drink to soothe his headache. Then Mother took a needle and thread and closed the wound. He grimaced at the pain, but made no sound. He always wanted to appear strong.

"These trees?" said Ham when she was finished.

"It was done deliberately," I said.

"Who would do such a thing?" asked Mother.

"I don't know for sure," I said. "But I have strong suspicions that it was some of our 'friends' from Nephil."

"You don't know that," said Ham. "It could have been anyone. Besides, even if it was Baldag, you have no proof that Ben-Tubal put him up to it. He could be acting of his own accord."

"True enough," I said, knowing it was futile to discuss the politics of Nephil with Ham. "If it makes you feel any better, I was the one who got wet first."

"Told you," said Ham, smiling slightly. I knew then that he was going to be all right.

While Ham rested, I set about freeing the rafts. Once I discovered that the felled trees were held in place by strong ropes that were deceptively hidden, this proved not to be as difficult as I feared. As soon as the ropes were cut, Ham's raft floated free. I had to partially disassemble the raft I had been steering because it was stuck fast and far too heavy to move intact. Once the individual logs were clear, I reassembled it in quick time. By then the day was fading. We ate a cheerless supper and retired for the night.

On the following day, I had reservations about whether Ham was sufficiently healed to travel. He claimed to be, however, so we departed at mid-morning. We were vigilant for the rest of the journey, but reunited with Father on the Plain of Nephil without further incident.

Somewhere along the return trip back up the Gihon Road with Ham, I determined that I would be the one to stay behind this time. Assuming that opposition would continue and perhaps worsen, I reasoned that one man alone would likely face the greatest danger next time. Since I was oldest, I decided that the one man should be me. Shem protested, but eventually deferred to my age. He and Ham left the next day.

Boredom set in almost immediately after Shem and Ham departed. I was unaccustomed to idleness and too restless to enjoy it. I paced around the camp, but dared not stray far and leave my post. From time to time, I heard strange booming noises in the distance, though I thought at first the solitude was playing tricks on my mind.

But one day as I was whiling away the time, I noticed that the water in the river seemed lower than usual. I had lived my whole life on or near the Gihon and had never known it to fluctuate much. The thought made me uneasy during the night.

When I awoke, the water level was considerably lower than the day before. I began to mark the level with sticks. The retreat of the water was clearly evident. As the day progressed, I became increasingly alarmed and wondered what new misfortune was about to befall.

All afternoon, I debated in my mind about what to do. But just about the time I had determined to head upstream and investigate, I heard a new sound coming from the opposite direction—what sounded like a cry for help. The first time I heard it I tried to dismiss it as the call of some strange bird. But as I strained my ears it came again and there could be no mistaking it. I hesitated for a moment, looking at the lumber and the falling river level. What else could I do? I had to see if someone was in trouble.

I followed the sound of the intermittent cries north and a little east toward the wooded ridge that bounded the river. At the top of a low hill, I stepped into a clearing where rings of upright stones had been erected. But this was not an ancient sacred place. I had spent my whole life living within a few miles of that spot and knew those stones had not been that way for long. Strangest of all, though, was that in the center of the inner circle a woman was kneeling.

"Hello," I called. "Are you all right?"

The woman did not seem startled to hear my voice, as if two strangers meeting like that in the forest, miles from the nearest village, was the most natural thing in the world. She stood and said, "I have lost my way."

"You *must* be lost to be here," I said. "We don't get many visitors anymore since ..." But I forgot what else I was going to say as soon as I was close enough to see who it was. "Don't I know you? You're Minnah, daughter of Keriath."

"I'm afraid you have me confused with someone else," she said.

"I wouldn't forget a face like yours." It just came out before I thought about what I was saying. Suddenly, I felt very embarrassed and hoped she couldn't see me blushing in the moonlight. "But you once kept my secret and I'll be glad to keep yours. Not that you necessarily have any secrets ... I mean, I wasn't trying to imply ... It's a warm night, isn't it?"

"Yes," she said, unfazed by all my awkward comments. "And you look thirsty."

"As a matter of fact, I am," I said, relieved to change to a different subject. "And I went trekking off from camp without my water flask."

"Well, then, refresh yourself," she said, pouring me a cup from her own.

I drained the cup in one big gulp. It was clear like water and sweet to taste, but it burned in my throat. "What is this?" I asked, suppressing the urge to cough.

"Forgetfulness."

"What?" I said, but my voice seemed to be coming from some great distance instead of from my own mouth. The full strength of the rising moon had turned the light gray stones to lustrous pearl. The strange thing was that they no longer looked solid, but had turned instead to a viscous liquid flowing slowly around the circle. I felt my knees starting to buckle and gave way to it while I could still make some effort at breaking my fall. Thick lipped, I asked, "What have you done to me?"

"It's a special draft from the potion-master," she said, kneeling over me on the ground so close that her hair spilled over my face. "Don't worry. It will cause you no lasting harm."

"But why?"

"They have their reasons," she said. Then seeing how worried I was, she added, "I am sorry." And she sounded like she meant it.

The last thing I remember was her saying to someone I could not see, apparently hidden behind the stones, "You won't hurt him, right? I have your word that you won't hurt him."

Of the next several days, I have little recollection. Every time I began to come to my senses, I was made to drink more of the potion. This was administered to me by some strange men from the east; I did not see Minnah again. I had been moved to a crude hut outside of the stone circles. It had been hastily constructed of branches, more for concealment than shelter. Then one day I woke up alone and groggy. My captors had inexplicably disappeared, leaving without any explanation of their motives for confining me or their sudden departure. As far as I could tell, I was unharmed and had suffered no ill effects apart from being famished. Their potion had been sustaining but not filling. I don't think I had eaten any solid food since the ordeal began, though I had no idea how long that had been.

Cautiously, I rose to my feet and made my way back to camp. When I could see from a distance that the lumber was intact, I breathed a sigh of relief. But then I saw the river—or I should say the empty riverbed where it should have been. Only scattered pools remained here and there where the channel was deeper. Fish trapped in the shallow waters were splashing in a vain attempt to escape. I realized that if I did not do something quickly, they would all soon die.

I ran up the empty channel and found the same scene repeated over and over. About two miles upstream, I rounded a bend and discovered the source of the problem. At that point the river ran through a narrow pass between the hills. Someone had dislodged an enormous quantity of rocks and earth and trees across the channel and obstructed the flow of the water. It formed a high wall behind which the river was backing up.

I scaled the wall with some difficulty and surveyed the situation. I don't think I had ever considered how great the flow of the river was until I saw how much had backed up in only a few days. Already a great body of water had formed behind the dam and the level of it had risen a considerable distance up the narrow valley between the hills. It must have taken thousands of men to do that in such a short period of time—or some devilment beyond my understanding.

I stood on the dam and tried to calculate how long it would take to clear such a massive obstruction. But I didn't need to wonder. A rumbling sound began to emanate from deep down inside the dam. In a moment, I realized what was about to happen and fled for my life across the dam. By the time I reached the bank, the middle of the dam where I had been standing was already bulging. As the dam started to give way, I scrambled desperately toward the safety of higher ground, feeling like I had never run so slowly. The dam collapsed with a deafening crash and the water poured forth with mighty power. All along the bank, the trees in the path of the torrent were toppled like twigs.

I made my way downstream, keeping to the ridge, and saw the damage that the water wrought on the bank was incredible. Great portions were eroded away and the river cut straight over the land where the bend used to be.

A sense of dread grew within me. Our lumber supply lay directly in the path of the onrushing waters. I ran downstream as fast as I could to see what had become of it.

Dusk was falling as I reached the camp—or where camp used to be, I should say. Every single log had been swept away.

Seventeen

I sat down on a rock just above the receding water line and looked out over the debris-choked mud bath that used to be our beautiful valley. *Gone,* I thought to myself. *It's all gone. How could we lose it all again?*

I had to find my brothers, but since I did not even know what day it was, I had no idea where to look. I checked my fingernails and felt my beard. Two weeks, maybe, since they left? But those were terribly imprecise measures. The moon was up soon, though, confirming that estimate was more or less correct.

My brothers will have reached Nephil by now, I thought. *They've probably started on their way back. If they didn't get stranded on the river by the low water, we'll meet in the middle somewhere.*

I traveled on into the night, slowly, though, because it was a dark night and difficult to see. When morning came, I was relieved to see that, though the river was overflowing its bank in places, I had left the worst of the damage behind. I had been worried about the camps of the people along the upper reaches of the river. Although it turned out the majority lay above the flood level, it wouldn't have mattered anyway because most of the campsites had been abandoned, including Aunt Libnah's. They had left without a word of goodbye or a hint about where they were going.

I slept a few hours in one of the empty campsites and hurried off the next morning at first light. On the second day, I reached the tents of Irad. His family was one of the few who had not moved away and they had not fared well, living in a low-lying area that was under about a foot of water. The river must have risen during the night and caught them unaware. They were so engaged in rescuing their belongings that they didn't notice me as I passed by. I couldn't help but laugh at how comical Fehud looked splashing around after his things. *Serves him right,* I thought, *after the way he treated me.*

The danger of looking behind you is that you can't see what is in front of you, so I didn't notice the woman on the road ahead until she startled me out of my gloating. "Do you think this is funny?" she said.

I looked up to see a young woman laden with an armful of wet clothes approaching on the road. It did not escape my attention that she was quite pretty, even in her highly irritated condition. "Why, no," I said. "I don't think it's funny at all."

"Hmpff," she said, depositing her burden on the ground beside the road above the water line. She picked up a robe from the pile and examined it. "Likely ruined," she said and threw it down in disgust. She turned her attention back to me and said, "Well, that would be easier to believe if you were making yourself useful instead of standing around gawking at others' misfortune."

"I'm in a terrible hurry," I said, which earned me a rolling of her blue eyes and a tossing of her golden hair. Why I didn't leave at that moment is a mystery that I couldn't adequately explain to myself. Somehow, in the few moments of that brief interchange, the paramount concern of my life suddenly became the desire to prove that she was wrong about me. So, before I knew what I was doing, I found myself adding, "But never in too much of a hurry to help someone in need."

The woman, however, was not waiting around to hear what I had to say, but was striding down the road after another load. She walked with such purpose that even with my long legs I had trouble keeping up with her. "Too bad about the river," I said, trying to make conversation.

"I don't suppose you know anything about it," she said.

"Someone dammed the river upstream and then the dam collapsed."

"It wouldn't surprise me," she said. "Lots of strange things go on upstream. Where did you say you were from?"

"Upstream," I mumbled, feeling uncomfortable about the direction our conversation was going, but not knowing how to extricate myself. Strangely, part of me didn't want to. I'd never met a woman like her and observed with interest that she wore the robe of a maiden even though she appeared to be a bit older than the typical age for marriage. I thought it best to make sure of her status, however, before I made an even worse blunder. "So, do you and your husband live close by?"

"I have no husband," she replied. But before a smile could form on my lips, she wiped it off by adding, "I live in the tents of my father Irad. No doubt you've heard of him. He's a very important man in our tribe."

"Yes, I have heard of him," I said, trying not to betray my disappointment and dismay as I realized to whom I had been speaking. This no doubt was Re-Aylah, the little girl who had freed me from Fehud's ropes when we were children—only she wasn't a little girl anymore. It hadn't occurred to me that she would have grown up, too, just like I had. She obviously hadn't recognized me either. And at the moment, it seemed much better that way.

About two hundred yards down the road, an intersecting path dipped sharply toward the river. "They say my father will soon be named to the Council of Elders," Re-Aylah was saying as she skipped lightly down the bank. "He would have been already, except for an unfortunate accident of relation. By the way, what did you say your name was?"

I was so flustered by then that I failed to pay sufficient attention to how slick the bank was due to the receding water. My feet slipped out from under me and I slid down right behind where she had just walked. But while she stopped at the bottom, I didn't, and the collision took us both into the river. As we came up sputtering out of the Gihon, I said, "I'm Jayfeth—your unfortunate accident of a relation."

"I might have known!" said Re-Aylah, indignantly. "I've heard you're nothing but trouble!"

"That may be true," I said, offering my hand, which she refused. "But don't judge me by what you hear. Make up your own mind."

"You haven't exactly helped your case today," she said, sloshing her way out of the water.

"I was trying to help—that should count for something," I said, plucking a linen undergarment from the water as it rolled past me. "Is this yours?"

"Give me that!" she said, snatching it from me.

"Do you want me to help or not?"

"Maybe that's not such a good idea," said Re-Aylah. "You said you were in a hurry. Perhaps you'd better be on your way."

"I see. I'm a troublemaker and you would prefer that I go make trouble somewhere else."

"I meant that if my father and brothers find you here they won't be happy to see you."

"Ah, nothing warms your heart like the love of your family, I always say." I took hold of an exposed tree root and scrambled up the bank.

"You are a very strange person," said Re-Aylah. "And that's my *own* opinion."

"Fair enough," I said. "Goodbye, cousin. Sorry for knocking you into the river."

I had much to occupy my mind after that. So although it was actually several hours later, it seemed like no time before I spotted my brothers coming along the road toward me. I drew a deep breath, dreading what I had to do next.

"Have you taken leave of your sense?" said Ham, greatly surprised to see me. "Why have you abandoned the lumber?"

"There is no more lumber," I said dejectedly and proceeded to explain to them what had happened. When I had finished relating the account, Ham cursed me for my stupidity.

"I forgot that you invented wisdom," I said defensively. "Why don't you enlighten me as to what you would have done differently—"

"Enough," said Shem. "It is not Jay's fault, Ham. Those who oppose us would love to divide us. We have to stick together."

"But what are we going to do now?" I said. "We're ruined and everyone is against us. I can't bear to see the look on Father's face when he hears this news."

"Don't underestimate the man," said Shem. "We're all safe and that's what is most important to him."

"I know what you're saying is true," I said. "But I remember how he grieved after the fire."

"I'm not cutting any more trees," said Ham. "I've had it up to here. I can't go through all that again."

"Maybe you won't have to," said Shem, stroking his beard thoughtfully.

"What do you mean?" I asked.

"I have an idea," said Shem. "What prevents us from salvaging it from the river?"

"It's already moving in the right direction," said Ham, picking up on Shem's idea. "As much as I hate to admit it, Shem may be onto something here."

"Assuming it wasn't all destroyed," I said.

"Don't lose heart brothers," said Shem. "Our enemies sought to do us evil, but perhaps the Lord will turn it to our good."

"What are we waiting for then?" said Ham. "Let's hurry back to Nephil. We have preparations to make."

We returned to the great city with all possible speed, trying to outpace the flow of debris. We continued late each night under the light of the waxing moon, sleeping as little as we could get by with. By the time we reached Nephil, we had devised a strategy about how to recover the lumber. Ham came up with a plan for an arm that would extend at an angle into the river, allowing water to pass under but funneling the lumber to shore where it could be transferred to land.

My apprehension about telling Father turned out to be worse than the telling itself. "Remember, my sons, this is the Lord's work," he said. "If the Lord wills it, it *will* come to pass. No hand is strong enough to resist his."

After pressing hard and sleeping only in snatches, we were quite fatigued. We spent the remainder of that day and night resting, rousing ourselves only long enough for one of Mother's excellent meals.

The next morning we set out to recover as much of the lumber as possible. Father and Ham remained behind to construct the water gate that Ham had devised, while Shem and I headed back upstream to survey the river for salvageable logs. Concerned that large numbers of logs arriving at the same time would overwhelm Father and Ham's ability to remove them from the river, our plan was to control their flow to Nephil to the extent possible. When we saw no logs for the first two days—only debris and water stained with mud—my heart sank from fear that the lumber had just been shattered and that we were watching it float by in small bits before our eyes. On the third day, though, we saw an intact log floating in the middle of the channel. I got so excited that I dove into the water and guided it to shore.

"Hardly a scratch on it," said Shem.

"I shouldn't be surprised now that I think about it," I said. "I just have to look at the calluses on my hands to prove how hard the gopherwood is."

"The Lord knew what he was doing when he chose this tree for the ark," said Shem. "He foresaw this day all those years ago.

"If this log survived, others probably did too," I said. "Maybe this will work after all."

With some reluctance, we pushed the log back out into the channel and sent it on its way. Shem said, "The Lord has guided it thus far and will see to it that it reaches its destination. We need to find out what happened to the rest."

As we continued upstream, we began to see more logs. As long as these were coming one or two at a time, we let them go, confident that Father and Ham could easily retrieve them at that rate. When we spotted several bunched up together, we took up a position in a bend of the river that brought them close to shore. We plucked as many as we could and dragged them up on the bank. Then we let them go again one at a time at intervals of few minutes each.

As the day progressed, we were able to make our way a little farther up the river. When night fell, we decided to sleep in shifts and I took the first watch. The moon was approaching full, providing enough light for me to pick out the logs as they came downstream. Halfway through the night I woke up Shem and took my turn at sleeping.

Sometime afterward, Shem shook me from my sleep. "Come now! I need help!"

Eighteen

I looked upstream and saw a huge mass of lumber approaching rapidly.
"What should we do?" asked Shem. "We cannot stop all that."

Without thinking, I said, "If we can't stop it, we'll have to go with it."

We plunged into the water and each of us grabbed onto one of the leading logs. We rode side by side in a straddling position. "We can't do this for long or our legs will be crushed," I shouted over the thumping and clunking of the logs as they jostled each other noisily. "Let's tie some of these lead logs together and form a raft."

With great difficulty we began securing the logs together—and that was my second bad idea in the span of a few minutes. It was dangerous work because the logs kept bumping each other and we were in constant danger of having our limbs smashed between them. Positioning them was difficult because they were quite heavy and we had no good way of getting leverage on them. Finally, though, we managed to get eight of the front ones tied together. Then, at least we could stand up and assess the situation. But we didn't like what we saw. Tying the logs together with us standing on them created additional drag and made them float more slowly. Other logs began to pass us on either side. We did not concern ourselves with them but rather with the main body that lay behind us.

"Now what?" said Shem.

"I don't know," I said.

"I thought you had a plan."

I didn't have time to think it all through," I said. "We don't even have anything to steer with."

"It wouldn't make any difference anyway," said Shem. "We couldn't move this whole mass. Besides, you know what's up ahead, don't you? We'll never make the turn ahead."

"This is the wrong place to be, isn't it? We'd better swim for it."

"Not from here," said Shem. "Let's see if we can make it to the rear. We'd better be on the upstream side when it hits."

We skipped quickly over the tops of the logs, trying not to put our weight fully on any one lest it roll. The logs shifted treacherously beneath our feet. About two-thirds of the way back, I stepped onto nothing and fell into the water. As I started to pull myself out, my left arm became pinned between two logs.

Shem was at my side in a moment trying to free me. The pain was intense, but we were nearing the bend and I knew that if I did not extricate myself quickly the injury to my arm would not matter anyway.

Sprawled out flat across the logs, I could get no leverage at all. Shem pushed as hard as he could, but the logs would not budge. By then, we were dangerously close to the turn. "It's no use," I said. "Leave me and save yourself."

"I won't leave you," said Shem.

"But there's no time!"

"If we perish, we'll perish together!"

At that instant the logs shifted again. The moment I felt the pressure off my arm, I drew it out of the water and was free. I looked over my shoulder to see that the leading edge of the floating pile was only a few feet from the outside bank.

"Run!" I yelled.

We reached the rear of the mass in a few moments, jumped into the water and swam like mad. The logs hit with a mighty crash. The front ones lodged into the outside bank and those that followed mounted on top of the ones ahead. Momentum continued to pile the logs behind onto the ones in front of them until they were all one gigantic logjam.

We reached the shore with the first rays of dawn and fell down exhausted on the sand.

"So much for the plan," I said.

"This is just a temporary setback," said Shem. "Now let me see your arm."

"Ouch!" I said as he examined it, bruised and swollen as it was between my elbow and shoulder.

"If you were a normal person, injuring your left arm wouldn't bother you as much," said Shem.

"If you were a normal person, you wouldn't have stayed around to help," I said.

He just shrugged and said, "At least it's not broken. Things could have turned out far worse."

"Things almost did turn out far worse," I said. "Thanks for ... well, thanks."

"Come on," he said. "Let's survey the damage."

There must have been four or five hundred logs in the jam. It was such a snarled mess that a more precise estimate was impossible. The pile had formed on the outside of a turn, creating some treacherous eddies at the base and forcing the water to squeeze through a narrow opening on the inside of the channel. Having already seen the devastating effects of what damming the river could do, I said, "We must not allow the channel to close completely."

We cautiously approached the obstruction from the upstream side. It was stable enough to climb on, so we surveyed the situation more thoroughly and made preliminary plans for how we wanted to proceed. "We will have to be very careful as we remove them, because some will be critical to the whole pile," said Shem. "We won't want to disturb those any sooner than we have to."

"I wish Ham were here," I said. "He's good at figuring things like that out."

"Well, he's not," said Shem. "So we'll just have to do the best we can without him."

We suspended two pulleys from trees overhanging the riverbank. As gently as we could, we removed a log that was laying on the top and rear of the jam. Pushing it out into the river we let it go, aiming it so that it would stay parallel to the channel. We knew that if one lodged crosswise, it could set into motion a chain of events that would be difficult to stop.

The process was slow and tedious. We stopped often to discuss the best order for removal, in constant fear of having the entire pile shift and collapse beneath us. We also had to watch behind us. Whenever we saw more logs approaching, we would cease working on the jam and guided the incoming logs through the channel. The last thing we wanted to do was to risk letting more logs pile up and shut off the flow of the river.

By the end of the day, we were both exhausted from climbing up and down and fighting the current. We had freed about forty logs from the pile and allowed about the same number of new ones to pass through the channel. I tried to take the first watch, but could not hold my eyes open despite the throbbing of my arm. Shem never woke up either, but fortunately, not many logs came through during the night.

We worked diligently over the next three days and had some progress to show for our efforts. However, the situation was becoming more precarious with each log that we removed. We knew that a moment might come when many would break free at once. Over lunch that day I asked, "What are we going to do when the jam starts to break up? Assuming, of course, that we aren't crushed when it topples."

"That's been bothering me all along, too," said Shem. "Do you think we could cut overland and head them off as they come around the bend?"

"My ideas haven't been working out too well lately," I said. "I'll go along with yours."

"This time, though, let's work from the back to the front."

"Agreed," I said. "It will be a long time before I stand on the front side of a log drive and try to stop them again!"

Having that conversation when we did proved fortunate. Early the next morning, Shem was on the bank hauling on the rope when I felt the log I was standing on shift ominously. "There they go!" I shouted, leaping for the taut rope and grabbing it with both hands, with Shem on the other end, leaving me precariously suspended over the collapsing pile as a hundred or more logs broke free all at once.

"Hang on," yelled Shem.

"You hang on!" I cried as Shem hauled me up and pulled me in.

"We'd better hurry," said Shem. "I don't know how much time we'll have."

We swam hurriedly to the opposite bank and took off running as fast as we could across country. I wished then we had taken time to explore that area. We were not sure where we were heading or what we would find when we arrived, but the terrain was not difficult and the distance proved to be only three-quarters of a mile.

"I know this place," I said when we arrived on the other side. "We camped here on our first trip down river."

"I remember," said Shem. "Ham nearly set his trousers on fire over there playing in the campfire."

"I've never seen him move as fast as he did hopping into the river when they started smoking. I laughed until my sides ached."

"I told him to be careful, but he never listens."

"Well, I'm listening," I said. "Have you got a plan?"

"Just a very simple one," said Shem. "Let's pluck all of the easy stragglers we can from the near side of the bank as they go by. Then we'll fall in behind the main body and work from the rear forward. We'll follow them downstream as far as necessary until we get them all."

Soon we could see them coming. We were able to get twenty or so by just wading out and dragging them up on shore. We set about retrieving the rest one by one. It was slow, tiring work and we would have been halfway back to Nephil by the time we were finished except that nearly half drifted out of the main channel in a place where the river widened and became trapped in the backwater. Since those weren't going anywhere for awhile, we followed the rest downstream until there was but one left in the water. We let that one go.

"Well done, brother," I said, feeling very self-congratulatory. "Shall we set these others afloat as we work our way back up river?"

Shem, however, did not look as happy as I felt. "Something is wrong," he said. "I think we should go back now."

"What is it?" I said. "Did you have a revelation?"

"No, not exactly. More like a feeling."

"That tells me a lot," I said and I'm sure he detected the irritation in my voice. It wasn't particularly directed at him—just frustration that he had an inner sense that I seemed to have no access to. "Let's go then."

We were about four miles downriver by then. Since we did not know the terrain well, we stuck to the bank of the river until we reached the point where we had crossed and then retraced our steps overland. We could hear the rushing of the water even before we could see the jam. In our absence, a large tree had lodged against the narrow opening of the channel and three new logs were already resting on it. What was worse was that this was not a gopherwood log, but a full-grown tree—probably one that had been uprooted by the torrent when the dam broke. Because its branches had not been stripped, it put up more resistance against the water and caught every bit of debris that floated into it.

"I was hoping you were wrong for a change," I said.

"I wish you were gloating about that right now," said Shem. "It's worse now than before."

With great difficulty, we were able to remove the three gopherwood logs that had lodged against the tree. But the tree itself we could not budge even when we attached the pulleys. The swift current squeezing through the narrow channel pinned it between the logjam and the near bank, holding it fast and creating a strong undertow that threatened to suck us down. To make matters worse, the volume of new logs coming downstream had increased again.

"It's no use!" I shouted over the roar of the rushing water.

"We can't give up!" yelled Shem. "Think! Think!"

I looked around to take stock of the desperate situation and noticed that some of the animals I had seen in the woods had followed us, apparently curious to see what all the commotion was. "The beavers," I said pointing. "Perhaps they can help."

I went over to the two largest beavers and began gesturing frantically, biting on a stick to make them understand what I wanted them to do. They looked at me and then at each other, wondering at my strange behavior. But somehow, I got the message across. They crawled out on the tree and began gnawing on the trunk. The branches, which had been so difficult for Shem and I to work around, proved no problem for their smaller bodies. While they worked, Shem and I kept watch for oncoming logs.

They had been working for the better part of an hour when I heard a loud snapping noise. The great force of the water had snapped the tree in two before it was completely gnawed through. Both ends of the middle were swept through the opening with the beavers still on board.

Alarmed, I swam to their aid as fast as I could. I had forgotten about the undertow, so I did not have a good breath when the current sucked me under. The crushing force of the water held me under for what seemed like a long time, but was surely only a few seconds. When I popped to the surface, I came up sputtering and coughing, half choked with water.

The beavers swam to my side looking perplexed.

"Ah, you were born and raised in the water," I said, feeling suddenly foolish at the realization. "You didn't need me to rescue you."

They looked at each other again and swam off, leaving me to my own embarrassment.

We resumed our work on breaking up the logjam the following day. The collapse of the pile the previous morning left the remaining logs more stable. That made the work easier and we proceeded over the next several days without further mishap. The last logs that we removed had been driven into the bank, which had subsequently collapsed upon them. These we dug out with the aid of some friendly badgers who were very adept at that sort of work.

Once the logjam was completely broken up, we spent the following days setting afloat the logs we had stored on the bank for safekeeping, beginning with those furthest downstream and working our way back upstream again. From time to time, we scratched notes into the logs, indicating the date and our location in the hope that Father and Ham would notice the inscription as they removed the logs from the river and not worry about us as much. By then, there were fewer new logs coming down the river. We hoped that this did not mean that there was another jam upstream, but we were encouraged by the fact that the water was flowing at its normal level. We had accounted for a substantial number of logs by then which was far better than we could have even hoped for a few days earlier. That only raised our expectations, however, and strengthened our resolve to recover them all.

Feeling like we could take more time, we made a more careful search as we proceeded upstream. Since we were entering a more populated area, we held to the Nod-side bank, thinking it better to avoid people as much as possible for awhile. Most of the logs we found in that section of the Gihon had become caught in various structures of the river either singly or in small groups. Some were just spinning harmlessly in eddies outside of the mainstream of the channel.

Around sunset several days later, we neared the tents of Irad and both of us knew what the other was thinking. "Maybe there won't be any logs around there," said Shem.

"You know we're not that lucky," I replied.

Nineteen

And we weren't. As we gazed from behind trees across the river, we could plainly see a log that had been stranded by the receding water in the fork of a tree just below Irad's camp.

"That won't be easy to retrieve without being noticed," I lamented. "Why couldn't it be on this side?"

"Like you said, we're not that lucky."

"Maybe we should just leave it," I said. "After all, it's just one log."

"Our duty is to recover every log possible," said Shem. "You shouldn't shrink back from a task the Lord gives you to do."

"You always say things like that."

"Besides, we're not committing a crime here. We have every right to be on the river doing this."

"I know that. It's just ..."

"What?" said Shem. "You're concerned about what Irad and his family think? I've got news for you. They already don't like us. They're not going to think any less of us for going after that log."

"Yes, but it never made that much difference to me before," I said. "Now, it's ... personal."

"Is there something you're not telling me?" asked Shem.

"Well, actually, yes," I said awkwardly. "I guess you'd better know—in case it comes up."

When I had finished relating my recent encounter with Re-Aylah, Shem said, "Why didn't you tell me this before, Jay?"

"It must have slipped my mind."

"Right," said Shem with a knowing smile. "I can't believe you knocked her into the river."

"It was an accident."

"Sounds like she wasn't entirely convinced of that."

"Would you stop it!"

"A little touchy about it, aren't you?" said Shem. "Well, giving them one more reason to dislike us doesn't change the fact that we still have to free that log."

"It's getting too dark to do anything tonight," I said. "Maybe we can sneak over there early in the morning and be on our way before anyone wakes up."

"Sneak?" said Shem.

"All right, a poor choice of words," I said. "I know we're not criminals. But the less attention we arouse over there, the better I'll like it."

We made a quick camp at a safe distance downstream, but it did me little good. Every time I closed my eyes I could hear the derisive laughter of my cousins echoing across years gone by and I recalled the reproachful look on Re-Aylah's face of only a few weeks ago. I woke long before dawn and lay listening to the night sounds, trying to dismiss the unsettling sensation that the crickets and frogs were mocking me.

When at last the eastern sky began to glow, my hopes for a concealing mist dissipated with the approach of a clear dawn. I roused Shem and said, "Let's get this over with."

The river always felt especially chill at that hour, so we did not tarry as we crossed. All was quiet in Irad's camp as we set about freeing the log. Although it was tightly wedged in the fork of the tree, we had encountered exactly that situation many times before and wouldn't have had any trouble accomplishing the task anywhere else. The trick, however, was doing it quietly when every move we made resounded in the morning stillness. It was tempting to just yank it out, let it go kerplunk in the river and then run like gazelles. That's probably what I would have done if Shem hadn't been with me, but he thought that would be beneath his dignity. I failed to see anything more dignified about the humiliation that would be heaped on us upon our discovery.

Despite the racket, we probably would have gotten away with it if not for the unfortunate fact that Re-Aylah was an early riser. Worse than that, she walked like a cat so that we didn't hear her approaching to fill her water jar until she said, "Lying in ambush to push an unsuspecting passerby into the river?"

"Uh, no," I said, startled. "We're the only ones wet this morning."

"So far," she said. "Let's keep it that way."

"I'm sure you remember my brother Shem. This is Re-Aylah, daughter of Irad."

"It's a pleasure to see you again," said Shem.

"I'm sure it is," said Re-Aylah. "Is that why you have come calling at this hour?"

"No, we're just passing through," I said. "As soon as we get this log into the river, we'll be on our way."

"What is it with you and throwing things into the river?" said Re-Aylah.

"I didn't throw you …" I said. "Oh, never mind." I could see she was having fun at my expense and any explanation I could offer would only make things worse.

But things got worse anyway, because the next thing I heard was a voice from the top of the bank saying, "Are these vagrants bothering you?"

It was my cousin Fehud, whom I had hardly seen since the day he waylaid me at Tel-Asher.

"These aren't vagrants," said Re-Aylah. "These are sons of Noah—Jayfeth and Shem."

"That's even worse," said Fehud. "What are you two doing lurking around our camp. Up to no good, I'm sure."

"We're glad to see you, too, Fehud," I said.

"They're rescuing logs in distress," said Re-Aylah, with a hint of a smile on her lips.

"Don't you need to be getting back to camp?" said Fehud derisively. "You know how Father hates it when his breakfast is late. And so do I."

Being dismissed like that clearly rankled her, but she said nothing. She just tossed her head and started walking up the bank—slowly, though, so she wouldn't miss anything. Fehud returned his attention to us and said, "Looks like you could use some help. Why don't I get some *rope*? The boys and I could make quick work of this situation."

"Thanks for the offer," said Shem.

"That's not what he means, Shem."

"Hah!" Fehud snorted. "I've always wondered why you didn't tell anyone."

Obviously, Re-Aylah had never disclosed her role in the affair. For a moment, I considered revealing it to Fehud just to embarrass her and get one up on her brother. Out of the corner of my eye, I saw that she was studying me and wondering whether I would expose her secret. But I had given my word—even if it was coerced a long time ago—and I decided to keep it. "I guess you'll have to keep on wondering."

"Oh, I concluded a long time ago that you were a coward," said Fehud, slowly advancing toward us. "You didn't tell on me because you were afraid I might do something worse. Not that it would have made much difference anyway. My father would more likely have rewarded me than punished me."

"What's he talking about?" asked Shem.

"I'd rather not discuss it," I said with a final, mighty heave on the pulleys. The log suddenly wrenched free, jerked us off balance and we let it fall to the ground. It landed with a splat that sprayed mud everywhere—including all over Fehud.

"Of all the—" said Fehud. "Why I ought to …"

"Looks like our work here is finished," I said, rolling the log into the water. "We'd love to stay and reminisce about old times, but we have a lot of work to do."

Shem scrambled out of the tree and both of us were in the river before Fehud could recover. I glanced back over my shoulder, past Fehud, to where Re-Aylah had paused at the top of the bank. From that distance, it was difficult to tell, but I thought she might be laughing to herself.

Further upstream, our progress slowed considerably. The river had overflowed its banks in many places so we had to extend our search well outside of the channel. It was in these areas that we located the majority of the logs that had not yet been accounted for. They had simply been stranded on higher ground as the river level receded.

After several more days, we neared our previous campsite. The destruction in that area of the river was extensive. Many trees had been toppled like twigs and even the course of the river itself had been altered. Although I knew that none of our lumber would be above that point, I persuaded Shem to press ahead up the river toward where the dam had been constructed to see if we could discover any evidence of who the culprits might be. We approached warily, but found no one in the area. At the mouth of the pass, however, we discovered places where the freshly-exposed rock appeared charred as if it had been shorn from its ancient foundations by fire.

"You're the learned one," I said. "What do you make of that?"

"I don't know," said Shem. "I've never seen anything like it."

"Nothing in the tribal history?"

"There are some references to strange fire going back to the time of

Enoch, son of Jared, but they're rather vague. I don't think they understood what was happening at the time. And the intervening centuries since the stories were first told have done little to clarify the events."

"You're not much help," I said off-handedly.

"How can I be?" said Shem, bristling. "I've been cut off from all access to learning. If I could discuss this with the elders, I might be able to offer some better explanation. As it is, they won't even speak to us. Do you know how bitter it is to have such a thirst for knowledge and not be able to satisfy it?"

"I'm sorry, Shem. I didn't mean it that way. You're always such a steady fellow, I forget that you're suffering like the rest of us."

On the opposite side of the river, we found hidden in the woods a large campsite that looked like it had recently accommodated a hundred men or more. We separated to make a careful search of the area, looking for clues about their identities. Soon I heard Shem calling me and found him bending over a small dead creature, the likes of which I had never seen. It had the body of a lizard, wings like a bird and a head like a serpent. It was about the size of my hand and naked, though it was impossible to say whether it would have been clothed with fur, scales, skin or feathers when grown. I reached out my hand, but Shem grabbed my arm and said, "Don't touch it. It's an abomination!"

"How can you call any of God's creatures an abomination?" I said.

"I'm not so sure that is one of God's," said Shem. "I sense something very evil here."

Despite my brother's misgivings, I felt pity for the creature. It clearly had not lived for more than a short time after its birth. Judging by the way its face and body were contorted, it must have suffered terribly in its brief life. Over Shem's objections, I picked up the creature and buried it in the ground.

We did not care to pass the night in that place, so we made our way back downstream to our former campsite, hoping that the familiar surroundings would give us some comfort. But the fact that it had been so terribly altered had the opposite effect. I lay awake long into the night thinking about the strangeness of it all.

As soon as we could see in the morning, we were off again. We had by then accounted for nearly every piece of lumber in our supply. Anxious to rejoin our family and see how they were faring, we made our way back downstream.

Occasionally, we found logs that had once again become stranded and set them afloat with a number inscribed into each to keep an account on our last pass through without having to wait for them. That way we would know if any did not make it to its destination.

When at last we reached the Plain of Nephil, we found that Father and Ham had been as busy as we were while we were gone. Ham's river gate had worked beautifully, but they had been able to rest little day or night as the logs kept coming in a steady procession. Although the logs had bunched up a few times, for the most part they had fared well.

Within five days, the last remaining logs had been accounted for. Thus, Shem's prediction had come to pass. Our enemies had sought to do us evil, but God turned it to our good. Virtually all the lumber had been transported intact to Nephil in a fraction of the time we had originally planned. What I had thought would take us twenty-five years had been accomplished in less than one. I could not help but worry, though, that the speeding up of our timetable was only an indication that the day of doom was all the nearer.

PART II:
PERIL IN THE DESOLATE LANDS

ONE

As soon as we were rested, Father instructed us how to lay out the lumber to start the construction phase of our great project. We had never seen any plans, and until then, had only a vague notion of what his intentions were. Apparently, the Lord had imprinted the details of the ark into his mind and that was sufficient for him. For the construction site, Father selected a flat, grassy area a quarter of a mile from the river. Nephil lay only half a mile to the east, so everything we would do would be in sight of its walls and all who passed by on the roads. After spending so much of my life secluded in the Highlands, it felt very exposed to me and I had to remind myself that it was for that very purpose I had suggested moving to Nephil in the first place. I have to admit, though, that once we were actually there, it didn't seem like as good of an idea as it did when we were back in the hills.

Father staked out the dimensions as follows: the length was four hundred fifty feet and the width seventy-five feet. When I first comprehended the enormity of it, my heart sank. All the work we had accomplished thus far in felling the lumber and transporting it began to seem as nothing compared with the task that lay ahead.

Seeing the look on my face, Father said, "It must be large so that all who fear the Lord may take refuge inside."

"But we are so few," I replied.

"My hope is that many will join us in constructing it."

"They haven't exactly been flocking to us to help so far."

"We've achieved all this with just the five of us, haven't we?" said Father. "Even if nobody helps, we'll manage somehow."

"It's just that I thought we were closer to being finished," I said.

"You should be thankful that we're not," he said with that portentous tone that always brought discussions to an end.

Thus we began hewing out beams and planks from the enormous stacks of logs. Even though the cured gopherwood split more easily than it chopped, it was still backbreaking work. Without the fine axes, wedges and saws we obtained from Nephil, I don't know if we ever would have made any progress.

As we had hoped—and feared—the Nephilim were curious about what we were doing. They came frequently at first and would remark something like, "He is building a monument to his god," or, "They say their minds are not sound." Whenever they came, Father would stop working and take time to explain what he was doing and why. Because of Merib's warning that there was a faction of opposition in Nephil, I initially feared that we would be harassed. However, Ben-Tubal's official policy toward us always remained one of tolerance and apparently his word held sway. So, while Father's warning seemed to have little effect on them one way or another, at least we were able to proceed with construction for some time without interference.

Living so close to Ben-Tubal's daughter without being with her was exquisite torture for poor Ham and he began inventing an endless succession of excuses to go into the city so that he could see her. Father caught on quickly, however, and insisted on accompanying him whenever he went. I feared that Father's strictness might drive Ham to sneak out at night, but we never caught him at it if he did.

After several months of watching Ham pine away, Father finally said, "Enough already. It's time you boys were married."

"But Father," said Ham. "I cannot hide from you the fact that I am already in love."

"You must not take a wife from the Nephilim," said Father. "I will seek suitable wives for you from *our* people."

"But why?" protested Ham.

"Because they are idolaters."

"She could change and serve the Lord."

"More likely, it would be you who would change," said Father. "You would be corrupted and fall into her ways."

"But what about our feelings for each other?"

"A feeling is like trying to grasp water," said Father. "It slips through your fingers and then it is gone. Set your heart on the things of God, Ham. Your feelings will take care of themselves."

All of Father's advice fell on deaf ears because Ham was as hard-headed a person as I ever knew. With countless arguments, he tried to persuade Father to change his mind until we were all weary of hearing about it. But Father was no stranger to stubbornness himself and nothing Ham could say would move him.

As far as possible, I tried to stay out of the middle because I had worries enough of my own with Father's announcement that he was going to find us wives. It wasn't that I was against marriage and I was not unaware of certain obvious advantages weighing in favor of having a wife. These, however, had often seemed negated in large part by some rather substantial disadvantages. Back when we still had interactions with other clans, I had known some husbands whose lives had been made miserable by the shrews they had taken as wives. Honestly, though, I had spent little time contemplating which way the scales would tip with regard to marriage in general and even less applying it to my own specific circumstance. Of course, it will be obvious that such cursory observations as I had made about the institution of marriage wholly failed to account for the caprice of love.

As Father and Shem made preparations for the journey, my feelings were hurt that he had not asked me to accompany him. When I complained, he said, "I don't think it is good to leave Ham and Shem alone together now. Ham listens to you—at least as much as he listens to anyone. I need you here to make sure he stays out of trouble." He nodded toward Nephil and I understood what he meant.

Mother also accompanied Father on that journey, which was unusual because she seldom traveled. This was her natural inclination, plus Father thought being at home was safer for her as the people around us became increasingly hostile. When Ham found out she was going, he said, "Don't tell me I have to eat Jayfeth's cooking."

"You don't look like you're in danger of starving anytime soon," I said.

"You'll survive," said Father. "Your mother has a special sense for matters of the heart. You might regret the match I make for you without her advice."

"I'd rather make my own match," said Ham.

"We've been through all that, so there's no need to bring it up again," said Father. "She's going and you're staying—and that's that."

Actually, Ham was not the least bit sorry to be left behind so close to Jirah. Day after day, he badgered me about it until I couldn't take it any more. "Go see her before we both die of your heartache," I said. "But you must not do anything to dishonor yourself or her. And you must remain within my plain sight on the wall."

Ham was so anxious to see Jirah that he would have agreed to any conditions. He sent word by way of the guard at the gate for her to meet him. When she appeared on the wall about dusk, he went to her. I propped myself up against the frame of the ark and watched them from a distance. I dared not fall asleep because I was afraid to take my eyes off them even though I could see one of her attendants nearby. But when they talked long into the night, I became very drowsy.

I awoke with a start before dawn. To my great relief, they were still visible above the parapet, their silhouettes illuminated by the moonlight. I cursed myself for my lack of vigilance and tried not to think about what Father would say if he knew I had allowed this.

At daybreak, Ham returned whistling like a songbird. I thought he would be worthless for work that day but he set about it with great zeal. When we took a break at mid-morning, he said, "Father has misjudged the Nephilim. They really are excellent people."

"In some ways," I said.

"In every way, if you ask me."

"But they're idolaters, Ham."

"What better way to win them over than to spend more time with them—or intermarry with them?"

"Does she want to be won over?" I asked.

"She's very curious about our ways," said Ham. "I'm sure that given enough time, she will change."

"Time with her is one thing that you will not have unless she is willing to convert first."

"Do you think Father would change his mind if she converted?" he asked.

"He's a reasonable man," I said, more from pity for my brother than conviction. In my heart, I was not quite so hopeful.

Although I had serious misgivings about it, I continued to allow Ham and Jirah to meet regularly as long as Father was away. Between my own watchfulness and the fact that Jirah was accompanied at all times by one of her father's servants, most often Takek, I didn't think they could get into too much trouble (although I was uncomfortable knowing that Ben-Tubal would be made aware of everything that was going on between them and wondered what would become of it). Ham was so happy that I didn't have the heart to stop him, though I did have to limit their times together or neither of us would have been able to get any sleep. Somehow, I hoped that if the relationship were allowed to run its course that they might see how little they had in common and lose interest in each other. I shake my head now to think how naïve I was to believe this.

One day as Ham and I were working, we saw a caravan approaching Nephil. By the way they were dressed, I could tell they were from our own clan. "Oh, no," I groaned. "It's Irad."

"I wonder what he's doing here," said Ham. "I didn't think he had much use for the Nephilim."

"Maybe he has some business to conduct with Ben-Tubal."

"Or else lodging a complaint with him."

"Knowing Irad, that's probably more likely," I said. "Let's work down by the river today and stay away from the main road. Maybe we can avoid them."

Only Irad and a few of the men went inside. The rest congregated outside the main gate. We turned our backs to them so we wouldn't have to see them staring at us. However, we couldn't help stealing glances from time to time to keep an eye on what they were doing. Soon, I heard Ham say, "Looks like we're going to have some company."

"Don't tell me," I said and looked back myself. "I was afraid of that. It's Re-Aylah and her sister Sirah. And if I'm not mistaken, that's their cousin Zehafilah. We ought to escape now while we have a chance."

"So what?" said Ham. "Why should we care about a few nosey women?"

"Not just any women, Brother. That Re-Aylah is about the most exasperating person I've ever met. She can't wait to come over here and make fun of us."

"How do you know so much about her all of a sudden?"

"Never mind that," I said. "Let's just look like we're busy and maybe they'll go away."

Within a matter of moments, the women were within speaking range. "Hello," said Re-Aylah. "Could we ask what you're doing?"

Reluctantly, I answered, "We are obeying God's command to my Father."

"Yes, that's what we've heard," Re-Aylah said. "But we would like to know *what* it is."

"Why don't you go ask your father," I said. "We explained all this to him a long time ago."

"But he never tells us anything," said Sirah.

"And besides," said Re-Aylah, "You did tell me to make up my own mind about you."

"Oh you did, did you?" said Ham.

"Not now," I muttered to Ham under my breath. "If you must know, it's an ark."

"What's an ark?" asked Re-Aylah.

"A boat," I said. "A large one. And we have a lot of work to do as you can see, so if you'll excuse us ..."

"If it's a boat, then why don't you build it down here next to the river so you won't have to drag it so far to the water? And how do you expect to navigate so large a boat when the Gihon is so narrow?"

"That's not its purpose," I said, painfully conscious of how dirty and sweaty and uncomfortable I felt standing in front of her.

"Then what is its purpose?" she asked.

"You're full of questions," I said.

"You're full of air," said Sirah.

"I'll vouch for that," said Ham.

"You're not helping here," I said, forcing a smile through clenched teeth. "I'm going to remember this next time you want to go see Jirah ..."

"Sister," said Re-Aylah. "Let's at least hear the man out."

"So where is the boat going?" said Zehafilah.

"Nowhere," I said. Realizing that did not sound very intelligent, I added, "I mean, I don't know where it's going."

"Let me see if I understand this correctly," said Re-Aylah. "You've spent forty-five years gathering the lumber to build a boat that is far too large for the river and are planning to go to no place in particular. You're joking with us, right?"

"I know it sounds crazy."

"If you are serious, then it's the silliest thing I've heard of in my whole life," said Re-Aylah. "Come on, girls. Let's leave them to their foolishness."

As they walked away, I could not resist yelling after them, "Father says a terrible disaster *is* going to happen. If it does—I mean *when* it does—you won't think it's so funny then."

They did not reply or even acknowledge they had heard my last comment. While I was looking after them and shaking my head, Ham came over and pretended to pick up something off the ground and hand it to me. He said, "I think these are yours."

"What?" I asked.

"Your eyeballs," said Ham. "I think they popped out of your head while you were talking to Re-Aylah."

"Don't tease a man with an axe in his hand," I growled, but he only laughed at that. "It's no wonder she's still not married at her age. Who could live with that?"

"And you thought Jirah and I were an unlikely pair. You may have tamed the behemoths, Jay, but you'll never tame that one."

"Why would I want to?" I said. "Just because you walk around all dreamy-eyed doesn't mean everyone wants to. I'm happy just the way I am. And if I ever do fall in love, believe me, she would be the last woman on earth I would choose."

"If the disaster comes, she might *be* the last woman on earth."

"That would be my luck."

"Deny it all you want to," said Ham, laughing. "The more you say, the more you prove my point. You couldn't hate her that much unless you loved her."

"You're impossible," I muttered and began taking out my frustrations on an innocent log. While I was swinging my axe wildly, an errant blow must have cracked the handle without me realizing it. On a subsequent swing, the axe head flew off, sailed fifty feet through the air, and landed on a pile of metal parts that Ham had obtained from the Nephilim. The terrible racket scattered the sheep in fright and they ran off bleating in every direction. By then, Ham was howling on the ground and I could hear the laughter of my kinsmen in the distance as well. I threw the worthless handle at my brother but missed, though he was laughing so hard I don't think he would have felt it anyway. Deeply humiliated, I sulked for hours behind a stack of lumber out of sight, pretending to be busy, until our kinsmen were gone.

TWO

When Father did not return in a reasonable time, I worried. Even when he sent a messenger after three months to say they were well but delayed, I remained concerned. Four more months passed before I was relieved to see their three familiar shapes on the horizon. However, I could tell by the way they carried themselves as they approached that they did not bear good news.

"It seems that every one of our kinsmen has turned against us," said Father. "We visited all the clans I could think of in the valley and plain, but not one of them wants to give their daughters in marriage to us. The only hopeful news we have to report is that the Ancient One agreed to intercede for us with Shalmish of the far northern country. He might be persuaded to allow one of his daughters to marry Shem. But even that arrangement is far from certain."

"What about Ham and me?" I asked.

"I'm sorry," said Father. "I've done all that I could do. The matter is in the Lord's hands. If it is his will, he will provide wives for you."

What was bad news for Father was good news for Ham. He begged me to talk with Father about Jirah, saying she was ready to denounce the idols and follow the Lord. Reluctantly, I agreed to do so and took Father aside one evening. When I told him what was on my mind, he was stunned and said, "Has the daughter of Ben-Tubal beguiled you as well?"

"You said yourself that none of our kinsmen would consent to let their daughters marry us," I replied. "Yet here is one who is not only willing but eager to marry Ham. And he can hardly think of anything else day or night besides the girl."

"You are overlooking one very important matter," said Father.

"I know what you're going to say. But if she is willing to turn away from idols and serve the true God, she won't be an idolater anymore."

"How can we be sure of her sincerity?" said Father. "I have been wrong about these people before."

"How can you be sure of any of us?" I replied.

"The proof of the tree is in the fruit that it bears."

"Well, then at least examine the fruit she bears before you pass judgment."

Father looked away from me toward the hills and said, "Though all the world turn against me, I didn't think my sons ever would."

I did not know if he was speaking to God, himself or me, but I took the liberty of answering. "Perish that thought. We'll never turn against you no matter what may come. Even Ham. If you put him to the test, he would choose you over the girl—though it broke his heart and cost him his only chance for happiness."

"Do you really think so?"

"I am certain of it," I said, though I was not quite as confident concerning my brother as I made out to be. Then I added what I thought would be the most compelling reason of all as far as Father was concerned. "And if she truly is willing to convert, then we will have saved an idolater from the coming destruction."

Slowly, Father said, "All right, then. I'll consider it. But first, I must inquire of the Lord before I give my consent."

We did not see Father at all during the following day. When he returned that evening, he appeared weak and shaken. What actually transpired between the Lord and him I did not find out until many years later. He refused to discuss the matter except to say that he would be willing to meet with the girl. And if her answers satisfied him, he said he would seek an audience with Ben-Tubal. Needless to say, Ham was overjoyed at this news. I was happy for him, but hoped that I had not inadvertently done him or our family a disservice.

Jirah, accompanied by Takek, met with Father the next day. She was considerably taller than Ham (for Nephila were exceptionally tall like the men) and statuesque, with ebony eyes and lovely dark skin so smooth and perfect that I could easily tell she had never done a hard day's work in her life. She wore a sapphire robe embroidered with silver thread and her wrists and ankles were adorned with much gold jewelry.

Father questioned her closely concerning her intentions toward the Lord. The answers she gave were satisfactory, though it was difficult to gauge her sincerity when so much could be gained by merely telling Father what he wanted to hear. Whatever the case, Father requested and was granted an audience with Ben-Tubal.

Now I had been wondering all along if the objections of my Father would be as nothing compared to those of Ben-Tubal. After all, Ben-Tubal was by far the richest and most powerful man I had ever known—maybe more than anyone who had yet lived. And we were but poor outcasts, shunned even by our own people. I would have thought we made poor suitors. To my surprise, though, Ben-Tubal was not only agreeable, but seemed delighted at the prospect of Jirah marrying Ham.

The wedding was an extravagant affair that lasted three days. On the first day was the customary exchange of gifts. Ben-Tubal, to his credit, did not embarrass Father by lavishing so many gifts on him that he could not reciprocate, though it was clearly within his means to do so. This was followed by a ceremonial bonding between the families, which was the universal custom of the people of that day.

The second day was given over to customs peculiar to the Nephilim. Separate parties were held for the bride and groom. At the groom's party, which I attended, were ten formal attendants (Shem and I were two, Merib a third, and the rest were Nephilim provided to us for that purpose, since we had no other friends.) The day began with "games" as they were termed. These were athletic contests—such as running, jumping and lifting heavy objects— that tested the strength and abilities of the participants. In running, I could not keep up with even the slowest-footed Nephilite (even though I was considered swift among my own people), but at least I was not embarrassed by my performance. However, when it came to feats of strength, I was humiliated. For example, I saw more than one Nephilite roll a rock the size of a lower millstone up a steep incline. I could not even budge it. Another man tied an iron bar into a knot using nothing but his bare hands. Even Ham, the strongest among us, was no match for even the least of them. They did not taunt us for our weakness, though, but seemed merely amused with us. It was all in good sport and there was much winking and ho-hoing among them about our lack of prowess. As I had begun to observe of their people, they were very childlike in many respects, which was quite a contrast to their physical power. You never knew whether to laugh at them or cower.

Later that day, the groom's attendants met in an inner room of the palace where each of us were expected to speak about the good qualities of the groom and tell stories to illustrate these characteristics, though some of the stories told were merely humorous. Shem and I, of course, had no difficulty coming up with plenty of anecdotes. And Merib had some that he had learned from his interactions with us. What surprised me, though, was how much the Nephilite attendants knew of Ham and our family that they related with details which could only have been provided by eyewitnesses. How much of this was accounted for by Ham's bragging during his visits to Jirah and how much was secret observation of our activities, I did not know.

All those in attendance heaped gifts upon the groom, including many objects of gold, which struck me as exceedingly generous coming from virtual strangers. Indeed, gold seemed to be in greater abundance every time I visited Nephil. I was later told that the second day usually concluded with dancing girls, but we did not have any. I assume this was at Father's request, not Ham's.

The third day was the high wedding day. The simple ceremony itself was conducted by Father. Ham and Jirah pledged their faithfulness to one another and to follow the Lord all the days of their lives. Then followed a great feast, the likes of which I have never seen. All Nephil turned out for it, though only the higher ranking were allowed admittance into the palace because there was not room enough for everyone in the banquet hall. Of these, only Baldag was conspicuously absent. I hoped it was merely because he didn't like us and not that he was up to something. The rest of the people feasted in the courtyard, which glowed brightly with the light of many torches. Musicians skilled in the lyre, flute, bow and all manner of other instruments played superbly as we dined. When I inquired about these, I was told that they were descendants of the renowned Jubal, father of all who make music.

There was such an abundance of food that I could not have eaten the smallest sample from each dish without becoming full beyond all measure. Given my previous experience with the rich Nephilite fare, I had tried my best to restrain myself from over-indulging—without much success. Feeling uncomfortably full and in need of fresh air, I decided to step out and escape from the crowd for a few minutes. While a chorus of excellent singers celebrated the occasion in song, I caught Merib's eye across the table, nodded toward the door and excused myself.

The east porch offered an expansive view of the Gihon valley. Watching the sunset cast the long shadow of the palace over the river put me in an especially reflective mood. When Merib joined me, I said, "We've come a long way since that day we first met in Latham."

"And now that our families are united by marriage, there's no telling how far we can go together," said Merib.

One of the servants came out and offered us drinks, though Merib declined. I looked out over the moonrise, raised my glass, and said, "May Jirah and Ham find much happiness together."

"Be careful with that," said Merib as I took a long drink from the cup. "It is very potent for your thin Highland blood."

That was no exaggeration. In only a few moments, I began to feel very light-headed.

"So tell me, now that Ham has come to his senses, will you?" Merib said, nodding toward the door that opened to the banquet hall. "Remember, I have other sisters."

I looked in the direction he indicated and saw the twins Mashea and Pashea standing inside. "Yes," I said, floating in a growing euphoria unlike anything I had ever experienced. "They are both beautiful. It would be difficult to choose between them."

"Perhaps you would not have to make a difficult choice," said Merib. "You know that among our people it is not forbidden to have more than one wife."

Mashea looked at me out of the corner of her eye. Her mouth turned upward ever so slightly, knowing that I was watching her. I was aware of my body in a way I never had been before. I could hear my heart beating in my chest, feel the blood coursing through my veins and sense the quickening of my respiration.

"The guests are all assembled and the feast prepared," Merib continued. "It would be as easy to celebrate two weddings as one."

Strangely, what had never entered my mind until then suddenly seemed overwhelmingly desirable. I was dangerously close to agreeing to the proposition on the spot—so much so that it startled me. And in that moment of hesitation, the feeling subsided like a tent whose poles are removed. I poured the rest of my drink over the balcony and said, "The food and drink are too much for my thin Highland blood, as you say. I will return to my tent to recuperate. Please give my regards to your father."

I wished Ham and Jirah well and took my leave. As I left the banquet hall, I felt the eyes of Mashea and Pashea upon me, but I did not look back.

Because of our concerns about the ark, Ben-Tubal had offered to post a dozen guards to watch over it during the wedding. I had misgivings about this, but realized that if Ben-Tubal wanted to do us harm, he could have easily overwhelmed us with the thousands at his command. So, I was not surprised to find everything intact when I returned.

"Go, join the festivities," I told the guards and they happily obliged. I lay down in my tent, head spinning and half-afraid that I might become nauseous. I propped myself up on my bags and sat there as motionless as possible thinking about Ben-Tubal's daughters, wondering if I had made the right decision by declining the opportunity presented to me.

A throbbing headache, which I felt sure was a result of the drink I had been given the night before, made for a rough start to the new morning. Strangely, rather than making me detest it, I felt a craving for it instead. While the sensation struck me as highly unreasonable, it was very compelling nevertheless. If I would have had a cup in front of me, it would have been difficult to resist. That had been my second bad experience with Cainite potions. I determined that there would not be a third.

In those days, it was customary for the bride and groom to spend a month alone together. They were relieved of all responsibilities and even had their meals brought to them if they desired. Jirah had elected to spend her bridal month in her father's palace—and I could not blame her for that. But Jirah's life was about to change dramatically and I feared that our crude encampment would be a poor substitute for the luxury of the palace. I wondered how she would fare away from the finery she had known all her life.

I did not have to wonder for long. About three weeks into Ham's bridal month, a messenger came to our camp with news from the Ancient One that he had arranged a wife for Shem. Her name was Ohlibah, from the clan of Shalmish, who lived on the shore of an inland sea of the same name located in the far northern territory.

I asked Shem how he felt about marrying a woman he had never laid eyes upon before. He replied, "If Ohlibah is the wife the Lord has provided for me, I trust that she will be an exceedingly fine wife." I admit that I was skeptical at the time. But I will also admit that subsequent events demonstrated clearly which of my brothers made the wiser choice.

When Jirah's bridal month was completed, we made preparations to travel north. Once again, the Nephilim offered to post guards for the ark in our absence. I suspect that there were many who were only too pleased to have this service provided. It made it possible for all of us to be gone at once, thus halting the work on the ark.

The journey to the Sea of Shalmish took three months. The trip itself would have been largely unremarkable except for the fact that it was the first opportunity for the rest of us to spend time with Jirah. Indeed, we could have made the trip in half the time if not for her, because she tired easily and was unaccustomed to the privations of travel. On the first night we camped, I overheard her saying, "What is that?"

"It's a mat," said Ham. "We sleep on them when we travel—"

"You expect me to sleep on that?"

"Just try it," said Ham. "It's really not that bad."

A few moments later, Jirah said, "It's lumpy and I can feel the hard ground underneath."

"You'll get used to it."

"I might as well be laying on a sack of rocks."

"It's only for a few weeks," said Ham.

"Weeks!" said Jirah. "I'll never be able to sleep on this. How am I going to be able to go for weeks without sleeping—especially with all this walking?"

"We only covered five miles all day."

"Can I help it if my feet hurt? And besides, this food is hardly sustaining for a long journey. Whoever heard of eating what you find along the way?"

And on it went until Ham was finally obliged to return to Nephil in the middle of the night to fetch cushions for her. These were not heavy, but bulky to carry on a long journey, so Father, Shem and I took turns relieving Ham from the burden. I wanted to tell Jirah to carry them herself, but I didn't wish to make things worse for my brother than they already were. Such were my first impressions of my sister-in-law.

After a long journey (that seemed even longer), we finally arrived at the Sea of Shalmish, which defined the northern border of Cush. Ohlibah was a petite, unassuming woman, and it will come as no surprise that her quiet spirit was a welcome change after twelve weeks on the road with Jirah. Only the immediate family members of Shalmish the Younger were present for their wedding and we merely caught glimpses of Shalmish the Elder the whole time we were there. They received us politely, but were markedly reserved in their interactions with us. No doubt they had hoped their daughter would marry better, but they were not prominent among the clans, despite being a numerous people. Even so, given our reputation, I suspect that Shalmish had to be persuaded against his will by the Ancient One to allow his daughter to marry a son of Noah, though what consideration he might have received in return I never knew. The clan of Shalmish did seem impressed with Jirah and the fact that she was Ben-Tubal's daughter, which I thought was a telling indication about their motivations.

Once the required ceremonies were completed, our respective families had little interaction during Ohlibah's bridal month. We camped at a comfortable distance from them and exchanged pleasantries whenever our paths happened to cross. Otherwise, we had few dealings with each other.

During the month, Father did not speak of his message from the Lord. But when it was time for us to leave, he imparted to them all that was in his heart. They received the news indifferently—as one would suffer to hear an elder recount exploits that had been told many times before. It should be noted that Ohlibah herself was not of the same mind as her family in this matter because she readily embraced the message. Undoubtedly, this was one of the primary qualities for which she had been chosen by Father Methuselah.

The Ancient One himself had been unable to make the journey. When we stopped briefly to see him along the way, it was clear that his health was failing and that he was too weak to travel. Not only were we concerned about his deteriorating condition, we found it unsettling to consider what that implied about the fulfillment of the prophecy.

We made somewhat better time on the return journey and found everything in order when we arrived back at the ark. With Ham and Shem both wed, that left only me unmarried, even though I was the oldest. While my prospects did not seem promising, the longer I spent in the company of Jirah, the less I minded.

THREE

I soon settled back into my old routine—long days of work and evenings around the campfire, punctuated by our weekly observation of the Sabbath. Since Father and Ham were clever at joinery, Shem and I were left to the backbreaking work of splitting beams and planks and hauling them to the construction site on Ham's cart. For this, we had taken entirely to using oxen instead of Naysa. The good burro was still very willing, but getting on in years and we hated to overtax his strength. However, we continued to use him for lighter jobs whenever we could so that he would still feel useful.

Gradually, Jirah adjusted to our family and we to her, though I cannot say the process was always easy. She and Ham made frequent trips into Nephil. Each time they returned, they brought more of Jirah's things from the palace until at length they were forced to put up a larger tent. It was splendidly furnished and spacious enough that several families could have fit inside comfortably. Father drew the line at servants, however, and would not allow her to have any in the camp.

I received many encouragements from Jirah and Ham to visit Nephil with them. Merib, by way of messengers, joined the chorus. I resisted, suspicious that they would only use the opportunity to try to engage me to one of Jirah's sisters—and I wanted nothing to do with that. Finally, though, boredom from the monotony got the better of me and I asked Merib to meet me on the wall of the city one evening.

The wall itself was largely ceremonial, not built for defense as walls were in later times. Its design was aesthetic and proportioned to call attention not to itself, but to the noble domes and spires of the city, like a fine setting enhances a jewel. It also restricted access to its three gates so no one could enter or depart the city unnoticed. Like much of Nephil, the wall was constructed of fine white marble. It stood fifteen feet tall and the craftsmanship of the stonemasons was superb. The seams between the blocks were practically invisible so that it appeared to be one giant, shining stone. On top of the wall was a walkway about ten feet wide and upon this Merib and I strolled.

"I see that you are making progress on the ark," said Merib.

"I suppose that is more evident to one who does not measure progress by each swing of the axe," I replied.

Instead of laughing at my joke, Merib said, "If the work is too difficult for you, why don't you speak to Ben-Tubal. He might command a hundred men to assist you if you ask him."

"Do you really think so?" I said, my heart rising momentarily as I considered the possibility. "Ah, but I don't think Father would allow it."

"Why not?" asked Merib. "Don't you want to finish it and be done?"

"It is not enough just to finish it," I said, avoiding a direct answer to his question. Part of me did want very much to be finished with it. At the same time, though, the thought filled me with dread, because I feared what might happen next. "How the task is accomplished is important. That means that only men who are committed may work on it. If they were just acting under orders, that would not be acceptable."

"Are you committed?" asked Merib. "Truly committed?"

"Why do you ask?"

"You told me yourself that you are not a seer. How can you be sure of what you have not personally seen or experienced?"

"Father heard this command directly from God," I said. "I am obedient to his vision."

"But if you are only following *his* orders, how is that any different from Ben-Tubal's?"

"It just is," I said, stubbornly refusing to concede his point.

"You can evade my question if you want—it makes no difference to me," said Merib. "But it seems to me that you are wasting your whole life in vain. Not all the seers in the world are in your family, you know. We also have prophets and they bring different oracles."

"Are these the Others you once mentioned?"

"Shhh," said Merib. "It is not permitted for us to discuss such things outside our people. Of course, that situation could be remedied quickly."

He nodded toward a private garden below, adjacent to the palace. Near the center lay a pool of water, and beside it Merib's sister Mashea was preparing to disrobe and bathe. Just in time, I averted my eyes and began walking hurriedly back toward the gate. "Why would you want to show me such a thing?" I asked as Merib caught up to me.

"Our people do not consider their bodies to be objects of shame," said Merib. "Is her beauty not pleasing to you?"

"Yes, she is beautiful," I said. "But her beauty has been reserved for another man's eyes. Surely there are prominent men among the Nephilim who would make more suitable husbands. Why would she want me?"

"Ben-Tubal greatly desires it."

"Why?"

"I do not know."

"I think you do know."

"Do you accuse the son of Ben-Tubal of lying?"

I studied his face for an answer, but he was as difficult to read as his father. At times like these, I never quite knew where I stood, so I chose to err on the side of caution. "No, I do not accuse you of lying. Please excuse my rash words."

His anger subsided and we stood there with an awkward silence between us. I finally broke it by saying, "I wish you would tell me what's going on here."

"Believe me, if you did know everything, you would wish that you didn't," he said and walked away.

Once the foundation of the ark was laid, we proceeded to build towers and scaffolding proportional to the height of the ark, which was to be forty-five feet tall. These were constructed in five sections—one fixed section in each corner extending at right angles twenty feet in either direction. The fifth, built on wheels, was movable for the construction of the exterior perimeter. Inside the base of the ark, we erected narrow columns at twenty-five foot intervals. All these we connected with ropes and pulleys so that we could hoist the heavy vertical and horizontal beams into place. It was difficult work, but there was visible progress which we all found satisfying.

"Looks like you're coming right along, Brother," came an unexpected voice behind us one day as we were working.

"Gomer!" said Father as the two men embraced. "I didn't know you were in these parts."

"I had to see the ark," said Gomer. "Everyone's talking about it. I must say, it's very impressive."

"Well, here's a hammer," said Father. "We could use your help."

"I wish I could, but I'm just passing through."

"On your way to … ?"

"To the land where the sun is born," said Gomer.

"Not you, too?" said Father. "Why would you want to go to Nod?"

"A new day is dawning there and the possibilities are endless," said Gomer, but Father only stared blankly at him. "You know, haven't you heard the song?"

"We don't hear many songs around here, except for the ones we sing for ourselves."

"Then allow me to enlighten you," said Gomer. "There are opportunities galore in the eastern lands, if half the tales I've heard are true."

"That's the problem," said Father. "Half of what you hear *isn't* true. And the other half has usually been exaggerated."

"But look at Nephil. Have you ever seen anything like it? And that's just the beginning. Where do you think all that gold comes from? I'm going there to get some for myself."

"No offense, but what do you need gold for? Don't you have better things to do than sit around and watch it shine?"

"You're missing the point, Noah," said Gomer. "It's not the gold so much as what it represents. I mean, you have all this to show for yourself. What do I have? Nothing. But when I strike it rich, things will be different. They won't call me 'Gomer the Accursed' anymore, but 'Gomer the Fortunate.' I can't wait to see the looks on their faces when I come back with all that gold!"

"Right," said Father. We had heard that kind of talk before. The last time, Gomer was going to make his fortune in the black wool trade, but the moths got to it. Or was it the blight? The schemes blurred together after awhile. When I was a lad, Gomer's stories thrilled me. But as I looked at him standing there with his outgrown tunic riding up on his pudgy middle talking about his next new plan to strike it rich, I couldn't help feeling sorry for him.

"I know what you're thinking," said Gomer. "But this time, it's going to be different."

"Yes, I'm sure it will be," said Father, trying not to sound patronizing. "What does Papa think about all this?"

"He, uh … doesn't exactly know yet. Didn't want to cause him any worry. It'll be more fun to surprise him when I come back rich. Won't he be proud?"

"He's proud of you now," said Father. "You know that. He's always believed in you."

"Not always for good reasons, though. I've had a run of ... well, you know. But I'll show him his faith in me was well-founded."

We prevailed upon Gomer to stay the night with us, partly in the hope that he would change his mind. Mother's cooking could have a very persuasive effect on those who had an appreciation for hearty food as Gomer obviously did. But in the morning, Gomer was resolute in his determination to go on, so we bade him farewell and watched him disappear over the bridge into Nod. Father tried not to show it, but I know he was deeply troubled by their parting. Before the day was out, he had dispatched a messenger to my grandfather Lamech. The price of messengers, which continued to increase each year, was up to a goat, which I thought was exorbitant. But it was an ill-tempered nanny that I never got on with too well, so I didn't mind as much.

Grandfather arrived about three weeks later. When Father related the full account to him, he shook his head and said, "That sounds like him. I should have known something was up."

"What do you think we should do?" asked Father.

"*You* don't need to do anything," said Grandfather. "You've got your hands full here. He'll probably get discouraged in a few months and come home."

"But apparently there really is gold in the east," said Father. "I'm more worried that he *will* find something. Remember the pearls?"

"Only too well. Those coastal ruffians watched him dive for a year. And when he got ready to leave, they waylaid him before he was a half-day's journey from their village. He was in a sorry state when he got home that time. The saddest part was that nobody ever did anything about it because of who he was. They just laughed at him."

"There may be worse characters than that in Nod," said Father.

"True, which is why I thought I would follow along behind—just in case," said Grandfather. "I'm getting old and have nothing but time on my hands anymore when Gomer's gone."

"We could use your hands here," said Father.

"I wouldn't be much good for hard labor anymore. And there's still a lot of the world that I would like to see before death closes my eyes. But I tell you what. When Gomer and I return, maybe we'll stay on for awhile and help. I've been intending to for a long time, but you know how things have been since your mother ..."

"I know, Papa. It hasn't been easy for you."

"I've done the best I could to raise him. That's all I can say."

"Believe me, I understand. And I admire you for it," said Father. "So how will you find him? He has a big head start."

"You know your brother. He usually leaves a trail. I'll just let this new venture run its course and try to stay close enough behind to help in case he gets into trouble."

Gomer's venture had been the closest thing we had had to excitement for some time. And with Grandfather's departure, monotony soon set in again. While my days were full with so much work to do, my nights were empty. Everyone had someone except me, and it was starting to weigh on my heart. Father and Mother had always been happy together and never had a cross word between them. Ohlibah was the ideal wife in every respect and she and Shem were very much in love. I was even starting to think that Ham didn't have it so bad, though I didn't feel that Jirah was quite my sort. Thus, even though I was tired each night, I had taken to staying up later and later— often falling asleep by the campfire because somehow being in my tent made me feel more alone.

On one such evening, when the others had long been asleep, I was reclining by the fire, occasionally poking it with the end of a stick for no other reason than to watch the sparks fly upward. I was starting to nod off when I caught a glimpse of movement among the shadows. A solitary figure approached from the Gihon Road, turned aside and headed straight for me, but a hooded cloak prevented me from recognizing the likeness. I scrambled to my feet in apprehension, knowing that it was far more likely to be an adversary than a friend. I was on the verge of calling out to warn my family when the figure entered the circle of the firelight and threw back the hood.

"Re-Aylah!" I said in astonishment.

"Quietly, please," said Re-Aylah. "I don't want anyone to know I am here."

I stood there dumbfounded, so Re-Aylah put into words what I couldn't say. "I know, you're surprised to see me."

"Well, yes."

"I can't say that I blame you. We've gotten off to a rather bad start."

"And you've come here to demand an apology?" I said.

"No, it should be the other way around," she said. "I've behaved rudely toward you, I'm afraid."

"If that's an apology, I accept it," I said, relaxing a little. "And I offer my own to you for my part. Why don't you sit down and refresh yourself. You must be hungry after your journey. We have lentil soup left over from supper and some curds. It's not fancy, but it is filling."

She ate hungrily—a quantity I thought extraordinarily large for a woman. I tried not to stare while she ate and drank, which was difficult to do without feeling like it was obvious that I was avoiding looking at her. But against my will my eye was drawn irresistibly back to her face and the luster of the firelight on her golden hair.

I kept my curiosity in check as long as I could. But when she finally finished, I said, "You didn't come all this way just to apologize, did you?"

"Not entirely, no," said Re-Aylah. "I've had something on my mind for the longest time. The terrible disaster of which you spoke when we last talked five years ago, what is it?"

"Five years? Has it been that long? I guess I've lost track of the time."

"It may not have seemed long to you, but it has to me. My heart has been troubled about it ever since."

Seeing the worry on her face wrought an amazing transformation on my heart. We had been at odds for so long that I had never considered that there might be another side to her. Her vulnerability made me long to comfort her and tell her that she need not fear, even though I knew what I had to tell her would not be comforting. I said, "Father says the Lord is grieved because people are turning toward evil and that a terrible catastrophe will befall."

"You mean on the Cainites, don't you?" She looked at me with heartbreaking earnestness, but I did not relent. "Not us. Please tell me he doesn't mean on *us*."

"I am sorry."

"Is there no hope then?"

"Father believes that if enough people return to the Lord wholeheartedly, doom can be averted. That's why we are building the ark. It serves as a witness to turn to him."

"And if they don't?"

"Then we will take refuge inside. Father says it will be the only safe place in the world when doomsday comes."

"These are hard words," said Re-Aylah, as much to herself as to me.

"It's difficult to understand why the righteous would be swept away with the wicked. I know your family is righteous and that's why they cannot accept the message."

"If only that were true," said Re-Aylah. "But the truth is that righteousness dwells on our lips only and not in our hearts."

"Even though they don't have much use for us, I know they're good people."

"When the eyes of other men are upon them, yes. But in secret, they do shameful things and justify them for the sake of honor."

"Surely it can't be as bad as all that," I said.

"Jayfeth, it was my father and brothers who burned your lumber. Some of the elders convinced him to do it, though he didn't need much encouragement. They thought Noah would get discouraged and give up on the ark."

This news stunned me, because I had always suspected Baldag of that despicable act. I could scarcely believe Re-Aylah's words that it was our own close kinsmen who had done it.

"Your eyes betray you," Re-Aylah said. "I don't blame you for hating me."

"You were very young," I said absently. "And besides, I don't hold you responsible for the acts of your father."

"But I knew of it. And I said nothing and did nothing to stop it. I even gave my approval because I thought he was doing the right thing at the time."

"And now?"

"Now I know that it was wrong and I'm sorry. As for the rest, I'm very confused. I hear your words and they frighten me. But I do not understand how your family alone can be right while all the rest of the world is wrong."

For that, I did not have an answer.

"I must go now. Goodbye, Jayfeth." She pulled the hood over her head and faded away into the shadows.

FOUR

The next day, I shocked my family by telling them that it was Irad who had burned our lumber. Ham was livid and said, "I say we go up there right now and burn their tents."

"I don't want to hear any of that kind of talk," said Father.

"It's only fair that they should drink the same cup they gave us," said Ham.

"That was many years ago and what's done is done," said Father. "Don't harbor bitterness in your heart—it's a worse fire than the one that burned the lumber."

I kept silent, but I have to confess that I was not wholly unsympathetic to Ham's sentiments. Finding out it was Irad reopened an old wound that had never healed very well. The fire had been a grievous loss from which it had taken us years to recover. Such a callous act deserved retribution. I replayed Re-Aylah's telling of it over and over in my mind rehearsing things I would say and do to Irad and Fehud in revenge. As the days went by, though, my outrage gradually subsided. I found myself thinking less about the lumber and more about Re-Aylah—much to my dismay.

One evening after supper, as Mother was mending Father's trousers by their tent in the fading twilight, I sat down beside her and watched for awhile. Despite her advancing age, her cheeks were full and rosy yet and her eyes still twinkled. Even with all the hardships she had faced, she remained well content with her life and I admired her for it. At length, I said to her, "How can it be that all my thoughts are consumed by the daughter of Irad?"

"What do you mean?" said Mother without looking up.

"Her father and brothers destroyed fifteen years of our labor. Her family hates us and treats us harshly. She herself mocked me and laughed at me."

"Yes?"

"What I mean to say is, I have no reason whatsoever to think about her. Yet I can't help myself."

"You think about her because you are angry with her and her family?"

"I am angry with their whole family. But she is the one I think about."

"Oh, then perhaps anger is not all you feel toward her." Mother put aside her mending, her eyes brightening as she looked at me. "Perhaps you also have feelings of love."

"I was afraid that you were going to say that," I moaned.

"You don't want to feel this way?"

"I'm not so sure that I want love at all. But if I were to love someone, why would I choose someone who thinks I'm a buffoon and whose family hates me? She is, of all women, the least likely for me to desire. It makes no sense."

"Ah, that's where you are in error," Mother said with a good-hearted laugh. "You are expecting love to make sense. But love follows its own unsearchable path." She twirled her finger around in the air several times to illustrate and then touched my chest.

"So what do I do?"

"Go to her. Tell her how you feel and see what she says."

"I have little doubt what she would say. She thinks I'm a fool."

"If she already thinks you're a fool, then what's the harm? You can do no worse in her eyes."

"I would be even more humiliated in my own eyes than I already am."

"Put away your pride, Jayfeth," she chided. "It has no place in matters of the heart. Besides, she may be more receptive than you think."

"Do you really think so?"

"The fact that you are in her thoughts at all is a good sign," said Mother. "After all, she did seek you out. And she has apologized for her role in all this."

"So, you think there's hope?"

"I cannot say. But if you don't try, you'll never know."

"I suppose that's true."

"Go to Re-Aylah and tell her all that is in your heart. At least then you will know."

Father thought this plan was ill advised. But since he had allowed Ham to marry a Nephila, he could hardly deny me the opportunity to seek out a wife from my own clan. Mother, bless her soul, took my side (if you could call it my side when I was so ambivalent about it) and persuaded him.

Shem accompanied me under the condition that I was to be given privacy in talking with Re-Aylah. That, of course, was making a big assumption. I had no idea how I was going to get her away from her family long enough to have a conversation with her.

I have to confess that being away from the camp was a relief as I had done no traveling since Shem's wedding several years earlier and my feet longed for the open road. We made our way at a leisurely pace along the Gihon Road because I was in no hurry. As long as we were on our way, I could maintain the fragile illusion that things were going to turn out well. I was in no rush to dispel my self-deception by actually going through with it. The farther we went, the slower my pace became until Shem started to lose patience with me because he was anxious to get home to his wife.

Even at that rate, we had to get there eventually. Late on the fourth day, Shem and I neared the tents of Irad. We crossed the Gihon and approached from the opposite bank in order to escape detection. In the place where we had observed them after the dam broke years earlier, we crouched and watched for an opportunity. Toward evening, a group of women came down from the campsite to the river to draw water and among them was Re-Aylah. My heart fluttered and I said, "I must be out of my mind to hope that she might consider me."

"Yes, you are out of your mind," said Shem.

"You're supposed to disagree with me."

"All right. She's madly in love with you and has only been pretending to dislike you."

"That's easy for you to say. You didn't have to work for your wife and you got an excellent one in Ohlibah. I don't know why I couldn't fall in love with a girl like her."

"Love?" said Shem. "Is that what you call this? It looks more like an obsession to me."

"Is there a difference?" I said and I wasn't making a joke.

"People generally get over obsessions. They wake up and realize just how silly they really were."

"You think you're so smart," I said. "But you don't know how I really feel. Why can't you be more supportive?"

"Oh, I'm supportive. No one cares about you more than I do, Jay. That's why I don't want to see you get hurt."

"I get the impression you think this is a bad idea."

"Oh? What makes you say that?"

"You don't have to be sarcastic."

"Listen to yourself," said Shem. "You've said that she's not even your type—quite apart from all the bad blood between our families that makes any chance you might have to win her hand in marriage virtually impossible."

"I know you're right. But I can't help myself. I'm ... I'm—"

"Obsessed."

"I think you mentioned that already."

"You're determined to go through with this, aren't you. Do you even have a plan?"

"Not really. I guess I'll just wait for her by the river when she comes to draw water tomorrow morning. Maybe I can catch her alone then."

When night fell, we crossed the river. At the spot where I noted that Re-Aylah had filled her jar, I wrote in the sand with my finger in small letters, "Jayfeth is near." Before dawn, while Shem waited downstream in the bend where I had knocked Re-Aylah into the river, I hid myself in some bushes and hoped that Re-Aylah would be the first to see my message.

Shortly after sunrise, I heard voices, which was a bad sign—more than one person was coming. I had difficulty seeing clearly through the early-morning mist, but it seemed to me that I could vaguely make out Sirrah standing near the spot of my writing. The thought came to my mind that I should just slip away in the mist while I still had the opportunity. A moment later, my fears were realized when Sirrah said, "Look—writing in the sand."

"Jayfeth is silly?" Re-Aylah said. "Who's making the joke?"

The other women gathered around and laughed. But of course, no one owned up to it. One of them said, "That's not 'Jayfeth.' It's 'jackass.'"

"There's little difference," said Sirrah and they all laughed again, even harder. My plan was going horribly awry and the urge to slip away grew until I could hardly restrain myself.

In the commotion, Re-Aylah's water vessel overturned. "You go along and get started," she said to the others. "You know how Father is when his breakfast is delayed. I will come as soon as I refill my jar." When they were gone, Re-Aylah looked around and said quietly, "Are you there?"

I stepped out from behind the bushes and said, "Jayfeth is silly?"

"When I understood the message, I knew the others would see it, too," said Re-Aylah. "I had to think quickly to divert their attention. So I blurred the letters with my toe and tried to make them think that one of them had done it as a joke."

"Ah, then you knocked over your own water jar intentionally to buy more time," I said, admiring her cleverness, if not her choice of words. "Thank you for not giving me away."

"So why are you here?"

With her typical directness, she had gotten to the point quicker than I had expected and my mind went suddenly blank. "Well, I uh ... You see, the thing is ... What I really wanted to tell you is ... "

"Yes?"

"I forgive you. That's it. I didn't want you to think that I held a grudge over any of the ... uh ... matters that you disclosed to me."

"You came all this way to tell me that?" she said, obviously touched. "That was very thoughtful of you."

I wanted to say more, but could not bring myself to utter the words. I just stood there shuffling my feet until, finally, the silence became so awkward that I said, "Well, I should be going now."

"Thank you, Jayfeth," Re-Aylah said and turned to leave.

"Wait," I said, in a sudden burst of courage.

"Was there something else?"

"I love you," I blurted.

"Love? You barely know me."

"That doesn't matter," I said, dropping to one knee. "Day and night you fill my mind. I can't think about anything else."

Was it surprise I saw in her eyes? Yes, but something else as well that gave me the briefest moment of hope before she dashed it by saying, "Jayfeth, please don't."

"I see." Whatever I had discerned in her eyes had vanished and it was plain that she was not going to respond in kind. "Of course, I had no reason to expect that you would feel the same toward me."

"It's not that."

"I know. Your father would never allow it—not to say that you would want to marry me anyway, which I know that you wouldn't."

"I am pledged to marry another," she said.

Stunned, I suddenly found myself wishing I were a thousand miles away where I would dig a big hole and jump inside and not show my face again among the living.

"I-I didn't know," I finally managed to stammer. I got back to my feet and, with my head hung low, said, "Your toe was right—I am a silly jackass. Please forgive my foolish words."

"Think nothing of it," she said. "How could a girl help but be flattered by your sentiments?"

"Thank you," I said. "That's a more gracious response than I deserve. So what man will have this honor?"

"My father has arranged with Ghurabbi and the other elders to engage me to a man named Baldag. He is the chief emissary to the Nephilim and a very important—"

"Baldag!" I said incredulously. "Baldag the fat? Baldag the home wrecker?"

"Jayfeth!"

"Baldag is a traitor. He hasn't represented anyone's interest to the Nephilim except his own—not to mention the fact that I believe he was responsible for kidnapping me, though you probably don't care about that. But you might care that he was probably the one who dammed the river and caused the flood of your camp, which you seem to have felt was my fault somehow."

"Stop it right now!" said Re-Aylah. "That's my betrothed you're slandering. Baldag is a great leader among our people and highly esteemed by the Nephilim as well. How dare you bring all these accusations against him. Do you have any proof of any of them?"

"Well, no," I said. "But I know they're true."

"Even though everyone else speaks well of him? Ah, yes. Once again, it's Jayfeth against the world. It must be difficult going through life as the only one who is ever right."

"As a matter of fact it is," I said.

"Arghhh!" said Re-Aylah in exasperation. "Goodbye!"

"Wait," I said as she walked away. "I—I didn't mean that. I don't really think that I'm always right. I was way out of line there. I don't know what came over me. I wish you well and much happiness. Really I do." But she did not turn around.

Shem did not have to ask how it had gone with Re-Aylah as it was written on my face. I bless him for not saying, "I told you so." As we made the long walk home in silence, I could not help but ponder the irony of the situation. The only woman I had ever loved was about to marry the only man I truly despised.

FIVE

s the months went by, I nursed my wounded pride and tried to rise above my humiliation. The days were tolerable enough as I could simply lose myself in the work. When the sun went down, however, the unwelcome visitor loneliness came calling and a cheerless companion he proved to be. Reaching my sixtieth birthday that year, I was well past the age when my people typically married and I remember thinking, "This is how men become bachelors." Before I loved Re-Aylah, I might have been well content with that lot. But once those feelings had been aroused and unrequited, they made me miserable.

I was not the only one around the camp with a heavy heart. As I paused from my work one day, I saw Father gazing across the river with a faraway look in his eye—and not for the first time. I asked, "What is it that troubles you?"

"I've been thinking about the people who dwell beyond the Gihon who have never heard the word of the Lord."

"You mean the Nodites?"

"Yes, and whoever else might also inhabit those lands. Since everyone here rejects the message, perhaps those others might accept it."

"You're right about that," I said. "There's nothing for us here except rejection."

"They at least deserve the opportunity to hear it."

"I have been very curious about those lands myself," I said, feeling the rush of excitement I experienced whenever I was about to embark on a new journey. "When do we start?"

"I'm sorry, son," said Father, shaking his head.

My heart sank. "You're taking Shem instead?"

"No, this time I go alone. I sense very great danger ahead and I do not want to put your lives at risk as well. You have plenty to contend with here."

I started to argue, but could tell by the set of his jaw that it would be futile. "So when will you leave?"

"The frame of the ark is almost completed," said Father. "That is the most difficult part. Afterward, the work will be easier and we will be able to spare a man. Then I will go."

About a month later, we laid the last crossbeam into place. Stepping back, we gazed in awe at the massive size of the ark. No longer was it dwarfed by the walled city of Nephil. From the top joists, we could look down upon all but the tallest spires and domes of the city. We congratulated ourselves heartily and praised God for giving us the ability to accomplish such a feat.

For the next several days, Father gave us detailed instructions about how to proceed while he was away—where all the interior walls were to be located, how to lay the decks, and cover the exterior. When I understood the extent of his instructions, I grew very concerned. "This will take years. You're not planning to be gone that long, are you?"

"I don't know. The Lord has not revealed that to me."

"You are coming back, aren't you?" said Ham. "Assure us that you *are* coming back."

"Where is your faith?" said Father. "I trust the Lord—whatever he has in store for me."

We shed many tears as he left—even Ohlibah and Jirah. The parting was especially painful for Mother, knowing somehow in her heart that they would not be soon reunited.

When three months had gone by, a messenger from Nephil came to our campsite.

"Hail, Son of Noah," said the Nodite. "I bring tidings from your father."

"Tell us," I said anxiously. "Is he well?"

"He is well enough," he said. "But he has much to tell you and wants to do so in person. He requests that you and Shem meet him at the crossroad under two dead oaks that is two weeks' journey due south of here. Ham is to remain behind to guard the women and continue the work. Under no circumstances are the women to enter the land of Nod."

That was all the information we could get out of him, so we spent the rest of the day making preparations. I was less excited about going than I might have been earlier in my life. The more I heard about Nod, the less inviting it sounded.

I retired early to my tent to rest before the long journey. When I heard a commotion in the camp, I looked out to see what was happening. It was Re-Aylah—and she was alone. When she realized that Father was gone, she turned to me and said, "May I speak a word alone with you?"

As we walked a few paces from camp, I asked, "Where is your husband?"

"I have no husband," she replied, her voice far from steady. "I was to be married three days ago. But I don't love Baldag. In fact, he scares me. So I ran away."

"Why did you come here?" I said, with more of an edge to my words than I intended.

Her head hung low. "I don't blame you for being angry with me."

"I'm not angry with you. I'm just ... well, I'm not angry. And you are welcome to stay with us as long as you like. You'll be safe here."

"But I have acted shamefully toward you and your family. I don't deserve this kindness. I ask only that you have your father pray that God might have mercy on me in the coming doom."

"I think if Father were here, he would tell you that God already knows what is in your heart."

She looked up, and I could see hope returning to her eyes. "Do you think so?" she asked and I nodded. She wiped away a tear from her cheek and said, "Then I will trouble you no longer."

"Where will you go?"

"I don't know. As far away from Baldag as I can get."

"Why don't you stay with us? If doom comes, this may very well be the only safe place in the world."

"After all I've done, I'm not worthy to even carry water for your camp."

"Please stay," I pleaded.

"I have nowhere else I can go," she said as a lone tear ran down her cheek.

We decided that Re-Aylah would stay in Mother's tent while Father was away. Mother was grateful for the company and they were a great comfort to each other. I myself was perplexed at this turn of events and wondered what would come of it. But I had little time to reflect because Father was expecting us.

As we departed early the next day, Ham was already at work, not at all disappointed about being left behind. He had grown very comfortable since marrying Jirah and was not nearly as adventuresome as he used to be in his youth. The surprising thing, though, was seeing Re-Aylah at his side helping. "You don't really need to ..." I started to say.

Re-Aylah interrupted, "If I'm going to dwell among you, I will not be a burden."

"What I mean to say is that the women usually concern themselves with ... well, you know, other matters."

"Do you think I can't handle the work?"

"Be careful how you answer that question," said Ham. "I can already see she's better help than you ever were!"

That was an argument I was clearly not going to win, so I gave it up and we went on our way. As a precaution, we started upstream along the Gihon Road like we were headed to Sethite territory. We didn't want our destination to be obvious—just in case the wrong eyes should be watching. As we walked along, I said, "I usually enjoy traveling, but I'm heavy-hearted about leaving today."

"Because of where you're headed or what you left behind?"

"Both, I suppose. But I was really thinking more about Re-Aylah."

"That's what I suspected," said Shem.

"I'm glad that we've been reconciled."

"But that's not all that's on your mind."

"Is it that obvious?" I asked.

"It's written all over your face."

"You told me I'd wake up one day and be over my obsession. I haven't yet."

"Maybe I was wrong about it being an obsession," said Shem.

"But I would be better off that way because there might be hope for a cure," I said. "When I first saw her last night, I hoped she had come for a different reason."

"Give her some time. That's my counsel. She has abandoned her marriage plans and turned her back on her family. It will take her awhile to sort everything out."

"I suppose you're right."

"Perhaps then she'll take pity on you."

"Thanks a lot," I said, but I laughed anyway.

Once we were well out of sight of the city, we crossed the Gihon, and headed east until we picked up what we reckoned was a main north-south road through Nod. Although we were correct in our assumption, the determination was not as straightforward as it might seem because the network of roads was more extensive than we expected. When we encountered forks and intersections, we chose the way that looked more heavily traveled as long as it was heading south. The forested area along the river valley gradually gave way to a hilly country with fewer trees. We did not meet many travelers along the way. The few we did encounter were mostly Nephilim, but they seemed well accustomed to seeing Sethites in Nod.

Toward afternoon, we were overtaken by a caravan of six wagons. The drivers, all Nephilim, drove the ponies hard. Shem and I hurried off the road for fear of being run over. The wagons were all laden with produce—more of the food-gathering parties like the one that Father and I had seen that night on the river years before. I winced to remember how that had turned out. We spent the first night on top of one of the knobby hills a short distance from the road, preferring the view it offered in case anyone approached.

As we proceeded further into Nod, the country became courser. We saw plenty of signs of human activity, but little that looked recent. On the contrary, the land seemed quite deserted. On the third day, we came upon a great tract of stumps, including many that were exceedingly large, where a once mighty forest had been reduced to a brushy wilderness.

The water in Nod was mostly brackish—a troubling discovery for someone who had never known anything but an abundance of fresh running water and sweet springs. We drank only what we needed each day and had no desire to drink one drop more because of the taste. The scarcity of wild animals was also unsettling. Except for an occasional rodent or crow, it seemed as uninhabited by animals as it did by people.

Nearly a week of hard travel went by before we saw our first Nodites. As we topped over a tall hill, we saw a large field of grain—millet as I later learned—laying south of the road. Fifty or so Nodites cut the heads while twenty or thirty others were engaged in separating the grain from the chaff. I was impressed by this, having never seen agriculture practiced on that scale before.

As we drew closer to where they were working, my attention turned from the harvest to the people themselves. I was reminded of the haunted look of the Nodite I had seen by the river that night and now I could see a whole people of the same countenance. They were shorter in stature than any race I had known—averaging little over five feet in height, and gaunt. Most of the men were bare from the waist up and their ribs were visible even at a distance. Nor were the women spared from the same haggard look. Their robes could not conceal the bony hardness underneath that was not at all befitting for women. Moreover, they were the dirtiest people I had ever seen—so much so that it was difficult to discern their true complexion, which I guessed might be somewhat darker than my own. The odor of their bodies was offensive—even at fifty yards—and their clothes were filthy and tattered. Their eyes, though, were the worst. They looked at us, but didn't really seem to see us. They had a vacant, lifeless stare that reminded me uncannily of the beheaded Nephilite I had seen as a youth.

We saw scenes of this nature repeated throughout the remainder of our journey. Although the purpose of the work varied, the conditions of the workers did not. But I began to observe at each work site that a person or several persons, according to the total number of workers, appeared to be in charge. Sometimes this was a Nephilite, though not always, for I also saw many Nodites functioning in that capacity. What distinguished them, as my eyes became accustomed, was that the overseers were clearly better fed and dressed.

We camped that night by the side of the road. Though I was tired from the hard day's march, I had difficulty settling into a sound sleep, thinking about everything I had seen. This turned out for our benefit, however, because far into the night, I sensed something was amiss.

Instantly wide awake, I saw a figure creeping toward Shem. I leaped on the man to restrain him from harming my brother. He fought wildly— kicking, scratching and biting—with surprising strength for his size. But Shem joined me in a moment. We were bigger than he and no strangers to hard work, so we quickly subdued him.

With his face to the ground and each of us pinning an arm behind his back, we questioned him. "What do you mean sneaking up here to harm us!" I said angrily.

"Easy Brother," said Shem.

I realized that the pressure I was applying to his arm must have been painful to him, so I relaxed a bit, though not enough to afford him any chance of escape.

"I only wanted food," he growled. I understood his speech, but the dialect sounded strange to my ears and was laced with vulgarities that I could only guess the meaning of. He added, "I would not have slit your throats."

I mulled that statement over in my mind and found it chilling to consider that the thought had even crossed his mind. Neither was I convinced that he had entirely dismissed the possibility.

"Aren't you one of the laborers we saw toiling in that field back there?" asked Shem and the man grunted. "How is it that you can gather food all day and still be hungry?"

"We don't gather for ourselves."

"Who then?"

"The Sons of the Gods, you idiots," he said.

"You say you gather for the Sons of the Gods, but I saw Nephilites in charge back there," I said. "I thought Governor Ben-Tubal ruled this land."

"The Governor is a good man. He gives food to the people. But the first part goes to the Sons of the Gods. It's much better here. We have something to eat and drink almost every day. If you work hard, you get to come here."

"This is a promotion?" I said. "That's hard to believe."

"You're not going to send me back, are you?" said the man.

"Back where?" asked Shem.

"No, I won't say the name out loud. Now either kill me or let me go. I don't care which."

"We have no intentions of killing you," said Shem. "Brother, hand me my pack. Let's give him some food."

I am ashamed to admit that my first inclination was to protest this. We had only a limited supply and the hope of finding more in that miserable country seemed slim. But as I regarded his plight, I felt compassion for the man and realized that he needed it far worse than we did. I poured some out and wrapped it in a cloth.

"So you plan to poison me by pretending to give me some of your food," said the man.

"We don't even understand what you are saying," said Shem. "We're only trying to help you."

The man looked at Shem in disbelief. "But why would you do such a thing?"

"Because it pleases God and it's the right thing to do," said Shem.

At this, we let the man up so that he could eat his food. But the moment we were off him, he ran away into the darkness with the food we had given him. I looked at Shem and shrugged, but there was nothing more that we could do.

The scratches on my throat where the man had clawed me stung from my sweat. Shem cleansed the wounds as best he could and applied ointment to them. But they were dirty cuts and remained red and swollen for several days. I stank so badly from wrestling with the man that I could hardly stand myself and was all the more miserable because of the unlikely prospect of bathing anytime soon. By then, of course, we were both beyond sleeping. We would have left right then, but the moon was hardly a sliver and we thought it unwise to continue in that forbidding land until we could see better. So we waited what seemed like a long time for first light.

Six

Neither of us felt much like talking the next day, so disturbed were we at everything we were seeing in that land. That people were living in such horrid conditions was previously inconceivable to me. Even more appalling was the realization that men could oppress their brothers so cruelly. How little I had known of the world living among the trees and meadows and clear-running streams of the Gihon Highlands! I longed to be there again.

As we walked along, I finally dared to say in the light what I had feared to say in the darkness. "I don't know who these Sons of the Gods are, but I would like to set them straight about a few things."

"Be careful what you wish for," said Shem.

"Why do you say that?"

"You never know whether you might meet up with them around the next bend. And they don't sound like the sort of people we'd get on with."

"You might. I think they might be prophets of the Cainites that Merib once told me about."

"That doesn't mean I'd have anything in common with them. Just because they're prophets doesn't mean they speak for the Lord."

"If not the Lord, then who?"

"That's a good question. But, then again, it may be something that Ben-Tubal just made up—a superstition to exert control over the people. There's not enough food to go around, so they've developed a system of rewards and punishments to control the distribution. And a false priesthood gives it legitimacy, so Ben-Tubal can maintain his popularity."

"You're just saying that because you've never trusted him."

"And you do?"

I thought it over a moment and said, "I'll concede that Merib always lets on like there's a lot more going on behind the scenes than meets the eye.

But Ben-Tubal has never been anything but helpful to us. It may be against my better judgment, but I have to admit that I like the man."

"You should listen to your better judgment more often," said Shem.

We began to pass by massive encampments that sometimes sprawled a mile or more along the road. The odor rising up from them was the most offensive I had ever smelled. Seeing them, I first began to realize that there were far more people in the world than I had previously imagined.

That night we took turns keeping watch, a practice we maintained during the remainder of our time in Nod. We were not attacked again, but whether this was because we were vigilant, I cannot say.

Two weeks to the day from when we had set out, we reached the great crossroad flanked by two dead oaks that we believed was the one we had been seeking. We did not find Father there, so we sat down and waited for him under the scant shade of one of the trees. Around midday, we spotted him coming toward us from the south. As he drew nearer, we saw that his eye was bruised and swollen nearly shut. We ran to him and said, "Father, are you all right?"

"It's nothing," said Father. "Just a friendly greeting from the inhabitants. Let's sit and talk for awhile while I catch my breath. I have much to tell you."

I noticed then that his pack was missing. I didn't have to wonder what had happened to it. "How long has it been since you have eaten?"

"My pack was stolen within days after I arrived in Nod," he said. "Ever since, I have been subsisting on whatever I could find, which turns out to be very meager in this place. But I brought some along they couldn't steal," he said, patting his stomach. "Your mother's cooking has taken care of that!"

"This is a horrible place," I said. "I had no idea how bad the conditions were here."

"Yes," said Shem. "We were attacked ourselves. If not for Jay's insomnia, we might not be here today."

"The scary part is that I don't think this is even the worst of it," said Father.

"The impression we got from the man who tried to rob us was that the people here consider themselves fortunate compared to conditions elsewhere," said Shem.

"I don't know how any place could be worse than this," I said.

"That's why I summoned you both," said Father. "As you can see, the people here are in deep distress. You couldn't have believed it if you had not seen it for yourselves. I can't begin to calculate how many souls there are in this land who need to hear the warning from the Lord. So I wanted you to know what I am up against here, because I plan to go throughout the length and breadth of Nod and preach to every last soul who will listen."

"I don't think that's a good idea," I said.

"When you say this, have you the things of God in your heart?" asked Father.

"But this is a dangerous place," I said. "We're concerned for your safety."

"Do you not yet understand, Jayfeth? If the Lord wills that my life be preserved, it will be preserved. And if his will is otherwise, I am more than willing to face whatever he has in store for me."

"Then let one of us go with you," said Shem.

"No, my son. It is good that you have this in your heart, but the work on the ark must continue. For now, I will go on alone."

I just shook my head and sighed, knowing there was no way to deter him once his mind was made up. Then I said, "There's something else you should know."

"What is it? Is your mother well? Is everything all right back at the camp?"

"Yes, everyone is well," I said. "But now we are one more. Re-Aylah has come to stay with us."

Father's face brightened. "I'm happy for you son. This changes everything. I will delay my plans and return with you at once to perform the ceremony."

"You're assuming too much," I said. "It's not what you think. She didn't come for me, but to avoid marrying Baldag and to be saved from the disaster."

"That in itself is cause for rejoicing," said Father. "See, I told you that if we persevered in spreading the word of the Lord, people would repent. It's just taking longer than I expected to see results. That reminds me of one other point I must emphasize to you, though. Under no circumstances are you to bring any of the women into this land."

"This is no place for a woman," I said.

"No, you don't understand my meaning," said Father. "They do not observe the same customs and propriety that we do regarding marriage. Sometimes, the women are just taken. It doesn't matter to them whether she is already married or what her wishes are—although I think a lot of them go willingly hoping for a better life. But even if she's not willing, they take her against her will if they want her."

"How can they get away with that?" I asked.

"As nearly as I can tell, they justify it as part of their religion," said Father.

"Let me guess," said Shem. "The Sons of the Gods tell them to do it."

"So you've heard of them too," said Father.

"Yes, but we really don't know any more than that," I said. "They're pretty secretive about it."

"I don't know much either," said Father. "But they must be very wicked to take for themselves such a blasphemous name—so be on your guard. Now, we'd all better be on our ways."

Father rose to leave. We tried to give him half our food, but he refused. "You'll need it for the return journey. I am about the Lord's work and will be content to live on whatever he provides for me."

Reluctantly, we watched him disappear over the hill heading west. Shem and I turned back north, walking as quickly as we could, anxious to cross the Gihon and put that horrid place behind us as quickly as possible.

That evening, a woman came to our campsite and stood just outside of the circle of firelight. "Are you the Sethites?" she asked.

I could not see her well in the shadows, but she looked somewhat taller than the average Nodite and there was something oddly familiar about her voice. Shem, who was closer to her, said, "We are Sethites. You sound as if you could be, too."

"I was, once," she said.

"You are either born into the tribe or you aren't," said Shem. "Why do you speak of it in the past tense?"

"A strange question coming from one whom the tribe no longer recognizes," she said.

"Is that your case as well?" asked Shem.

"No, it's the other way around," she said. "I no longer claim my place in the tribe."

"Why?"

"I'm sure she has her reasons," I said, as the realization of who she was began to sink in. "Are you going to make her stand there all night while you quiz her? She's probably hungry."

"Of course," said Shem. "Sorry. Please come and sit by the fire. Are you hungry?"

The woman stepped into the circle of the campfire and I saw that it was, in fact, Minnah—still as beautiful as ever even as disheveled as she was. She sat down opposite us and said, "Yes, I am hungry. I've been hungry every since the day I set foot in this wretched place. I would do anything for food. *Anything you like.*"

The desperate look in her eyes left no doubt what she was willing to offer. "Please do not mistake us for wicked men," said Shem. "We'll gladly share our food with you, but not for a price."

"Suit yourself," she said and greedily accepted a large helping of the dried fruit and nut mix that we carried on journeys. Why I didn't turn her away was a mystery even to myself. After all, she was an adulteress, had abandoned her husband to take up with an evil man, and had even gone so far as to aid in kidnapping me. But I searched my heart and, strangely, found I was neither angry nor bitter toward her. One small wink she had given me as a boy somehow covered over everything else she might have done in her life—a testament, I suppose, to the depth of feeling that even the smallest act of kindness inspired in an outcast like me. So I kept silent.

While she ate, Shem said, "You have us at a loss. You seem to know us, but we still don't know who you are."

"I'm nobody," said Minnah and she was looking right at me, wondering why I didn't say anything.

"That's a funny name," said Shem.

"She doesn't want to talk about it," I said.

"All right," said Shem. "I was just making conversation."

When she had finished eating, she said, "Do you have any *grack*?"

"I don't know what you are talking about," said Shem.

"My guess is that it's a drink," I said. "The Cainites are skilled at making potions, aren't they? You drink *grack* and it makes you feel good, right?"

"*Grack* makes you forget," said Minnah.

I looked at her with pity, knowing that with her past, forgetting would be a welcome relief. As gently as I could, I said, "We don't have any *grack*. And if we did, we wouldn't give it to you. *Grack* is bad. It makes you do things you shouldn't do. And if you are not careful, it will kill you, too."

"With the way my life is going, that might not be such a bad thing," she said. "I gave up everything for my lover and now he has tossed me aside like refuse. I can't go back home and there's nothing to live for here."

"Come with us to the ark," said Shem. "You'll find sanctuary there."

"Sanctuary?" she said. "There's no sanctuary for me in Cush —only shame. As long as I'm merely 'missing,' it raises enough doubt to keep alive the possibility that the ugly rumors aren't true. But if I ever return, the whole affair will be exposed. I can't let that happen. It would kill my father—and my husband."

"So might worrying about where you are," said Shem. "And besides, you can't keep running forever."

"I can't think about forever," said Minnah. "I just survive from day to day."

"Well, at least think about it for the night," said Shem. "You will be warm and safe with us by the fire. Tomorrow might bring new hope."

Minnah did seem to sleep peacefully for awhile—probably the most restful night she had passed in months. But watching her sleep made me all the drowsier myself. After awhile, I couldn't hold my eyes open any longer.

When I awoke, Minnah was gone—along with most of our remaining food. "Of all the ... well, that's gratitude for you!"

"Forget it," said Shem. "I have a feeling she's going to need it far more than we do."

I was in an ill humor all that day. Not only was I hungry and tired, I felt foolish for having been taken in by Minnah yet again—and all the worse because it happened while I was supposed to be keeping watch. To his credit, Shem didn't rub it in. That night, we ate the last few crumbs we had left, which only served to whet our appetites. We went to sleep on very empty stomachs.

About midnight, we heard the sound of heavy hooves coming up the road from the east and saw in the distance what appeared to be a man riding on the back of a bull. As they approached, though, we saw that it was not bull and rider, but rather one beast—horrible to behold. It had the body and legs of a bull, but the appearance of a man from the waist up!

We cowered in the shadows as the terrible beast sped by us. As it passed, a fit of trembling shook me as such I have seldom known.

When it was gone, I looked at my brother and could see that he was just as appalled as I was. "What on earth do you think that was?" I whispered.

"I don't know," said Shem. "But I just had a thought. What if the Sons of the Gods aren't ... human?"

The next day, still shaken from the terror of the night, we felt very weak and hungry indeed—so much so that we had difficulty maintaining the pace we wanted over the next few days. Once we left the inhabited area, we found some sour green apples. They were so tough we could hardly chew them and they gave us bad stomachaches, but at least they provided some sustenance or we might have collapsed on the road.

The last few days in Nod were a test of endurance. I have little recollection of them except for constantly willing myself to go forward. Finally, the countryside began to look more familiar and we were greatly heartened to sense that we were nearing home.

When at last we reached Nephil, we paused only long enough to drink deeply of the sweet water of the Gihon before we crossed the arched stone bridge back into our beloved Cush. By the time we reached sight of the camp, however, we could tell something was wrong. Instead of the joyful reunion we had been looking forward to, we were met with the news that Re-Aylah was gone.

SEVEN

"Gone!" I said. "What do you mean she's gone?"

"What do you think 'gone' means?" said Ham. "She left."

"But why?"

"She wrote this note. Read it for yourself."

Re-Aylah, to the family of Noah,

I cannot stay with you any longer, so I am leaving and will not be back. Tell Jayfeth I will fondly remember all the times we had together, especially playing as children at Tel-Asher. If only we could relive that day, I could be happy again. But if you were in my place, you would do the same. I see now that you were right and I have no choice except to say farewell and thank you for your kindness.

"That's it?" I asked. "She didn't say anything else?"

"She never gave any indication," said Ham. "She seemed quite content. But when Jirah and I returned, this is what we found."

"Returned?" I said. "From Nephil I presume. A fine guardian you turned out to be!"

"How was I supposed to know?" said Ham. "And even if I had been here, could I have prevented this? She's of age and can make her own decisions."

I was so distressed by this news and weak from hunger that my knees went weak. In disbelief, I sat down right where I was and did not move until at length a bowl of porridge, warmed-over from breakfast, was brought to me. I had to practically force myself to eat it. Even though I was nearly starving, my appetite had left me. It didn't help to see Mother so distraught, because she had grown quite attached to Re-Aylah. She and Ohlibah had been at the river washing clothes and had only learned of Re-Aylah's departure not long before Shem and I returned. Ohlibah did her best to comfort her, but she would not be consoled. Needless to say, it was not the happy homecoming we had expected. I retired to my tent in the middle of the afternoon and slept clear through the night.

I can't say I was refreshed in the morning, but I couldn't sleep any more. Even though I still felt tired and weak, I could think of nothing else to do except get up and start working on the ark. Since everyone was afraid to say anything, we worked in silence for most of the morning.

When we stopped to eat lunch, Shem sat down beside me and said, "You're very quiet today."

"There's not much to say. She's gone and I'm still here," I said. "I don't know why I'm surprised. I've known all along I had no chance with her."

"It's too bad," said Shem. "And you were making such good progress with her, too. She could actually speak to you without spitting on the ground."

"You always know the right thing to say," I said, chewing on a mouthful of bread. Although I had been hungry for most of a month, I wasn't enjoying it very much. "What I don't understand is how she could leave without saying goodbye."

"Perhaps it was too painful for her. The way she talked about her childhood, she was obviously very emotional about it." Shem stretched out on the grass and leaned on his elbow. "So what happened at Tel-Asher anyway?"

"I'll tell you. Our cousins took me prisoner. They tied me up with ropes and went off and left me. Fehud thought it was very funny. But Re-Aylah set me free."

"How come you never told me about that?" asked Shem.

"Do you have to ask? I was very embarrassed about the whole thing."

"I see your point," said Shem. He rolled on his back and closed his eyes as he sometimes did in the middle of the day—whether to meditate or nap I do not know. Then he added thoughtfully, "It's funny what people recall when they're under stress."

"It does strike me odd that she would bring it up now," I said. "Unless …"

Shem sat up and we looked at each other.

"You don't suppose she was trying to tell us something," said Shem.

"She is very nimble-minded," I said, unfolding the note I had absent-mindedly stuffed in my pocket. "If leaving wasn't her idea, she would have tried to find a way to tell us. Maybe the reference to Tel-Asher means that she was being taken prisoner. And reliving that day means being set free."

"Possibly," said Shem. "But what does she mean about you being right?"

"She did tell me once that I always thought I was right, even if everyone else believed differently. I was talking about Baldag at the time."

"He would definitely have a motivation to do something. But how would he know to look for her here?"

I cast a suspicious eye toward the tent of Ham and Jirah. "I don't doubt that most everything we do finds its way to the ears of Ben-Tubal. And is not Baldag his right-hand man?"

"We must be very careful here, Jay," cautioned Shem. "These are intriguing speculations. But reading between the lines hardly constitutes solid evidence on which to make such serious accusations."

"You're right," I said. "But what would prevent me from at least making an inquiry of Ben-Tubal? I'll just ask for his assistance in locating Re-Aylah—without any other speculations—and see what he says. He's always favored me."

"His daughter *is* our sister-in-law."

"Right. So I believe he will act with restraint—whatever the truth. And speaking of his daughter, I think we would be well-advised to keep our suspicions to ourselves."

"Agreed," said Shem and immediately went to ask Jirah if she could get me in to see her father right away. He told her to say that our family, being very fond of the girl, was distressed at her leaving and would be grateful for any assistance he could provide in finding her. Jirah seemed more than happy to do this, apparently relishing the opportunity to help without having to do any physical work. I always did my best to give her the benefit of the doubt. If she did sometimes pass information along to her father, I hoped that she did it unwittingly and not to be deliberately hurtful.

Late that afternoon, I appeared in the court of Ben-Tubal to plead for his assistance. I was informed by one of the functionaries in charge of protocol that Ben-Tubal was now to be addressed as "His Excellency." He looked the part, too, sitting on his new throne inlaid with gold and precious jewels— twice as opulent as the one before. "So much gold!" I remember thinking, but only for a moment before Ben-Tubal addressed me sternly.

"You know that Baldag has been my emissary to the sons of Seth for these many years," he said.

"Yes, Your Excellency," I said. "Although I always thought it was supposed to be the other way around."

He glared at me and continued, "Yet you did not fear to assist the daughter of Irad in this matter. Do you think the disgrace of such an important man is a matter to be taken lightly?"

"Not at all, Your Excellency," I said. "But she came to us seeking refuge and the customs of hospitality among our people dictated that we give her sanctuary. Not only that, but she is also our close kinswoman. How could we have refused her request for help?"

"We also have customs," said Ben-Tubal. "They deal most severely with any woman who would disgrace a man in this way."

"Even if it becomes known that such a man is not honorable?" I had no prior intentions of taking this line of reasoning, but his anger caught me off guard and the words came out before I fully considered them. Immediately, though, I regretted saying them.

"How dare you insult the emissary!" said Ben-Tubal, rising so quickly that his robe flapped with the movement.

Towering over me like that, he cut a very intimidating figure. But since I had started down that path, I could not turn back. Trying not to cower, I swallowed hard and said, "My intention is not to slander your official, but to plead for leniency concerning the girl's offense by making you aware of the extenuating circumstances. I have reason to believe that Baldag has acted treacherously to our people—without your knowledge, I'm sure. He has abused his position of authority for his own personal gain. And you can add kidnapping and adultery—which I have personally witnessed—to his list of offenses. In fact, I have often wondered why a man like you would have anything to do with a man like Baldag."

Ben-Tubal bent close, and in a harsh whisper that only I could hear, said, "Sometimes a man like me needs a man like Baldag."

At that point came a long, uncomfortable silence. My boldness in his presence may have been foolhardy, but I suspected that little of what I said came as a surprise to him. However, it was one thing to know (and possibly approve) of a man's secret deeds and quite another to be forced to deal with the accusations in public. All eyes in the court were upon Ben-Tubal. For the first time ever, I saw him discomfited as he looked around the hall. I guessed that he was balancing the continued usefulness of his official against the strange respect which he held toward our family. Apparently those two considerations weighed equally in his mind so that he could not render a decision. Finally, he said, "I will take the matter under advisement. Now leave my presence." He slumped in his chair, rested his head on his right hand and waved me away with his left.

EIGHT

Deep in thought as I was leaving the palace, I heard a voice in the long, arched corridor quietly say, "Sir, may I venture a word with you." I was surprised to feel his hand on my shoulder because the Nephilim rarely touched each other except as an invitation to love play. But when I turned to look, it wasn't a Nephilite at all, but one of the palace servants. A smallish man with narrow-set eyes, he glanced nervously around and then led me down a hallway to his quarters.

Once behind the closed door he said, "Don't you remember me?" I studied his face but could not recall ever setting eyes on him. "I am Dayak, the man whose life you saved."

"I'm afraid you have me confused with someone else," I said. "Not only did I not save your life, I'm quite sure we have never met."

"But you did save me," said Dayak. "When you were a youth, you and your father interceded to Ben-Tubal for a man who was cruelly oppressed by a Nephilite at the Gihon River. I am that man."

"Why yes, of course. I remember you now." Actually, although I well remembered the incident, the man in front of me seemed hardly of the same species as the one I had seen in the river that night. "So, it has gone better for you since then?"

"On the same day that the Nephilite was executed, I was promoted to serve in the palace. I have plenty to eat and excellent quarters as you can see."

The room was sparsely furnished by palace standards, but I had no doubt they were incomparably better than his former living conditions. "I'm glad that our petition caused Ben-Tubal to compensate you in this way."

"His Excellency is a just man, sir," Dayak said. "But also very practical. Having me here ensures my silence about the incident. He knows I won't make trouble. Make no mistake, however. The oppression of our people continues and worsens by the day."

"I have just returned from Nod and was appalled at the misery I saw there."

"Then you can well understand how good a turn you did me. I vowed that if I ever had the opportunity to repay the kindness that was shown to me by Noah and his son that I would risk everything, even my life, to do so. That time has come."

"We couldn't accept any payment for speaking out against injustice and cruelty," I said. "Besides, we lack nothing—except an abundance of friends. So I would be pleased to count you as one and could think of nothing that would reward us more."

"Ah, but you're wrong again," said Dayak. "I do have something you lack and would dearly like to have." He lowered his voice to a whisper. "I know where the daughter of Irad is."

"What! Please tell me!"

"You have already guessed most of it. Baldag was enraged when the daughter of Irad fled. You know he has a terrible temper. I overheard him talking with His Excellency in the council room a few weeks ago. When Baldag learned that she was with your family, he watched for an opportunity to seize her. While she was alone working on the ark yesterday morning, Baldag told his men to make it look like she left of her own free will, although it was actually a kidnapping. I know this because I have friends in Baldag's charge—and believe me, he is not universally well-liked. The girl is being taken to an outpost in Havilah, the land beyond Nod. There she will be held prisoner until such time as he can decide what to do with her."

"That scoundrel! I'm going to confront Ben-Tubal about this outrage right now."

"Sir, think about it," said Dayak. "Is such a course likely to achieve success? I don't know whether His Excellency knows of the kidnapping, but Baldag is one of his top officials and you saw how harshly His Excellency answered you. I would not advise putting it to the test."

"You're right," I said, restraining myself. "I suppose the only thing to do is to go to Havilah and rescue her."

"A rescue yes," said Dayak. "But you can't march straight through Nod to get there. All roads there will be watched and you will be stopped before you are out of sight of Nephil."

"Then what hope do I have of saving her?"

"Perhaps this one. My father and his mates calculated that it was possible to reach Havilah from the west. He contemplated escaping that direction to free lands, but died before he was able to attempt it."

"That's easily said. But how do I get west of Havilah without crossing Nod? Doesn't Nod extend all the way to the sea?'

"True enough," said Dayak. "But what if you were to circumnavigate the Forbidden Land?"

"Around Eden?"

"Yes, and approach from the opposite side," he said, tracing a crude map with candle grease on an old rag. "No one would expect you from that direction."

"But even if that were possible, it would take months. By then, it could be too late."

"I have a plan," said Dayak. "Unrest is brewing in the northern territories and the coastal region. I will make sure that this report reaches His Excellency's ears in such a manner that he will think of no one else to send but Baldag. I have friends in that area who will stir up trouble to keep Baldag occupied for a long time—for not everyone is loyal to His Excellency and the resistance is growing. And neither is Baldag as favored as he once was. His Excellency is beginning to wonder if Baldag has outlasted his usefulness. Baldag knows this full well and will be anxious for any opportunity to prove his worth."

"Has Ben-Tubal's power really grown so great among the Sethites that he could consider ousting his emissary, even as despicable as he is?"

"His Excellency is not the power you need to worry about," said Dayak.

"What do you mean?"

"Surely you know that His Excellency doesn't rule at his own pleasure."

"If not his own, then whose?" At this Dayak glanced nervously about his room, though we obviously were quite alone. He whispered, "The Sons of the Gods."

"Please pardon my ignorance, Dayak. I keep hearing this term, but I have no idea who these men are."

"Why, they are not men at all. They are spirit beings, though they can take the appearance of men when they choose. But it is said they prefer to inhabit the bodies of living creatures—especially humans."

"The Others!" I said, greatly astonished. "The Sons of the Gods are the Others—the Watchers that the Ancient One spoke of. Why didn't I see that before? So they really do dwell among men."

"*Rule* over men would be more correct, if you take my meaning. Their desire is to enslave us."

"The plight of the Nodites is very grim indeed."

"I don't just mean the Nodites," said Dayak. "Many of your brethren may be found there now as well. They go seeking riches and a better life. But that's not what they find."

"They see Nephil and assume the land beyond the river is full of gold."

"The Havilah does have much gold, but the mining of it is toilsome and guards have to force the labor. That's where the maiden is being taken—to a garrison at the gold mines in Havilah. I think she will not be mistreated for fear of Baldag who has vowed to deal with her personally."

"Is that also where the Sons of the Gods dwell?" I asked.

"No, Enoch-Nod is the seat of their power."

"So, Enoch-Nod is an important city then, like Nephil?"

Dayak laughed. "I am surprised that you know so little. Two score Nephils could fit inside Enoch-Nod with room to spare. But while it surpasses it in size, do not suppose you want to see it on account of its beauty—for it has none. You must avoid Enoch-Nod at all costs. It is a very dangerous place."

I thought all that over for a moment and still had so many questions. But one was overriding because it hit so close to home for my family. "I still don't understand how His Excellency fits into all this."

"Who do you think the Nephilim are?" asked Dayak. "And how did you think they came to be?"

"I suppose they're descendants of their ancestor Cain."

"Yes, but not just any descendants," said Dayak. "The Sons of the Gods have been selecting the best men and women from among the Cainites for these many generations and have been breeding them as a man might breed livestock."

"For what purpose?"

"To create ever more suitable bodies for them to inhabit."

I shuddered at the thought. "You mean His Excellency ... ?"

Dayak shook his head. "Not to my knowledge. They seem to prefer working behind the scenes—at least for now."

"So what keeps them from ... you know, whatever they do—to just anybody."

"I don't think you need to worry about being possessed by them. Your family must have some strong magic. No one, not even His Excellency, seems able to have his way with you."

"It's not magic—not in the sense you mean it anyway," I said.

At this, we heard the sound of footsteps in the hallway. "Someone is coming," Dayak said. "We have delayed too long. If they find you here it will not go well for either of us. Quickly, let yourself down through the window."

I hurried to the window and was glad to see it was not far above the ground. "Thank you, Dayak. I will not forget what you have done." As I sat on the ledge with my feet out of the window, I added, "Why don't you come with us on the ark? Father says that a terrible disaster is about to befall the earth. But if you join us, you will be spared."

"I owed your family a huge debt," said Dayak. "I was pleased to repay you for your kindness by risking my life to tell you these things. But when Baldag is dispatched to quell the rebellion, I will consider my obligation discharged. As for your god, I neither know him nor fear him. Rather, I fear the Watchers and have no desire to incur *their* wrath. I plan to do whatever I can to preserve my own comfortable life in this place." The footsteps grew closer and I could delay no longer. "Now go, before you are discovered."

"Nevertheless, the offer stands," I said. "Goodbye."

I held onto the ledge with my hands and lowered myself out the window. My feet were only three feet from the ground, so I let myself drop down into the palace garden and tried to act as if everything was in perfect order as I made my way to the street. I don't think anyone saw me and I was able to make my way out of Nephil uncontested.

As I walked the short distance from the city to our tents, many thoughts raced through my mind. I knew my family would be anxiously awaiting news from me, so I had to think quickly. I was very concerned that if one word of my conversation with Dayak reached the ears of Ben-Tubal, it would ruin any hope I had of rescuing Re-Aylah and might well cost Dayak his life. So, in those few minutes, I determined two things. One was that I would tell them only of my audience with Ben-Tubal, and not mention Dayak. The other was that I would leave secretly that night by myself to rescue Re-Aylah.

I related to my family what had transpired with Ben-Tubal and how he had spoken harshly to me. I asked Jirah, "Why didn't you tell me your father was so upset?"

"Baldag is an important official—how could you be surprised?" said Jirah indignantly. "You asked to see His Excellency and I got you in. I didn't say he was going to be in a good mood."

"It wasn't very smart of you to attack Baldag's character anyway," said Ham, jumping to Jirah's defense. "It sounds like you've made things worse instead of better."

"I had to make some case in Re-Aylah's defense. I didn't say anything that I didn't know in my heart was true. And you know I'm right. Whose side are you on anyway?"

"Your side, of course," said Ham, backing down a little. "Just questioning your tactics, that's all."

"Let's not quarrel among ourselves," said Shem. "We're caught up in a struggle that's a lot bigger than we are, so we're bound to feel the squeeze. Let's just make sure we're always standing on the side of right."

To this we all agreed, and Jirah offered, "I'll talk with him when he cools down a little. You can't imagine the pressure he's under."

Oh yes I can, I thought to myself. *If he's dealing with—whatever the Others are—I'm sure he has his hands full.*

That night, when everyone else had gone to bed, I took Shem aside and told him everything—for he was the most trustworthy man I have ever known besides my father. When I disclosed all that I had in my heart to do he fell on my neck and embraced me. I left him in anguished prayer for my safety. Little did I know how sorely I would need those prayers before my ordeal was ended.

NINE

I left Nephil about midnight by the North Road, thinking it best to disguise my true intentions as far as possible. I knew, too, that if Dayak succeeded in getting Baldag dispatched to put down the insurrection, then the North Road would likely be the path he would take. So when morning came, I inquired at every village and tent if the inhabitants knew the whereabouts of the daughter of Irad. Though I knew full well they did not, I hoped my inquiries would reach Baldag's ears. In the afternoon I took a crossroad that led due east toward the coast. If Baldag were intent on learning my location, the last report he would have would be that I was heading in the opposite direction of where I was really going.

When night fell, I backtracked and headed west, trying to put as many miles behind me as possible before morning. But before I regained the North Road, I heard ahead of me the voices of men arguing. I slipped off the path and stole up quietly to a camp I had visited earlier in the day. The leader of the clan was saying, "But why does he want to know?"

"It's not your place to ask why," said a rough-looking Nephilite whom I recognized as one of Baldag's thugs. By the light of the campfire, I could see five others of the same ilk, at least one other of whom, judging by his height, was a Nephilite as well.

"Then neither will I answer your question," said the chief elder.

"Come now, be reasonable," said the Nephilite. "We only want to know if he was here today or not."

When I heard that, I shuddered. My plan had succeeded almost too well. Baldag *was* looking for me and in far closer pursuit than I had imagined.

"It's bad enough that he extorts produce from us—"

"That's not extortion," said the Nephilite. "It is tribute for his protection."

"Protection from what?" asked the chief.

"Surely you know there's a bad element about."

"Yes, and it arrived in our land at the same time you foreigners did," said the chief. "How do you account for that?"

The Nephilite laughed coarsely. "Ho-ho! You think your feeble insults matter to me in the least? But beware. That bad element may come in the night when you least suspect it and burn your tents to the ground—with you in them. Sleep well, if you can!"

The band of men stormed off toward the east with many menacing looks toward the people. I remained motionless on the ground until they were gone and lingered to hear the ensuing discussion since it closely concerned me.

One of the clan said, "You have acted unwisely, Upschad."

"What are you, Moshabaya, a cowering old woman?" said Upschad.

"You mistake prudence for cowardice," said Moshabaya. "Why put our families at risk for the sake of this man?"

"If Baldag wishes to find him, that alone is sufficient reason for me. Whoever Baldag is against, I am for."

"But who is this son of Noah that we should protect him?" asked another man. "Aren't we right in saying that Noah is a lunatic? The tribe has shunned him. Why should you protect him?" Several around the fire grunted in assent.

"As for whether Noah is in his right mind, I cannot say," Upschad replied. "But he has done us no harm. His only crime that I ever heard of was making unauthorized prophecies—which, in my opinion, is a dubious accusation. Who knows whether the Lord spoke to him? He's probably a better man than all of you, if this is your attitude. Besides, I wouldn't turn over one of my goats to those brutes. Time was when we would not even speak to such as these. This clan used to know the difference between right and wrong. But now ... well, I'm glad your fathers are no longer among the living so they cannot see what a sorry state you've come to. Mark my words, if you follow the path of expediency over righteousness, no good will come of it. And we won't—not as long as I'm chief of this clan."

"That may not be for long," murmured the man nearest me.

The assembly broke up and most of the men retired to their tents—but not all. Three milled around just outside the circle of firelight, not far from where I remained concealed in the tall grass. They spoke in low voices, but were close enough that I could hear most of what was being said.

"I'm telling you, we're courting disaster by defying Baldag." I could not see his face, but I recognized the voice of the one named Moshabaya.

"Upschad clings to the old ways."

"Yes, Grishna," said Moshabaya. "And the old ways aren't suited to these new dangers."

"But what can be done?" asked Grishna. "He's still vigorous and no doubt will be around for a long time to come."

"By then it might be too late," said Moshabaya.

"Then what do you propose?" said the third.

"First, I think you ought to go after the Nephilim, Arnon. You've spent time among them. See if you can smooth things over."

"I can do that," said Arnon. "But that doesn't solve the main problem."

"Leave that to me," said Moshabaya. "It's about time for a change of leadership around here."

"He won't step down quietly," said Grishna.

"If he continues to oppose Baldag, then we might not have to do anything," said Moshabaya. "His personal grudge will be his own undoing. But we'd better make it known that the rest of us have chosen the right side, or the wrath of Nephil will fall on all our heads, instead of just Upschad's."

Arnon strode past without seeing me. I waited until Moshabaya and Grishna were gone as well and carefully made my way around the camp, more anxious than ever to be on my way. But before I had gone half a mile, my conscience began to nag at me. With Baldag's men in close pursuit, I urgently needed to move on. However, I couldn't justify leaving the man who had sought to protect me without trying to warn him. So I turned back, determined to advise him of the conspiracy within his clan.

When I returned, the camp was still for the hour had grown late. Only Upschad was visible, in deep thought squatting before the fire and staring at the dying embers. I cleared my throat so I wouldn't startle him as I approached from behind. I squatted beside him and said in a hushed voice, "Do you know who I am?"

Upschad glanced sideways and said, "If you are who I think you are, you should not be here. It is not safe." His gaze went back to the fire.

Now that I was close, I realized he was much older than I had thought— perhaps older even than my Grandfather Lamech. His flowing hair and beard showed surprisingly little gray and his back no hint of bowing. But his eyes could not conceal the accumulation of years. And, more than that, his demeanor was clearly forged when the world was younger and the people more noble.

"Those who seek me are moving away from here—at least for the moment," I said.

"They are not the only ones you need to worry about."

"Yes, I know," I said. "That's why I am here, because you are also in danger."

"You speak of Moshabaya and the others? I am not unaware that they are scheming against me."

"Then shouldn't you take your loved ones and those who are still loyal and flee?

Upschad looked at me in a way that made me ashamed for having suggested it. "I might have expected braver counsel from your father's son."

I searched for words to reply, but they failed me. Thankfully, Upschad continued, "Even though I'm too old to put up much resistance, I'm too proud to run. Besides, Moshabaya and the others are still young. Who will teach them wisdom if I flee? Perhaps they will yet recognize their folly. So tell me, is it true that disaster is coming on the earth? I believe that is the prophecy for which your father was shunned."

"I'm not a seer," I admitted, compounding, so it seemed, my shame. "But my father says that it is."

"And do you believe it?"

I started to answer without thinking, but stopped myself. The honest answer to that question was more complicated than a short answer would allow. I had already insulted the man; I did not want to be flippant as well. "I believe that he believes it."

"That is not the same thing," said Upschad.

"Everywhere we turn, we are met with skepticism and opposition. It's hard not to have some doubts. But if you knew my father, you would know that believing in him is very nearly the same as believing the prediction. If he said the sun would rise in the west tomorrow, I would expect that it would."

"Then he is not mad?"

"No. At least I do not think he is, though I know his message is hard to hear."

"As I suspected then," said Upschad. "The reports that have been spread about him are lies. It is a sad day when righteous men are discredited and evil men are exalted."

"Like Baldag?" I said. "You are quite right in your opinion of him. I speak from personal experience."

"So do I. He's engaged in a dangerous game, playing our people off against the foreigners, and the clans against each other. And now my own son ..."

His voice broke off, choked with emotion. I gave him a moment to regain his composure and prompted, "Your son?"

"Are you familiar with the village of Latham?"

"I know it well," I said. "We have close family ties there—or, at least we used to."

"As do we. Keriath the chief saw that the strength of his clan was failing. He had produced no sons to take his place—only a daughter—and had no man in the village he thought worthy to be his heir. So he looked outside, to me, and sought to engage my son Giblith to his daughter."

"Minnah," I said, making the connection.

"Then you, too, have probably heard the rumors?" said Upschad. "That Minnah secretly loved another—this accursed Baldag. Try as he might, Giblith never felt like he could make her forget him. And Baldag, being without honor, did nothing to discourage her. I presume it was his way of exacting revenge on Keriath for overlooking him as his successor and on Giblith for taking the position that Baldag thought should have been his own."

"That sounds like him."

"And then one day Minnah was gone—vanished without a trace. Many people said she had run off with Baldag, and I have to admit that I feared they were right. But Giblith refused to believe it and wore himself out looking for her all over Cush. And even when Keriath died of a broken heart, Giblith wouldn't give up his search, despite the fact that the village was in turmoil without a leader. But three weeks ago, word came to us that Minnah was dead—she had been captured by rebels to use as leverage against Keriath because he was friendly to the Nephilim. I am ashamed that I was actually relieved to hear that she was dead instead of being with Baldag. But I still blame Baldag for coming between them. If things had been better at home, she might not have been so vulnerable."

I thought about this story and tried to resolve the contradictions. I had seen Minnah less than two weeks ago and knew for a fact that she was not dead. The report had to be mistaken—or a deliberate fabrication made up by Baldag or even Minnah herself to cover up their sins. The problem was that it was one of those lies that was more convenient for everyone than the truth and I was momentarily tempted to keep silent. Giblith could save face and take his place as chief of Latham. And Minnah could just slip off into oblivion, which is what she wanted to do. But while it was convenient, it was still a lie. I could not let it be perpetuated—not to mention that it let Baldag off far too easily. "Minnah is not dead," I said. "I have seen her myself just recently in Nod and can attest from personal knowledge that she had enough food to sustain herself for several days."

"So she was able to escape from the rebels?"

"I don't think she needed to escape," I said.

"You mean the rebels let her go?"

"Sir, I don't know how to tell you this, but I don't think she ever was captured by the rebels. It was just a deception to cover up the awful truth. Your suspicions about Minnah and Baldag were not unfounded. In fact, it is worse than you feared. Minnah not only had feelings for Baldag, she has been acting on them for a long, long time. But when Baldag found a younger woman—one he could openly wed—he cast Minnah aside like refuse."

After a moment's silence, Upschad said, "This news is worse than the last and painful to hear."

"I'm sorry to bear you ill tidings," I said. "Baldag has hurt a lot of people, including some who are close to me. He's the reason I'm here right now looking for Re-Aylah. I don't know if it will ease your pain, but I believe that Minnah is sorry. She has been a victim too—though not an innocent one. I don't think she ever wanted to hurt Giblith. And, believe me, she's now paying a very heavy price for her sins."

"Is she?" said Upschad. "And how much would she have to suffer to atone for her sins? Would it ever be enough?"

"I don't know. How much would be enough for any of us?"

"Well, I for one am weary of living in a world that values honor so little. You have given me much to think about—not the least of which is whether to tell my son what you have disclosed to me. As for you, you should go now, before someone sees you and reports your whereabouts. My eyes are closed. I will not see which way you go from here."

"I would not be afraid if you did," I said as I rose to leave. "Thank you, Upschad."

TEN

Since I knew Baldag's men were looking for me, I left the roads and set out across the Setti Plain, bearing to the northwest and avoiding villages. When dawn came, I hid myself and rested because I had not slept in two nights. This was my pattern—sleeping during the day and traveling at night—as long as I remained in the inhabited areas.

By the sixth night, I reached the lower foothills. Being back in my beloved Highlands so invigorated me that I traveled on through most of the next day, no longer feeling the need to move under the cover of darkness. I veered my course due north, and within a few days, I reached the place where the hills curved to the northwest. Looking down on the Jade Forest, I longed to go see Tor and his family, but knew that I could not afford the time. So, I set my face to the west and stepped onto soil that I had never trodden. As for whether I was the first or last man to do so, only the Lord knows.

I kept to the lower foothills, generally seeking the westernmost route I could maintain. Food and water were plentiful, which was a relief after my journey to Nod. Why people suffered from such hunger when the world abounded with food was beyond my understanding.

Occasionally, through gaps in the firs, I could see the Jade Forest to my right and below me. To my left and above me, though I could not see it, lay Eden on a plateau at the top of the Highlands. Being so close to Paradise filled my soul with longing. At the same time, though, a deep sense of my own unworthiness gnawed at me anytime my path ventured too close to the summit.

Four days later, around mid-morning, I became aware of the faint sound of rushing water in the distance. The hills had become steeper and the going more strenuous. By degrees, I had been forced further to the north than I had intended. The sound grew louder as I proceeded, and at midday, I topped over a hill and beheld a marvelous sight. A waterfall, at least three hundred feet high, cascaded down the face of a sheer bluff into a pool below. Ahead of me, directly in my path, was a mighty torrent of water that was not fully explained by the waterfall. A vast spring gushed from the base of the bluff to greet the downpour in a frothy cauldron, saturating the air with a billowing mist.

Most amazing of all, though, was that I thought I caught a glimpse of what appeared to be a young girl in the falls—not standing, but suspended in the air. I say young, but not of age, for she seemed in that sense timeless. She played and laughed in the spray, though she did not appear to be wet. Or maybe it was that her essence was of the water, so that being wet was in no way unnatural to her. I cannot be sure as this assessment was formed in an instant. When she looked up at me with big, liquid eyes, she smiled and vanished into the mist. As to who or what she was, I cannot say, because I could find no trace of her or anything in the vicinity that would even verify her existence, though I searched diligently. But I know she was something more than a trick of the sunlight dancing on the spray. I should say that although I was surprised by the apparition, she by no means alarmed me. The place exuded such an intoxicating air of goodness that I knew I had nothing to dread. Only long afterward, when I had a chance to reflect, did I realize how strange the experience was—and I suppose anywhere else it would have been. But so near to Eden, it seemed like a perfectly natural occurrence.

When I realized that nothing more was going to be seen of the girl—at least not by my looking for her—I took stock of my situation. Considering the volume of water, I guessed that I was looking at the headwaters of the Tigris River. The channel was rocky and the current swift, so I decided to seek a more suitable crossing place and found one about two miles downstream. The water was even colder than the Gihon—due to the spring, I suppose. It had a delicious taste and I drank my fill as I crossed.

On the other side I found, much to my delight, a whole network of springs. These streamed upwards from the ground through fissures in the rocks. In some places the streams shot up dozens of feet into the air. Only in later times did I contemplate the pressures inside the earth that could cause such an effect. Indeed, how could the fountain that was said to be at the center of Eden flow so abundantly situated at the highest point in the land unless some great power were forcing it up?

Those springs closest to the river were cold water, but not more than a few hundred feet away, I discovered hot ones as well. These spewed forth intermittently from deep inside the earth with a great whoosh, and the combined effect of the rushing, spewing and streaming waters made an exceedingly pleasurable sound.

I sat down and soothed my weary feet in a pool of hot water. This yielded such gratifying results that I searched out a larger pool, stripped myself and soaked my whole body in it for a long time. When I grew hot, I took another exhilarating dip in the river. In this way I passed a most pleasant afternoon.

While the rocks were smooth and did not hurt my feet, I knew it would be too hard a place to sleep for the night. So, toward evening, I reluctantly tore myself away to seek a suitable campsite. A grassy clearing not far away served the purpose perfectly. After eating, I slept better than I had in some time.

I awoke greatly refreshed, and with one long look behind me, pressed ahead. Over the next two days, the terrain became increasingly more rugged. To avoid the steepest of the inclines, I had to bear further and further to the north. Then I came to a place that could not be crossed at all because the way was blocked by towering columns of hexagonal rocks—smooth, black, and cool to the touch. Pressed together in an interlocking vertical pattern, they formed a wall which I followed so far that I began to be concerned that the barrier might go on without end. My fears were relieved, however, when the rock wall ended abruptly after about six miles.

As I passed around the north face, I noticed that the columns were decreasing in height to form what looked like steps leading up to the summit. Curious, I began to climb.

I was unprepared for what I saw when I reached the top. The barrier was not made as a wall, but rather appeared to be a causeway of gigantic proportions. To my left in the distance, I could just make out the waterfall. To my right, an exquisite garden perched in steep terraces on the bluff—tended by whom or what I don't know. But my eyes could not linger on these exceedingly fair sights, because my mind had already turned to what lay just over the hills ahead of me—Paradise! The road I was standing upon led straight to her heart and a longing to go there seized me.

Ah, yes, the road. I was awed by its massive size—the part that I could see was at least a dozen miles long, nearly an eighth of a mile wide and hundreds of feet above the ground. But it ended abruptly where I was standing. "A bridge to nowhere?" I wondered.

I recalled that the Father and Mother of all left Eden by the Eastern Gate—not to the north where I stood. Then I remembered what Father told me about God himself coming down to earth and walking in the Garden. Perhaps that was the very path he trod when he came down from the heavens! Perceiving that it was holy ground, I prostrated myself. After a time, I unsteadily descended the stairs. Greatly shaken, I could eat no food the rest of the day.

From there I headed due west, desiring to keep some distance from the Forbidden Land. By evening I felt so drained that I did not even bother to pitch my tent. The next morning I awoke hungry. Fruit grew abundantly in that place, so I helped myself to all the bananas and pears I wanted and soon felt like myself again.

I continued in a westerly direction all that day and into the next. On the day after that, I began to bear back to the south somewhat and discovered another wondrous thing: a field of multi-colored rocks arranged like a courtyard garden. I had to turn aside to see that wonder, if only for a little while. What first captured my attention was a series of gigantic crystals protruding from the ground to heights well exceeding my own. Some were as clear as water, but most were colored; I do not think there was a shade that was not represented. Beryls, amethysts and emeralds threw out shafts of light in every direction and the refracted sunlight dazzled my eye.

I made my way slowly between them, taking care to avoid stepping on the more delicate crystals that covered the ground like clover, so I would not crush them (and because the sharp points on some of them hurt my bare feet). As I examined the place more closely, I could see far more intricate structures—some as fine as the hairs on my head—in a lacey network like a spider's web. As I passed, I turned to look again and saw the same through a large crystal which enlarged it by some optical phenomenon, so that I could see every detail I had missed the first time.

I was so intent on viewing this from every possible angle that I accidentally bumped into an adjacent crystal. When I did so, it vibrated, emitting a deep hum that pleased my ear—no, not just my ear, but as if I heard it with my whole body. The vibration it made set some of the others nearby to sounding in different pitches. I answered back, trying to match the tones I was hearing and found that my voice alone was sufficient to set them vibrating. This so delighted me that I burst into song. I tell you the truth, all the sons of Jubal could not match the music I made there that day!

I continued in a westerly direction for the rest of that day and on into the next. By the following afternoon, however, I could see that the hills were beginning to bend away to the southwest and I followed their course accordingly.

I do not have time to recount all of the other wonders I beheld in those weeks that I passed so near to Eden, but I must relate one more incident that occurred when I was camped at the westernmost point on my journey. I had not been asleep for long when I was awakened by a disturbance in the meadow nearby. To my amazement, I discovered a multitude of animals gathering themselves into a circle under the light of the full moon. They seemed to be waiting for something and I realized that they were all looking at me. As I advanced, the circle opened momentarily to allow me to enter and then closed up behind me. I stood in the center and they prostrated themselves on the ground before me according to their form—whether furred or feathered or whatever manner of animal it was. As they rose, the circle began to move from my left to my right, all of them directing their eyes to the sky. I looked up as well, but did not see anything other than what I would ordinarily see in the night sky when the moon was full. Whether they saw something else I do not know.

The animals circled faster. As they did so, each began making noises in whatever manner befitted it, quietly at first and gradually increasing in volume. Soon a rhythm emerged from the cacophony of sound. The deeper-voiced animals, like the lions, bullfrogs and boars, alternated in a pulsing rhythm. *Roar—croak—grunt. Roar—croak—croak—croak. Roar—croak—grunt—croak—grunt—grunt —grunt.* Then the smaller furred animals yipped, chattered and cooed, their voices rising and falling in unison. The birds chirped or warbled or called according to their kinds. Surprisingly, the result was not at all unpleasant to hear. Rather, it struck a chord deep within me, a place in my heart of which I was only dimly aware. I joined my own voice to the chorus, lifting my hands to the sky. As the animals ran, crawled and flew faster and faster, I gave myself over to it, spinning and dancing with all my might. At last I fell to the ground exhausted. The animals pressed around me and I let them touch me as they eagerly wanted to do.

When I awoke, the sun was already well above the horizon and I lay in the center of the clearing all alone. As to the meaning of this strange ceremony, I can only speculate. Perhaps the animals somehow knew of what my family was doing and wished to pay us honor. Or perhaps they recognized the image of the Creator in whose likeness I had been made. Whatever the case, I could not help feeling that on that night I came closer to what the Creator intended for his creatures than perhaps I had at any other time of my life.

ELEVEN

With my late start, I did not make very good progress that day. As I continued southward, I sensed by early afternoon that I was approaching another body of water which turned out not to be a river but a swamp with hundreds—maybe thousands—of tiny islands covered with marsh grasses and drooping trees. The view was blocked, so that I could not tell how wide it was—a hundred yards or a hundred miles. Crossing it looked like a gloomy, miserable business and my heart sank. I didn't feel up to swimming and wading after my long night and planned to make an early camp on the north bank for the night. But then I noticed a huge reptile napping in the shallows and I coaxed him into giving me a ride. From the armor on his back and his powerful tail, I knew it must be a crocodile—the first I had ever seen. We made several miles of progress before nightfall, which came early there, and camped on one of the larger islands that was about an eighth of a mile in diameter.

The crocodile and I continued like that for three days. I was beginning to wonder if we were ever going to reach the end of the wetland when we came rather suddenly to a river, unnamed and uncharted. I prevailed upon the crocodile to carry me across so I wouldn't have to swim. When I sent him back on his way, he seemed far more pleased about it than I was. While not the friendliest animal I have ever encountered, he nevertheless had proved to be a trustworthy ferry and it was good to have some living thing as a companion—even a scaly one. I was not sorry, however, to leave the dreary swamp behind. I was tired of being wet and longed to see the sunshine again. There wasn't much sunshine to be seen yet, however, because the late-afternoon shadows were already growing long, so I did not go much further that day. The mangos and papayas of that country were good, so I ate my fill and soon fell into a deep sleep.

After five more days, I began bearing more to the southeast, keeping the receding Edenic plateau in view over my left shoulder. In two more days, I emerged into a grassy land that was flatter than any country I had seen since I left the Setti Plain. At last, I had reached what I assumed to be the Havilah. I headed due south for three days, guessing according to Dayak's rough map that I still carried with me, and made excellent time in that nearly featureless terrain. Then I headed east in the uncertain hope that Dayak's calculations were accurate.

The transformation of the landscape was abrupt and grew steadily worse as I traveled toward the rising sun. To my dismay, I discovered that food and water were even scarcer in the Havilah than in Nod, which I wouldn't have dreamed possible. I carefully rationed my provisions, but hunger was not the biggest problem; water was practically nonexistent in those parts. The springs were dry and the streambeds dusty. And I had, at best, only a three-day supply in my flask if I conserved strictly.

How aptly named was the Havilah—the Sandland—for a more barren wasteland you could not imagine! It made Nod seem like the lush Setti Plain by comparison. I saw no living thing—plant or animal—only desolate expanses extending as far as I could see in every direction. It was not as hot as some later deserts came to be (because temperatures were more moderate everywhere then), but there probably never has been one as bleak.

Late on that first day, I reached what had once been a stretch of forest. All that was left, though, were denuded trees, stripped bare and toppled like twigs on the ground, all pointing toward me as I advanced. The destruction, whatever it was, had come from the east. Since the footing was treacherous in that broken landscape, I stopped around dusk for the night.

By the end of the second day, I left the trees behind and came into a region that might once have been a thriving savannah, but now was only a coarse dust kicked up by my plodding feet. Since I no longer had to worry about obstacles, I traveled on through the night to preserve my perspiration.

Somewhere around midnight, I saw up ahead what I thought at first were the stumps of small trees and assumed I was nearing another band of former forest. When I got close enough to see more clearly, though, I stopped in my tracks. They weren't clumps of stumps, but skeletons—very large ones—of what appeared to be elephants. Strangely, there was not even a trace of skin or hide to be seen, as if the destruction had completely obliterated their covering. And, like the fallen trees, they all faced westward. The herd appeared to have been in a headlong flight of terror when sudden death had overtaken them.

The eerie silence and the sight of their bones glowing in the sickly pale moonlight very nearly unnerved me. Only the need to pick my way carefully through the graveyard restrained me from breaking out into a run because I was loathe to accidentally bump into one of the skeletons in the dark.

I have seldom been so glad to see the sun as I was on that following morning. But although it chased away the night terror, it hardly brought any comfort by fully illuminating the desolation. Being surrounded by so much death was oppressive, but I could go no farther after a long day and night of hard traveling. I pitched my tent and fell into a fitful sleep.

I awoke sometime in the afternoon and scanned the bleak horizon. *It hasn't improved any since this morning,* I thought. But then in the distance something caught my eye—a shimmering like sunlight on water. I hastily grabbed my things and was quickly on my way, anxious to replenish my rapidly-dwindling water supply.

When I had walked for an hour, I thought, *It must be farther than it looked.* I picked up my pace, hoping to reach it by nightfall. But as the sun began to sink low in the sky, I had the sickening realization that I was never going to reach it. It was only a trick of the sun on the sand. I picked up handfuls of sand and flung them into the air in frustration.

I continued on through the night and stopped to sleep for a few hours at midmorning. The mirages became more frequent and I tried to ignore them. But I couldn't help getting my hopes up momentarily whenever I saw one. By the afternoon, I was seeing no more skeletons. I can't say that I had grown accustomed to them, but they no longer shocked me as they had that first night. In fact, they seemed almost preferable to what I then began to see— ghostly gray shadows on the ground. Not even the bones of these creatures had survived the heat. All that remained was the outline of their ashes. I shuddered when I came across some that appeared vaguely human in form. Whatever had happened, I was getting closer to it.

And then there was a place, miles wide, where there was absolutely nothing save a hard crust that appeared to be many inches thick. This, clearly, was where the strange fire had originated. It had burned so hotly that it had melted the very dust of the earth and fused it into a dark, crystalline mass, unlike anything the earth had ever seen. The next thing I knew, I was running, unaware that I had even made the decision. All I could think about was getting to the other side, and I didn't care about how much effort or sweat I expended in the process. When at last I was past it, I couldn't help but make a bigger demand on my water than I had rationed for the day. But

I was feeling quite ill by then—some lingering sickness of the land, I suppose. And I knew if I didn't find water soon, it wouldn't matter anyway.

By careful rationing, I made my three-day supply of water last five days all totaled. As I wrung the last drop of water out of my flask, I tried not to despair at how desperate my situation was. I found it hard to believe that only a few weeks before I had been in the very shadow of Eden drinking my fill of the sweetest water imaginable. What had wrought such destruction I could only guess, but my suspicions centered on the Sons of the Gods. It seemed that whatever they touched wasted away. I shuddered to think how utterly wicked they must be. But I was way past the point of turning back, so I tried to push those thoughts out of my mind and pressed on.

My tongue swelled and my mouth dried to the point that I could hardly swallow. During the day, my extreme thirst made it difficult to sleep so I passed the seemingly endless time as best as I could under the shade of my tent. At night when I traveled I was so weak that I could only move at what seemed like a tortoise's pace. Staggering forward for nights on end, I prayed for strength—pleading not so much for my own life (for by then death seemed almost preferable) but for the life of Re-Aylah. I could not bear the thought of her suffering at the hands of Baldag in that horrible place.

At the limit of my natural endurance, I reached a point where I became separated from my suffering. In the place where suffering had been, I found not peace exactly, but a sense of detachment—like it was happening to someone else besides me. Knowing that I was nearing the point of death and resigning myself to it gave me an odd sense of tranquility. Accepting my fate did not cause me to give up though. This should not be confused with bravery, because bravery implies a choice, which I did not have. Rather, since I thought I was going to die anyway, I merely resolved that instead of lying down, I would meet death falling forward.

TWELVE

efore that moment arrived, I saw a glint of reflection as if upon
water. *Surely another mirage*, I thought, the delusions seeming ever
more real due to my deprivations. But I hadn't been seeing the
mirages at night, and as I moved closer, I could see even through my delirium
that it was, indeed, water at last. With my final remaining strength, I reached
the pool and knelt to drink.

The first taste, however, proved a terrible disappointment, for I later
learned that this was one of several shallow pools that collected water
pumped from the gold mines. In those days, the water table all over the earth
was generally higher than it is today, so only diligent removal of the water
made even shallow underground mining possible. By the time it reached pools
like that one, the contamination from the mining operation and the high rate
of evaporation rendered it unfit to drink by anyone except the desperate. It is
little wonder, then, that it made me nauseous. But apparently it was enough
to save my life.

For a long time, I lay beside the water unable to move. Every time I
looked up at the nearly moonless sky, the stars swam before my eyes. As the
night advanced, though, I summoned my strength to take stock of the
situation. Across the sludge pond to the east, I could see what appeared to be
structures. At last, I surmised, I had reached the gold mines of the Havilah.
And I hoped that in one of those buildings I would find Re-Aylah.

I circled the pond. (Even though I could have waded across, I had no
intention of crossing it because I didn't want that foul water touching me.)
The darkness of the night worked to my advantage as there was little cover
otherwise. If my approach were seen, all my efforts would have been in vain.
On the opposite side, I located a trench that led toward the structures. I
stayed close to this (but not in it) in case I needed to duck down out of sight,

bending low to keep from presenting a silhouette against the horizon. As I drew closer, I got down on my hands and knees and crawled.

Here and there I saw wooden boxes above the ground, which I correctly guessed were entrances to the mines. Not far away, several dozen low buildings, crudely constructed of wood and thatch, served as barracks for the miners. At the south end of the compound stood a much larger building made of stone. I was greatly heartened at the sight of this because it fit Dayak's description of the garrison where Re-Aylah was being held prisoner.

At a loss to know how to proceed, I climbed a nearby rock pile to get a better view—a vantage point that felt very exposed, but I had to be able to see what I should do next. Even looking down from above, however, I could see no good way to get to the garrison without being spotted. The breaking dawn found me there still, debating what to do as men drifted out from the barracks. Many of them came over to the trench and relieved themselves in it. I gagged at the realization that I had drunk downstream from a latrine— no wonder it tasted so bad!

The men formed lines outside of the garrison and each received one helping of food that seemed insufficient to sustain the hard day's work that I knew each of them was performing. They looked haggard—more so even than the agricultural workers I had previously seen in Nod. These looked like walking dead men. The curious thing was that most of them were wearing items of gold jewelry—apparently in compensation for their labors. Seeing filthy men starving to death with gold chains around their necks struck me as one of the strangest sights I had ever seen.

Then one man in particular caught my eye, but not because he wore any jewelry. He was considerably older, though taller and more robust. I knew that frame in a moment for it was practically my own—my grandfather Lamech.

My mind reeled at this unexpected turn of events. Momentarily, I considered sneaking off again to collect my wits. But, desperate for water and food, I suspected my chances for success would not improve by delaying. So, for lack of a better plan, I decided to pretend that I was a slave in order to get close to Grandfather. Since most of the slaves were shirtless, I stripped off my tunic and concealed it under some rocks along with my pack. I climbed down from the mound and approached from behind one of the mine shaft openings. Stooping my shoulders in an attempt to hide my height, I shuffled off to the garrison with the other men. My appearance— gaunt and dirty after the hard crossing of the wasteland—no doubt helped me to blend in with the others.

I didn't go straight to Grandfather, thinking it best to bide my time until the proper moment so that his surprise at seeing me wouldn't give us both away. Instead, I got in line with the other slaves and received a bowl containing a gruel of crushed and boiled grain. Judging from the smell, the grain was starting to spoil. But, since I had not eaten for several days, I picked out the dirt and ate it anyway. Even though it was hardly more than a couple of mouthfuls, it was all I could do to keep it down. I swallowed hard and took several deep breaths, knowing I needed the sustenance. All the while, I kept my eye on Grandfather. When it came time for the men to work, I took careful note of what shaft he entered and followed along behind.

I have no desire to recall the horrors of the Havilah gold mines, but my account would be incomplete without some description of them. The narrow, oppressive shafts were poorly ventilated, and a dirty dampness pervaded the entire complex of tunnels. At intervals, men turned hand cranks at pumping stations, hour after hour, to force water up through leaky metal tubes and out of the shafts. Otherwise, the mines filled with water and could not be accessed. Near the surface, the air was chilly, but became uncomfortably warm as I descended into the deeper recesses. Because the mine shaft branched into many passages, I soon lost track of which way Grandfather had taken. I was standing at one of the forks trying to decide which way to go when one of the guards cursed at me and shoved me down a passageway, so that my decision was made for me. The tunnel ended at a rock wall where a man was laboring with a pick axe. Running diagonally across the wall was a vein of gold ore as wide as my hand.

"What should I do?" I asked, but I will not repeat the answer that he gave me. So I said, "Please bear with me. I've only just arrived and don't know what is required."

Disgusted, he tossed the pickaxe at me and grunted, "Dig."

Breaking rocks with a pickaxe made gopherwood seem like pine. Sparks flew with each blow of metal on quartzite and splinters from the shattered rocks stung my body. I worried that an errant chip might blind me, so I squinted my eyes all day. (Indeed, I noticed many in that place who had lost their sight or who were maimed in other ways from the grievous work.) The tunnel was not tall enough for me to stand up at my full height and this fatigued my back. Given my already weakened condition, I might not have lasted even one day in that awful place if I hadn't been accustomed to hard work.

The longer I stood in the shin-deep water, the more the soles of my feet softened and the rocks hurt my feet. Since no water was ever offered to us, I finally just cupped my hand and drank from the muddy water I was standing in because I was so thirsty.

After I had worked for awhile, my fellow slave took notice of how hard I was toiling. He said gruffly, "Are you trying to get us all beaten?"

"Of course not," I said. "I'll work harder."

"You idiot! That's not what I meant. You're working too fast. If you keep it up, the guards will expect us all to work harder and will not spare the rod if we fall short."

"Oh, then I'll slow down." This reproof actually wouldn't have been necessary anyway, for I found myself tiring quickly. I could hardly catch my breath because the feeble torchlight seemed to be robbing the tunnel of what little stale air it contained.

The man looked to be about my age, though it was difficult to tell for sure; obviously he had led a hard life. That seemed to be about the average age in the mining camp. Not many older men were there—they either earned the right to move on or died young from the harsh conditions.

"I'm Jay," I said, trying to be friendly.

"Shut up and work," he said.

As I labored, he made frequent suggestions about what I could do with the pickaxe, most of which would have been quite painful, as well as some recommendations about placement of the shovel that would have been physically impossible. As I dug, my fellow slave separated the gold ore from the matrix with a hammer. The gold went into a bucket, while the matrix went into a cart. When the handcart was full of matrix, he pushed it up the passageway. Larger carts passed by regularly, collecting the waste, hauling it out and dumping it on the piles. When the man returned, he indicated that he would take his turn on the pick, which was the harder labor, while I worked at separating the gold ore from the matrix. If all the shafts produced such prodigious quantities of gold, it would boggle the mind to consider how much was produced in a year. Before that day, I had never given much thought to the riches of Nephil. But, ever afterward, the cost of its production weighed heavily on my mind.

After awhile a guard came around and collected the gold from us. As long as the eyes of the guard were on him, my fellow slave worked diligently. But the moment that the guard left, he resumed his slower pace.

When I sensed that morning had passed, I asked him when we could expect lunch. He laughed at me. When I realized there would be no lunch, hunger gnawed at my stomach all the worse. At long last, the guards barked out the signal that the workday was ended. Exhausted and half choked from the damp dust, I was so relieved to be above ground again that I welcomed the sight of even the barren landscape of the Havilah.

Supper followed the same pattern and menu as breakfast—long lines for lukewarm gruel. I pinched my nose to keep from smelling it and quickly finished it off. By then, my insides were in such turmoil that I endured a long ordeal at the latrine, followed by another. By the time I returned to camp the second time, the men were lined up in front of barrels with their bowls in their hands. I could tell from the looks on their faces and the way they acted that it was *grack* or something like it. As much as I longed for something to drink that wouldn't turn my stomach, I nevertheless resolved that I would have nothing to do with it.

While the others were getting drunk, I milled around looking for Grandfather and found him off to the side with another fellow. As I passed by, I said as casually as I could, "May I have a word with you?" He turned and followed me for a couple of steps before I said, "Try not to look surprised, Grandfather."

His eyes flew open wide as he recognized me, but he did his best to conceal it. He asked, "How is it that you have come to this awful place?"

"I should ask you the same thing," I said. "We've had no word from you since your last visit. We've been worried."

"My search for Gomer brought me here. And here I have remained." He nodded toward the man he had been standing by. Only then did I recognize Gomer; I wouldn't have known him without being told. His physical condition had deteriorated to a mere shadow of what I formerly knew him to be. Seeing how badly he had wasted away moved me with pity.

"He has fallen under the spell of the Sons of the Gods," said Grandfather. "I looked all over this land—in horrible places I will not even speak of. I found him here about a year ago suffering terribly as you can see."

"We must get him away from here," I said. "The sooner the better."

"You do not understand the nature of the problem. He could leave any time he wants, as could any of these men. The slaves number in the thousands and could easily overwhelm the few scores of guards if they chose. Or one could simply sneak off when the guards were not looking."

"Then they're afraid to cross the wasteland. I don't blame them. I wouldn't attempt it again myself."

"You crossed the western wasteland?" said Grandfather, looking at me in amazement. "No wonder you look so gaunt. I did not know it was possible to survive the desolation of the western crossing, although your presence here proves that it can be done. But that is not what keeps them here—and there are other ways out. I've had my eye on the southern route. A man could survive there if he used his wits."

"Then why *don't* they leave?" I asked.

"The bitter truth is that they prefer to serve their masters rather than the Lord."

"I hear your words, but I don't comprehend them. How could they prefer this?"

"You are thinking as one who serves the Lord, and that is good," said Grandfather. "We follow him because he cares for us and wants what is best. And what is best for us is a whole-hearted commitment to him, for he wants the whole man. The so-called Sons of the Gods, on the other hand, hate men. They require nothing of a man beyond what is useful to them. Therefore, the men are otherwise free to indulge in whatever gratifies their desires, without regard for whether it is right or wrong. As you can see, they pay a heavy price for their freedom, which is a far worse form of slavery."

While we were talking, Gomer got in line for *grack*. "Shouldn't we stop him?" I asked.

"It is no use. He must make the decision for himself." Grandfather watched sadly as his son downed his bowl. Gomer's countenance changed quickly and he got the wild look of grack intoxication in his eyes.

Across the way a fight broke out between two men. Rather than restraining them, a crowd circled around them and watched until one man beat the other unconscious. Then they drifted away, leaving the defeated man bleeding on the ground without the least regard for his condition. When the crowds were gone, Grandfather carried the injured man to the barracks. He laid him on the floor—for there were not even mats to sleep on—and examined his wounds. He said, "I think he will be all right when he sleeps it off."

Grandfather looked at me and observed that I was shaking—appalled at the cruelty that was everywhere evident. He put his hand on my shoulder and said, "You have a tender heart, my son. See that you do not ever lose it."

We went back outside and stood around, trying not to listen in on the loud, course talk the other men were engaged in.

"Is your father well?" Grandfather asked.

"When I last saw him he was well, though I fear for him. He's going all over Nod telling people to repent, and that's not making him very popular."

"I don't doubt that, but may the Lord protect him. And what of Father Methuselah?"

"I'm sorry to report that his health is failing," I said.

"Then the fulfillment of the prophecy draws near," said Grandfather. "How I wish I could see him again before he goes to his fathers."

"Then of course you must come with us."

"Us? You are not alone?"

"I have reason to believe that Re-Aylah may be a captive here."

"Not my Sunshine! Tell me no harm has befallen her!"

"I don't think so," I said. "At least not yet."

"It did not occur to me until now that you were not looking for me."

"But Grandfather," I said, feeling a pang of guilt. "We didn't know that you were in need of rescue, or we would have stopped at nothing."

"Of course, my son. I know that. I can leave any time I want as I have already said. But you search here in vain, for I assure you that I have not seen her or any other woman in this camp. A woman would not last a day here among these depraved brutes."

Then I related the full story to him. He was particularly troubled by my account of the strained relations between Father and Irad. He said, "Was it not enough that Gomer has come to ruin? And now to hear that my other sons are at odds. What a bitter cup I have been made to drink!"

"The fault is not ours, I assure you," I said.

"I do not blame you," he said. "I know my sons. One is stubbornly independent and the other is too ambitious for his own good. That is not a good mix."

"No, it isn't," I said. "Anyway, my hope is that I might find Re-Aylah in this garrison, or one like it, and rescue her."

"Then perhaps all is not against us, for you have stirred my recollection. Several weeks ago, there was a commotion in the camp with the arrival of several wagons. I remember it well because it was in the middle of the night. We do not get many visitors here, as you might well imagine. So perhaps that could have been the arrival of Re-Aylah."

"The problem is getting inside to see if she's there."

"With that, I can help," said Grandfather. "I have the uniform of a guard, which I had planned to use for my own escape."

"Where did you get that?" I said amazed.

"The people in this place are altogether corrupt. You can obtain anything for a price."

Grandfather led me around to the backside of the barracks. Behind some loose boards, he had hidden a uniform which he gave to me.

"Shall I go in tonight when everyone has gone to sleep?" I asked.

"No, wait until tomorrow," said Grandfather. "If you go in boldly in broad daylight, you will not as easily arouse suspicion. The guards come and go frequently in this place. If you act like a guard, they will think you are a guard. But you must be very careful, for the guards will be most anxious to avoid displeasing Baldag by letting Re-Aylah escape."

I quickly tried on the clothes to see if they would fit. They were tight, but I managed to squeeze into them. Then we hid them again, since it would not have been good to be found with such articles in our possession.

While we were thus engaged, great revelry had spread throughout the camp. I will not describe the detestable ways in which the men degraded themselves, because such things are shameful to even speak of. By mutual agreement, Grandfather and I split up so as not to attract any undue attention to our relationship. Grandfather went to find Gomer and I retired to the barracks to sleep as I was exhausted. I lay down on the floor in a corner and shut my eyes against the barbarity.

THIRTEEN

I awoke before the other men who had straggled and staggered in throughout the night. Stepping over their stupefied bodies laying on the floor, I went outside and looked around. When I was sure no one was watching, I put on the guard's clothes.

As I approached the garrison, I tried not to think what a foolhardy venture I was undertaking. I knew that in all likelihood I would be caught and abused to death by the guards—or at best be forced into real slavery. But as I had not even the slightest conception of another plan, I advanced hoping that Re-Aylah was inside so that my life might not be forfeited in vain.

I climbed the steps and entered the door unchallenged. On both sides of the landing ran corridors with many doors on either side, which I assumed were the guards' quarters. Straight ahead, another flight of steps led upward. When I saw two men talking at the top of the stairs, I braced myself. Knowing they had seen me, I dared not do anything to arouse their suspicions. So, I walked boldly up the stairs. When I reached their level, I nodded, intending to walk on by.

"Where are you going?" said the shorter of the two. He was a squatty man and quite hairy, so that his chest and upper back were covered just like the beard on his face.

"I'm—I'm reporting for duty," I stammered.

"You're new here, aren't you?" said the taller guard. He spoke with a raspy voice and had a jagged, poorly healed scar on his cheek.

"I just arrived."

"From where?" said the taller, who may well have been a Sethite.

"From Nephil," I said.

"You must have messed up real bad to get sent here," said the hairy one.

"And you'll be messing up again if you wake up the Captain this early in the morning," said the man with the scar. "He's sleeping one off and won't be happy if anyone disturbs him. This is the end of the line, you know. You can't afford to mess up here."

"There's nowhere to go from here but down, eh Bulgeh?" said the hairy guard.

"And we do mean *down*," said Bulgeh and they both laughed. "You wouldn't enjoy breaking rocks in the mines all day."

I forced myself to laugh with them and said, "No, I'm sure of that. So just tell me what to do."

"Go wake up the prisoners," said Bulgeh.

"There are rods in the closets," said the other.

"If they don't move fast enough to suit you, give them a good whack," said Bulgeh.

"Yeah, you might as well make the best of it," said the second. "It's about the most enjoyment you can have in this place."

"Whack the prisoners," I said feigning enthusiasm, though probably not convincingly. "Sounds like fun."

As I walked back down the stairs, I breathed easier. So far, the plan was working. But I still had no idea where Re-Aylah was—if she was there at all.

While I was taking a rod out of the closet, a door on the opposite side of the landing opened. Out came another guard, and behind him I could see stairs that led downward. "Which one of you dogs is supposed to relieve me?" he called up the stairs. "First watch is over."

"I'm coming. I'm coming," said the hairy one. "It's about time I had some more fun with her."

"You're a fool, Shrog," said Bulgeh.

"Hey, all he said was that we weren't to lay a finger on her," said Shrog. "And I haven't."

"But I'm telling you he's liable to not like the dirty talk," said Bulgeh. "He's got a mean streak, that one. You never know what's going to set him off."

"Ah, she's lucky she doesn't get worse than that," said Shrog.

"You tell him that to his face when he gets here!" said Bulgeh.

As Shrog retorted with an obscenity and disappeared down the stairs, I did my best to conceal both my elation and my anger. Here at last was proof that Re-Aylah was being held in the dungeon below, though it pained me to speculate about what she had endured. But I kept my wits about me and went on with my business.

At the hut where only a short time earlier I had been a prisoner, I stood at the door and yelled, "Get up, you lazy dogs! Sluggards will suffer the rod for breakfast!" I spied Grandfather and he winked at me. Then I repeated this at all the other barracks. Seeing the prisoners cower in fear as I passed by gave me an odd feeling. Only a day before, I had been working right alongside them. The uniform and the rod made all the difference.

As the men filed out groggily, I found Grandfather again and whispered, "I'm going to pretend to hit you. Cry out like you're in pain." As we neared where Bulgeh was standing outside, I faked a blow to Grandfather's back and he yelled like I had really struck him. Bulgeh laughed and said, "I see it didn't take you long to get the hang of it. I think things will work out well for you here."

While the prisoners were eating their scant mouthfuls of cold gruel, I followed my nose to the mess hall where the guards ate. It was no palace banquet, but the food was at least edible and the portions ample. I ate more than I had eaten in the last two weeks combined until I nearly made myself sick. I also concealed a small loaf in my uniform for Grandfather and Gomer.

When it was time for the men to begin their work, we headed toward the mines. Suddenly, a voice behind me said, "Hey, who do you think you are?"

I turned to see the man I had worked alongside of the day before. Alarmed that he had recognized me, I could think of nothing to say.

"How come you've been made a guard so quickly?" he asked.

"The Lord has blessed me," I said, not knowing what else to say.

"A bribe's more like it."

"See here. I'm a guard now. You shouldn't talk to me that way."

"All right, all right."

"Don't be lazy today," I said. "Work hard—and not just when we're watching. Maybe I'll put in a good word for you."

He seemed pleased with that prospect and headed into the tunnel. I sighed with relief and waited at the entrance until Grandfather and Gomer approached. Then I followed them inside.

Grandfather knew the mines well and went to a passageway that afforded us some privacy. When we were alone, I produced the loaf I had hidden. Grandfather gave thanks, broke it and they ate it hungrily.

Gomer looked at me strangely as he ate. "Don't you recognize me?" I said. "I'm your nephew Jayfeth." His blank stare didn't give any hint of recognition.

"He is not in his right mind," said Grandfather. "The grack has done this to him. Sometimes evil spirits seize him and torment him grievously."

"Is there any hope?" I asked.

"Hope is all I have. But he must make the decision for himself. I cannot make it for him."

I shook my head in pity as they picked up their tools and began working. Watching them while I stood and did nothing felt very strange, but we had to make it look convincing. I said, "I have located Re-Aylah."

"Is she well?" asked Grandfather.

"I presume so, though I have not actually seen her. But I have learned that she is being held prisoner on the lower level."

"Do you have a plan?"

"I'm going to try to get the duty of guarding her tonight," I said. "When no one is watching, I'll set her free and then come back for you."

"I cannot leave Gomer," said Grandfather.

"Of course I mean to take him with us."

"He will not go," said Grandfather.

"You'll go with us, won't you Gomer?" Gomer just stared blankly at me. He was as thin as me by then and his eyes were dark and sunken. Around his neck hung a gold chain and he wore a gold ring on his right hand. He had found gold after all, but those few baubles had cost him his dignity and freedom. "You know who I am, don't you? I'm not a guard. I'm your nephew Jayfeth."

Slowly, Gomer nodded. "Right," I said. "It's settled then. We leave tonight."

Gomer huddled in the corner, looked down and shook his head.

"I don't understand," I said.

"I can't go," Gomer croaked.

"Do you like it here?" I asked.

I looked questioningly at Grandfather, who said, "No, he hates it here. They all do. But their minds are filled with fears of the consequences. And they are all quite addicted to the grack. They suffer terribly if they go even one day without it."

"What they've said about me all along, it's all true," Gomer lamented. "I am unlucky. And unlucky people meet terrible fates."

I went over to him and put my hand on his shoulder. "I wouldn't call any man unlucky who had a father who loved him this much." That seemed to help. He looked up after a moment and nodded.

"So, what do I do?" I said. "I can't just abandon you both here."

"You are not abandoning us at all," said Grandfather, reassuring me. "I choose to stay here of my own free will as long as there is any hope of saving my son from this dreadful fate. You, on the other hand, must rescue my Sunshine."

This did not feel right to me at all, but there seemed to be no other solution. The three of us embraced and slapped each other on the back for a long time.

"Now go," said Grandfather. "If you stay too long, you will arouse suspicion."

I made a point of staying away from Grandfather's tunnel for the rest of the day. I contemplated speaking with the other guards about him as well as the man I had promised to put in a good word for, but thought better of it. Once they linked me with the escape of Re-Aylah, anything I might have said on their behalf would surely have had the opposite effect.

I stashed food at the noon and evening meals and filled my flask from a barrel of clean water next to the garrison. Retrieving my pack from the dumps, I re-hid it behind the barracks where the uniform had been. Then I waited until the shift change that I assumed would come at dusk. When I saw one of the guards entering the garrison as the sun was setting, I seized the opportunity. Grandfather nodded to me as we exchanged one last glance. My eyes grew misty, but I braced myself and followed the guard inside.

The guard coming off duty was already waiting at the top of the stairs and there was little conversation between the two because he was anxious to get onto whatever diversions awaited him. I was again surprised at their lack of discipline and hoped that it could be used to my advantage.

"Say, there must have been a mix-up," I said as the new guard started down the stairs.

"What's that?" said the large-featured man, who spoke quite slowly.

"Watch duty. Looks like we're both down for it."

"I'm going to guard the prisoner," he said, not seeming to understand.

"That's just it," I said, trying again. "So was I."

He grunted in reply.

"That means there would be two of us."

"Two of us," he repeated. "I suppose you're right."

"One too many, if you ask me."

"Ask you what?"

"If you thought we needed two men to guard one prisoner," I said.

"I didn't ask you that."

"No, but if you did, my answer would be that one was plenty."

"One what?"

"One guard."

"Oh," he said and started again for the stairs.

"What I'm saying is that I'm willing to take this shift and you can have the night off.'

"I wouldn't have to work then?"

"Not tonight."

Finally, he understood and shuffled back outside without a word of thanks, though it's strange I should have expected one. I felt badly about deceiving him in that way, but Re-Aylah's life was far more important.

The small lamps only dimly lit the narrow stairs. They led to a short hallway, at the end of which stood a stool and a large wooden door with a sliding panel that was used to pass food. I was greatly relieved to see that nobody else was around. As I unfastened the bars that held the door shut, I congratulated myself for my bravery and cleverness. *This wasn't so hard after all,* I thought as I strode through the door. *Maybe this will finally earn Re-Aylah's affection ...*

Slowly, a distant awareness of my face pressing against cold stone made itself known to my mind. I opened my eyes and realized that I was lying on the floor of the cell and was alone. As I started to get up, the back of my head throbbed. Touching it with my hand, I found it wet with blood and almost lost consciousness again. Taking care not to make any sudden movements, I rose to my feet. When I saw an old board laying near where I had fallen, the situation became all too clear—Re-Aylah had mistaken me for a true guard and turned *my* rescue into *her* escape.

FOURTEEN

I shut the door, barred it again and crept stealthily back up the stairs. When I reached the landing, I heard footsteps coming down the steps from the officers' quarters. Quickly, I slipped into the closet because I didn't want to let anyone see me in my bloodied condition. When they stopped outside the door only a few feet away, it occurred to me that they might be coming to get equipment and I wondered what I was going to say if they opened the door and found me there. As it turned out, they didn't, but what I heard next was almost as bad.

"What new man?" said one who must have been the Captain.

"The one who just came in from Nephil." I recognized Bulgeh's voice speaking.

"I don't have any orders about a new guard from Nephil. Bring him here. I want to question him."

As soon as they were gone, I cracked the door and made sure no one else was coming. In a moment, I was outside gathering my things. I wasted no time, knowing they would shortly discover that their prisoner had escaped. Our only chance was to make the most of a very limited head start. The problem was that I had no idea which way Re-Aylah had gone. I didn't even know how long I had been unconscious, but I didn't think it was more than a minute or two. Even running for her life, she couldn't have gotten far.

I climbed up the backside of one of the tailing piles—out of sight of the camp—hoping for a better view. The moon was new and did not cast much light, but there wasn't much cover either. I strained my eyes until they hurt. Then, away to the south, I glimpsed a slight flicker of movement. I couldn't tell for certain if it was her, but nothing else I knew of lived there. In the distance beyond, I saw some mounds and what looked like a tree line on the southern horizon—the first living trees I had seen in what seemed like ages. Re-Aylah was very intelligent; she would head for the cover.

I ran as fast as I could to try and overtake her, my head pounding with every step. But even though I had always been fleet of foot, I still had a lot of ground to make up. And before I had gone very far, I heard a commotion in the camp behind me—not the din of revelry, but angry voices shouting. Our flight had been discovered much sooner than I had hoped.

I then faced a dilemma. My natural inclination was to run even faster. But if I had seen Re-Aylah out in the open, I feared that they would see me as well. So, I reasoned that stealth was better than speed. If they didn't know where I was, they would lose time organizing bands and searching. If they spotted me, though, they could marshal all their forces in one direction. Therefore, I forced myself to crawl on my hands and knees and hoped that by then Re-Aylah had reached the low hillocks I had seen between the camp and the tree line. They, too, appeared barren, but would obscure her from view if she held to the ravines.

Crawling tired me much faster than running and soon scraped my hands and knees raw. Behind me, the searchers shouted as they fanned out to look for us. Judging from the number of the voices, the prisoners were being pressed into the search as well—no doubt with a promise of a reward for the man who found us and a threat of punishment if they failed to capture us. As they drew closer, my instincts urged me to jump up and run for it. I fought the panic rising within me and held to the ground, knowing that if they spotted me it would mean certain capture.

At last I reached the first ravine and felt safe to start running again. But these zigzagged tortuously, so that it took me a long time to make it through them. I didn't want to expose myself any more than I had to by crawling over the top of one mound to get to the next ditch. My pursuers, however, did not have to worry about concealment and thus continued to gain on me. What had made the trenches I could not even guess. It was as if something beyond the size of human comprehension had scoured the land with gigantic claws. Inside the trenches, I could hardly see anything at all. I stumbled often and more than once slammed headlong into a hidden bank when the course of the ravine veered. My sides heaved from exertion and my lungs burned for air, but I didn't dare to stop. By then, my pursuers had also reached the ravines. I could only hope that the need to search more carefully there would slow them down a little.

After what seemed like a long time, I suddenly found myself out of the hillocks and into a flat clearing. I groaned at the realization that the mounds did not extend all the way to the trees as I had first supposed. I crawled again—this time on my belly because I was afraid to rise even as far as my knees. At that agonizingly slow pace, I pressed ahead foot by foot.

The eastern sky began to lighten perceptibly and my heart sank. If the approaching dawn found me still in that exposed area, I was doomed. So, I determined to use what remained of the night and my strength to make a dash for it. The trees were less than two miles away and I hoped that, even if my pursuers spotted me, I could reach cover before they caught up to me. I ran as fast as my legs could move and made the edge just as the first rays of the sun broke over the horizon. I collapsed on the ground gasping for air. I didn't know whether I had been seen, but I could go no further until I caught my breath.

As the faint light of dawn began to penetrate the woods, I realized that the trees were sparser than I had thought and would not hide me very well. Quickly, I changed out of the guard's uniform, which was badly soiled anyway, and put on my own clothes. I didn't want to make the same mistake with Re-Aylah again! With a couple of mouthfuls of bread and two swallows of water, I was on my way, running swiftly, but at a pace I knew I could sustain for awhile.

I had no idea where Re-Aylah was, though I knew she must have been very weary and would likely be looking for a place to rest. I speculated about how far she might be ahead of me. She had a head start and undoubtedly had made better time in reaching the woods. Even with my most optimistic appraisal, I guessed she had to be at least an hour ahead of me, probably more. And I dared not call out for fear of bringing our captors down on us. When I considered all this, the chances of finding her began to seem very slim indeed.

As the morning wore on, I heard no sound of pursuit behind me. I didn't know how long they would continue to look for us, but hoped that the logistics of supplying food and water for so many men in that remote place would soon discourage them. However, I suspected that when Baldag learned the news, a more exhaustive search would ensue.

Once I was certain that I was not being closely followed, I felt I could make a more careful search for a sign to show that Re-Aylah had passed that way. By late afternoon, though, I still had seen nothing to give any indication that she was within a hundred miles of there. I hoped that she was just being clever and taking care not to leave any tracks. In my heart, though, I feared that she might have struck out in an entirely different direction. These were not my worst fears, however, because more insidious doubts began to disturb my mind. After all, I had not actually seen her for certain. As I thought more about it, I could not recall even hearing her name spoken by the guards—nor Baldag's for that matter. I had just assumed from bits and pieces of conversations and circumstances that she was there. But could I have heard only what I wanted to hear?

When night fell, I stopped, since I couldn't risk missing a sign in the darkness. Exhausted after hard flight for a night and a day, I found a brushy thicket, lay down on my mat and fell asleep.

My body did not want to wake up the next morning. My head still throbbed and every muscle ached. By much effort, though, I finally roused myself. While I ate a bit of my provisions, I tried to figure out what Re-Aylah was thinking. Cush lay to the northeast and I assumed that's where she would want to end up. But Baldag would certainly know that and would likely concentrate his search on those north-south routes, so she would want to avoid them. Going west was even more dangerous as my own experience had taught me. But I didn't know if she was aware of how ill-advised crossing the western wastelands unprovisioned would be. A third possibility was that she might backtrack toward the mining camps. It had in its favor being the unexpected thing to do, but I suspected that she would want to get as far away from that horrible place as she could. As I eliminated the possibilities one by one—admittedly on the barest of reasons—I came back around to the south. Since the last direction I had seen her (or thought I had seen her) traveling was south, I decided to continue on that way until I had reason to do otherwise.

The further I went along, the more living things I saw. It was no Paradise to be sure, but was certainly more inviting than anything I had seen in quite a long time. Still, I saw no signs of Re-Aylah and began to despair of ever finding her.

About mid-morning I heard a noise away to my left. I stood still and listened intently, fearing the pursuers were back on my trail. As I strained my ears, though, it sounded more like an animal moving through the brush.

I hadn't gone far when I heard it again—this time much closer. I looked and saw a tawny dog coming toward me. Grateful for some companionship in that remote place, I called to him, hoping that with his superior sense of smell, he could assist in searching for Re-Aylah.

Warily, he approached until he stood only a couple of feet away, his muscular shoulders twitching with what I thought was excitement at seeing a man. I reached down to pet him, but he growled and snapped at me. My hand smarting and bleeding, I backed away slowly, keeping my eyes firmly fixed on his. I had never before in my life seen an animal behave that way toward a human, and I sensed something was terribly wrong. Then he barked, and to my dismay, his bark was answered by others.

The next thing I knew, I was running with a pack of vicious dogs in close pursuit. I crashed through the brush, heedless of the brambles tearing at my skin. The first dog had held back, waiting for the others to join him. But now they were gaining on me rapidly. Looking back frequently over my shoulder, I did not see the ferocious dog that had circled ahead until he was almost on top of me. I turned quickly to my right and headed into a ravine, hoping to find some shelter there because I knew I could not outrun them. What I found instead was a sheer bluff with no outlet. I was trapped.

The dogs approached slowly and fanned out around me to prevent any possibility of escape. They had no need of speed now because they knew their prey was cornered. The ground all around me was littered with the jumbled bones of previous victims. Obviously, I was not their first quarry, but probably their biggest and already they were salivating. With my back against the bluff, the situation seemed hopeless.

Just then, I heard a voice above me say, "Jayfeth?"

"Re-Aylah?" I said, shocked. "Thank God!"

"Why are those dogs attacking you?" she said. "Do you have that infuriating effect on everything you come in contact with?"

"I've had a lot of practice with you," I said. "But if you help me get out of this mess, I promise I'll do better!"

"See if this will support your weight." Re-Aylah threw down a vine, but it didn't come down quite to within my reach. She pulled it up and began tying another one to it. The dogs, who had retreated momentarily at the sound of another human voice, moved closer again and snarled menacingly.

"I'm not trying to rush you or anything, but how are you coming up there?" I said.

"Try this," she said, lowering the joined vines. As soon as the end reached me, I grabbed hold of it and climbed as fast as I could. It felt none too secure, but anything was better than staying down there with the dogs.

When they saw that I was eluding them, the dogs were outraged. They jumped up in the air and snapped at me. I was just about ready to hurl a curse at them when the vine slipped and I nearly tumbled back down into their midst. But after I slid a few feet, it held fast again. I redoubled my effort and quickly reached the top.

I had never been so glad to see anyone in my life as I was to see Re-Aylah at that moment. I started to embrace her, but felt awkward about it and stopped myself. She didn't seem to know quite what to do either. Finally, she broke the embarrassing silence by saying, "I thought you were supposed to be able to communicate with animals."

"I can," I said. "Well, usually anyway. But those dogs didn't seem to be in the mood for conversation."

"No, they didn't. So we'd better be moving along before they find their way up here."

When we had run a couple of miles, we stopped to rest. After we caught our breath, Re-Aylah asked, "I'm very curious. How is it that you came to be in this forsaken place?"

I briefly related my account to her about how we figured out that she had been kidnapped, of my travels around Eden and the crossing of the Havilah wasteland. I concluded with my arrival at the mining camp, finding Grandfather and Gomer, and my rescue efforts. "And that's when you whacked me over the head."

"I'm greatly embarrassed," she said. "I had no idea it was you. I feared for my life and when I saw the opportunity to escape, I seized it."

"The hardness of my head is well known among my kinsmen, so I don't think I've suffered any permanent damage," I said. "It occurs to me now, though, that we must be very careful not to become infected by the violence all around us."

"What do you mean?"

"The world is becoming such an evil place that it would be easy to become violent along with it."

"But you know how Baldag and his men have mistreated me," she protested.

"Yes, and I have often consoled myself with thoughts of what I would do if I ever got hold of him," I said. "But if I did all that my hands found to do, I would risk becoming as corrupt as he is."

"Next time, you might try letting me in on your scheme then," she said defensively. "Perhaps some violence could be avoided."

"I was not rebuking you."

"Hmpf."

We had been reunited for only a few minutes and already I had offended her. Trying to recover, I said, "The note you left us was very clever."

"Do you really think so?" she said. "I had to think fast. Baldag's men said they would harm your family if I didn't cooperate. So I tried to let you know without tipping them off."

"I'm sure they had no idea. But Shem and I figured it out almost immediately."

"So what do we do now?"

"You've been going south," I said. "I don't know if Baldag's reach extends all the way to the sea, but continuing in that direction seems as good a plan as any to me."

"Before we go anywhere, let's have a look at your hand and head," she said, taking my hand in hers. Her touch gave me such an indescribable thrill that my trials paled to insignificance. That one moment was worth it all. Indeed, I found myself perversely wishing I were more severely injured just to prolong her tending to my wounds!

Fifteen

After we had eaten, Re-Aylah and I resumed our southward course. As far as we could tell, we were no longer being chased, so we took our time. Though I had no idea what lay ahead, I didn't care. I was well content just to spend time in Re-Aylah's company. Although we were in a hostile land and faced many hardships, I recall those days with special fondness.

Since we didn't want to attract attention, we lit no fire when we camped at the end of each day. We talked and laughed late into each night with only the moonlight shining upon us—an effect that made me feel freer with her than during the day. All too soon, it seemed, the evenings would pass. Then she would retire to the tent while I slept on my mat under the stars and dreamed of what might be.

The country we passed through was a strange one. Besides the behavior of the dogs which I could not explain, I saw many other unusual sights. On the second day, for example, we came across the carcass of a newborn fawn born with two heads. I also saw many other anomalies, such as featherless birds and animals with various kinds of deformities. I confess that my mind was so preoccupied with Re-Aylah that I didn't give proper attention to investigating these things. Otherwise, I might have understood certain matters sooner than I did.

As we were walking along on the fourth day following our reunion, we heard a deep grunting sound not far ahead of us. We slowed our pace and approached cautiously. Topping a small rise, we saw a fearsome monster at least thirty feet tall. His rows of sharp fangs and scythe-like claws would have been frightening enough. But when I saw what he was doing, I was appalled. The beast was standing over the half-eaten body of what appeared to be some kind of deer. Blood smeared his pebbly olive face and spattered his pale underbelly. He was so engrossed in his gruesome feast that he didn't even notice us gaping at him, so we crept away unnoticed. The sight of flesh eating flesh deeply disturbed us both. We walked for a long time in silence and after that, we were more alert.

On the following day, we began hearing the sound of many animals wailing in the distance. As we drew nearer, we sensed we were approaching an inhabited area. Peering through the brush, we looked out over a river—the Pishon—on the opposite side of which stood a building that was surprisingly large for such a remote place. Surrounding the building were row after row of cages in which all kinds of animals were being confined. Two rough-looking men were going from cage to cage, jabbing the animals with pointed sticks for no apparent reason. The animals cried out in pain and some snarled at the men. Most of them looked half-starved and in very poor condition. I was shocked by such cruelty and told Re-Aylah that I intended to do something about it.

"I don't think that's a good idea," she said. "We might end up worse off than they are."

"We can't just leave them here to suffer," I said.

"But what concern is it of ours?"

"Father says that all of creation is our concern. If one suffers, all suffer. We have been given dominion over this world and part of that responsibility is to protect its creatures."

"I've only recently escaped from my own cage and have no desire to end up in another," said Re-Aylah.

"Fine," I said. "I had no intention of asking you to go with me anyway. Such work would be far too dangerous for a woman."

"You didn't seem to feel that way when I was saving you from the dogs," said Re-Aylah.

"Uh ... good point," I said. "Sorry."

"Well there's something," said Re-Aylah. "A man admitting he was wrong. Perhaps there is hope for you after all, Jay."

We kept watch from a distance until long into the night while the men drank themselves stuporous. When the last two had staggered into the building, I said, "I'm going now."

"You mean *we're* going now."

"I thought you didn't want to risk capture for the sake of these animals."

"It's not for the animals," she said, and I smiled to myself.

We made our way down the thicketed slope, which was no easy feat in the darkness. A foul odor hung thickly in the evening mist. I tried not to think about why the river smelled so bad and was glad we didn't have to swim it since we had spotted canoes laying on both banks. The Pishon was narrow there and easily crossed, so we were soon on the other shore opening the cages and freeing the captives. I talked quietly to the animals as I released them, but they didn't give any indication at all of understanding me. Some even growled, though that seemed understandable given their treatment at the hands of men. I hoped that the guards were drunk enough that they wouldn't hear the commotion.

There were about two hundred cages in all, but the latches were simple and we made quick work of it. In the last cage was a forlorn cougar. When Re-Aylah had freed it, she whispered, "You were right. This was a good thing to do."

"That's something," I whispered back. "A woman admitting that a man is right."

"Hmpf," she said. "Let's get out of here before I change my mind."

"First I want to get a look inside. There might be more in there."

"You *are* crazy," she said, but followed me anyway.

We entered a long corridor that was dimly lit by torchlight. The sound of snoring on either side gave evidence that we were walking through the sleeping quarters. We had only seen half a dozen different men during the afternoon and evening and we hoped that was the extent of the force there. Silently, we crept down the hallway, hardly daring to even breathe for fear of waking one of them.

At the end of the corridor, we came to a heavy wooden door. I put my ear to it, but could hear nothing stirring within. The sound of the latch scraping seemed alarmingly noisy in the silence and Re-Aylah glared at me. I shrugged as there was nothing I could do. I pulled the door slowly toward me, just enough to get a peek inside. When it creaked loudly on its hinges, it made me wince. I spat on my fingers and rubbed the saliva on the hinges, diminishing the squeak to a more bearable level.

As soon as the door cracked open, I looked inside and was appalled to see a half dozen tables on which were laid dead animals in various stages of dismemberment. At the same moment, the smell hit me. No wonder the river smelled rotten—that must have been where they dumped the carcasses. Yet I could ascertain no purpose for such terrible cruelty.

Badly shaken, I started to turn away when something caught my attention—the glint of reflection from the eye of one of the animals. Only the eye of a living creature glistened so.

I whispered into Re-Aylah's ear, "Stay here and keep watch. But don't look inside." Of course, she looked anyway.

I opened the door a bit further and slipped inside. Dodging baskets of discarded limbs and entrails, I picked my way slowly between the tables. I held the cloth of my tunic over my mouth and pinched my nose to keep from gagging. Only the moonlight through the high windows provided any illumination.

At the back of the room, I found a wolf laying on its side held fast by straps to a table. The thong around its neck was so tight that it could scarcely breathe. I doubted that his captors would have cared if it strangled to death during the night; their intention for it in the morning was all too clear.

I released the two straps that held its hind quarters and shoulders and then carefully unfastened the one around its neck. The moment it was free, it bolted from the table, upsetting a tray of instruments that fell to the floor with a silence-shattering clang. The wolf rushed out of the door past Re-Aylah, while I stood there momentarily paralyzed with panic that everyone in the compound had been awakened by the sound.

The moment passed with no alarm sounding, so I hurried back toward the door so that we could make our escape. As I reached it, though, we heard a noise down the hallway and looked at each other.

"Someone's coming," said Re-Aylah in a panicked whisper.

I looked quickly around the room, but no other doors were to be seen— only the open windows situated high on the walls. I hoped, though, that if we stood on the bench beneath that we might just be able to reach one. We left the door standing open since we could ill afford to make any more noise while someone was stirring, and jumped up on the heavy wooden counter. I clasped my hands to make a step for Re-Aylah and then boosted her up to the window. While she crouched on the ledge, I jumped as high as I could and grasped the sill, but did not have a sufficient grip to pull myself up. As my fingers slipped, I dreaded the thud of landing back on the bench because it would surely draw attention to us. But just as I was about to lose my grip, I felt Re-Aylah clasping my wrists and hauling me up with surprising strength.

The ground outside the building sloped southward so that it was lower than the floor inside—farther than I wanted to jump. A sprained ankle at that moment could have been deadly. So, Re-Aylah lowered her body out of the window and held tightly to the sill while I slid down her body like a rope to break my fall. When I was safely on the ground, she lowered herself as far as she could and then dropped into my waiting arms. Suddenly, unexpectedly, had come a situation that I had previously only dreamed of. I couldn't bring myself to put her down immediately—and she didn't ask me to. As I held her there, she looked into my eyes in a way that she never had before.

A cry of alarm spoiled the moment. The empty cages had been discovered. Instantly, I set Re-Aylah on her feet and we ran for our lives. But the contingent at the compound was small and unable to mount much of a pursuit, if indeed they pursued us at all. By the time we had gone five miles, we knew we were safely away and slowed our pace to catch our breath. Dawn followed soon after and we stopped for breakfast.

As for Re-Aylah, whatever fleeting moment we might have shared back at the animal compound had passed. She resumed her usual demeanor toward me—friendly, but slightly detached. Indeed, I began to wonder if I had just imagined something between us out of wishful thinking.

As we sat facing each other, Re-Aylah suddenly shrieked. Before I could turn around, I was knocked to the ground and rolled onto my back. I looked up to see a wolf straddling my body—the wolf we had rescued the night before. All I could think of was the irony of freeing that great beast only to be killed by it.

Instead of doing what I thought it would, though, the wolf licked my face and nuzzled me.

"It's all right," I said. "It means me no harm."

When I could finally get back on my feet, I could see it was an unusually large she-wolf, with exquisite silver fur that was longer than my fingers—a fact I could appreciate more fully when I was not laying flat on my back looking up at her. As we watched her, the wolf turned circles and cried, trying to communicate something.

"So what is she saying?" asked Re-Aylah.

"I'm not certain," I said. "But that bark sounds like 'master' to me."

"Can you really talk to animals or are you just making it up to impress me?"

"It was lonely growing up after our kinsmen turned against us—no offense. So I made friends with the animals. With the way I've been treated all my life, I have often preferred their company to humans."

"Oh, thanks!" she said.

"I wasn't talking about *you*, of course," I said sheepishly. "I just meant that relating to animals is mainly a result of spending time with them and observing their ways. For example, I can tell that this wolf has spent much time with humans."

"What makes you say that?"

"Look at her eyes," I said. "I can't explain it, but being with people makes them more than what they were. You can always tell by their eyes."

"And what do you see when you look into *my* eyes?" asked Re-Aylah.

Her question caught me off guard. I looked, not knowing if she was serious. Her eyes, how they danced! But whether it was from passion or playfulness, I couldn't say. I would have given anything to plumb the depths of their blueness. I looked away, embarrassed, and said, "You're mocking me."

"Mocking? No, just testing," she said clearly enjoying herself. "You're the one who claimed to read eyes."

"The females of some species are harder to read than others," I said with an exasperation that was not entirely feigned.

"So, what does the wolf mean—that her master did this to her?"

"Perhaps she now regards *me* as her master."

"How typical of you to assume that," she said.

"You're misunderstanding me again."

"And *you* have understood *me*?"

I made no response, for by then I was bewildered by the whole conversation. I just shook my head and gathered up our things.

Although we were both tired, we wanted to put more distance between ourselves and the compound before we slept. When we tried to return to our southward course, however, the wolf blocked our way—not menacingly, but resolutely. This was puzzling and even a bit disturbing. I felt sure, though, that I did not want to make her angry. So we followed her nudging, which took us in a more southeasterly direction.

The wolf had a general sense of which way she wanted us to go. But from time to time she would stop, circle around and sniff, sometimes making minor course alterations. As morning gave way to afternoon, she seemed to grow surer of herself and her pace quickened. Re-Aylah and I, however, were exhausted, so we camped long before the shadows began to lengthen in spite of the wolf's urgings. The wolf finally acquiesced, but paced around the camp restlessly barking "Master" over and over. She was so anxious to move on that I thought she might leave us behind. I recall thinking that it might be for the best, because I still had no idea where she was leading us. For all I knew, it might have been to the very stronghold of the Sons of the Gods.

SIXTEEN

I presume the wolf's impatience continued long into the night. I cannot say for sure, however, because as soon as I pitched the tent for Re-Aylah and we had eaten a portion of our food (which was running alarmingly low), I fell asleep under a low tree. I was awakened only once when the wolf howled, a plaintive sound that stirred my heart in sympathy for her. As far as I could tell, whoever or whatever she was calling did not answer.

"It's all right," I said in the direction of the tent, half hoping that Re-Aylah would be frightened enough to come running to me for protection. "It's only our friend's heartsickness." As I said it, I realized why I identified so much with the sound. At times, I felt like howling myself.

We set out early the next morning, continuing our southeasterly course. The wooded, rolling hills gave way to an unfamiliar terrain with sandy soil and thin, bunchy grass. Here and there, scaly, branchless trees stood in groves. What I remember most, though, was a growing hint of sweetness in the air that seemed to be the very aroma of excitement: we were nearing the Great Sea.

The she-wolf no longer hesitated at all, at times running on ahead until we completely lost sight of her. But she always returned to make sure that we were following. About midday, we topped a sandy hill that was higher than most. As we reached the crest, we saw at last the Great Sea in the distance. The wolf could restrain herself no longer and raced toward a peninsula that jutted out into the water.

Overwhelmed by the enormity of the featureless horizon, I stared at the tourmaline intensity of the sea until my eyes watered. Finally, I glanced at Re-Aylah and could tell that she was as moved as I was. Neither of us spoke, but soon we found ourselves running toward the sea. I knelt on the sand at the edge, cupped my hands and took a drink. It was warm and strong like a stout ale, (not unpalatably salty as it afterward came to be). I waded in up to my thighs and let the warm water caress my weary feet and legs. It felt so good that I dove in and submersed myself entirely. When I came up again, I saw that Re-Aylah had followed my lead and we splashed around in the water for a long time. I had not bathed thus in all the time since I entered Havilah and I knew it had been even longer for Re-Aylah. After the scarcity of water in that arid land, swimming in the ocean was a luxurious and welcome sensation.

We were so caught up in playing that we didn't see the solitary figure approaching from the peninsula until he had very nearly reached us. Re-Aylah spotted him first, and then I looked up to see what had caught her attention. He was of small stature, with long white hair and beard. His wizened face indicated great age. At his side, the wolf pressed against him, matching him step for step. Her meaning now was clear. She had led us to *her* Master.

I came up out of the water, pulled my hair back and wiped my face as best I could. "Greetings, Venerable One," I said, embarrassed to be meeting a stranger with my clothes dripping wet.

"Thank you for returning Moonbeam," said the old man. "I have missed her these many days."

"Rather, it was the other way around," I said. "She was the one who led us to you."

He regarded us with an eye that was so penetrating that I began to grow uncomfortable under his stare. It made me wonder how much of our experiences it would be wise to reveal without knowing more about him.

"I am Jay," I ventured. "May I inquire who you are?"

"That is of no consequence," he said. "What I want to know is what happened to Moonbeam. I can see that she has suffered much."

"We assure you it was not at our hands," said Re-Aylah. "Rather it was Jay who rescued her from the evil men who captured her. You ought to be thanking him instead of accusing him."

"Nevertheless, I perceive that there is much that you are not telling me," said the old man.

"We also have suffered much from the schemes of wicked men," I said. "Our bad experiences have made us cautious."

"The enemy of the wicked will find a friend among the righteous," he said. "You are welcome here. Follow me."

He led us along the length of the peninsula. At its highest point, it was only about ten feet higher than the level of the sea. Above the beach line, grass grew in abundance and a few sheep were grazing. On the furthest prominence of the peninsula stood a low building of dressed gray stones, ancient in origin. But now it appeared to be abandoned except for its lone occupant.

"What is this place?" I asked.

"It was built in the days of your forefathers long passed," said the old man. "When men began to call on the name of the Lord, they built this place to keep vigil. But they are all long gone and no one calls on the name of the Lord anymore."

"I do," I said.

"We do," corrected Re-Aylah.

"I would hear more about that," he said. "But first I will show you to your rooms and get dry clothes for you. I do not get many visitors here and those who come find the accommodations rather austere. But perhaps the hardships you have encountered will make this seem quite comfortable."

He provided us with linen undergarments and robes of spun wool that was the softest I had ever touched. When I had dried and changed, I laid down on the bed and fell asleep immediately.

Sometime later, the old man knocked on my door and summoned me to supper. We dined on a thick soup made of kelp and something that resembled cucumbers. We talked as we ate, and based on his comments, I regarded him at first as a servant of the Lord. Thus, I told him the better part of our account without reservation and he was keenly interested in all that I had to tell him of the oracles.

"Are you then among the sons of the prophets?" he asked.

"I myself am not a prophet," I said, the familiar sting of shame burning in my cheeks. "But my father and brother are and I report to you faithfully what they have told me."

"Jay has many other excellent qualities, though," said Re-Aylah. I was greatly heartened that twice in recent hours she had rallied to my defense.

"I am sure that he does," said the old man. "But my soul thirsts for new oracles."

"Our story is told," I said, trying to change the subject. "But we still don't know who you are. Please tell us what your name is and from what tribe you are descended."

"If you must know, I once was known by the name Meshullah," he said. "I, too, am a descendant of Seth. But when I came to this place, I renounced all that. I took a vow that as far as this world is concerned, I have no identity and am without genealogy. I consider myself only a priest of Melchi."

At this, I grew uneasy, since I had told him much in the confidence that he was a follower of the Lord. But this sounded like one of the gods of the pagan Cainites. "Who is Melchi?" I asked.

"The one who will come," said the priest. "An ancient prophecy says that before Melchi comes, a prophet will precede him and prepare the way. I had hoped that you were that prophet."

"As I indicated, I am not a prophet," I said, resolving to be more cautious around him. "And neither do I know anything of this Melchi."

"Nevertheless, you have told me much that interests me," he said. "You long to return to your people and I would very much like to see this ark of which you have spoken. So, I propose to take you there myself."

"That's kind of you to offer," I said. "But the way is long and dangerous. And we have bitter enemies."

"But if we travel by boat, we might avoid detection by your enemies."

"By boat?" I repeated. "I hadn't thought of that."

"Around Cape Shur and up the Gihon," said the priest.

I still wasn't sure if we should trust him. However, he had been hospitable up to that point. And seeing as how we had no plan for crossing Nod, I looked at Re-Aylah and shrugged.

That night I slept better than I had in a long time and awoke greatly refreshed just before sunrise. I looked for Re-Aylah in her room and in the dining hall, but didn't find her. I inquired of the priest, who was cooking breakfast in the kitchen. He nodded toward the eastern patio.

Re-Aylah sat upon the low stone wall, her arms encircling her drawn-up legs and chin resting on her knees, profiled against the rising sun. Emboldened by her recent comments on my behalf, I said, "I've never seen anything as beautiful as the rising sun in your hair."

"Please don't, Jay," she said without taking her eyes from the sea, which at that hour looked like liquid topaz.

"I don't understand," I said. "I thought—well, I hoped—from the way you were talking and acting that your feelings toward me might be changing."

"Feelings?" she said. "Feelings change like sunlight upon the water. See, already it is not the same as when you first spoke."

And she was right, for by degrees the dawn was transforming the sea from topaz to emerald. I said, "My father once told me much the same thing."

"Your father is a wise man," said Re-Aylah.

"I cannot help the way I feel."

"Perhaps not. But feelings are not enough."

"You want riches and prestige in the tribe?" I said. "I am sorry, I have none to give you."

"Do you think me so petty? You only prove my point."

"And what exactly *is* your point?"

"Can't you see? I do not wish to be merely the object of your adoration."

"I thought women appreciated adoration."

"I am not just *a woman*, Jay. I am Re-Aylah."

"Of course you are," I said, failing to grasp her point. "Is it not enough that I think the sun rises in your hair and that your eyes put the blueness of the sky to shame?"

"No."

"Then what more do you want from me?"

"Your respect," she said and walked back inside.

None of us spoke much during breakfast. The priest was naturally a man of few words. Re-Aylah and I, on the other hand, just didn't know what to say because an awkward silence had fallen between us.

After we finished eating, we prepared to leave, packing the boat with enough food to last us many weeks, along with items from the temple so that the priest could perform his rituals while he was away. By late morning, we were ready. Before we left, though, the priest wanted to say goodbye to Moonbeam. He explained that she would not be coming with us as she did not travel by boat. We found her laying among the lambs a short distance from the house. Realizing that the priest was leaving distressed her, but he spoke comforting words and stroked her fur to calm her.

"Has she no mate?" I asked.

"She is a special breed," said the priest. "I do not think there are any more of her kind. The old order of things is passing away and the new order is lesser than the former."

"That is sad," said Re-Aylah.

Re-Aylah and I let Moonbeam and her master have some time alone together. As we walked toward the boat, I said, "When I was crossing the Havilah wilderness and dying of thirst, I saw mirages that appeared like water in the distance. They looked so beautiful and inviting. But when I reached them, I found that I was only seeing what I wanted to see."

"There is a big difference between an oasis and a mirage," she said.

"I want no more of mirages, Re-Aylah. If you will lead me to your true oasis, I will drink my fill and be satisfied." She took my arm in her hands and we walked along in silence. I dared not open my mouth again and risk spoiling the moment.

SEVENTEEN

Soon we embarked, heading due south until we were out of sight of the shoreline before turning east. There were no sailboats in those days since there was not enough wind to make them practical, so we traveled under our own power. The boat was cleverly designed, stable enough to stand up in, with a draft so shallow that it glided across the water with minimal effort. The priest took the first shift of paddling to show us how it was done. After some time, he handed the paddle to me, but I offered it instead to Re-Aylah. The priest looked at me disapprovingly until he saw how much it pleased Re-Aylah, so he said nothing.

The exhilaration of the open sea enthralled me. Not only the days, but also the nights in the boat were fantastic—especially the first. There was no moon, and stars filled the sky and the water, so that I lost all frame of reference. At times, I had to hold onto the side of the boat to steady myself. I felt as if I were floating through the heavens, almost close enough to the stars to reach out and pluck one as you would pick an apple off a tree.

Looking into the water, I saw that some of the stars appeared to be moving. I realized that it was not just the stars reflecting off the surface of the water. Sea creatures that glowed with their own light glided alongside the boat. Long into the night, I watched them with delight and even put my hand into the water to try to catch one, but they were too quick for me.

Three times each day—morning, afternoon and evening—the priest knelt down in the bottom of the boat and offered prayers to Melchi. I don't recall exactly how these prayers went, because the words made little sense to me. It would be something like:

Oh great Melchi,
Wellspring of the sea
And the seed from which all fruit is born.

The word unspoken says all.
Ancient, but ever young,
Victim of death and victor,
May your coming be soon!

And so it would go. Each night he lit candles and each morning he burned incense. I asked him what the meaning of all this was, but his answers were vague. These rituals and recitations had been passed down from the priests who had come before him since the world was young—so long ago that much of their significance had been lost. All he could say was that when Melchi came, everything would be understood.

Re-Aylah and I swam every day, sometimes more than once. The water was remarkably buoyant, and with no current or wind to fight against, we had no trouble keeping up with the boat. When we were done, we changed clothes in the tiny cabin and hung our wet clothes to dry on the sides.

Our boat attracted a great variety of sea creatures who were curious about us. When I was not paddling or swimming, I spent much time hanging over the side of the boat watching them. There were fish as small as my fingernail and some as large as the boat in all colors you could imagine. One strange animal had a mushroom shaped head and legs that hung like the branches of a willow tree and was every bit as large. I was particularly taken with a kind of sleek gray fish that was taller than me and very intelligent. They would swim alongside the boat and leap up out of the water ten feet into the air. They even let Re-Aylah and I mount their backs and ride them as a man would a horse. The priest, however, did not venture into the water.

On the fifth day, we saw a disturbance in the southern horizon. It disappeared, but a short time later we saw it again—closer. A fountain of water sprayed into the air and something swirled in the water—something quite large. The sight alarmed me, recalling Father's experience on his rite of passage. I exclaimed, "It's a leviathan!"

"I think not," said the priest. "In fact, I have not heard a report of a leviathan sighting in many years. My guess is that the great creature has passed into legend."

"Of course," I said, trying to hide my embarrassment. "I was just teasing Re-Aylah."

"That was very convincing," said Re-Aylah. "Perhaps the elders will ask you to perform it as a drama at the annual festival."

"And you can play the part of the ferocious beast," I said, and Re-Aylah laughed.

"We should be cautious nevertheless," said the priest. "This is a whale. Although they are gentle creatures, they are huge. A flick of its tail could capsize the boat."

The next time the whale surfaced it was less than a quarter-mile away and I began to get a better idea of its enormity. I hadn't thought it possible for a living creature to be larger than a behemoth. But the whale was—not in length, but certainly in girth. And there was no question in my mind that if the two could be weighed in a gigantic scale, the whale would have easily tipped the balance. We stopped paddling and sat motionless in the water, not wanting to startle him. What looked like a giant shadow passed underneath the boat, turning itself in the water and exposing its white underbelly as it glided by. I was amazed at how agile it was for its great size. Then it floated slowly to the surface and poked its head out of the water only a few feet from the boat. It was grayish blue in color, with a head the size of a building. His mouth was so wide that it could have swallowed the entire boat sideways in one gulp. On his back was an orifice by which it apparently breathed rather than through gills. It emitted a series of clicks and squeals for communication. I could not tell what he was saying, but a long, plaintive moan suggested great sadness.

"Have the effects of the Curse reached all the way to this remote place," I wondered. I reached out my hand and tried to comfort him.

"Do not despair," said the priest. "Melchi is coming. He will restore all things, so take hope!"

When the whale was some distance away, he sprang out of the water and fell back again with a crash. It made a tremendous splash and even several hundred yards away it rocked the boat so that we had to hold onto the sides.

Two days later, the sea ahead changed color to a deep red hue. As we advanced, we could see a giant mass of kelp blocking our way and extending for miles in either direction. The priest looked concerned and said, "We will have to go around it."

"That will take a lot of time," I said. "What do you think we should do, Re-Aylah?"

"I think we should try to go through it, rather than around," said Re-Aylah. "If it proves too thick we can always back out."

"I agree with Re-Aylah," I said.

So, against the advice of the priest, I guided us into the kelp bed. Immediately, we felt the drag on the boat and the priest warned us again, saying, "This is unwise."

The priest's advice notwithstanding, I continued forward. Although it took some extra exertion, we progressed several hundred yards into the kelp bed. The further we went, however, the thicker the kelp became. Our forward motion slowed to a crawl.

Re-Aylah looked at me and said, "The kelp is too thick. We should turn back."

"We can make it," I said. Not wanting to humiliate Re-Aylah—or so I thought—I stubbornly pressed onward until we were very nearly at a standstill.

She leaned over and said quietly so that the priest could not hear, "Don't do this on my account. Didn't I say that we should turn back if the way became too hard?"

"Yes you did," I said. "So if there is any blame to be affixed, it rests on my shoulders."

"You're doing it again," she muttered and sat down, annoyed. But I did not listen.

By then, gaining even a yard at a time took all the force I could muster. To my dismay, even those tiny gains began to erode. Finally, we did not move at all and I had to admit that we were stuck.

"Did I not tell you this would happen?" asked the priest.

Ignoring that comment, I jumped into the water to try to clear away the kelp. I hoped that I could yank it out of the way and clear a path. But the stalks proved to be very tough and difficult to untangle. "Do you have anything sharp?" I asked.

All the priest had were two small cooking knives. So Re-Aylah joined me in the water and we began cutting our way through the kelp bed stalk by stalk. Though the stalks were tough, the leaves were tender. Out of curiosity, I popped one into my mouth and found that it was good to eat. "At least we won't starve," I said trying to cheer Re-Aylah.

"Maybe you can *eat* your way out of here," she said.

The progress we made in this manner was agonizingly slow. We worked hard all the rest of the day and gained maybe two hundred more yards. Around sunset, we crawled into the boat exhausted. My left hand was sore from gripping the knife. Even though it was heavily callused from years of hard work, being in the water all day had softened it up. Then a terrible realization dawned on me and I said, "Let me see your hand."

Re-Aylah slowly extended her right hand. Just as I feared, it was as raw as it could be. She had never once complained, though I could see by her eyes that she was in considerable pain. "Do you have any salve?" I asked the priest. When he was out of my hearing, I said, "You don't have to prove anything to me. You've already impressed me a hundred times over."

Re-Aylah nodded, but didn't say anything, struggling as best she could to keep her chin from quivering. When the priest returned, I applied the ointment as gently as I could to her hand. She winced, but did not cry out.

After I had finished treating her wound, I said, "I'm sorry I got us into this. I should have listened to you both."

The priest put his hand on my shoulder and said, "Melchi has his own ways. In his time, he will act."

"And if not?" I asked.

"He is still Melchi."

The priest brought out some bread and wine. The wine helped to take the edge off the pain in my hand and soon I fell asleep.

Stiff and sore from the previous day's exertion, I didn't greet the new day with much joy. Our predicament did not seem any more hopeful with the light of dawn. It only reminded us that the kelp bed still extended as far as we could see. My wet clothes had not dried during the night and I exhaled audibly as I put them on. When I came out of the cabin, I saw Re-Aylah gathering her things to change.

"No," I said. "You can't go back in the water until your hand heals."

"But I want to help," she protested.

"I would insist on the same thing for my brothers," I insisted. "Or my friend."

She accepted this, but only reluctantly. I climbed over the side of the boat and started hacking at the kelp. The water stung my stiff fingers. But since I had no one to blame except myself, I couldn't complain. The priest manned the paddle. After I cleared a few yards, he would take one stroke and then wait while I cleared more.

I had not been working long when the priest said, "Something is coming."

I looked in the direction he indicated and saw a disturbance in the kelp on the left side of the boat. "What is it?" I asked.

"I do not know," said the priest. "But it's bigger than you are."

Once again, the first thought that crossed my mind was the leviathan. I scrambled back into the boat, even though I knew it would not offer much protection from such a monster. To our great relief, though, it was only a sea cow. Apparently, my splashing had aroused her curiosity and she had come to investigate. Then I got the idea to enlist her help in freeing the boat. I tried to explain it to her, even slipping back into the water to show her how to push the boat, hoping that she would mimic me. But when she swam off, I shrugged my shoulders and went back to work.

Not long afterward, however, the sea cow returned—this time with a herd of others. Apparently, she had understood after all. Two of them pushed from behind, while two more swam underneath the boat and lifted it up on their backs so we were barely skimming the water. The others in the herd swam alongside us and rotated in when the first ones tired. With their impressive power, we made steady progress and by midday, we cleared the edge of the kelp. The whole herd made great squealing noises, then turned and swam back to their home.

After they were gone, I stood up in the bow of the boat and looked out over the open sea ahead. To no one in particular, I said, "Well, that wasn't so bad." As soon as the words were out of my mouth, a wet tunic hit me in the back of the neck. I didn't have to turn and look to know who threw it.

After two weeks of traveling steadily eastward, we reached what the priest called Cape Shur, a large prominence of rock that extended far into the sea. We landed in the bay that it sheltered and re-supplied our provisions because we had eaten all of our fresh fruit and we were starting to run low on fresh water. My legs were happy to be on dry land even for a short while, but we did not linger because we did not want to be seen. Within a couple of hours, we were on our way again, carefully navigating our way through the submerged rocks that ringed the cape.

From there, we began to bear northward. When we had been at sea about a month, stopping only once more to re-stock our provisions, we reached a great coral bed that sparkled from vivid rose to hyacinth blue. We picked our way carefully, as some grew all the way to the surface and we did not want to risk running aground. Some of the islands in the archipelago were large enough to have gotten out of the boat and walked around upon. Stretching our legs would have been a relief after weeks in the boat, but we decided against it for fear of damaging the fragile coral. I did spend some time swimming around the reefs. The water stung my eyes a bit when I opened them, but the sights I beheld were well worth it. The fish were more brightly colored than those of the Gihon and of incredible variety. They showed no fear of me whatsoever and swarmed around me in fantastic numbers, flashing in the shimmering shafts of sunlight. In one place, a hungry grouper mistook my trousers for seaweed and tried to eat them. We had quite a struggle, which I was losing badly. But just as I was about to concede my pants for want of air, he apparently decided that they didn't taste very good and spat them out, sparing me unbearable embarrassment in front of my traveling companions.

When we were past the coral beds, we made excellent time for the next three days. The priest reckoned by the stars that it was time to turn back to the west. He deliberately overshot the mouth of the Gihon so that we could approach it from the north, which we all agreed would be safer.

Entering the Gihon undetected, however, proved impossible because the area was inhabited. About a dozen men from the village situated on the northern bank met us in boats and forced us to land. As we went ashore, all I could think of was Gomer and the pearl bandits.

Eighteen

The village of Zeitgon, as that place was known, consisted of about four dozen thatched huts surrounding a wooden dock for loading and unloading boats. The villagers were a rough-looking lot of brooding characters descended apparently from some other son of Adam besides Seth or Cain. And from the looks of his offspring, he wasn't the pride of his father.

"We only wish to pass up the river in peace," said the priest.

The swarthy man in charge, who wore a patch over his right eye, said, "And where would you be heading?"

"Our destination would be our own concern," I said. "But to show our good will, I will tell you that we are on our way to Nephil."

I could see out of the corner of my eye that Re-Aylah was questioning why I had revealed this. But Nephil was the only significant place I knew of along the Gihon, so it would not be difficult to guess where we were going. I hoped that by openly disclosing what was easily presumed, it would appear we had nothing to hide. I also thought that if these people were under the control of Nephil, we might be able to use our close relations with Ben-Tubal to our advantage. But as soon as the words were out of my mouth, I could tell that they had the opposite effect.

"Nephil, is it!" said one of the men. "What good will is that? I say we kill them all right now."

There were murmurs of approval in the crowd, but the leader appealed for calm and said, "That proves nothing. I've been to Nephil myself, but that doesn't mean I'm in league with Ben-Tubal."

Before I could respond, Re-Aylah spoke up quickly. "If that is your concern, then put your minds at rest. I have only recently been imprisoned by one of his top men. I managed to secure my freedom and am now on my way home to rejoin my people."

While Re-Aylah was speaking, an old woman pushed her way through the crowd of men. Bent but not frail, she pointed her bony finger at me and said, "I know who you are."

"Well," said their leader. "Tell us so that we may benefit from your wisdom. Or shut up and get out of the way."

"If your father were alive, you wouldn't talk to me that way," croaked the woman. "Nevertheless, I will tell you—not because you're my son, but for the good of the cause. I saw this man among the tents of Pashbah some months ago. This is a son of Noah."

I could tell by the grunts and scowls of the crowd that this wasn't going to count in my favor either. Regardless, there was no use trying to deny it, so I said, "You are correct in saying so. But you have me at a disadvantage because I do not know you or your people."

"I am Nasha," she said. "And the Zeitgonians lead the resistance movement in the coastal lands. When the time is right, we will rise up and overthrow the Nephilim and regain control of our land."

"You talk too much, old woman," said the man with the patch. "Now we *will* have to kill them for what they know."

"And this is my son Havijam," said Nasha undaunted. "Although the way he speaks to me, you would never know that I am his mother." Next, she regarded Re-Aylah and said, "So you are the one he was looking for? I don't blame you for running out on the fat pig Baldag, though I'm not sure you have improved your lot."

"It's not what you think," I said.

"You're not married then?" said Havijam. "Good. Then I will claim her for myself."

"What Jayfeth means, is that he and I are only engaged to be married," said Re-Aylah.

I looked at Re-Aylah and tried not to betray my astonishment, though I knew that she was only trying to protect her virtue from the brute Havijam.

One of the other men spoke up and said, "Remember his kinsman who came looking for pearls? I bet this one is the same way—weak and stupid."

"Jayfeth is not weak," said Re-Aylah, taking hold of my arm.

"What about the other part?" I whispered.

"Just go with me on this," she muttered. And then she said out loud, "We love each other and look forward to many happy years together. I must decline your offer."

"How about a fight?" said Havijam, his one good eye flashing ferociously wherever it fell. "Best man gets the girl."

"The wise man is not hasty to resort to violence," Re-Aylah said with remarkable calm in her voice. At the same time, though, I could feel her fingernails digging into my arm. "We're peaceful people, aren't we Jay."

"Yes," I said, steadying my voice over the pain in my arm. "We came in peace and would like to depart in peace as well."

Havijam moved closer and said, "A coward, eh?"

"A servant of the Lord," I said, struggling for calm.

"The god you serve must be very weak if you won't even fight for your betrothed."

"Re-Aylah isn't a prize to be won in a fight. And as for the Lord, he is not weak, but patient and merciful. However, you will taste his power soon enough if you don't repent of your violence, because a doom is coming on all the world."

At this, he slapped me hard across my left cheek. It stung like fire and it was all I could do to restrain myself. But what little good sense I possessed— and Re-Aylah's hand—held me back from letting Havijam provoke me.

"Just as I said," Havijam retorted. "A coward."

"This is not the welcome that Dayak said we'd receive here," said Re-Aylah. It was a blind guess, and she had calculated the moment of disclosure for maximum effect. When Havijam hesitated, she pressed the point. "You do know who I'm talking about, don't you?"

"What difference would it make if I did?" said Havijam.

"None," said Re-Aylah, "unless saving a man's life still counts for something. At least Dayak seemed to think so when Jay saved his life."

The murmuring began again, but this time it was directed toward Havijam, who was beginning to have second thoughts. "You might have said as much to begin with. We could have avoided this ... misunderstanding."

"I didn't want to brag," I said.

"I've decided to let you go," said Havijam. Then he turned to Re-Aylah and said, "Too bad you're already spoken for. He's not half the man I am. I could make you happy."

"Not unless you jumped off this dock with a rock around your neck," Re-Aylah said under her breath.

To all of us, Havijam said, "We have many spies. If you divulge anything you have seen or heard here today to the wrong person, you will feel the knife of Havijam!" From the menace in his voice, I didn't take that as an idle threat.

Without another word, we three entered our boat and embarked as hastily as possible. "Give our regards to Gomer," Havijam called out after us, which brought a chorus of laughter from the crowd. But at least we were away unharmed.

As we headed up the river, I said, "All right, I'll admit it. Making the connection between Dayak and the Zeitgonians was brilliant."

"Thank you," said Re-Aylah. "And I'm proud of you, too. I know that it was difficult to let him provoke you like that without responding. But if you'd done what he wanted you to do, things might not have turned out so well."

"I could have taken him," I said.

"And all the rest of them, too?"

She had me there, so I changed the subject. "By the way, what you said about us being engaged ... ?"

"The choice between Havijam and you *was* difficult," Re-Aylah said with a wry smile.

"You shouldn't tease about something so important."

"What makes you think I'm teasing?"

"That's the problem—I never know!"

"Isn't that part of the fun?"

"Fun for you," I said indignantly. "But I would prefer that you just say plainly what you mean."

"All right," said Re-Aylah. "If your proposal still stands, I accept."

"Please don't torment me if you don't really mean it."

"I can't say it more plainly than that, Jay."

"You're serious?"

"I wouldn't ask so many questions if I were you," she said, dismissing my inquiry with a wave of her hand.

Then the priest, who had been silent all that time, said, "I know little of love and affairs of the heart. Since I renounced this world, I have kept myself from such things. If the silly talk and antics I have witnessed on this voyage are any indication of what I have missed, then I have chosen wisely indeed."

"This is nothing," I laughed. "You should have seen us when we didn't like each other!"

Where the Gihon met the sea, we found ourselves on a wide, sluggish river that seemed hardly the same as the one I had known from my youth. However, after a week of traveling through lowlands lined with moss-draped cypress trees, like so many gnarled and bearded old men guarding the river, the Gihon narrowed and the current strengthened, making paddling more difficult. The number of dwellings we passed by increased, and since we thought it best to be seen as little as possible, we hid the boat in an isolated tributary, covered it with brush, and continued our journey on foot. Knowing that the area surrounding the river was more likely to be inhabited, we struck out north, away from the river, for a day before turning back to the west. The priest could not travel very fast or far in a day, so we made slow progress through the Lower Gihon Valley. But with no further hindrance, we finally arrived safely back at our camp in a matter of weeks. There was much rejoicing at our return and even more about the news of our engagement.

My first glimpse of the ark, however, tempered my happiness somewhat. My brothers had not been idle and had made considerable progress while I was away. The time of the ark's completion was drawing ever nearer. In my heart, I feared what that meant.

Nineteen

It will be obvious that my rescue plans—such as they were—had still another glaring flaw that had yet to be reckoned with. They completely failed to take into consideration the reaction of the one who had caused all the trouble to begin with, namely Baldag. My sole focus had been rescuing Re-Aylah and returning to my family, and I had made no plans about what I would do beyond that point. Foolishly, I deceived myself into thinking that, having outwitted Baldag once, we would be left alone. Of course, it did not take him very long to learn that Re-Aylah had returned. On the third day following, we awoke to find ourselves surrounded by a hundred armed men and Baldag himself heading the contingent. We were trapped between our tents and the ark, with no evident means of escape.

"Hand over the girl," Baldag demanded.

"I wouldn't hand one of our goats over to you," I said with contempt.

"Let me restate that," said Baldag, with deadly glee. "Hand over the girl and I will entertain your plea for leniency, instead of killing your whole family right now."

"We won't beg for your mercy," said Ham disdainfully. "Abducting the girl against her will was a serious offense. You should be begging for our mercy instead. Besides, we all know that this is an empty threat. You wouldn't dare to harm the daughter of Ben-Tubal. And we are his kinsmen by marriage."

"Are you so sure he would object?" said Baldag. "He is most displeased that his daughter has betrayed him."

"What!" said Jirah. "Are you going to let him talk about me that way?"

"We'll handle this, my little Tigress," said Ham.

"Perhaps I can help change His Excellency's attitude back in your favor, because you know I have His Excellency's ear," said Baldag. "But first give me my wife."

"She's not your wife," I said. "And she never will be."

I felt Re-Aylah slipping past me and I caught her by the arm just in time. "Let me go," she said, trying to shake free. But I held on tightly.

"Hah!" Baldag sneered. "Now who's forcing her to do something against her will? She wants to go with me."

"It was a mistake for me to come back," said Re-Aylah. "I didn't think he would go this far. I'm endangering all of you by staying here."

"I don't care," I said. "I would rather die than hand you over to him!"

"And what about your mother and brothers and their wives?" asked Re-Aylah. "Would you sacrifice them, too? I can't let you do that."

"I would rather fight," said Ham as the circle of men began to close in around us.

"It's me they want," Re-Aylah pleaded. "Turn me over and save yourselves."

"No," said Shem. "Let's retreat into the ark. We'll be safe in there."

The next moment we were backing up the ramp. Mother led Re-Aylah by one arm, Ohlibah took her by the other, and the priest pushed from behind, while my brothers and I placed ourselves between them and Baldag's advance.

"What about my honor?" said Jirah, lingering with us. "He has insulted me."

"Jirah has a point," said Ham. "This does seem cowardly to me."

"It's three against a hundred," I said. "My apologies to your wife, but that's not very good odds."

"What protection will the ark provide anyway?" said Ham. "It's not even fully enclosed yet."

"In here, the Lord himself will protect us," said Shem.

Baldag laughed as he started up the ramp. "If you think this miserable pile of sticks will stop me, a curse be upon you and your god! I take whatever I want and do whatever it pleases me to do."

"We'll see about that!" shouted one of the men with Baldag, stepping in front of him.

"What? Giblith!" exclaimed Baldag as his eyes went wide with terror. I remembered the man I had seen with Keriath all those years ago when the Nephilim first came to Cush. Apparently, he had infiltrated Baldag's guard and had been waiting for the right moment to exact his revenge. Giblith was powerfully built like his father Upschad—the kind of man that other men look up to. Baldag's face went pale as he realized that his doom had befallen him. Before he could react, Giblith wrestled him down the ramp. They rolled down to the ground with Baldag fighting wildly for his life. But Baldag's years of indulgence had caught up to him at last. And Giblith, in the heat of a man robbed of all he held dear, easily overpowered him. I saw the flash of a knife, but only for an instant before Giblith, with one upward thrust, plunged it deep into Baldag's chest. "That's for Minnah!" he cried. And those were the last words that Baldag ever heard.

All this happened so fast that Baldag's men were temporarily stunned. His chief henchman recovered quickly, however, and before we could rally to Giblith's aid, he stabbed Giblith in the back with his spear. Several other men started toward them to finish Giblith off before Jirah cried, "Stop it!"

An enraged Nephila is not a person to be ignored and the men hesitated as she continued. "Leave that man alone. He is the only one here today who has acted honorably." She glared at Ham who was standing dumbly beside her. "Baldag has misled you into thinking that he was doing His Excellency's bidding in many shady dealings with the sons of Seth, even going so far as leading you into committing an act of treason today."

The word "treason" had a dire effect on the men. They all knew the penalty and the dread showed on their faces. One of them spoke up and said, "We was only follerin' orders, Yer 'Ighness. Me an' da boys never went in for da rough stuff. But we din't 'ave much choice 'cause disobeyin' orders 'int tolerated neither."

"That's what I thought," said Jirah. "Now listen to me. All of you who are loyal to His Excellency gather around me and defend your princess. And all who want to be counted as traitors can rally around your slain commander. Perhaps you will be lucky enough to die in battle instead of being flailed alive for your crimes."

The vast majority wasted no time in forming a semi-circle around the ramp, spears pointing outward. The remaining handful of Baldag's loyalists, seeing they were badly outnumbered, fled over the bridge into Nod, some on horseback and some on foot, led by the man who had struck down Giblith.

Jirah said to the man who had spoken up, "I want the names of all those traitors. They will be tracked down and dealt with according to the laws of the land."

"Yes, Yer 'Ighness," he said.

"And as for those of you who have chosen wisely, I will speak to His Excellency about an amnesty decree, provided you have not committed any further crimes."

"That's my little Tigress," said Ham, nudging me. "Very impressive, don't you think?"

"You haven't heard the end of this yet, Bear Cub," said Jirah quietly to him. And her tone made it made clear he hadn't.

"Bear Cub?" I said.

"It's ... personal," said Ham.

"I don't want to know," I said. "We should see to Giblith anyway. He's badly hurt."

Giblith had slumped to the ground beside Baldag and was staring blankly at the sky, mumbling. Shem and the priest examined his wound. Stepping back a few paces, out of Giblith's hearing, Shem simply shook his head.

"We have physicians in Nephil," said Jirah. "Perhaps they can help."

"I have some training in the healing arts myself," said the priest. "He is mortally wounded. I am sure of it."

"How long does he have?" asked Ham.

"He is strong," said the priest. "He might last a few hours, but no more."

"So all we can do is try to ease his suffering?" I said.

"He keeps calling for his father," said Shem. "Maybe that would help."

"Upschad's village is not that far away by horseback," I said. "If these men ride their horses hard, maybe they could bring Upschad back in time to see his son one last time."

At the mention of Upschad's name, the men who were still standing around hung their heads and shuffled their feet uncomfortably.

"Speak up if you know something," commanded Jirah.

"Well, dat's a sad tale dere, Yer 'Ighness," said their leader. "'Int no one dere to send fer no more. Dat same feller what done in da son, done in da pap, 'bout six months back. Pois'n it was. Made it look like old age, but it weren't. We was real broke up to 'ear it 'cause he weren't a bad sort. Weren't no cause fer it. Dey gotta new chief now and he aren't likely to come trottin' down 'ere to cry over this feller, if ya' know what I means."

I was very sorry to hear about Upschad, though I can't say I was surprised. I'm sure Moshabaya and the others were only too happy to see their leader gone—and may have even been conspirators in the crime.

We carried Giblith inside the ark and tried to make him as comfortable as possible. His labored breathing continued, but he didn't respond to us until about mid-afternoon when he opened his eyes. His voice was quite weak and raspy when he gave us this charge, "Tell Minnah I forgive her. Tell her I still love her."

"I will," I said. "I'll do everything I can to find her and tell her. I promise."

"Father, I'm coming to you now," said Giblith. And those were his final words before he died.

"He saved my life," said Re-Aylah, deeply moved.

"He saved all of us," I said. "Upschad would have been proud."

When we emerged from the ark, we saw that no one had come to claim Baldag's body. Shem said that we should see to his burial as well as Giblith's. Even though I knew he was right, I was loathe to touch Baldag's corpse. But somehow we got it loaded into a cart alongside Giblith and carried them about two miles upstream to a quiet hillside meadow overlooking the river.

As we covered their lifeless bodies with stones, I felt great pity for Giblith. He should have been chief for many years. He should have been happy. He should have fathered many children and watched them grow up in peace. Instead, his life had been ruined by betrayal and then tragically cut short.

Even toward Baldag, I did not feel as I would have expected. For though I despised him in life, I felt no joy in his death. Ham, however, showed no sympathy. "What a fitting end Baldag has come to. He got what he deserved."

"It isn't good to gloat over the death of your enemy," said Shem. "This man suffered from the Curse just as we all do. May we not fall prey to the same evil that overtook Baldag."

"It's ironic," I said. "They were bitter enemies in life. And now in death they lay side by side."

"There's probably a lesson to be learned there," said Shem.

"That the same fate overtakes the righteous and the wicked?" said Ham. "It seems unjust to me."

"The wise men say that it will go better with the righteous," said Shem.

"If only we knew for sure," I said.

TWENTY

Jirah wasted no time in seeking to have her good name restored among the people. On the following day, Ben-Tubal issued a proclamation. Upon investigation, Baldag had been discovered to be a traitor and disloyal to His Excellency. He disavowed any connection with the treacherous acts committed by Baldag and completely exonerated our family in the matter concerning Re-Aylah. Furthermore, he said that any accusations made regarding Jirah and her alleged disloyalty were false and slanderous. Anyone who was caught repeating them would be punished most severely. Thus ended the unfortunate saga of Baldag and Giblith, except for one piece of unfinished business—the promise to find Minnah and relate to her Giblith's dying words. The problem was that I had no idea where to find her.

Not long afterward, Father returned unlooked for. We were overjoyed to see him, but alarmed to see how thin and haggard he looked. The extended mission to Nod had not been easy for him.

When I told Father all that had transpired since I had last seen him, he was amazed and praised God for watching over us. Hearing about Lamech and Gomer, though, and the wretched conditions in which they were living at the mining camps, distressed him greatly. Before my tale was told, I knew that he had already made up his mind to go there.

In turn, Father related all that had happened to him. He had traveled throughout the land of Nod, warning of the coming doom, but to no avail. In every town and village he visited, the message was rejected and the people refused to repent. He had been beaten on three different occasions (a detail he told us boys later but spared Mother from the telling). Nevertheless, he remained confident that if only the Lord would stay his hand long enough, eventually the message would prevail.

When Father had finished, I said, "I have saved the best piece of news for last. Re-Aylah has consented to marry me."

"I always had a feeling about you two," said Father, delighted. Not only was he quite fond of Re-Aylah, the fact that I was still unmarried at my age had been weighing on his mind for many years. He hugged both of us and then said to Re-Aylah, "I am thinking that we should seek your father's blessing upon this marriage. I know that relations with my brother haven't been what they ought to be, but perhaps this will bring healing to our family at last."

Re-Aylah and I agreed with his counsel, though not without secret misgivings on my part—and even more so when Re-Aylah persuaded him that it would be best for him to remain behind. I would have welcomed Father's presence because the thought of facing Irad and his clan without him filled me with dread. But I was so anxious to please her that I would have gone along with anything she said.

The next day, Re-Aylah and I set out along the Gihon Road. As we walked along, I thought about what I was going to say and tried to guess how Irad would receive us. News of our coming apparently arrived before we did, for a delegation awaited us when we arrived at his camp on the third day following. At first, I hoped that they were coming to welcome us—until we drew close enough that I could see their faces. Then I knew it was not going to go well.

Re-Aylah started toward Irad to greet him with a kiss. But when he scowled at her with contempt, she shrank back.

"Greetings, Uncle," I said, but my voice didn't sound nearly as stout-hearted as I had imagined beforehand. "Re-Aylah has consented to marry me and we have come to seek your blessing upon our marriage. Please accept these gifts in seal of the bonding of our families."

Ignoring the gifts I set before him, Irad walked up to Re-Aylah. Now that our intentions had been revealed, my hopes rose momentarily that they would be reconciled. But his icy scowl quickly dashed that notion.

"Father, please ..." Re-Aylah started to say, but Irad spat in her face. Then the whole clan turned their backs on us and walked away.

Re-Aylah stood bravely while I gently wiped the saliva from her face. Then she could control herself no longer and cried bitterly while I held her. We left our ceremonial engagement gifts laying on the road and trudged back toward Nephil in silence.

The evening after we returned to the ark, Mother came to me while I was tending the livestock and said, "I would like to talk to you about Re-Aylah."

Since it was not like Re-Aylah to let someone else speak for her, I immediately became concerned. "Please don't tell me that she has changed her mind about marrying me."

"No, she didn't say that," said Mother, choosing her words carefully. "But she is in deep distress about being disowned by her family."

"I can understand that. And as her husband, I will do everything in my power to comfort her."

"But given what she is going through now, do you think the time is right for marriage?"

"What do you mean?" I said. "Doesn't she want to go through with it?"

"She has given her pledge and is prepared to fulfill it," said Mother. "However, I'm not so sure she's ready. If her heart is broken concerning her family, how can she give her whole heart to you?"

"But Mother, don't you see how desperate I am? I would give anything for even a small piece of her heart."

"And would you really be content with that?"

"Yes!" I said. But as she waited for me to think about it, I knew the question deserved a more thoughtful answer. Finally, I said, "No, I would soon want more."

"Then my advice to you is to not rush into this. Give her some time to heal."

"But what if she changes her mind? Getting her to this point has been no easy feat."

"Easy?" said Mother. "I've told you before not to expect love to be easy. Besides, would you really want her to marry you under these circumstances?"

"I would want her to marry me under any circumstances."

"Even if part of her feels like she's being forced into it because she has nowhere else to go?"

I sighed. "I know you are right, but it's hard."

"Look, Jayfeth. Your father and I have been happy these many years because each of us has always put the other's needs ahead of our own. There's a time to cling with all your might, but there's also a time to let go. And believe me, the letting go is by far the harder part. I think you need to examine your motives because all I hear you talking about is what you want and what you need. I warn you, my son, if you are not careful, you risk destroying the very love you long for."

These words stung me. I struggled with them late into the night.

The next day I went to Re-Aylah and said, "I release you from your pledge to marry me."

"What? Don't tease me," she said, caught off guard by my clumsy bluntness. "Teasing is my privilege, remember?"

"I do remember. But this isn't a joke—I wish it were. What I mean is, the man who sought to harm you is dead and you are under no obligation to marry me. You are free to go or free to stay or free to do whatever you decide to do."

"I'm afraid you've taken me by surprise," she said, turning away. "I don't know whether to feel grateful or hurt."

I reached out, tentatively, and touched her shoulder. "I'm not trying to make you feel either way. I'm ... I'm just trying to do what's best for you."

"This wasn't your first marriage proposal. How do I know it won't be your last?"

"I'm going with Father on a long journey to the mining camps. If I return ..."

"You mean 'when' you return," she said.

"*When* I return, we can talk about our future together if that is your wish."

"And your wish as well," she said. "It's possible that you may not always feel the same way toward me."

"That thought has never occurred to me," I said in all earnestness.

"You're a good man, Jay," Re-Aylah said. "I don't know what is wrong with me that I don't seize the opportunity before it passes me by." She pulled away and I let her go. I saw little more of her prior to our departure.

Father spent much time during the days before we left talking with the priest. When I had some time alone with him, I asked, "What do you make of the priest's beliefs?"

"Honestly, I don't really know," said Father. "He acknowledges the Lord as the Most High God and this Melchi he speaks of is closely bound up in that belief. But as for who or what Melchi is, I cannot say. I don't think the priest himself knows for sure."

About a week later, as the priest was walking around the work site, he happened to run his hand along a rough cut board and got a splinter. It was not a serious wound at all, but the priest had a profound reaction. Looking at his bleeding palm, he mused, "This means something."

"Yes," said Ham. "It means that you should be more careful where men are working."

Shem glared at Ham and then tended to the priest's wound. Afterward, the priest surprised us by announcing that he would be leaving the next day.

"But if you believe our message about the coming doom, why don't you stay with us and be saved?" asked Father.

"I do believe it, though my eyes will not see it," said the priest. "A new order is coming, but I belong to the ancient order of things. Besides, Moonbeam will be most anxious until I return."

"What of Melchi?" said Father. "Aren't you concerned that your priesthood will die out?"

"The priesthood of Melchi is not of this world, nor does it depend on my service," said the priest. "The priesthood will last forever because Melchi lives forever."

As we could see that his mind was firmly made up, we did not try further to persuade him. Jirah procured a small boat for him from Ben-Tubal and we stocked him with provisions for his return journey. We strongly urged him to allow us to accompany him, but he insisted on going alone. With no small amount of sadness, we saw him on his way the following morning. As he departed, Re-Aylah whispered something in his ear that made him smile, but no amount of coaxing would make her reveal what she had said. I was glad, though, to see her acting more like herself. We waved to the priest from the stone bridge as the Gihon carried him past the wall of Nephil and around the bend of the river out of sight. We did not see him again.

TWENTY-ONE

ather and I had been making our own preparations. I didn't relish the thought of returning to the mining camps, but neither could I bear the thought of my grandfather and uncle living in that awful place. I hoped that Father could rescue them where I had failed. In my eyes, there was nothing he could not do. Within the week, we set out for the mines of Havilah. Rather than heading south as I expected, we traveled up the Gihon Road until we reached the Latham Road before crossing the Gihon. During his many wanderings Father had discovered a northern route through Nod. The distance was greater, but the way was not so desolate, which Father ascribed to its closer proximity to Eden. Whenever we came to any inhabited area, Father would stop to preach. No matter how hard he tried to persuade them, however, they continued to ignore his warnings.

On the third day after we crossed the Gihon, we came to a sizeable village on the far bank of the upper Euphrates, which we crossed by way of a shallow ford. We were met there with open hostility, and one man in particular seemed intent on inciting the people against us. "This is the man who has brought this curse upon us," he shouted. "Ever since he came the first time, our women have been childless."

The crowd grumbled in agreement. But when Father spoke again, his voice was remarkably steady. "There *is* a curse on us and we all bear part of the responsibility for it. So if you want to know why the Lord has brought this judgment against you, look no further than yourselves. But if you repent of your wickedness and devote yourself to Him, you will receive blessings instead of curses."

"See!" said the man. "He admits that his god is responsible."

"My god is God," said Father. "What you call gods are not gods at all, but only bits of wood and stone and metal, though I will admit that there are dark powers behind some of these. But they should be avoided at all costs."

"Now he insults our gods," said the man. "What do you say?"

"Rid the earth of him!" came the reply.

They picked up stones and hurled them at him. One of them caught Father in the forehead and opened up a gash over his right eye. He staggered backward, but didn't fall. Then he steadied himself, and when he addressed the crowd again, it was with such power that the people shrank back. "Listen you scoffers! Why the Lord bears with your rebellion so long is beyond my understanding. But do not be deceived into thinking he will not act, because it is only out of his great mercy that he did not destroy you long ago. His forbearance will not last forever, though, and you are only storing up punishment for yourselves. This present judgment will seem as nothing compared with the one to come!"

With blood streaming down his face, the prophet strode through the midst of the crowd. No one dared to lay a hand on him, so great was his wrath. As I followed along several paces behind, even I was afraid to speak to him until we were a long way down the road.

We continued on without further incident into less populated lands. Since Father seemed ill-disposed to talk, I occupied my mind with the words of the man at the village about the curse that had fallen upon them. Since I had been isolated from village life so long, I wondered how widespread the barrenness might be. And what of my own family? Although my brothers had both been married for some time, neither of their wives had yet born children. As I thought about it, I could not remember how long it had been since I last heard the sound of a child's laughter. When Father's wrath had subsided, I asked him what he thought about it.

His face became very grave and all he would say was, "I fear that we're running out of time."

After several more days of traveling almost due west, the flinty hill country grew more rugged as we approached the southeastern foothills of the Eden Plateau. Then one afternoon, we could hear running water ahead—a sweet and unexpected sound in Nod. Emerging through a narrow pass, we saw the river tumbling over the rocks from high above toward the plain below. An arch of solid rock just above us spanned the river, framing the scene like a temple doorway. I looked at Father and he read the question on my face. "It's the Pishon."

"Not this," I said. "The Pishon I crossed at the animal compound was as dirty and dead as it could be."

"The river does not defile itself," said Father. "It begins as clean water, regardless of what happens downstream."

The arch stood about thirty feet high and twice that wide from base to base. The surface was smooth but not polished, and wide enough for two companions to walk comfortably abreast. It was not constructed of blocks like the one in Nephil, but was all of one great stone with the surrounding rock. Neither was any mark of chisel or hammer to be seen, yet it could not have been more perfectly suited for the purpose of crossing the stream. In a way I could not explain, it reminded me of the causeway I had seen many scores of miles away to the north of Eden.

"Is it natural?" I asked. "Or was it made?"

"Both, perhaps," said Father. "I think it belongs to the first days—a time when you would not have made such a distinction."

We camped there for the night, but lit no fire. Somehow it didn't seem fitting in that place. The music of the Pishon cleansed the air of all other sounds, lulling me into a peaceful sleep, and I rested better than I ever had before in Nod.

The next morning, I awoke early, greatly refreshed, which I suspect was due to some healing property of the water. Father showed similar effects, looking as if he had shed years of care overnight. Needless to say, we were reluctant to leave that place, but our pressing errand did not allow us to linger.

However, it was not my desire to stay that made me hesitate to set my foot on the arch to cross to the other side. Rather, it seemed to me to be a holy place. A sense of unworthiness to be treading upon such sacred ground gave me pause. It was a feeling vaguely reminiscent of what I had experienced on the causeway, but not nearly so intense. Father assured me, though, that it would be all right and I followed slowly behind him. It occurs to me now that something about him ever belonged to such timeless places.

The summit of the arch afforded us a spectacular view. Below us, the Pishon splashed down through the foothills at a pleasantly noisy slope from the Eden Plateau. If only I could have had a glimpse of the fountain from which it issued! To our left, we could see a wide expanse of the plain below and the opening arc of the Pishon's great loop to the east before turning back to the southwest and heading for the sea. Away to the west and south spread the Havilah wasteland. Even from a great distance, its utter barrenness was apparent. As we walked along, I said, "Do you know what happened there in Havilah? I've never seen such desolation."

"Not for certain," said Father. "But the elders used to recount legends about the awesome powers of the mighty ones of old."

"Mighty ones? You mean mighty men or … ?"

"'Or what' is a good question. Apparently, they could take the form of men, but they weren't really human. They came from beyond this world. Some say they were appointed by God to administer certain affairs of this world after the Fall. Some were said to have been cast down to earth in the rebellion or summoned by the dark arts of men. Regardless of how they got here, legend has it that they taught men many things, including the art of making strange fires. They say they could make them burn cold or consume some things and not others. So, when men first began to covet gold, they used this skill to clear the land and make it easier to get at the gold. But men's thirst for knowledge and wealth has always been insatiable. In their greed, they turned to ever more dangerous practices and smote the land with such a force that it wrought a devastation that has not healed for many generations."

The path led downward toward the plain. We zigzagged between the rocks, never straying far from the noisy Pishon. I said, "When I was a boy, you once told me that not all knowledge is good. I never quite understood what you meant, because how could knowing the truth be bad? Is this the kind of knowledge you were talking about?"

"It's not so much that some knowledge is bad," said Father. "It's that some is beyond us. When you were just a little boy toddling around the camp, I didn't let you swing an axe—not because the axe was bad, but because you were so small that I didn't want you hurting yourself."

"I can understand that."

"But there is even more to it than that. You have always counted yourself unfortunate because you are not a seer. Yet, there is a side to it that you don't perceive. Before the Lord spoke to me, I hadn't a care in the world. But once God revealed the coming doom, I have carried a heavy burden ever since. How can I rest from building the ark and warning others while I possess such knowledge? And because you know this, too, you have a burden as well. And so do all who hear the sound of my voice—though I pray it is for their salvation rather than increasing their guilt. That's the point. With knowledge comes responsibility. To know a thing is to be responsible for a thing—and to be judged accordingly. Such is man's lot ever since the Mother and Father of All ate from the forbidden tree of the knowledge of good and evil."

"Surely you are not suggesting that ignorance is better," I said.

"No, but the man who would be wise must constantly strive to use his knowledge for good. And that is a difficult path to follow, because there are ways that may seem good to a man which result in destruction. Then his so-called wisdom proves to be folly."

We emerged from the foothills by midday. Reluctantly, we left the Pishon Valley behind and set out across the plain. The land grew barren again and we conserved our rations accordingly. We picked up a road leading southwest, which Father felt confident would take us to the mining camps in four or five more days. We had not gone far, however, when we saw a solitary figure shuffling toward us in the distance. Father and I looked at each other and we both knew immediately that it was Grandfather. The fact that he was alone could only have meant one thing.

We ran to Grandfather and embraced him, but our relief at seeing him quickly turned to sorrow.

"Where is Gomer?" asked Father, though we already suspected the answer.

Grandfather just shook his head.

"I should have come sooner!" Father cried as the realization pierced his heart. "I should not have delayed!"

"There was nothing you could have done," said Grandfather, consoling him with a hand upon his shoulder. "He wasn't himself for a long time."

"Why should I be surprised that I cannot save the people," Father lamented. "I couldn't even save my own brother."

"I know, my son. It's a bitter cup we have been made to drink. But perhaps you will find some comfort in this. Before Gomer died, he repented, though he paid bitterly for his freedom from grack. When the madness left him, we escaped from the mining camp and were returning home. Alas, he had no physical strength left to go on with. Two days ago, he just laid down and died. But I say better to die free than live in that wretched condition. You saw him, Jayfeth. Do I not speak truly?"

"Yes, Grandfather," I said. "It was horrible. Leaving you both there like that was one of the hardest things I've ever done."

"But you did the right thing and saved my Sunshine," said Grandfather. "And let me tell you, they weren't happy when they found out she was gone."

"That didn't help Uncle Gomer," I said.

"Oh, but you did help him," said Grandfather. "He was better after you came. Seeing you sparked memories of his former life. I am convinced that was what gave him encouragement to throw off his bondage."

Hearing this gave me some consolation and I hoped that Gomer had found in death the peace that eluded him in life.

After we ate and drank a little, we began to slowly retrace our steps. When we came to a crossroad, Grandfather started to take the eastern path, but Father tried to steer him gently northward. "No, Papa. This is the better way. That road leads toward Enoch-Nod."

"Yes, I know," said Grandfather, resisting his assistance. "I have traveled widely in this accursed land. I know very well where it leads."

"You must not go *there*," said Father. "I have not even ventured there myself because I have heard that it is evil beyond description."

"Do you think I don't know that?" said Grandfather, becoming more agitated. "That is why I *must* go. Someone must confront the Sons of the Gods about the suffering they are inflicting upon the people. Enoch the Righteous did it and drove those demons into submission for generations. Now someone must speak up for this generation. My time on this earth grows short. I have nothing to lose."

Father paused for a moment while he weighed those words. "What you are saying is true. But I do not think you are the one to go. In your condition, you might not even withstand the journey—much less a confrontation with such as these."

"Do not underestimate a grieving father's wrath."

"I know you're grieving," said Father gently. "But don't throw your life away in vain when you are sorely needed at home. Your son Irad has made me his enemy. Perhaps he will listen to you. Let's return home so that you may rest and recover. Then I will go to Enoch-Nod and do all that you have said."

Having already lost one son, Grandfather could not resist this argument. Slowly he nodded in agreement. Whatever remained of his strength he would use to reconcile his surviving sons. With one last look in the direction of Enoch-Nod, he raised his eyes to the heavens, lifted his hands and said, "These evildoers have robbed me of my son, O Lord. Do not let Gomer's death and all the other misery they have caused go unavenged!"

We returned by way of the Pishon arch. Grandfather was very weak, and even at our very slow pace, the ascent was almost too much for him. But his efforts were well rewarded with the full day we spent under the span. The Pishon cascade proved tonic for him and he was much the better for having lingered there. When we set out again, he had a spring in his step that I had not seen for many years.

"I've always liked traveling," he said as we went on our way. "You know what I'm talking about, don't you boy."

"Yes, Grandfather, I do. There's nothing quite like the thrill of seeing new places. And always the promise of something interesting just around the next turn."

"I see a lot of myself in you."

"I take that as a compliment."

"Half compliment, half curse," he said. "I have always had a knack for finding trouble. Looks to me like maybe you have inherited that knack as well."

"It does seem that way sometimes."

"Well, when trouble comes your way, just keep moving forward. Like you say, there is always something new around the next turn—and it just might be for the better."

We took care to avoid inhabited places on the return journey. Although it took longer, Father did not want any unpleasant encounters with the Nodites to add to Grandfather's burden. Thus, we arrived home about four weeks later and found things in good order.

Within a few days of our return to Nephil, Grandfather said that he was ready to go visit Irad. Although Father offered to go with him, Grandfather said that since relations between our families were not good, it would be better if he went alone. Since the way was not difficult and Grandfather was much improved, Father consented to his wishes.

Meanwhile Father sought and received an audience with Ben-Tubal to request a letter of recommendation for his trip to Enoch-Nod. He went alone and when he returned, I asked, "Did you get it?"

"He gave it to me, but very reluctantly."

"Reluctantly?"

"He said he was concerned for my safety, because he knows I do not hesitate to speak the truth. But I think there was more to it than that. I thought I saw fear in his eyes."

"Dayak told me that the Sons of the Gods were the real power behind Ben-Tubal," I said. "But if he is afraid that giving you this letter might anger them, why did he grant your request?"

"I think there is something that a man like Ben-Tubal fears more than anything," said Father. "And that is being diminished in his own or anyone else's eyes. Refusing my request out of fear of displeasing his masters would be an admission that he is not the man he thinks he is."

As for Re-Aylah, I kept my distance from her as much as possible, avoiding conversation and even her glance if I could help it. After being so close to her for an extended period of time on our return journey from the mining camps, I felt like I was being pulled in two directions. I longed to be with her, but being close to her only reminded me of the love we almost shared. That was worse.

TWENTY-TWO

When Grandfather returned from the tents of Irad, he again looked very old and tired. The cares he had cast off at the Pishon cascades had re-gathered themselves and seemed to weigh heavier than ever on his shoulders. "Your brother's heart is hardened against you. I tried with many words to convince him to be reconciled with you. He said that for my sake he would not harm you. But he was not willing to forgive you for all the wrongs he said you have done him."

"Wrongs!" said Father indignantly. "He spit in your granddaughter's face and made her an outcast. And he destroyed fifteen years of my hard labor without provocation. What 'wrongs' does he feel need righting?"

"Ones that you can never set right, I fear," said Grandfather. "He has been overlooked for selection to the high eldership again and he thinks it is because your prophetic ministry and Gomer's misfortunes have given the family a bad name. He thought that winning the favor of Nephil through Re-Aylah's marriage to Baldag might advance his prospects, but that, too, proved ill-fated."

"So he can sell his daughter like cattle and treat us any way he wants to further his reputation."

"I'm not taking his side, Noah. I'm just trying to help you understand his point of view."

"The more I understand it, the sicker it makes me," said Father.

"Yes, he is proud and ambitious to the point of folly. I ask you, though, to bear with the failings of your brother. Have I not had enough sorrow in my life to contend with? Do not let my gray head go to the grave burdened by concern for what will happen between you two when I'm gone."

"Insofar as it depends on me, he has nothing to fear—nor did he ever."

"Very good, then," said Grandfather. Then he added with a note of optimism that could only spring from the hope of a desperate parent, "And perhaps Irad might yet have a change of heart someday."

"Perhaps," said Father, but he did not sound so hopeful.

Soon after this, Father made ready to leave for Enoch-Nod and his departure was a bitter one. With all the terrible reports we had heard concerning that place, we feared for his very life. Even Father, who was ever undaunted by the persecution of men, seemed apprehensive about going and I supposed that is why he had never yet ventured there in his wanderings through Nod.

"Have you had a premonition about Enoch-Nod?" I asked.

"Not a premonition," said Father. "The Lord hasn't shown me any specific visions about that place. Nevertheless, I have a foreboding of calamity. My heart tells me that unspeakable evil lurks in Enoch-Nod and I am loathe to draw near to it."

"Then why go?"

"Shall the hordes of Enoch-Nod be deprived of the opportunity to hear the word of the Lord because I lack the courage to go there? No, I won't shrink back from the charge God has given me—especially not now when the time draws so near. Besides, I have promised to attempt this thing. I owe it to my brother to confront his tormenters."

When he said goodbye to Grandfather, their parting was particularly grievous. They embraced as if knowing they would not see each other again and our hearts were all broken.

As soon as Father had gone, Grandfather announced, "I, too, am leaving. My time is almost upon me and I wish to see Father Methuselah again before I die."

Since I alone remained unmarried among my brothers, there was no doubt but that I would be the one to accompany him on the long journey. I was surprised, though, to hear Re-Aylah say that she wanted to go as well. I started to protest, but when she said, "He's my grandfather, too," there was nothing I could say.

Because we were all concerned about Grandfather's ability to travel far on foot, Jirah arranged for a carriage and driver. The carriage was one of the new kind that the family and officials of Ben-Tubal had taken to riding in. Drawn by two ponies, it was comfortable and well-provisioned. Re-Aylah sat in back with Grandfather and saw to his needs, for by then he had become quite feeble and prone to fits of coughing. In spite of his condition, Re-Aylah made him laugh often and that was good to hear. I, on the other hand, spent most of my time up front with the driver, trying to avoid Re-Aylah insofar as that was possible in such close proximity.

One day, I overheard Re-Aylah say, "Grandfather, do you think there is any chance that Father will have a change of heart toward me? Since you're a prophet, I was hoping you would have some knowledge concerning this."

"I am sorry to disappoint you, my Sunshine, but that is not how the gift works. I do not see everything, but only what the Lord chooses to reveal." He wheezed and the phlegm rattled for several long moments before he was able to continue. "Besides, it is not good for a man to know too much of the future. Such knowledge is too heavy a burden for him to bear."

"So is being disowned by your family," said Re-Aylah glumly.

"Do you regret the decisions you have made?"

She thought about it for a moment and said, "I don't know. I regret the consequences."

"Ah, you want it both ways."

"Why can't I have it both ways?"

"If you could have it both ways, you would want to have it three ways. There would be no end to it. All you can do is make the best decisions you can and go on with your life. As long as you are not content with the way things are, you will never be content."

When we arrived at Tabor Spring, the Ancient One received us warmly, though the rest of our kinsmen treated us like outcasts. I was dismayed to observe that Father Methuselah had failed considerably since I had last seen him. But reuniting with his son after a long absence seemed to renew his strength somewhat. The same could not be said of Grandfather Lamech, however. By then it was clear that he would not be making the return journey.

Re-Aylah and I stayed on for several weeks because we saw that Grandfather's time was very near—though we did not speak of it to each other. Methuselah and Lamech spent much time together, reclining side by side in the tent or sitting by the spring. They reminisced about days gone by and conferred about what the future held until Grandfather Lamech's breathing became so labored that he no longer had the strength to walk or even speak.

Then one day, Grandfather summoned Re-Aylah and me to his side. Reclining on a mat in his tent, he managed to say, "The time has come for me to go the way of all the earth. Do not grieve excessively, for my years are many and bitter and it is a great relief to set them aside. If only the suffering could end with me ..." His voice faltered as a spasm of coughing seized him. Re-Aylah laid her hand lovingly on his shoulder to comfort him. Finally, he caught his breath again and continued. "Alas, the Lord has revealed to me that dark days lie ahead for both of you as well. Do not lose hope, however, for in the end you will prevail. And if you tread the path together, the way will not be as dark and you can taste what joy may be found along the way." He took my hand and placed it on top of hers. Re-Aylah nodded and blinked back her tears. She bent over and kissed him on the forehead. Then he closed his eyes and breathed his last.

I might have wished for something more—to see his spirit rising from his body, or a light or a sound, any sign to give evidence that something good lay beyond that moment. But all was still, and I hoped that stillness meant peace for him.

No one in the clan offered us condolences. Indeed, no one spoke to us at all beyond what was absolutely necessary for performing the burial ceremony. It was soon accomplished, however, and we took our leave of the Ancient One not long after. Seeing his poor state of health, I was reluctant to leave. However, he said that his clan took good care of him and he assured me that we would see each other again. Whether he said this from prophetic knowledge or merely as a comfort to us, I do not know.

As we departed, I started to take my accustomed seat beside the driver. But Re-Aylah beckoned me to sit in back with her. I hesitated, but couldn't think of a plausible reason to decline her invitation.

Once we were underway, I said to her, "I want you to know that I don't consider Grandfather's last words binding upon you."

"Even though he was a prophet?"

I marveled at how, even through our sadness, she could still make me smile. "He said himself that it was not good for a man to know too much of the future."

"And just how long *will* you wait for me, Jay?" This time, she was earnest.

"I'm *not* a prophet," I said. We rode on in silence, with ill tidings of dark days ahead weighing heavily on our hearts.

When we reached the ark, everyone was saddened—though hardly surprised—to hear the news we bore. Jirah had one of her father's messengers dispatched to Irad, for none of us had any desire to go there ourselves bearing sad tidings. With Grandfather gone, our estrangement seemed very likely to worsen. Jirah also had one sent to find Father in Enoch-Nod. We had as yet received no word from him and we hoped and prayed that things were going well.

But such was not the case. Weeks went by and still Father did not return. Then, one evening, Merib came to me quietly in the camp and said, "I have some news for you that you will not be glad to hear. The messenger His Excellency sent to Enoch-Nod has returned, but he did not find things as they ought to be. Your father told him that although he appeared to be a guest of the Sons of the Gods, in reality he was being held prisoner in the Tower of the Watch and was not at liberty to leave."

"What does His Excellency say about this?" I asked.

"He is making a full investigation into the matter. If it is found to be true he will do whatever he can to win your father's release. Since your father was traveling under His Excellency's letter of recommendation, he considers this matter personal."

"If this is the way the Sons of the Gods operate, then why does His Excellency have dealings with them at all?"

Even though we were alone, Merib looked around as if someone might be listening. In a voice that was barely above a whisper, he said, "It will not always be so. Nephil, the magnificent city, is nearly completed and His Excellency's power is firmly established. Now he has turned his thoughts to even loftier matters—to acquiring the deep knowledge and the attainment of immortality. When these are within his grasp, nothing will stop him."

"There is no one like him," I said, considering the meaning of these words. "But though his reach is long, I don't think these are within even *his* reach."

"You should know by now not to underestimate him," said Merib.

"Yes, well be that as it may, I appreciate all his efforts on Father's behalf. And I think that I, too, will go there myself to see what can be done."

"You must not do that," Merib warned. "You do not know what you are dealing with."

"Thank you for your counsel," I said. "I will take it under advisement." But even as the words were coming out of my mouth, I had already resolved in my heart to go.

PART III:
THE ABOMINATION OF ENOCH-NOD

ONE

Three weeks of hard travel eastward took me into the interior of Nod and through masses of people past counting. The conditions they were living in were even more squalid than those I had seen before in northwestern Nod and the odor of their uncleanness hung in my nostrils. But something else lurked behind the smell of human filth. It revealed itself haltingly—first in traces and then in whiffs—until finally the reek of it grew so strong that it overpowered and engulfed what was merely foul. The stench compared with no other I had ever encountered—an acrid odor that hung over the entire region.

For several days, I had made no camp for fear of being assaulted. I slept only in snatches when weariness overcame wariness. I had been thinking for three days that I ought to have reached the city, but was afraid to ask the inhospitable people for aid or directions. Walking through brushy hills covered with encampments that seemed interminable, I unexpectedly topped over the last one. And like a man stumbling onto a viper, I could see the city coiled below in the valley of the Euphrates River: Enoch-Nod, the great and terrible mother of abominations.

The buildings were of astounding size, stretching some five miles along the river and at least two miles wide on either side of it. A horde of tents, pitched together in a jumble so vast that their number could not be guessed, surrounded the city. At the core of Enoch-Nod, on the near side of the river, stood the largest and most imposing building of all—the Tower of the Watch, a six-sided monstrosity that must have stood close to a thousand feet tall. Nothing in my previous experience prepared me for its colossal scale. All the buildings of Nephil seemingly could have fit inside that one. Its skin of black porous stone reflected no light, as if a grotesque shadow of Sheol, discontent with the grave alone, claimed also that portion of the living world and thrust itself against the calcined umber sky. Columns of dark windows gaped like the mouths of corpses impaled upon scaly metallic spires that made a travesty of adornment. Where abode the Sons of the Gods I did not have to wonder. With a shudder, I headed toward it.

On the far side of the river stood the cause of my stinging eyes and irritated skin. The towering chimneys of the immense smelting factories and forging furnaces poured forth prodigious quantities of noxious smoke, as I suppose they had done ever since Tubal-Cain first practiced the fiery crafts. And though I had never before given much thought to where our implements came from, I could never afterward use one without pausing to think about where they were forged. Of the functions of the other buildings, I could only guess, but some were undoubtedly devoted to the plying of darker arts. Of these sorceries, I will mention only what is absolutely necessary, for it is not good to speak too much about such things.

At first, I had hoped to reach the center of the city and somehow find Father by nightfall. But my view from the hill had deceived me and the distance was further than I had judged. As the shadows deepened, so did my sense of alarm. Even now, so many years later, it is difficult to recount that night wandering lost through the streets of Enoch-Nod—a despised stranger in a hostile land.

Before I arrived, the fact that I had no plan had given me only a vague sense of uneasiness. For comfort, I had reminded myself that I had no real plan for rescuing Re-Aylah until I got to the mining camps and that had turned out well. But whatever hope I had taken in that comparison deserted me like a pleasant dream upon waking to some harsh reality. Her prison had been little more than a hut on the edge of the wilderness guarded by a few undisciplined men who were only slightly less disinterested than the slaves they watched. This, however, was an unassailable stronghold in the very heart of the enemy's land. All the unheeded warnings about that place echoed through my mind and each step forward seemed only to heap folly onto foolishness.

The gathering gloom emboldened the tent dwellers as they forsook whatever slight sense of modesty or propriety that perchance had lingered in that place while the sun shone. A riot spilled out into the streets, so that I had difficulty making my way through the throngs. Everywhere I looked, people relieved themselves openly in the streets with no regard whatsoever to modesty or sanitation. Combined with the sulphurous smoke of the furnaces, the whole city reeked so badly that I could hardly breathe. Most of the people appeared intoxicated to the point of mania and enflamed with an insatiable lust. Men and women alike cast off all restraint, while the others took little notice of their shocking perversions. I hurried through the crowd, keeping my face forward so that I might not sin with my eyes.

Even though I was moving as fast as I could, a young man passed me. What I noticed particularly about him, apart from the fact that he was shoving people aside who got in his way, was that he looked quite agitated and was carrying on an animated conversation with no one who could be seen. He had a wild look in his eye—one that did not look quite human. When he noticed me, he smiled a hideous smile that showed more of his teeth than was natural and my blood ran chill. Then he resumed his talking, though the only word I could plainly make out was "kill."

Several paces ahead, he stole up behind an unsuspecting older man whose back was turned. I caught the momentary glint of torchlight on a metal blade. But before I could do anything or even shout, he plunged his knife into the old man's back. As the old man reeled, the young man snatched the cup from his hand and slipped away into the crowd.

When I reached the older man, I could see that he was mortally wounded. I knelt beside him and cradled his head in my arm. He was trying to say something, so I leaned my ear close to his lips. "He stole my grack," the man rasped, his voice rattling in his own blood.

"But you're dying! Is that all you have to say?"

I do not know if he heard me; his eyes were already staring far away. A few moments later, his head slumped, and I knew he was dead.

To add to my great dismay, I seemed to be the only one who had taken notice of the murder. I cried out to those passing by for help, but everyone ignored me. I said to one man standing nearby, "Doesn't it matter to you that this man was murdered before your eyes?"

"What concern is it of mine?" he said. "I didn't know him."

"Don't you think he at least deserves a decent burial?" I asked.

"The carts will be along in the morning to haul off the dead bodies to the furnaces," he said, irritated with my questions. "And I'd be moving along if I were you, stranger, or they'll be carrying you away too!"

I didn't feel right about leaving him there like that, but what else could I do? I could see no suitable place for burial and had nothing with which to cover him. So I found a place off the road that was out of the way and dragged him there in the hope that one of his kinsmen would pass that way and mourn for him. At the time, I did not notice that I was covered with his blood.

I endured the rest of the night as a nightmare from which I could not awaken. Badly shaken, I reached the first buildings. Immediately, I lost behind them the landmark for which I was aiming. Unable to collect my thoughts above the deafening din of revelry, my sense of direction deserted me. Drumbeats reverberated off the walls and my ears were filled with shrieks and moans and laughter unlike any others I have heard in this world or wish to hear again. Dazed, I stumbled through streets and alleys trying to find my way, driven onward only by a longing to find my father, no longer to rescue him—for I had already despaired of that—but so that in him I might find some measure of comfort in that godless land.

Suddenly, I emerged into the great expanse of the courtyard encircling the Tower of the Watch. Between the Tower and me stood a platform with a table in the center surrounded by a crowd of people. A sect of priests, wearing robes of crimson trimmed with saffron, intoned malevolent incantations while a woman lay on the table, bound hand and foot like a lamb about to be sacrificed. I could not understand what the priests were saying, but I thought I grasped the purpose of their ceremony well enough.

What I thought I could do alone against so many, I don't know. But I had already witnessed one murder that night and I was determined not to stand by and witness another. Forcing my way through the crowd, I rushed up on the platform and shouted, "Stop!"

The priests stepped back in surprise, except for the chief priest who held his ground. My eye was drawn to the figure emblazoned on his shaven head—the image of a serpent. It was, at once, both horrible and fascinating to behold. I had a hard time looking away, even as I reached for the ceremonial knife to cut the woman free. But when I looked at her face, I got a surprise of my own. "Minnah?" I said in astonishment. "Run. I'll hold them off as long as I can."

"What are you doing?" she said, looking neither fearful nor relieved. "You'll ruin everything."

Minnah's reaction was hardly what I would have anticipated. Paralyzed by indecision, I stood over her not knowing what to do. In that moment of hesitation, the priests recovered and a half dozen guards seized me. I suddenly remembered my charge and shouted back at her, "I have something I need to tell you." But they carried me away before I got the chance. From the looks of things, I would never have another.

Getting inside the Tower of the Watch proved no further problem, for there

I was taken prisoner and held under guard in an anteroom on the first underground level. No one offered me anything to eat or drink, though I was made to sit for hours. Neither did they speak a word to me. Weary and dejected, I hadn't the pluck to ask any questions.

About mid-morning, I was taken to the office of the Captain of the Guard, a stoutly-built man of harsh countenance called Saur-El. At first, I mistook that for his name, though I later learned it was his title. The guards made me sit on a low stool with my hands bound tightly behind my back. Saur-El loomed over me, circled slowly and regarded me with contempt. After the bizarre events of the previous night, I was beginning to come to my senses. Their rough treatment had left me in an ill mood, so I said, "What's the meaning of this?"

He struck me across the face with the back of his hand and said, with remarkably little emotion in his voice, "I will ask the questions. You will answer. Who are you?"

"I am nobody—only a stranger here."

He swung at me again. I tried to duck my head, but he caught me just above my left eye. "There is no point in being evasive. I know who you are, son of Noah."

"Then why ask?" I said, knowing it would bring another blow. This time it was to the back of my head.

"I will ask. You will answer," said the Saur-El, his voice still flat. "Why are you here?"

My strength was failing and I was having a hard time catching my breath in the stifling air. Since my identity was known, my errand would not be hard to guess, so I answered, "I came to seek the freedom of my father. I understand he is being held prisoner here."

"In that, you are mistaken," said the Saur-El. "Your father is a guest here."

"Then take me to him and we'll be on our way."

This brought yet another blow to my face, though I didn't know why. I was amazed that the Saur-El could remain so calm while beating a man, but it surely came from much practice. He said, "I'm afraid it is *you* who are not at liberty to leave."

"What have I done but save the life of a woman?" I said. "Shouldn't you rather be honoring me?" He struck me again, harder than before and I thought for a moment I might pass out.

"Honor you, a murderer?"

"Murderer?"

"Do not deny it," he said. "We have witnesses who saw you kill a man in cold blood on the outskirts of the city. Why, you are still covered with his blood!"

"I only stopped to help ..."

"And this knife was found in your hand," said the Saur-El, caressing the ritual knife that was apparently to have been used on Minnah. "No doubt it was the same knife used in the murder. Stolen from the temple, I'll wager. We can add theft of a sacred article to your list of offenses."

By then, I was seething. Mustering what remained of my strength in defiance, I said, "This is an outrage! I see you serve your masters well, calling what is good evil and what is evil good. They are not Sons of the Gods, but sons of dogs. A curse be on them and on you as well!"

That outburst apparently brought a final and decisive blow, though I don't remember it. Dimly, I recall being dragged down several flights of stairs and thrown roughly into a dark, damp cell. The sound of the heavy door clanging startled me back to consciousness. It was a fearful sound for anyone and all the more to one who had been accustomed to roaming freely all his life. I never knew quite how much I relished that freedom until it was taken away.

Two

Only a sliver of torchlight leaking through a slit in the door made it possible to see anything at all in the windowless dungeon. Groping my way around the cell, I was alarmed to find it only eight feet square.

"There's been a terrible mistake!" I cried, pounding on the door. "I'm innocent. Come back and let me explain." But my pleas went unanswered.

Fighting back panic, I searched the gloom for a means of escape. The walls and floor were constructed of rough cut stones, ill fitted and shoddily mortared. Foul water seeped through many cracks, infusing the cell with an oppressive dankness and leaving not a dry place to sit.

I tested the walls wherever the mortar was deteriorating, but couldn't find a single stone that could be budged. Perhaps if I had a tool, I could have excavated my way through given enough time. But I had been stripped of all my possessions and not even so much as a chamber pot had been provided to me. I examined the cell again more thoroughly, probing each crevice gingerly—half to spare my knuckles and half for fear of touching something loathsome in the hollows. When at length this yielded no promising results, I sat down on the floor with my back against the far wall and stared at the door.

How long I remained thus I do not know. Marking time was impossible in that sunless place. I saw no person and heard no sound except the drip of water, which soon magnified in my ears until it was more than an annoyance. Wet and chilled from the dampness, I felt as miserable as I ever remember being.

After what seemed like a long time, I began to sense that I was not alone. I looked carefully around the cell, for by then my eyes had adjusted to the dim light, and I saw that the far corner seemed to be a living shadow.

"Who's there?" I whispered, trying not to betray my fright.

No answer came, unless it was a faint scratching on the stones. I cowered, not knowing what manner of evil it might be. My prison, however, was far too cramped to ignore whatever might be lurking there. So I braced myself and drew near.

It was only a rat, I found to my relief. In fact, I was so desperate for the company of another living thing that for a moment I considered making a pet of him.

"Hello, my little fellow," I said, extending my hand. But when he hissed at me, I thought better of it. I shrank back to the opposite corner and waited, hoping that he would go away. His pitiless eyes remained fixed upon mine, however, and I knew that I would have no peace or sleep as long as he was in the cell. So, I decided to drive him away, little understanding how daunting that seemingly simple task would prove. When I tried to scare him, he only flashed his teeth at me. I wished for a stick or something to poke at him. Since I had nothing of the sort, I took off my tunic and wrapped it around my hand. When I reached down to pick him up, he lunged at me. Somehow, though, I managed to seize hold of him. I could feel him biting my hand through the cloth, but forced myself to hang on while I stuffed him back through the hole. He was surprisingly strong for his size and it took great force to expel him. I stopped up the hole by cramming my tunic tightly into it and sat down breathing hard, my hand stinging like fire from the rat bites. Cold and utterly alone, I huddled in the dark and prayed for deliverance.

I must have dozed for a minute, because the next thing I remember was being awakened by a stabbing pain in my ankle. I jumped up and realized with horror that the rat was gnawing on it. Before I could recover my wits, he scurried off into the darkness, but I did not see which way it went. I rechecked my tunic and my heart sank to find it was still in place. The rat had more than one way in—perhaps many, making it impossible to prevent him from entering.

I had no choice but to keep vigil. With preternatural cunning, however, the rat bided his time, knowing that I must eventually sleep. As hard as I tried to stay awake, fatigue finally got the better of me, because I had traveled hard and slept little for weeks. But when I drifted off again, the rat gave me such a gash to the thigh that I would never forget it. Again he was gone before I could do anything to defend myself.

An abhorrence fell upon me such as I had never known. I paced the cell, then circled it, reversed directions and then jumped up and down—anything to keep myself awake and avoid the terror that waited for me to drop my guard. But eventually I wearied of this futile exercise, for I knew I could not keep it up indefinitely.

So, then, a new plan formed in my mind: to feign sleep and draw the creature out. What I intended to do to him, I kept secret even from myself, lest I lose my nerve. For I, who never was one to even swat a fly, began to have murderous thoughts in my heart toward the rat.

I sat down, leaned back against the wall and pretended to go to sleep. But the rat—or the malevolent spirit that guided it—apparently saw through my deception. He did not show himself for hours, until finally true slumber overtook me. I had no sooner drifted off when the rat dropped from somewhere above me onto my head. I awoke screaming and flailing my arms. Again he was gone before I could catch him.

I cannot adequately describe the horror that ensued. For this cycle repeated itself times uncounted—whether for days or weeks I do not know— until sanity deserted me. From some distant corner of my mind, I began to observe myself as if I were someone else. With about as much interest as someone seeing a new kind of insect for the first time, I thought, *So this is what happens when a man goes mad.* I had what felt like an animal awareness of finding and eating an occasional crust of stale bread that was left for me by some unseen hand through the door slit and lapping foul water between the cracks in the floor (only a few feet from where I had to relieve myself) when overcome by thirst. All the while, I struggled to stay awake and postpone the torture of that embodiment of spite. So intense was my loathing that it sharpened my senses beyond tolerance. A distant drip became the scurrying of tiny claws on stone; a slight flicker of torchlight in the hallway created the illusion of movement in the shadows; and any faint stir of air might simulate rat whiskers brushing against my skin. These delusions made me even more wretched than I already was and I had not a moment of peace even when I was not directly under attack.

Then, at my lowest point of despair, came the echo of a woman calling as if from a dream. The balm of her voice was like a salve to my afflicted mind. The mere sound of it soothed my fears as a gentle hand awakens a sleeper from a bad dream. Slowly, I became aware that the voice was speaking my name. It seemed luxurious on her lips, as if it contained more sounds than it ever had before, something like "Zhayfeth," though that does not do it justice. Barely daring to hope, I rose to my feet and said weakly, "Who's there?"

"I am Sheshi-Behura."

Hearing another human voice stirred emotions so deep they cannot be described. All I can say is that at that moment, my vexation of mind receded and a semblance of reason returned to me. "Sheshi-Behura," I said. "Please open this door and let me out."

"I cannot do that," she said.

"Don't leave me in this awful place. I beg you to help me."

"I *have* come to help you," she said. "I have been appointed as your Advocate before the Council."

"There's been a terrible mistake. I've been falsely accused."

"The evidence is against you," she said. "But I will return soon and then you can tell me your account of the matter."

"You're not going to leave me here?" I pleaded. "I cannot bear another moment in this dungeon."

"I will see what can be done about better accommodations," she said. "But for now I must go."

With that she was gone, but not before she had given me a possibility to cling to that the dungeon would not be my tomb. I lay down on the floor and slept.

Several hours later, I awoke with a start thinking the rat must surely be upon me, but he was not. Although my joints ached from sleeping on the stone floor, I otherwise felt better than I had since my imprisonment. I remembered Sheshi-Behura, and checked my recollection to verify that she had not been merely a dream. Eagerly I watched the door, anticipating her return and listening intently for her footsteps. After what seemed like a long, long time, I heard her light footfall on the stairs. Leaping to the door, I called, "Is it you, Sheshi-Behura?"

"It is I, but you may call me Sheshi."

"Very well, Sheshi," I said. "Were you able to win my release?"

"You do not understand our ways. A defense must be made for you before the High Council of the Watch."

"I am innocent."

"That remains to be determined," she said. "But in order to make your case, you must tell me exactly what happened. Do not hold anything back."

So I told her the account of my arrival to Enoch-Nod. When I had finished, she said, "The man who was murdered was a stranger to you then?"

"I'm quite sure I never laid eyes on him before."

"I see," she said. "Then robbery was your motive."

"My motive for what? I told you I did not murder the man."

"I meant the reason that you went to him."

"You think that I would rob a man while he was dying in my arms?" I asked.

"You said yourself that he was neither your kinsman nor your comrade. What other explanation could there be?"

"I was only trying to help him," I said. "I felt compassion for the man."

"You expect me to believe that? More importantly, do you expect the Council to believe it?"

"It's the truth."

"If that is the truth, your defense would be better served by a lie," said Sheshi. "The sentence for robbery is much less severe than for murder. You might only lose your hand."

"That's the best I can hope for?" I asked.

"Compared to the alternative, you would be very fortunate to receive this punishment."

"After what I've been through, death might be a relief," I said bravely, though I did not truly believe my own words.

"I didn't say death. There are punishments that would make you beg for death."

"What kind of Advocate are you?" I said. "Your words bring me no comfort."

"I will go, then, and disturb you no longer."

"Wait!" I cried. "I didn't mean that the way it sounded. My circumstances have made me neglectful of courtesy."

"What is it that you want then?"

"To get out of this cell."

"As I told you before, I am working on that," said Sheshi. "In fact, I must be going now, as I have an appointment with the Saur-El."

Desperately searching for something that would delay her departure, I said, "Before you go, could you bend down by this slit in the door so that I may look upon you?"

"Why?"

"Please," I pleaded. "Just let me see your face."

She stooped and put her face close to the narrow opening. Even if I had not been so starved for the sight of another human being, I would have found her lovely. Her black hair glistened like the soft approach of evenfall and bowls of moonless night sky graced her eyes.

"Why are you weeping?" she asked.

Until she said this, I didn't realize that I was. "I'm overwhelmed by your beauty," I said, hoping that she could not see me well in the dim light, for I was suddenly ashamed of my own uncleanness. Then I whispered, "Please help me!"

Her delicate features appeared unaccustomed to being touched by such an earnest plea. For a moment, she seemed unsure of herself. Then she recovered her composure and said, "I will help you. But to do so, I must go for now."

The waiting became almost unbearable. When what seemed like hours had passed, though it may not have been that long, I spotted the rat on a ledge, watching me. He made no move to attack and neither did I stir, knowing that if I started toward him he would disappear again. I preferred knowing where he was, even if it meant enduring his uncanny stare. I don't think I was imagining things when I say that he was studying me. Finally, he bared its teeth in what might have passed for an evil grin. As he disappeared into a hole, I shuddered to think he had discovered some weakness in me.

After what felt like days, but may have only been a few more hours, I heard heavy footsteps descending the stairs and braced myself as the door opened to reveal four guards. The one in charge said, "Come."

As I was led up the stairs, I was told that I was being moved at night to protect my eyes after the long period of captivity in darkness. Indeed, even the pale light of the dying, smoke-obscured moon hurt my eyes. I did not care, though. After the dungeon, I welcomed even the noxious night air of Enoch-Nod. Being out of the cell so exhilarated me that I briefly contemplated making a run for it. The four guards, however, looked formidable. And since things seemed to be looking up, I decided to see what would happen next.

I was taken to a bathhouse near the Euphrates and allowed to wash. Where the water came from, I do not know (certainly not straight from the polluted river because it was surprisingly fresh—a great luxury in that land). Afterward, when I had been given clean clothes, I began to feel more like myself again.

Beyond the southern courtyard of the Tower of the Watch stood an imposing mansion and to this I was taken. A dozen wide stone steps led up to the entrance, a smoke-stained mahogany frame carved with many strange beasts and mysterious symbols. Inside lay a great room with an open stairway on the left wall leading up to a second-story balcony. An indigo rug woven with a star field and images of constellations covered most of the floor. Near the foot of the stairs, a short hallway led to the studio of Sheshi-Behura. She met me there and the guards left us. Candlelight illuminated the room, including a small table that was set for us. In a corner alcove, I saw numerous scrolls—more than I had ever seen in one place. (Wouldn't Shem have loved to get his hands on those!) Altogether, it was quite a welcome contrast to the rest of Enoch-Nod.

I sat at the table opposite Sheshi, while servants brought us food. Like the Nephilim, the elite of Enoch-Nod used utensils and I was glad to have had some exposure to their proper use, though I would have preferred not being slowed down by them. In my haste to satisfy my hunger, I could not later recall much of what I had eaten—only that I could not eat as much as I thought I wanted because my stomach wouldn't accommodate it all after being half-starved for so long.

From time to time, I thought I caught Sheshi's eyes lingering upon me. Whenever I noticed, though, she would quickly look down. I remember wondering if it were more than just fascination with a stranger from a foreign land—and I surprised myself by hoping that it was.

Only after I had eaten my fill did I realize that my appetite had made me neglectful of the grace that had been shown me. "Where are my manners?" I said, rather sheepishly. "If I should thank you a thousand times for getting me out of that cell, it would not be an adequate beginning."

"I was happy to do so," she said in dulcet tones that stuck honey-like to her speech in ways that enchanted my ears and solaced the gravity of her words. "But do not let your change in accommodations make you think that all is well. You still face very grave charges and your prospects for being found innocent are not promising."

The wine had started to go to my head, but her sobering counsel was more than ample motivation to push the cup and plate away. Realizing that my very life might hang on some useful bit of knowledge, I resolved to find out as much as I could. "So tell me about this place," I said, indicating our surroundings.

"This is the House of Hura, High Priest of the Morningstar," she said.

"Are you his servant then?" I asked.

"I am his daughter."

"Forgive me," I said, deeply embarrassed. "I meant no offense."

"I took none."

"You must think the worst of me—first accused of murder and then insulting the daughter of a great dignitary. I should have guessed your relation from your name. And that you were no ordinary person from your beauty." These last words were spoken without forethought. And, as I was saying them, I worried that I might be committing another blunder.

To my relief (and I will confess also to my gratification) she blushed and lowered her eyes. "I do not think the worst of you," she said. "In fact, I have never met anyone like you before. You are ... different."

"In what way?"

"In the way that you tried to help the man you are accused of killing, for example. I cannot get out of my mind how you tried to assist someone who was a stranger to you."

"It was nothing, really," I said, shrugging. "I only did what anyone would do."

"No, it is not what anyone else would do. A thousand men might have walked by him without stopping, but you did."

"It never occurred to me *not* to stop," I said. "Unfortunately, it didn't help him—or me."

In that way, we talked late into the evening. I should say, rather, that I did most of the talking—in spite of my resolution to find out more about her. She plied me with many questions about my life and land, and carried away by her rapt attention, I was only too glad to oblige. Indeed, she seemed to think that everything I said was interesting, funny, or profound. When I saw by the servants' yawns that the hour had grown late, I realized that I still knew practically nothing about her or Enoch-Nod.

As I was preparing to leave, I said, "I apologize for keeping you up so late. I know you have important work to do tomorrow—like trying to save my life."

"It was my pleasure," she said. "Who could tire in such company?"

"Then you do believe I am innocent?"

"Does it matter to you?"

"Shouldn't an Advocate believe in the innocence of the person she is defending?" I asked.

"If an Advocate's answer is all you want, then 'no.' What your Advocate believes is of no consequence. I would make a case for you regardless. Goodnight."

THREE

I wondered what other kinds of answers there could be as the guard escorted me to my new quarters in a dormitory not far from the House of Hura. The room, though simple, seemed extravagant compared to what I had just been accustomed. It even had a couch and that night I slept far better than I had since I left home.

The mid-morning sun, tarnished though it was, greeted me when I awoke. As I lay on the couch wondering what the new day would bring, there was a knock on my door. Food was brought to me, as it was each day at regular times, unless I was dining with Sheshi. She summoned me frequently to advise me about my case. She summoned me as well on days when she had no news, although at first I failed to grasp all that implied.

During these visits I was able to learn more about her—slowly, though, for in many respects she remained quite secretive. Following in her father's footsteps, she was studying to be a priestess in the Cult of the Morningstar. Her duties as Advocate were part of this process, because all of the initiates were required to study at law. Once the basic studies were mastered, she said she would advance to ever more profound areas of learning. The ultimate goal of this training mystified me, however, because her words were full of indefinite references to "awakening" and "enlightenment." It had a ring to it, though—especially when the words were in Sheshi's mouth. Despite my upbringing and my questioning nature, I would be lying if I denied that I felt a certain attraction toward the practice and the practitioner.

One afternoon several weeks later, she led me to a balcony on the fifth and highest story of the house. As we sat on an ornamental bench overlooking the river, I marveled at the massive iron bridge below that dwarfed the stone bridge in Nephil. Across the Euphrates lay the great factories of Enoch-Nod, with the red glow of their chimneys reflecting off the smoke in the afternoon sun. By then, I was beginning to grow accustomed to the air and at that height, it felt somewhat clearer and fresher. And as long as I was with Sheshi, it was easy to enjoy myself a bit and forget that I was, in fact, a prisoner. Trying to get her to tell me more about her religion, I said, "So tell me, what is the ultimate goal of the awakening?"

"To achieve the divine nature," she said, pleased that I was showing an interest.

"That's the part I don't understand. How can a mere mortal be like God?"

"By ascending the enlightened pathway."

"But won't the enlightened pathway just lead you to being an enlightened mortal?"

"The divine nature is immortal."

"That may be true enough," I said. "But what makes you think that the divine nature is attainable by mortals?"

"The reason you have difficulty with this is because you always want evidence. Sometimes you have to open your eyes to your inner sight." She took my face in her hands and gently closed my eyes with her fingers. "Now, clear your mind of all thoughts."

I tried to oblige her, but even when I shut out the background clamor of the factories, I was still conscious of the softness of her hands on my face and the almost imperceptible sound of our breathing. And when I realized how much I was enjoying the sensation, I began to be embarrassed at this new level of intimacy. "I don't see anything," I said, feeling a need to fill in the silence. "I don't possess the sight."

"Because you do not follow the enlightened pathway."

I opened my eyes again and said, "To follow the enlightened pathway, I have to open my eyes to my inner sight. But to open my eyes to the inner sight, I have to follow the enlightened pathway. It sounds to me like we're going in a circle."

"Life is a circle."

"That sounds very nice. But if it were true, we'd never get anywhere."

"Where is it that you want to get to?"

"I'm not sure," I said with a smile.

"If you don't know where you're going, then it doesn't really matter, does it?"

"I'll know it when I get there," I said. "It's hard to explain, but my life has felt more like a river than a circle. It keeps sweeping me downstream toward an inevitable destination."

"That sounds so fatalistic," said Sheshi. "It's like everything has already been predetermined for you. But if you followed the enlightened pathway, you would not know such limits. You could become one with the divine nature and plot your own destiny. You would be like the gods yourself, knowing all things. All mysteries would be revealed and all power would be yours. Nothing would be beyond you."

"I'm sorry. I just have a hard time accepting all that. Unless I can experience something, it doesn't seem real to me."

She shook her head and said, "Why must you always question everything?"

"Why must you always believe everything?"

She rose and stood overlooking the parapet, apparently caught off guard by the question. "You do not understand the joy of the enlightened pathway."

"Do you?"

"Not yet," Sheshi admitted with a note of sadness. "But someday I will."

I stood up next to her and said, "Are you certain of that? All I've seen in this land is misery."

"I do not know what you are talking about."

"How could you miss it?" I said. "All over Nod the people are suffering terribly."

"I have not been all over Nod. I— I seldom leave this complex."

Although I found her naivete hard to comprehend, one look at her face erased all doubt that this was news to her. What a sheltered life she must have lived in the temple complex. She was a prisoner almost as much as I was. I said, "Then perhaps you should venture out sometime—if you truly want to be enlightened."

"Leave me now," she said, signaling to the guard. "I wish to speak no more of it today."

As I walked away, it occurred to me that we should not part like that. As I turned around to beg her pardon, I saw her take out a vial concealed in her robe. With trembling hands, she drank from it.

The guard took me by the arm and escorted me back into the house, saying, "Come on now. Her diversions are no concern of yours." His tone was polite, almost friendly, with none of the course language Saur El's men used, which probably was a requirement for serving in the house of a priest.

"Is it grack?" I ventured.

"Of course not," he said in a hushed tone. "Grack is for the rabble. The priests reserve the good stuff for themselves."

"So, it's expensive then?"

"They pay a price," he said. "Make no mistake—they pay a very high price!"

The following day, Sheshi met me at the door when I arrived at her house. She seemed serene again, though I thought I could detect a trace of care in her face that had not been there before. As we crossed the star field rug to a part of the house I had not been in before, she said, "About the matters we discussed yesterday, I fear that there has been a misunderstanding. You were right in saying that the people are suffering."

"So you took my advice and went out to see for yourself?"

"No, I asked my father about it," she said as we entered a long hallway leading toward the back of the house. "He explained that the High Council of the Watch is helping people all over Nod to alleviate their suffering."

"Well, I *have* been all over Nod and I've seen it with my *own* eyes. It doesn't look like help to me—unless you call slavery, starvation and mind control 'help.'"

"You shouldn't speak that way!" Sheshi admonished.

"Why not?"

"They will hear you."

"And what will they do—'help' me like they're 'helping' your people?"

"You are incorrigible."

"And you are gullible."

"Perhaps I am—for believing that you are a good man."

"So telling you the truth makes me a bad man?"

"Your version of the truth."

"Truth has no version," I said. "It's just the truth. And it is no respecter of opinions about it."

"In Enoch-Nod, it is different," she said. "The opinion of the High Council of the Watch is all that matters. And Father says that right now, the opinion is against you."

"But I have you as my Advocate. I'm sure you have had lots of experience with difficult cases like mine."

"You *are* my experience," said Sheshi.

"You mean I'm the first—and only?" The expression on her face confirmed that she was not joking. My heart sank. After that, I shut my mouth and tried not to think about how bleak my prospects looked.

At the end of the hall, a staircase wound down around the perimeter of a dimly-lit vault. I was only vaguely aware of the surroundings—an altar, candelabras and a half dozen acolytes who were attending them—because my eyes were transfixed by the figure seated on the chair in the center of the room. More specifically, it was the emblem of the serpent emblazoned on his forehead that I could not take my eyes off of as we reached the floor level. It left me no doubt of where I had seen him before. With a sickening realization, I said, "Don't tell me—this murderer is your father?"

"A strange accusation coming from a man in your position," Hura replied calmly. His voice had a richness and cadence similar to Sheshi's, which I had begun to identify as a characteristic of the well-born of Enoch-Nod.

"That woman you sacrificed was a friend of mine," I said indignantly.

"That's not exactly how she described the relationship," said Hura.

"Well, so she was more like an acquaintance, really. But that's not the point—."

Hura raised his hands as if to calm me with a gesture. "Come now. Don't you owe me the courtesy of investigating the facts before you make such unpleasant accusations?"

He nodded toward one of the acolytes tending a censer. I looked and saw that it was Minnah—still very much alive. Recovering from my astonishment at seeing her there, I finally managed to say, "Well, if you aren't one for turning up where you're least expected. I am pleased that my efforts at saving you were not in vain, Minnah."

"That name no longer has any meaning for me," she said. "I'm now called Ell-Esa."

"Very well, Ell-Esa. Seeing you reminds me of a charge I was given that I was afraid I wouldn't be able to fulfill. I have a message for you. It's from Giblith."

"I don't want to hear it," said Ell-Esa.

"But I promised him I would tell you," I said. "They were his … last words." She tried not to show it, but I could tell that this was the first news she had heard of Giblith's death. "He wanted me to tell you that he forgave you," I continued. "And that he loved you—to the very end."

"Why tell me this?" she said bitterly.

I had been expecting a more grateful reaction and wasn't sure how to respond. "I—I thought you would want to know."

"So that I would spend the rest of my days feeling guilty? So that I would rush back to Cush and throw myself on his grave? I'm sorry to disappoint you, but I don't want his forgiveness. And I don't need your pity. I have a new life now and no intentions of ever going back."

"But Cush is your home," I said. "You can't run away forever."

"You know what they do to women like me. My looks won't save me from that fate anymore. And the only one who I thought truly loved me for who I am turned out to be the worst one of the lot."

"You won't have to worry about him anymore, either," I said, still probing for some show of emotion. "Giblith killed him."

"I can't say I'm surprised—or sorry."

"Even though Giblith and Baldag both died over you?"

"There you go again trying to shame me," said Ell-Esa. "But you don't understand what it's been like to be beautiful."

"No, I can't say that I do."

"When I was younger, I could get away with anything because I had a pretty face," she said. "But I'm telling you it's turned out to be a curse having looks that men would kill for. The High Priest of the Morningstar finally helped me understand that. The women have always hated me because they were jealous and the men have always lusted after me. I'm not saying I'm proud of all the things I've done, but I'm no worse than the hypocrites who would stone me if I go back. No, I'll stay right here. The Cainites don't care about my past. They accept me just the way I am, which is more than I can ever hope for in Cush. As a matter of fact, it's more than *you* can ever hope for in Cush. We're not so different in that respect because you're an outcast, too. That's something to think about—if you ever get out of the predicament you're in here. Now if you'll excuse me, I have my duties to attend to."

Once again, Ell-Esa—Minnah—had caught me completely off guard. I remember thinking that I should have said more on Giblith's behalf. He deserved better and my silence at that point seemed to dishonor his memory. But I knew she had a point. Even I had been guilty of treating her differently. One wink from her when I was a boy made me overlook behavior in her that I wouldn't have tolerated in a man or woman of lesser beauty.

While I was still mulling over my complicity in the whole affair, Hura said, "As I was saying, you did not even know what it was that you interrupted that night. It was not an actual sacrifice, but the symbolic death of the initiate to her old life. You were making an assumption because your god requires blood sacrifices. Rather barbaric, don't you think?"

How he had learned this, I don't know. But he had deftly exposed a secret reservation about the sacrifices that I had long harbored in my heart.

My moral high ground, already shaky, felt as though it were giving away beneath my feet. I didn't know what to say.

"Yeesss," Hura continued, drawing out the word and nodding his head because he could see that he had hit the mark. "You seem to have a keen interest in the affairs of prophets and priests—an interest that unfortunately goes unfulfilled since you are not numbered among them by your own people. Too bad your current circumstances are not more favorable. A promising young man like you might find better acceptance into the priesthood of the Morningstar, where the innocent are not slaughtered for the sins of the guilty and a man can advance on his own merit, rather than being hampered by social status or relying on the whim of a capricious god. It is a shame, yes. But at least you can stop exaggerating the differences between us. They are not so great as you think. My ancestor Cain—may his name be revered— also abhorred the bloody sacrifices required by your god. His brave stand is not forgotten here in the city he founded. And the mark that was given to him for shame, I now bear proudly in his honor."

I stood there dumbstruck, mesmerized by his words and by the serpent on his skin which seemed almost to have a life of its own.

"We are not the savages that the sons of Seth have deemed us to be," said Hura. "It grieves me that we have been so misunderstood by your kinsmen—a feeling with which, I daresay, you are not unacquainted. If only you were at liberty to settle among us, you, too, would find acceptance and solace, as Ell-Esa has, instead of persecution and hostility. Now was there something you wished to discuss with me?"

Any other time, I could have thought of a hundred questions, but by then I had forgotten why I had gone to see him in the first place. His words seemed more sensible and respectful than any I was accustomed to hearing outside of my immediate family and I was completely taken in by them. Everything I had previously known and believed about the Cainites suddenly seemed like a grave misunderstanding.

Seeing that no questions were forthcoming, Hura said, "Very well then. I return you to the charge of your Advocate. I urge you to listen carefully to her and follow her advice. Your fate depends upon it. Sheshi has been a very apt student and will be very resourceful in your defense." He smiled with fatherly pride at her. She closed her eyes momentarily and smiled, drinking in his praise. As we walked up the stairs, I remember thinking how lucky I was to have them on my side.

FOUR

y encounter with Hura left me feeling very unsettled and wondering whose side I was really on. Within a short span of time, it seems I had been plucked by the roots like a flower and transplanted to new soil—not alien and barren, but strangely familiar and carefully prepared. However, while conditions might have seemed favorable to take root and bloom where I had been transplanted, this flower was homesick. What little sense of security I had recovered since being freed from the dungeon had dissipated like a morning mist. I wished for something solid to hold onto to steady myself. As far as I was concerned, there was nothing in the world more solid than my father. Beyond deep affection that made me want to see him, I *needed* to see him—my fixed, immovable landmark by which I could re-orient my soul. I had been asking Sheshi every day when we would be reunited. At the time, she put the delay off to the vagaries of their legal system. But I redoubled my efforts and my pleas became more frequent and fervent. Finally, Sheshi made the arrangements and Father was allowed to visit me in my room.

"Is your mother all right?" he asked. "And your brothers?"

"When I last saw them, yes," I said. "But I am sorry to report that your father Lamech has gone the way of all the earth."

Father nodded his head sadly and said, "The messenger bore this news to me some time ago."

A moment of silence passed between us before I asked, "Were you able to appear before the High Council?"

"No," said Father. "I was apprehended on the day I arrived in Enoch-Nod. I have been treated well under the pretense of being an honored guest, but my movements are completely restricted. I have petitioned the Council for an audience but to no avail. Even Ben-Tubal's letter has as yet brought me no satisfaction. And what of you? What are these charges that have been leveled against you?"

I told him about my experiences on the night I arrived in Enoch-Nod. When I reached the part where I cursed the Sons of the Gods, his face became very grim. "What you said was not good. There are forces at work here beyond our understanding. It is not good to slander such beings."

"You're right," I said. "That was bad judgment. Perhaps I have misjudged many things."

"It's not like you to give in so easily," said Father, eyeing me carefully. "Have they broken your spirit so completely?"

"No—at least I don't think so. I've just had a lot of time on my hands to think, that's all."

"And what have you been thinking?"

"That maybe the Cainites aren't such bad people after all—just different."

"I hope you've never understood me to say that being different is bad," said Father. "God made us all different and whatever God does is good. It's rebelling against the word of the Lord that's bad."

I turned away, wandered over to the table, and fumbled about absent-mindedly with my things, somehow feeling that a measure of detachment would blunt what I had to say. "What if the word of the Lord doesn't seem good?"

I couldn't see him with my back turned, but I know he bristled at the suggestion. Nevertheless, his voice was controlled when he spoke. "What do you mean?"

"Like the doom you're always talking about," I said. "What pleasure does he take in frightening us with such warnings—or worse yet, in following through with it? And what about animal sacrifice? You know how that's always disturbed me."

"Sometimes we have to trust in the Lord even when we don't understand."

I knew he would say this even before he said it, which only added to my agitation. "And just where is the Lord? Why did he not hear my prayers when I was in the dungeon? Why hasn't he delivered me?"

"Jayfeth, you know the Lord is *always* with us. We can talk with him anytime and anywhere."

"You he talks to," I said. "Me he has abandoned."

"Jayfeth—"

"Maybe Cain was right in refusing the animal sacrifices," I said, giving full vent to my anger. "Why should the innocent die for the guilty? And why should I serve such a god when he doesn't care about me!" When the words were out of my mouth, I could scarcely believe I had said them. I dared not look at Father for fear of seeing the horror on his face.

"What kind of lies have they bewitched you with?" he said. "Have you forgotten that Cain murdered his own brother? And these people venerate him for it!"

I never studied like Shem did, but even I knew that. Why it had temporarily slipped my mind, I cannot say. Suddenly, though, the things I had just said seemed as foolish to me as I'm sure they had to him. "Of course," I said, abashed. "I don't know what I was saying."

"Don't you think I know how hard things have been for you—being the son of a prophet and yet not a prophet; being born of a leading clan and yet an outcast; loving and not being loved? But perhaps the Lord has allowed these things to happen to you to show you what is in your heart. Because it seems to me that resentment over what you *don't* have has been eating away at your soul and blinding you to all the things you *do* have."

At that moment, we heard a guard in the hall talking in a loud voice to the attendant. "Who authorized this? Get that man out of there right now. I'll be speaking to your superior about this."

As the attendant escorted Father away, he turned and added gravely, "I don't know what they're trying to do to your mind, son, but be assured that it won't be for your good. And whatever you do, do not underestimate the cunning of your adversary!"

Father had never spoken to me thus—at least not since I was a child—and his words cut me to the quick. I was ashamed at my behavior and crushed at having lost face in his eyes. So like a man who has tried on new clothes that make him look ridiculous, I discarded my more favorable assessment of the Cainites and put on caution as my garment again—just in time, as it turned out, because I was soon summoned to the House of Hura. When I reached the mansion, Hura and Sheshi were talking on the stairs. My arrival interrupted a serious conversation, and before they realized I was there, I heard Hura saying, "I know you meant well, but that was ill advised."

I listened to see if she would defend herself against whatever this accusation was, but she only lowered her head in acquiescence. When I cleared my throat to let them know I was in the room, Hura acknowledged me with a nod and added, "Your duty is clear. See that you do not lose sight of it."

"Yes, Father," said Sheshi.

As Hura turned and walked slowly up the stairs, Sheshi took me into her studio. I wondered why there were no attendants around as there usually were. When I saw the grave look on her face, I asked, "What is it that troubles you so?"

"It's …" she said, then hesitated. She drew a deep breath and started again. "The trial has been set for this week."

"Isn't that good?"

"You still don't understand, do you?" she said. "Can't you see that their minds are already made up against you? If your father were not a great prophet and carrying a letter of recommendation from Governor Ben-Tubal, the sentence would have been carried out long before now. But do not let the fact that they are going through a trial deceive you into thinking you will escape punishment."

Her face was so sad that I almost felt sorrier for her than I did for myself. "Is there no hope then?"

She did not answer right away, but turned instead toward the window. "In deciding such matters," she said, closing the curtain, "the Council takes many factors into consideration. More than just the circumstances of the case."

I watched her move softly through the warm glow of the lamplight, running her fingers lightly across an open scroll. She did not meet my gaze with her eye, but with her thought, aware that I was not displeased with what I saw. "Go on."

"If an accused person came from one of the ruling families, say. That fact could tip the balance in his favor."

"Regardless of whether he actually committed the crime?"

"Sometimes the facts are open to interpretation," said Sheshi, pausing long enough to light the censer, filling the room with the fragrance of jasmine.

"What does that have to do with me, an outcast from the Gihon Highlands? I'm not from one of the ruling families."

"It is not blood alone that is recognized," she said, completing her slow circuit of the room.

"You mean marriage? But which of the noble daughters would marry a poor foreigner—and an accused murderer at that?"

She stood right in front of me, so close that I did not have to strain my ears to hear her whisper, "I know one."

Speechless, I watched her lift her eyes to meet mine. "Love me, Zhayfeth, and you will lack for nothing you desire."

"But this is…" I fumbled with my words. "What I mean to say is …"

"Why do you hesitate?"

"Well, for one thing, there's the matter of the coming doom that has been prophesied," I said, straining to regain my composure. "If it comes, there will be only one safe haven—in the ark."

"Then I will come with you," she said.

"I would like that very much," I said. "But you cannot come as my wife."

"You are not attracted to women?"

"Oh, it's not that."

"Then it is me that you find unattractive."

"It's not that either," I said. "I think you know the opposite is true."

She looked at me questioningly for a moment and then said, "You did not tell me you were already married."

"I'm not married."

"Engaged then? I understand that among your people that is very nearly the same."

"I am not engaged either."

"Then what is that look that I see in your eye?"

"My heart belongs to another," I said.

"Then why are you neither married nor engaged to her?"

"Her feelings …" I began, with no easy answer for her question, "are not the same for me."

"Then I ask you again, why not make *me* your wife?"

I turned away and leaned on the table with both hands to steady myself. "It's not that simple."

"Why? What could be simpler?" she said, following me. "Would you be better off pining away in a dungeon for a woman who does not love you?"

"Not if you put it like that," I said. "But I haven't given up hope of winning my freedom. If that can be accomplished, I might yet win Re-Aylah's heart as well."

"Then take me as your wife now and be set free. Then, if this other woman has a change of heart, you may take her as your wife as well. I am not so selfish that I wouldn't share you with another for the sake of your happiness."

"That is not our way," I said.

"What is your way, Zhayfeth? The way of unrequited love? The way of wanting what you can never have?"

"No," I said, for I had no other answer.

"Then love me," she implored, embracing me. "I pledge that from the rising of the sun to its setting, I will seek nothing but to serve your every need. And from moonrise to moonset, I will fulfill your every desire. I will withhold nothing from you. You shall be as god to me and I will worship the very ground you tread. And I will be your goddess, the very object of your desire. I will be the woman you have always dreamed of."

Oh, the cunning of the enemy of my soul! For in that moment such temptation seized me as I had never before known. If my father's rebuke hadn't still been ringing in my ears, I might very well have succumbed. But in the moment when I resisted the desire that raged within me, my eyes were opened to a terrible folly within myself. For the first time, I saw clearly what I had been doing to Re-Aylah that she found so repulsive. I had erected an idol to her in my heart—no less real than the ones these people bowed down to. I was blinded from seeing the true person, replacing her with some idealized woman I had invented in my mind. No wonder Re-Aylah recoiled. I pulled away from Sheshi and said, "I am sorry."

"Then I have failed." Sheshi hung her head and began to weep softly.

"Failed?" I said. "I haven't even had my trial yet."

"Just go," she sobbed.

A great sense of uneasiness kept me awake long past midnight, wondering if I had made the right decision. Looking back, I see that that night marked an irrevocable choice in my life. I had cast my lot with the Lord, with my father, and if she would ever have me, with Re-Aylah. There would be no turning back. Indeed, I couldn't have turned back if I wanted to. The paths diverged from that point and the bridge to the fork not taken was burned behind me. Not that there would never be doubts—for I was, by nature, often tormented by them. But having passed, if barely, that one test, the next would necessarily be different.

Eventually, I must have fallen asleep, because the next thing I remember was that the door to my room burst open and in came the Saur-El with a dozen of his guards.

"Get up," he said. "You are to be moved at once."

The ominous tone in his voice and the fact that he had brought so many men with him meant that whatever they were planning would not be for my benefit. "Where are you taking me?"

"To a location more suitable for a criminal like you."

"What about my trial? It is supposed to be this week."

"I'm afraid there has been a slight delay," said the Saur-El. "The date has been rescheduled for *ten years* from this week."

Hearing that, I bolted for the door, but the guards were on me before I took two steps. The Saur-El bent down beside where my face was pinned to the floor and said, "Resisting the reasonable request of the Captain of the Tower Guard? You're list of offenses is growing longer, Sethite. That little act of defiance will add at least seven years to your trial date. But you don't need to worry about that. You won't survive that long. The High Council has something special planned for you. Take him to the pit!"

FIVE

They bound me with ropes, suspended me by my hands and feet from a long pole, and carried me through the courtyard and across the bridge to the south side of the River Euphrates. With my back to the ground and looking up through the crowd of guards, it was difficult to make out much of what I was passing. But the rhythmic rumblings, punctuated by periodic exhalations of steam, gave me little doubt that we were heading toward the furnaces.

The ringing of hammers on anvils indicated that we were very close before we entered a long, low building at the end of which was a passageway that led deep underground. The din of the forges faded as I was toted down a series of dimly lit ramps. But even in that poor light, I could see that the walls were unnaturally smooth, excavated by some process that apparently left the surface impermeable to water or we should have been immersed before we got ten feet underground so near the river.

Not only was the tunnel dry, it was also hot, and grew increasingly so as we went until it became stifling. Still, down we went, passing other tunnels that branched off from the main one, until I realized that the whole city of Enoch-Nod must be connected by subterranean passageways like a gigantic ant colony.

My hands and feet swelled to the point of being quite painful, so that each step of the guards became harder to bear. Finally, though, the passageway leveled out and we came to a massive iron door. I remember wondering why they needed a gate of that size so far underground, but my thought was interrupted by the guards muttering to themselves that they intended to go no farther. Even they feared what lay on the other side. They beat on the door and yelled until at last it opened. With much cursing for their own lack of haste, they threw me roughly inside and left hurriedly.

As the door slammed behind me with a resounding clang, I heard a throaty laugh pitched so low I would not have thought it possible to come from a human being. I looked up at the largest man I have ever seen—head and shoulders above even the tallest of the Nephilim—and quailed to think of strength that could swing a slab of iron the size of that door like I could open the gate to our sheep pen.

"I am Krell," he said, in a voice that was considerably kinder than I expected.

"I am Jay," I offered weakly, not knowing what else to say.

"Yes, I know," said Krell. "I've been expecting you."

He bent down over me with a knife in his hand. For a moment, I thought that he was going to kill me right then. Instead, he cut the ropes that bound my feet and hands, saying, "You won't be needing these."

As I rubbed my throbbing hands and feet, the idea of running for it passed briefly through my mind. I'm sure this was not hard to guess, so Krell added, "Do not think about trying to escape. The only key to that door is the one I carry around my neck—unless you think you can snatch it from me."

He led me down a corridor past rows of closed doors. From inside of some of the cells, I could hear muffled moans of pain and cries of anguish, even through the heavy, windowless doors. I shuddered to think that a similar fate likely awaited me.

The hallway led to a chamber with a vaulted ceiling well-suited to Krell's proportions. At one end of the room was a large table at which a meal had been prepared. He indicated a chair for me to sit and eat with him. Although I was apprehensive, he did not seem to be the sort of man that you wanted to risk offending. With my feet dangling above the floor, I sat across from Krell and ate. The food was tasty enough and the ale strong, but not overpoweringly so. Emboldened by the show of hospitality, I said, "You know who I am, but I don't know who you are apart from your name. Are you the jailer?"

"In a manner of speaking," said Krell. "But my title is Chief Executioner. And this is your last meal."

I gasped and nearly choked on my bread. After a couple of coughs dislodged the crumb, I managed to squeak out the words, "Apparently, I've been sent here by mistake. I haven't even had my trial yet."

"Trial? I received no instructions about a trial."

"But I was supposed to have at least ten more years. No—seventeen!"

"If you ask me, you're better off this way," said Krell. "Go ahead and get it over with."

"I want to see my Advocate Sheshi-Behura."

"You should have been more amenable to her advice before. It's too late for her to help you now."

"Can I at least see my father?" I asked. Father was a very persuasive man. If anyone could get me out of that predicament, he could.

"No," said Krell. "I'm afraid that will not be possible either. You shouldn't have been allowed to see him last time. He puts foolish ideas in your head and now you're worse off for it. You should try thinking for yourself next time. But then, I suppose there won't be a next time, will there? Eat up, now. It will make you feel better."

"I've lost my appetite," I said.

"So, you're ready then?"

"Wait! Maybe just a few more bites," I said and continued eating, chewing very slowly. "So you would kill me just like that?"

"It's my job."

"And do you enjoy your work?" I asked, incredulous that someone could actually have a job doing something so abhorrent.

"It's not so much the actual killing," said Krell. "Any brute can kill. For me, it's the pain and suffering that count. I consider myself an artist. I know just what to do to inflict the greatest amount of anguish on the condemned. I study them to find their most vulnerable points and search out weaknesses that can be exploited. For example, I see that you are a left-handed man, with callused hands and better fed than most I see. That would suggest an entirely different approach than I would take with someone else. Not everyone would see that or know how to expose your most sensitive nerves. In fact, no one could do it better than I, which is why I get all of the special cases. Would you like another loaf of bread?"

I accepted, though it was all I could do to keep putting food in my mouth. When I spoke again, my voice was still less manly that I hoped, but I could no longer blame the breadcrumb. "So, it's to be slow torture then?"

"No, not for you," said Krell. "That was just wishful thinking."

"That's a relief," I said with an audible sigh.

"You won't think so by the time *he* is finished with you—and I do mean *finished*."

Krell's tone made it sound so terrible that I suddenly found that I could not swallow my mouthful of bread. I finally had to wash it down and even then, it seemed to stick in the back of my throat. "Who is *he*?" I asked with trepidation.

"The Exalted One," said Krell. Reading the blank look on my face, he added, "The Morningstar, of course. Who else would I be speaking of?"

"The Morningstar isn't a star?" I said rather stupidly.

Krell shook his head and said, "Do they not teach you anything in your land?"

"They tried to, but I'm afraid I wasn't a very diligent student."

"The Morningstar was the one who opened the eyes of the Father and Mother of all."

"You mean the Serpent?"

"Oh, don't call him that—unless you want to insult him," said Krell. "Besides, it's no longer an apt description. The body he now indwells has grown huge through the devouring of so many. When you see him—and you *will* see him very soon—you will see him as a dragon, with claws like knives and teeth like spears, snorting fire."

"You say that he inhabits this body," I said, stalling for time. "Then it is not his own?"

"Why, he is a spirit being, as are all of his company," said Krell. "What bodies they had in their own realm I cannot say. But they have none in ours so they must use others. Rather, I should say they have no bodies *yet*. However, it is said that very soon they will."

"How can that be?" I asked.

"I do not know the process, for it is not wise to pry into the affairs of the gods. Somehow through their sorceries they have discovered the secret of mating various kinds."

I thought about some of the abnormalities I had encountered in my various travels and about the gruesome experiments being performed at the animal compound. "Now that you mention it, I have seen some strange things which make more sense in light of what you have just said. But what would be the purpose of creating such monsters?"

Krell leaned over the table and said in a low voice, "I would not tell you this otherwise, but you will soon be dead. So why keep it a secret from you? They are like eunuchs, with no ability to produce offspring. Since they fell out of favor with the Terrible One and were banished from his presence, they have been seeking a way to gain the advantage, for they are outnumbered. But if they can find a way to propagate themselves and become a race, then they can increase their numbers and overthrow the Terrible One."

"But what does this have to do with humans?" I asked.

"They need a kind to intermarry with. Next to them, humans are the highest order beings." Then he added with a wink, "And, frankly, they are quite taken with our women."

Krell's words so filled me with horror that I didn't know what else to say. The Terrible One he spoke of could be no other than God Almighty and this plan to create a demonic race would be an unspeakable abomination in his sight. At last, I began to understand the urgency of the impending doom that had been revealed to my father. This could not be allowed to come to pass.

By then, I was so distraught that eating was out of the question. "I see you're quite finished," Krell said. "Good. We'd best be getting on with it. Just leave those dishes. It wouldn't be hospitable to make you clean up and then kill you."

He led me down another passageway. I followed him dutifully, though I am not sure why. As we descended, I felt the heat intensifying again.

We soon came to a ledge and stopped. Krell said, "This is where we part ways. I will lower you down by this rope. When you get to the bottom, just wait. The Exalted One will come to you in his time."

"You expect me to climb down this rope and just wait for the dragon to come and devour me?" I asked.

"I could throw you down instead," said Krell. "But you would probably be killed or severely injured by the fall."

"What difference would it make if I am to be dead soon anyway?"

"He prefers to devour his victims alive," said Krell. "The more terror he can inflict upon them, the more he seems to enjoy it. It makes the meat bitter, which is just the way he likes it."

"Is there any chance at all for me?" I asked. "Of defeating the dragon or escaping his clutches?"

"None that I can see," said Krell. "Nothing on earth can match the dragon for power and cunning—certainly not a puny man like you. And as for escape, there are only two ways out. One is the tunnel that leads to the dragon's lair and the other descends to the lake of fire."

Given those two choices, the latter sounded preferable. I said, "What's the lake of fire?"

"Do you not know that deep inside the earth it is hot beyond imagination?" said Krell. "The Watchers have discovered a way to tap into this heat that is so hot it melts rocks. It fires their furnaces and powers their factories. But do not think that you can escape that direction, for you would be incinerated before you got anywhere near it. On the other hand, dying that way might be preferable. You might make it far enough to avoid having the dragon feast on your roasted body. He will not go near the lake of fire himself because of an oracle that is the one thing that he fears. Now get down this rope before I lose patience with you. I can see that you are only stalling to prolong your life."

Why I climbed down that rope and into the darkness below I cannot say. I thought briefly about trying to flee back up the passageway. But to do that I would have had to go through Krell. Since I only came up to just above his waist, that seemed impossible. Still, a man fighting for his life may perform amazing feats of strength and it might have seemed preferable to die that way. But those who say such things were not in my place. They did not see how imposing the man was, nor did they hear the authority with which he spoke. He was neither dull-witted nor slow as giants in later ages came to be. Rather, he was awe-inspiring in every respect.

Like a frightened child obeying his father or a cringing soldier obeying his king, something within me responded to his command. If I had to die, I wanted to die bravely and not as a whimpering coward. But as I descended into the black heat of the pit, my resolve withered. It was deeper and darker than I expected and I had the unsettling sensation of being suspended over nothing. I had very nearly changed my mind and decided to climb back out when my foot hit the floor. Immediately, he jerked the rope out of my hands. I was trapped.

"Krell, tell me that you will keep watch with me until the dragon comes," I found myself saying.

"I am sorry, little one," he said. "Even Krell does not dare to be near when the dragon is at his work."

With that, he was gone and I was alone in the dark with the dragon.

Six

As my eyes adjusted to the darkness, I detected the faint reflection of fire to my left. Approaching cautiously, I peered inside a passageway that twisted sharply to the left and down, disappearing into a cauldron of molten rock about a hundred and fifty feet below where surface encrustations of slightly cooler rock rolled like ships tossed upon seething waves of magma. "The lake of fire?" I wondered. All those campfire tales of a fiery place of darkness and torment suddenly became very real to me. And I found no consolation in recalling that it was supposed to be the place to which the wicked dead were condemned. Hastily I withdrew, unable to withstand the heat unshielded for more than a few moments because I felt like a loaf of bread baking in a stone oven.

As I groped my way around the circumference of the pit, only sheer, smooth walls met my touch except for one wide opening. However, when I took a tentative step forward into the blackness, a sense of unmitigated dread stopped me in my tracks. That tunnel led to the dragon's lair. Whatever slim hope I had momentarily entertained of escape in that direction faded into despair. Retreating to the place I had originally descended, I wilted on the spot and acquiesced to my fate.

Already I was sweating profusely and the heat of the surrounding rocks was rapidly turning my discomfort into anguish. I fixed my gazed on the tunnel across from me, straining my eyes so that I might see my doom approaching. In that feverish swelter, the shadows cast by the lake of fire took on the semblance of apparitions. It was only a trick of the eye, I kept telling myself, not specters, but failed to convince myself. Despite the heat, I began to shake—part from fright and part from heat exhaustion.

A constant low rumbling, felt as much as heard, and the intermittent hissing of steam sounded the dirge for my interment. However, it was no eulogy of praise that I heard through my delirium—rather accusations.

Regret for every wrong I had ever committed and every unkind word I had ever spoken assailed me in that tomb. Why, it had only been a few hours earlier that I had blasphemed the very character and person of God Almighty. Now he had brought me to the fitting end of a doubter and evildoer. Since the impending punishment was so well deserved, I feared to call for deliverance on the name of the one I had maligned. But from a seared heart through parched lips, I found myself mumbling, "Mercy, God, have mercy."

By then, I had stopped perspiring, my body wrung out like a rag. Too weak to sit up any longer, I leaned over on my side and waited for the otherworldly beast to carry me away. When, lo, I saw in the tunnel a far distant light—not still, but moving closer. The dragon was drawing near, a furnace of fury, stoked with hatred, and bent on destroying all who did not serve him. A scream of terror rose within me, but withered in my desiccated throat. With no strength left to fight, I shut my eyes and hoped that death would overtake me quickly—and that I would not open my eyes in the next life to find that my circumstances had not improved.

Out of the darkness, I heard my name echoing through the tunnel. It was a familiar voice, but surely only the delusion of a dying man hearing the sound he most wanted to hear. Against all fear, I opened my eyes, fully expecting to see the terrible monster ready to devour me. But behold—it was Re-Aylah!

At that same moment, she spotted me, too. Rushing to my side, she poured water into my mouth from her flask, cradling me in her arms, for by then I could hardly even sit up by myself to drink. I clung to her and wept like a baby.

When at last I regained a bit of my composure and felt my strength returning, she said, "Come, let us leave this dreadful place. Can you stand?"

As she helped me to my feet, I could not take my eyes off of her. "What happened to your hair?" I said. "And why are you dressed like a court servant?"

"You told me yourself that Nod was no place for a woman," said Re-Aylah. "I did my best to hide that fact."

"How on earth did you find me here?"

"I'll tell you on the way. But Sheshi-Behura said that we must not delay. We don't know how much time we have. Are you able to walk?"

I nodded and she put my arm around her shoulder. Leaning heavily upon her, we entered the tunnel—the place I had so dreaded only a short time earlier. But I would have followed her anywhere at that moment—even into the dragon's lair.

As we walked along, Re-Aylah quietly explained how she came to be there. Ben-Tubal, hearing of our plight, had determined to come to Enoch-Nod to personally seek our release. At Jirah's urging, His Excellency had been persuaded to allow Re-Aylah to come along with his entourage. Their arrival in Enoch-Nod coincided more or less with my transfer to Krell's charge. When Sheshi-Behura learned that I had been taken by Saur-El, she had become alarmed. So, she sought out the Nephilim to ask for their assistance in rescuing me because she feared that a diplomatic solution might come too late.

"But why you?" I asked.

"Who else would risk venturing into the devil's den to save you?"

"Good point," I said. "I suppose that makes us even now as far as rescues are concerned."

"You're forgetting the dogs," said Re-Aylah. "I think this puts me one up on you. But who's counting?"

The tunnel was longer than I had imagined, and not just because distances seem greater underground. At some point, we had actually crossed under the river, so that we were back on the north side of the Euphrates when a flicker of light caught my eye. "What's that up ahead?" I whispered, alarmed that the dragon might have come for me after all.

"It's Sheshi-Behura," said Re-Aylah. "What did you think it was?"

"Never mind," I said. "By the way, I hope you haven't jumped to any conclusions about Sheshi and me."

"Do you mean a conclusion like she's in love with you?"

"You know about that? Nothing came of it, I assure you. How did you find out? Did she tell you?"

"I don't have to be told things like that," said Re-Aylah. "After all, I am a woman."

"You're not just *a* woman," I said. "You are Re-Aylah."

"Very good, Jay. You *are* learning."

Sheshi waited in a doorway that was so well disguised that it would have been impossible to see if you did not know exactly where to look. Seeing Re-Aylah and me together must have been difficult for her and it showed on her face, but she didn't say a word. Up a series of ramps and stairs she led us until we reached another door that she opened by some concealed mechanism. Being out of the pit was a relief, but those new surroundings were hardly comforting—a vast complex of subterranean chambers connected by winding tunnels. Without Sheshi's familiarity with the passages, we would have become hopelessly lost.

As we ascended, we began to see crimson and saffron-robed priests engaged in sorceries so terrible that I am loathe to relate them. However, without some understanding thereof, this account would be incomplete and the subsequent events incomprehensible. As I have previously recounted, I had begun to piece together a vague conception of the perversion that was underway, but the full scale of the operation was now revealed in its awful entirety. For there, in the nether regions deep below the Tower of the Watch, an execrable alliance was being forged.

Surely man is more than bone and flesh alone. Who could deny that he also consists of an immaterial nature—a spirit, if you will—that distinguishes him from inanimate objects, and by immeasurable degree, from animals as well? Some men may be said to possess a greater spirit, and some a lesser, but all possess a portion; otherwise, they would not be human. But while man's spirit is an essential part of his nature, his spirit has been dominated by the flesh—though I do not think it was intended to be so. A different realm also exists where the opposite is true—where spirit holds sway. And, if a rift separates men and animals, between men and the spirit beings who populate the other realm lies an abyss. Therefore, betwixt the two worlds—material and immaterial—a thick curtain has been drawn, though perhaps in the days of Adam it was less so. For some men, like my father, the barrier may seem more veil than curtain, because God opens their eyes at times and enables them to see beyond. The all-important distinction, however, is that this gift is initiated by God. The prophets of the Lord did not take this office upon themselves (as I was all too painfully aware), nor did they communicate with any being other than the Lord or his designated messengers. Not so the sorcerer. Whatever his guise, he can be recognized by his trespass against the boundary fixed between the realms. Despising the ordained order, those fallen spirits stand at the door, so to speak, and seek admittance where they ought not enter. There, conjurer and conjured embrace in an unholy communion. The priests and priestesses of Enoch-Nod were such sorcerers, and that place— the Tower of the Watch—was the nexus between the two realms, where learning transgressed the line into the occult and the spiritual degenerated into the demonic.

But the sorcerer's first step is a misstep—and a fatal one. Having breached the barrier for his own purpose, the sorcerer's curse is that he must, inevitably, be bent toward the purpose of the forces he has admitted. The atrophied spirit of a man is no match for the power of a being whose primary existence is spirit. The human servants of the Watchers were certainly no exception. Whatever seemingly noble motivation that had started them down the enlightened pathway—the longing for knowledge or yearning to touch the great beyond—had long since been twisted into another kind of craving, an intercourse of a forbidden kind, and one that was reciprocated by the spirit beings themselves. Whether it was because the spirit beings had been banished from their native abode or for some other reason unfathomable to humans, they seem to have had a peculiar fascination with the realm and affairs of men. So, in spite of the yawning chasm that separated the two realms and the taboo that should have caused the spirit to resist carnalization and the human to recoil from demonization, both sides were busily at work building bridges across the gap in the netherworld of Enoch-Nod.

I am treading here, I admit, with uncertain footing, speaking of matters which I, among offspring of prophets, rank among the least qualified to expound. Yet, how else could I explain the gruesome and unnatural contortions of a demoniac's face which looked like a novice taking up a musical instrument for the first time; or the levitation of one of the priestesses five feet off the ground with no visible means of support; or the guttural utterances of chants in a language that was never meant to be heard on earth; and, especially, I shudder to recall the macabre surgery that was joining the head and torso of a man to the body of a goat? (What an abomination!) Even so, this was only a foretaste of the abomination yet to come. For there was another sound that came echoing through the chambers—the most familiar and worldly of all I heard there, but that only made it more upsetting. It was the bawling of a cow in the throes of a difficult birth. And the cry that went up from her calf as she delivered was unlike anything I have ever heard or wish to hear again.

All this I took in with no more than brief glances and chance overhearings as we made our way along the twisted passageways. A better man might have confronted the cultists and rebuked them for their devilry. But having only recently sojourned in the land of blasphemy myself, I hardly felt competent (had I thought of it at all) to lecture them. Indeed, sickened as I was by what I observed, my only thought was to avoid notice.

Sheshi's status as daughter and heir-apparent of the High Priest of the Morningstar enabled us to accomplish this without incident for some time. No one challenged us or even paid attention, engrossed as they were in their dark arts. For this I was thankful, because I was already weak and tiring quickly of the steep ascent. As we reached the upper chambers, though, we heard a commotion below.

"Do you think they've discovered that I have escaped?" I whispered fearfully.

Sheshi hurried us into an alcove and we listened intently. "I do not think so," she said at last. "It sounds more like exultation than dismay." Her face showed relief, though her hands trembled. I thought to myself, and not without good cause, that she did not look well.

A little further up, the passageway split again and Sheshi said, "Here we must part for now, Re-Aylah. Beyond the door at the end of this corridor is where Ben-Tubal's entourage is quartered. You will be as safe there as anywhere."

"Why can't I go with her?" I protested, not wanting to be separated from Re-Aylah and preferring Ben-Tubal's protection to whatever lay down the other, more ominous-looking tunnel.

"Do you think it would be wise for a condemned prisoner who has just escaped to risk being seen in public right now?" Sheshi admonished. "You must hide for awhile and let His Excellency seek clemency for you."

"And if he fails?"

The anguish on Sheshi's face was more than ample reply. I had been so obsessed about my own fate that I had given no thought about what this was costing her. I shut my mouth and argued no more.

SEVEN

The corridor we took was narrower and wound through out-of-the-way places that appeared little-used even by the cultists. Though we saw no other persons or any sign of activity, I had a growing sense of foreboding that I could not explain as we proceeded. Finally, we came to what appeared to be a dead end and I thought for a moment that Sheshi might have lost her way.

"At the pinnacle of the Tower is a place where you might be able to escape detection for a time," Sheshi said, haltingly, as she seemed to be debating within herself about how much to disclose. "But to reach it ..."

"Yes?"

"To reach it, we must pass through a certain place."

"A dangerous place?" Sheshi nodded and I said, "I can't imagine a place more dangerous than the ones through which we've just come."

"This one is," said Sheshi, her voice barely a whisper. "It is the Inner Sanctum of the Watchers. Your life will be in grave peril—and mine."

"I thought you were on good terms with ... them."

"After I just helped you escape?"

"I see your point," I said.

"Even if that were not the case, you should not make the mistake of lumping them all together. The cults may be in alliance, but they are not all of uniform purpose—and that can be dangerous."

"But they don't have to know. I'll keep your secret."

"Aiyah!" she said. "They are Watchers—don't you know! They don't need to be told. They can read people, like a person reads a scroll. I have made a practice of opening myself up to them. I do not know how long I can keep myself closed."

"Then let's go another way," I suggested.

"There is no other way," said Sheshi. "Everywhere are spies except in the place where they least suspect. They are distracted by the arrival of Ben-Tubal or they would have found you out long before now. Our only chance is to sneak past them while they are occupied with other matters."

Sheshi's knowing touch in just the right place on the wall revealed a hidden door that gave way with a slight push. Soundlessly, and with profound trepidation, we slipped inside. A short flight of stairs led to a vestibule behind a long wicker screen that partitioned a staging area for their rituals. Dark lay the hall in a dismal cloak of gloom that smothered the light offered by the circular fire pit in the center of the polished, black marble floor. Twenty chairs, and outside of those a like number of columns, circled the smoldering coals. And upon the chairs were seated—I shudder to recall—the Watchers!

They looked like men; at least they had the outward appearance of men. But that was the most unsettling part. I never realized until that moment how little the form of man had to do with his humanity. Even with their faces shrouded in the shadows of their cowls, a difference was manifest. Although it is difficult to describe in words, a child could have seen it—if any child were left in the world. Yet, it was so subtle that one of them might pass through a crowd unnoticed if he wanted. The best I can describe it is that their expressions lacked nuance, the natural display of sympathetic emotion—like the flicker of the pupil when eyes meet or the almost imperceptible nod of acknowledgement when listening to someone speak. Likewise, the language was easily understandable, but lacked a certain familiarity. It was communication without communion. There was something cold, remote and bloodless about them—a high, haughty superiority that seemed to demand prostration and cringing from lesser beings. I wondered briefly what had become of the Nephilim whose bodies these Sons of the Gods now inhabited—if they had forfeited them completely or whether some vestige of their former selves remained. The latter possibility seemed the less likely, for I detected no trace of anything with which it would be possible to relate on a truly human level. The things before me were wholly alien.

As we entered the Inner Sanctum, an unholy council had just begun. Though we made no footfall, the pounding of my heart felt loud enough to be audible and I had to make a conscious effort to quiet my breathing. The one who seemed to be their leader was saying, with all the vivacity of the last exhalation of breath before death, "You all know why the Nephilite Governor is here. What are we going to do with the prophet?"

"We cannot just let him go, Semjaza, if that is what you are suggesting," came the challenge from a broad-shouldered one across the circle.

"What more can we do than has already been done, Azazel?" asked Semjaza.

"We need more time," said another, whose back was toward us as we slipped along quietly behind the screen. "The son is weak and very nearly ready to succumb. The priest's plan will work, I tell you."

"It's too late, Jomjeel," said Semjaza. "He has been dispatched to the Master Executioner. I could not delay because the signs portended betrayal."

At the word "betrayal," Sheshi halted, pressed herself against the wall and went rigid with fright. We were still some fifty feet from the doorway she had indicated—too far to reach before being detected, which now seemed more imminent and inevitable than ever. Not knowing what else to do, I took Sheshi's hand and tried to revive her.

"That is unfortunate," said Jomjeel. "This son was our best chance to influence the father."

"The prophet would not have been swayed regardless," said Azazel.

"Doubtless you have a better idea," said Semjaza.

"You should have listened to my advice and disposed of this matter a long time ago," said Azazel.

"That's easy to say." Stiffly, Semjaza got up and paced the floor as he talked. "But you can see for yourself that he has the seal. You know very well the limits."

"Respecting the seal is a sign of weakness," Azazel sneered.

"No, it is a sign of intelligence," said Semjaza. "We cannot risk provoking the Terrible One now while we are yet outnumbered. We could lose everything."

"Soon, we will not be outnumbered," said a voice I had not yet heard.

"So you say, Rameel, but I see no evidence." Semjaza knelt down and thrust his hand into the burning embers. I watched, horrified as he removed it, still smoldering, and showed it to the others. "See, this body is almost used up. Already it has lost the ability to feel. I weary of constantly changing from weakling to weakling."

"We are making progress—" Rameel started to say before Semjaza cut him off.

"What you call progress looks like nothing more than freaks to me," he said, sitting again. "We need a vessel more worthy of the treasure it bears."

"And you will have it!" said Rameel. "I am trying to tell you we have had a breakthrough, just today."

"Go on."

"You just said yourself that these bodies are weak," said Rameel. "We have wasted far too much time manipulating flesh alone. But now we have succeeded in making a body that is more than flesh!" The room went totally silent for a moment as the Council processed the implications of this statement. Then Rameel added, "I should say that much of the credit goes to Azazel and his men for their skill in metallurgy."

"These are bodies of metal?" asked Semjaza.

"No," said Rameel. "This is beyond metallurgy, beyond husbandry and the mating of different kinds, beyond anything that's been done before. We have created something entirely new—a calf of living gold!"

Excited murmurs (if you could call the sound "excited") echoed around the room. Sheshi was still catatonic, but the Watchers were so intent on the matter at hand that I began to hope again that we might escape detection.

"Silence!" said Semjaza, and immediately quiet was restored. "There will be time enough for celebration when the deed is accomplished. That, however, is by no means a certainty. As you well know, the Exalted One has grave reservations about our endeavors."

"That's only because he does not know the pleasure of these human women as we do," said Azazel.

"The Morningstar is the *archos*—may he be praised," said Semjaza. "If the condescension of this liaison with humans is difficult for us, how much more for him? But he has not forbidden us as long as we do not interfere with his designs. So, if what Rameel has said proves to be the solution for which we have been searching, we should apply all our efforts toward the end of increasing our numbers. Then, we will be able to overthrow the Terrible One and all of the universe will be ours to rule!"

"It will only be a matter of months before we are ready to proceed with human women," said Rameel. "But we will need a vast supply because they will not survive the birth."

"That can be arranged," said Semjaza. "For now, though, I suggest that we do nothing to arouse suspicion until the time is right. Thus, let us send the prophet away, for I divine that it would be better if he were kept unaware of our plans."

"That will make Ben-Tubal look like he has prevailed over us," said Azazel.

"That can't be helped," said Semjaza. "But he is still useful—for a little longer at least. Now, let us have a look at your handiwork, Rameel—and gaze upon the future of the universe!"

The Watchers made for the door that Sheshi and I had entered only a few minutes earlier. Without even the screen in between we would surely be seen as they passed by. There was nothing to be done except to pick Sheshi up in my arms and carry her to the far end of the chamber while they exited on the other side of the screen.

At the door, the Watchers hesitated and Semjaza said, "I smell something."

I had little doubt that it was the sweat of fearful intruders. But Azazel unwittingly diverted suspicion by saying, "It is the burnt flesh on your hand, Semjaza. Go on, we are wasting time."

As they departed, Sheshi and I reached the stairwell and collapsed on the floor.

For a long time, we sat without moving as the pool of fear that had engulfed us slowly drained away. What a strain it had been for Sheshi to keep herself closed to the Watchers, I can only imagine, but gradually a semblance of life returned to her face. "We have a long climb ahead," she said at last. "Let us begin our ascent."

I looked closely at her face, drawn and deathly pale. "You are in no condition for that kind of exertion."

She considered that assessment for a moment and said, "You are right. But you should have no trouble finding your way now. This stairway leads only to the pinnacle and opens to no other floor. You should be safe there—for awhile at least. Tonight is not a night for watching."

"And what will you do?"

"My father's house is the least suspicious place for me to be—and the place where he can best protect me if need be. They already suspect something, so I must make ready my own escape. You heard them."

"Now that you mention it, yes, I did hear them," I said, with an edge in my voice that I could not conceal.

"I know what you are thinking."

"I may be a bumpkin from the hills," I said, "But the hills aren't *that* high. What did the Watcher mean by 'the priest's plan'? Has all this been only a scheme to turn me away from my father and God?"

"You have been manipulated, yes," Sheshi slowly admitted.

"And you were part of it?"

"I am so sorry, Zhayfeth," she said and began to weep. "I never meant to hurt you—I swear it. I do love you. That much was true and they didn't count on that. I know I can never have you—not in the way I want. But you have to believe that I'm telling you the truth now. My life is forfeit because of what I have done for you."

Sheshi's confession so moved me that I could not harden my heart against her. I put my hand on her shoulder and said, "I do believe you. And you shall have sanctuary with us. Even if I don't make it out alive, tell my father all that has happened—Re-Aylah will vouch for you—and you will dwell in our tents."

"Do not speak of your own death," she said. "You will survive this ordeal. Has your god not ordained it? As for the rest, I must face what has been ordained for me."

As we parted, Sheshi told me to watch the window of her studio. When she placed a lighted lamp there, that would be the signal that it was safe to come down. I made good progress running up the first twenty flights, but had slowed down somewhat by thirty, still weak from all I had endured. At forty, I was breathing hard and at fifty I stopped to catch my breath and think for a minute, because it occurred to me that I had no food or water. I briefly contemplated going back down, but quickly dismissed the idea. Things had gone far better than they might have up to that point and it was not worth risking otherwise for a meal—even if I had any good prospect of finding one. After that, I went slower. At seventy, I began to wonder if I would ever reach the top. While I was reassuring myself that the steps could not go upward unceasingly, I lost count. I was breathing so hard by then that I couldn't remember the last number of which I was certain, or even make a good estimate of how many more flights I climbed. But at last, I reached the top and lay down on the roof, sides heaving.

After a few minutes, I sat up and took stock of my surroundings. Above the foul air that settled near the ground of Enoch-Nod, the stars shone and it seemed almost peaceful. The roof was flat and surrounded by a three-foot-high parapet. It contained a great variety of equipment—shiny metal and glass instruments bearing strange markings (a kind of celestial mathematics, I suppose). Arrayed on tables were numerous sky maps and diagrams plotting the course of the sun, moon and stars—a motif that seemed everywhere repeated in Enoch-Nod and was apparently of paramount importance to the

Watchers. Whether these marked portals back to their own domain, delineated a method of divination, or served some other purpose, I do not know.

I made my way over to the edge of the roof and peered over the side to locate the House of Hura and immediately recoiled at the shock of seeing how high I was. With no small exertion of will, I fought back dizziness and forced myself to look again. The haze of dirty air made it difficult to see clearly the objects below. Dimly, at times, I could make out the faint outline of Hura's mansion, but was alarmed to realize that if there was a light shining in Sheshi's window, I wouldn't have been able to see it.

Every few minutes, I checked again, hoping that conditions would improve, but to no avail. I was haunted by the thought that the lamp might be burning brightly, only obscured by the poor visibility, and that I might be missing my one chance to escape. Eventually, weak and exhausted, I dozed off to sleep.

I awoke with a start, thinking I heard voices. I momentarily dismissed the notion, remembering Sheshi's assurance that the roof would not be in use that night. Just a fragment of a bad dream, I thought. But then I heard it again and this time the otherworldly voices emanating from the stairwell were unmistakable. The Watchers were coming!

EIGHT

F rantically I searched, but there was no place to hide and no way to escape without sprouting wings. In desperation, I peered over the parapet and spotted a narrow ledge, not more than eighteen inches wide. It was only about three feet below me, but it was a thousand feet above the ground. "Oh, no," I groaned. But I only hesitated for a moment. I had no other choice and no time to waste. So over the battlement I scrambled and ducked down out of sight just as two Watchers emerged from the stairwell. Narrow ledges at great heights are not generally good places to practice such acrobatics—especially for people like me who are not known for their grace. I nearly lost my balance in the process and only my tenuous grip on the crenel saved me from an ungainly dive onto the courtyard far below.

After I had repeated "don't look down" to myself at least ten times, I opened my eyes and risked a peek through the opening. Seated at their instruments gazing into the night sky, they were, in the purest sense, "watchers," reading the heavens like a scholar reading a scroll.

After some time, the taller of the two said, "What do you make of it, Baraqijal?"

"As you say, Kokabel, it appears to be a comet."

"But what of the interpretation?" asked Kokabel.

As Baraqijal plotted the position of the comet on his chart, he said, "Before I answer, I would know what you think of the course we have chosen."

"Some aspects seem promising," said Kokabel hesitantly. "And yet ..."

"Go on. The others cannot hear us. And you know you can speak openly with me."

"That is true—and the very reason I have brought you here tonight, even though it was not a night to watch. So I will tell you that I have a great uneasiness, despite the optimism of the others."

"Your misgivings are not unfounded," said Baraqijal. "I divine that this comet is a portent of ill for our band and not for good."

"Aargh," said Kokabel. "I feared you would say this. You, above all, are most skilled in the divining of signs in the heavens. But though my skill lies more in observation and calculation, I am not unacquainted with your art. You have validated the conclusion I had already reached."

A long silence fell between them as they stared at the heavens unaided by their instruments. My legs started to cramp from crouching in that awkward position, but I dared not move a muscle for fear of startling the pigeons that had settled to roost only a few feet away. They stared at me with a wariness that left no doubt that they were ready to take flight at the slightest provocation. I gritted my teeth and held on, hoping the Watchers were not planning to stay up there all night.

At last, Kokabel said, "Do you ever wish you could go back?"

"Such thoughts are futile," said Baraqijal. "You know we cannot go back."

"But if the signs are against us, what shall we do?"

"What can we do? The constellations do not lie."

"Is there no way, then, to change what fate has decreed?"

"Only a great convulsion of the heavens and earth could alter it now."

"But would the convulsion turn in our favor?" asked Kokabel.

"Our only chance is to *make* it turn in our favor," answered Baraqijel with a note of finality that filled me with dread.

Without another word, the Watchers left the roof. The moment it was safe, I climbed back over the parapet, scattering pigeons in the process and vowing that if, by providence, I survived that ordeal, my feet would never willingly leave the security of solid earth again.

When my wits had sufficiently recovered, I wondered about the sign that had so alarmed the Watchers. Cautiously, I put my eye to the instrument through which they had been looking and, lo, the sky was inside the device! In the center was a star with a strange tail that I assumed was the omen they had spoken about. Fascinated, I sat there transfixed for a long time, until I finally tore myself away to look at the star map. There was the fresh notation that Baraqijal had made concerning the ill portent. It was in the constellation of the water-bearer.

The seeing devices gave me an idea. I searched through the equipment until I found one that could be held easily in the hand and looked into it. What was far appeared near in it, too—not to the same degree as the larger ones, but suitable for what I had in mind. I aimed it at the House of Hura. Though I still had some difficulty penetrating the haze below, I could clearly see lights, but not, I felt sure, in the corner where Sheshi's studio lay. In this way, I passed what was left of the night, checking every quarter hour or so and observing the stars in the time between. When morning came, I used even greater care, so as not to present a silhouette against the sky. About an hour after daybreak, I finally saw the signal I was awaiting—the brightly burning lamp in Sheshi's studio.

I replaced the seeing device where I found it and descended the stairs. My apprehension about encountering more Watchers grew with each step. By the time I reached the bottom, my pulse was racing—and not just from exertion. Cautiously, I peeked into the unholy place and was relieved to see that it was empty. On the opposite side of the room, the double doors that served as the main entrance were standing open, beyond which a short corridor led to the much larger assembly hall, though most of that was hidden from my view. I wasted no time retracing my steps around the screen and fumbled with the door for only a moment before it opened. I hurried as fast as practical down the tunnels, hoping not to meet anyone, to the place where Re-Aylah had separated from us. At the end of that shorter passageway was a door. While I searched for a hidden mechanism, I heard noises stirring from somewhere below. "Trapped again," I berated myself. When I turned to see if anyone was coming, I leaned against the door and it opened, sending me sprawling backward on the floor of the suite where Ben-Tubal and his men, along with Re-Aylah, were gathered. How quickly I had forgotten that a door could be just a door.

"There you are," said Re-Aylah, helping me to my feet. "I was just reassuring our friends here that you would be along presently."

Ben-Tubal shook his head at me. Then his men knew it was all right to laugh, which they did, heartily, at my expense. He said, "The first day I set eyes on you, I said to myself, 'There is a boy whom trouble follows like his shadow. And when it isn't following him, he goes chasing after it!'" Then the men laughed all the harder.

"I'm glad to see you, too," I said. "Do you have anything to eat? I'm starving."

"That's a man," said Re-Aylah, salvaging for me what remained of their breakfast. "Always thinking of his stomach—"

"As I was going to say," interrupted Ben-Tubal. "Trouble has found you once again, son of Noah, and you had better listen to me or you'll have more to contend with than this woman's tongue. I will be summoned momentarily to appear before the High Council of the Watch to plead your father's case. They think you are dead. I do not know how they have been prevented from apprehending that you are, in fact, very much alive—because practically nothing escapes their notice. Whatever the explanation, I am not inclined to dispel their misconception if I can help it. Appealing for one will be easier than for two. Therefore, I propose that you change clothes and try passing yourself off as one of our servants as your cousin has done. I would offer you the robe of a Nephilite, but I don't think that would look convincing unless you plan to grow some in the next five minutes—though with the way you are eating, anything is possible."

"Thank you for your kindness, Your Excellency," I said. "But there is something you should know about these ... whatever they are. They have plans to—"

"Do not speak of it," he said in hushed tones. "I know very well the situation we are facing here. In fact, I have been coping with it since before you were born. Believe it or not, things could have turned out much worse for humankind if not for my skill in governance and diplomacy. But there was a limit to what I could do. After all, they raised up the Nephilim for the sole purpose of serving them. A hammer cannot forge itself, as we say. But if that hammer be swung by another hand ..." His voice trailed away for a moment before he continued. "Well, now is not the right time. We are in their stronghold and the matter before us is a delicate one. It could very well turn out that chasing after your family's trouble will lead to trouble of my own."

"I understand," I said. "And I am more grateful than you could know. So, I am embarrassed to ask one more favor of you."

"But that will not prevent it, I am sure."

"You wondered how I managed to survive. It was only through the assistance of the daughter of the High Priest, as I'm sure Re-Aylah has told you. Sheshi now fears for her own life and would seek sanctuary in Cush."

"The daughter of Hura—egad, man!" exclaimed Ben-Tubal. "He is more dangerous, in his own way, than the Watchers. And she is the apple of his eye. This I will *not* do."

"But after all she has done for me, I cannot just abandon her."

"You are irreformable, master troublemaker, and I do not have time to explain all the reasons why this is a bad idea. But since we must come to some quick understanding on the matter, I'll make this one concession. If perchance she came to abide in the Gihon Valley, which I think is a *very* unlikely possibility, I would look the other way. That is not sanctuary, mind you. And she must make her own escape. I will not lift one finger to help. This is my final word on the matter. Understood?"

"Clearly understood, Your Excellency. Thank you."

"Now change and quickly," he said. "She will be here any moment."

NINE

I barely had time to don the plain robe of a servant before Sheshi came to escort us to the assembly hall. She nodded knowingly at me, but said nothing. As we came into the presence of the High Council of the Watch, Re-Aylah and I had no difficulty hiding behind the Nephilim entourage, tall as they were. Yet even though we were screened from sight, I could not help feeling exposed in an inward way, as if they might be able to *feel* my presence. Father was already in the hall, and though he did not see me, I was comforted by knowing he was there. Hura also was in attendance to observe his daughter's debut as Advocate.

In contrast to the sparse inner sanctum, the assembly hall was opulent beyond description. The effect was overwhelming—not for its artistry, but for its extravagance. The floors and pillars were of the finest onyx in Havilah and the walls were overlaid with gold. In the middle of the chamber was a raised dais and bar, also of gold and encrusted with precious jewels. Upon the bar were carved blasphemous images, at the center of which was a depiction of the sun subservient to the stars. Behind the bar on thrones of ebony sat the High Council of the Watch. Mercifully, their faces still remained mostly obscured by the shadows of their cowls, but I would have recognized those inflectionless voices anywhere. Behind the dais was a gallery, where some two hundred more of their band were seated in the shadows. The floor of the chamber had no chairs, so we were obliged to stand before the intimidating assembly. From the center of the dais, the Watcher called Semjaza spoke. "In the matter before us today, a prophet from the land of Cush has come to Enoch-Nod. It would be of no consequence to us if not for two reasons. The first is that the prophet has been inciting the people wherever he goes. The second is that his son was accused of unprovoked murder. That matter, however, has been recompensed in a manner befitting—". He halted in mid-sentence, fixing his eyes on Sheshi. When he said, "I suspected as much," the color drained from her face and I thought she might faint.

"The Morningstar—may his name be praised—in his divine wisdom, determined to spare the young man," said Hura, stepping in to steady her. Considering the circumstances, his voice was remarkably calm.

"Strange that he would reveal this to you alone," said Semjaza.

"I am his servant," said Hura with what sounded like a hint of rebuke. A long, almost unbearable silence followed, with Semjaza and Hura locked in a contest of wills. I was amazed at Hura's boldness and fearful of the power that made him so. Finally, Hura conciliated to a degree by adding, "The Morningstar's ways are inscrutable. Who am I to question them?"

That seemed to placate Semjaza for the moment. He looked in my direction and said, "Come out and stand beside your father."

I don't know how he sensed that I was in the hall, but there was no point in trying to hide any longer. Father looked at me, eyebrows raised, as I took my place next to him and I shrugged my shoulders. The Watchers in the gallery murmured at seeing me alive. To quiet them, Semjaza raised his charred hand (the sight of which was enough to unsettle my hastily eaten breakfast). "Now let us continue," he said.

Sheshi had recovered a little by then and Hura whispered something to her. He nudged her forward and she said, tremulously, "Celestial Majesty and esteemed members of the High Council, His Excellency Ben-Tubal petitions to speak on behalf of the prophet."

"And his son," whispered Hura.

"And his son," said Sheshi. "His Excellency claims this right as a privilege of his office and as their kinsman by marriage."

Semjaza nodded his assent and Ben-Tubal advanced a few paces. "Thank you, Celestial Majesty. It is true that I am related to this man by the marriage of my daughter to his son. But I stand before you today and appeal on his behalf not as his kinsman, but as a witness to his character. I have known this man for nearly one hundred years now and have found him to be honest and upright with regard to his conduct. There is no one like him in all the land. While it is true that his beliefs differ from ours, you know that I have always upheld a policy of tolerance insofar as it would not be detrimental to the governing of the people."

He paused for a moment and Semjaza said, "So noted."

"And as for the son," Ben-Tubal continued, "I have known him ever since he was a young boy. In all that time, I have never seen the slightest inclination in him toward violence. In fact, he is so tender-hearted and delicate that many among our people consider him effeminate, accounting for the fact that he is still unmarried at his age."

"That's not true!" I said out loud.

Ignoring me, Ben-Tubal continued, "You can see by looking at him that he is hardly capable of committing the crime of which he is accused. I ask you, therefore, to release these men to my custody. I will personally guarantee their conduct."

"We will confer on your request and render a decision," said Semjaza.

I turned to Sheshi and whispered, "Don't I get to say anything in my own behalf? I didn't like Ben-Tubal's defense."

"The testimony of the accused is not considered valid since there is every reason to suspect that he would lie to save himself," she replied. "But take heart, because if anyone can sway them, His Excellency Ben-Tubal can. The higher ranking an official, the more weight his testimony is given. And outside of the High Council and my father, none ranks higher than His Excellency."

The conferring of the Council was not a verbal one. Their eyes rolled up in their sockets, so that little but the whites were showing as they withdrew their minds and deliberated in a plane of existence inaccessible to us. The uncanny silence was worse in its own way than enduring their voices. And considering that my life was hanging in the balance, the waiting seemed slow indeed.

At length, Semjaza said out loud, "The Council has reached a decision. The words of Your Excellency have persuaded us to release these men to your custody—with the understanding that they are to leave Enoch-Nod forthwith and cause no further trouble."

"Thank you, Celestial Majesty," said Ben-Tubal. "We will take no more of your time and be on our way."

I breathed a huge sigh of relief. After months of captivity and uncertainty about my fate—including the lowest points of despair I had experienced in my life—I was about to walk free.

"Wait!" said Father to Ben-Tubal. "I did not have the opportunity to address the Council."

"What are you doing?" I said under my breath. "Let's just get out of here while we have the chance!"

"This is what I came to do," Father insisted. "I promised the Lord and your grandfather that I would."

"For what?" I said. "Do you really think you'll change their minds?"

Father ignored my question and stared at Ben-Tubal. His Excellency agonized for a moment, his jaw clenched so tightly that you could see the muscles straining. Then he nodded his head with a jerk toward Sheshi, who turned back to the Council and said, timorously, "The prophet petitions to be heard. His Excellency respectfully requests that you give him audience."

The appearance of Semjaza's face at that moment is difficult to explain. If he had been human, I might have said that he was glaring, but his stony features betrayed no such emotion. It was something *behind* his eyes, if that makes sense, that radiated a menacing intensity. Finally, he grated, "Speak."

"High Council of the Watch," Father began. "It is true that I have traveled throughout the length and breadth of this land preaching repentance to the people. It was not an occupation that I took upon myself at my own initiative, however. Nor would I have repeatedly placed myself in peril if it were not a message of dire importance that I received directly from God Most High. Ever since the Father and Mother of all were banished from the Garden, the curse that was invoked upon them has been advancing far and wide. In these latter days, the effects of the curse have worsened considerably. The people are suffering terribly and are dying in great numbers—a thing unheard of in the days of their fathers."

"What is your point?" Semjaza said impatiently.

"The point is that if the one transgression in the Garden brought a terrible curse upon the earth, how much more devastating will the punishment be if a whole people sell themselves to do evil? I have been warning the people about nothing less than the impending destruction of the world!"

"We're not going to sit here and be admonished by this servant of our enemy, are we?" said Azazel, with echoes of support from the gallery.

"Restrain yourself," said Semjaza, an unnatural tic sporadically affecting the right side of his face. "Now is not the time."

"His Celestial Majesty is right," said Hura, stepping forward unexpectedly. "These speculations may be easily dispelled, for they spring from certain misunderstandings which, with the Council's indulgence, I would like to clarify."

The recording of Hura's words does not fully convey the effect that they had on his listeners—at least the human variety. Without actually hearing him speak, it would be impossible to adequately sense how persuasive he always sounded. It was little wonder that he had risen to such high position. With those few words, he had already created an expectation that he was right beyond anyone's ability to question him. And if his audience would only listen to reason—*his* reason—they would soon be enlightened as well.

"I was not present in the Garden," continued Hura. "But I know one who was. And he gives a different account of the events that have just been described, because the Cushite has omitted certain crucial facts. The Father and Mother of All were flawed by the hand of their maker—deliberately, I might add. They had been given the spirits of children, a naivete that prevented them from achieving their ultimate potential of perfection. And why, you may ask, would he withhold the one characteristic that could enable them to attain the divinity they so richly deserved? 'Why, indeed?' I say again, because it is a question of paramount importance—the fate of men and angels hangs on the answer." There was a long, dramatic pause as Hura turned and looked directly at Father. "Because he suffers no rival to his glory. Am I right?"

Father did not answer, but the Watcher called Azazel spoke up. "Never were truer words spoken," he said to murmurs of assent from several Watchers in the gallery.

"Yes, not even his own prophet can deny this," said Hura. "The Terrible One covets all the praise for himself. What would it have cost him to acknowledge that he was first among equals?"

"Nothing," Azazel answered again.

"Nothing at all," said Hura. "But he was not content with that. No, he demanded that all other beings prostrate themselves continually at his feet. Those who were too noble to abase themselves in this way had no choice but to depart from his presence. And it was fortunate for mankind that they did. When the Morningstar—may his name be praised—came to earth, he took pity on the humans and opened their eyes to see how they were being misused. So, what you call 'banishment' was in reality a liberation. Thanks to our spirit guides, we humans may now pursue our own destinies, unshackled from the bonds of ignorance and servitude."

"And the price we pay is death," said Father, unaffected by Hura's oratory. And it was good for me that he wasn't, because hearing Hura speak always confused me.

"You are nearly six hundred years old," Hura replied. "And but a youth compared to your grandfather. Death hardly seems to be making any demands on you."

"A man does not die with the first meal he misses," countered Father. "But with the accumulation of days without eating, starvation will eventually overtake him. Likewise, if you liberate yourself from the source of life, death is bound to follow sooner or later."

"If you're going to die anyway, then what have you gained from all your groveling, prophet?" said Hura contemptuously.

"A peaceful conscience. And the hope that when my days are over, my spirit will find rest."

"My conscience is clear," said Hura.

"Your conscience is seared," said Father. "It's been bent in the wrong direction so long that you don't even hear it anymore."

"At least I haven't wasted my life in a vain hope that amounts to nothing more than wishful thinking. If the spirit world you're looking forward to is so wonderful, why would anyone seek to escape from it, as so many of this present company have done? As for me, I'll take the here and now in the flesh."

"Then you'd better make the most of your time, for it is growing short," said Father. "Judgment is coming very soon."

"You've been saying that for over a hundred years now," Semjaza interjected, his face twitching more noticeably, though he seemed unaware of it. "Still, nothing happens. Why? Because you have been laboring under a delusion. The Terrible One no longer cares what happens to this world or its inhabitants. His experiment failed when humans became enlightened and he has moved on to other amusements. The Watchers are the best hope for mankind now."

Then Baraqijal rose and said, "If I may have leave to speak ..." Semjaza nodded and Baraqijal continued, "We all know that the prophet's argument is without merit. Yet the impending catastrophe of which he warns should not be dismissed lightly, because an evil portent has appeared in the sky."

"You picked an inopportune time to divulge that information," said Semjaza.

"The prophet appears and so does the sign," said Baraqijal. "What could be more opportune than that? Perhaps he has some knowledge that would be useful to us."

"Well, what say you, prophet?" said Semjaza. "Do you have any oracles for us?"

"I was commissioned to warn my fellow human beings, not rebellious spirits," said Father. "But if you want a word from the Lord, here it is: The Lord rebukes you, O Watchers of skies and men. You have fallen from heaven and soon you will fall from the earth. The Abyss awaits you, where you will be shackled in unbreakable chains until the end of time. And I also have a message for you, Hura, to take to your Master. You were the Son of the Dawn, but you have chosen darkness instead. Therefore, blackest darkness has been reserved for you where you will be tormented by fire for eternity for all the torment you have caused!"

This threw the assembly into great confusion. No small number of the Watchers wanted to kill Father at once, but many were reluctant because of his seal (whatever that was; it was invisible to me). Still others fell to debating the omen in the heavens. All those unhuman voices talking at once made a sound horrible to hear, like boulders scraping together. When Semjaza stood to try and restore order, his cowl fell back on his shoulders. By then, the tics had worsened to full-fledged contortions, far beyond what could have been accounted for by facial muscles alone. His features distorted to such grotesque proportions that I thought his skull might crack under the strain. Above the din, in what might have passed for a shout (not for volume, but for intensity), he said, "Get out! Do not show your face here again. We have the power to destroy you. We will make you suffer beyond what you could possibly imagine!"

TEN

Despite the threats, no one dared to lay a hand on Father as he turned and strode from the hall because the spirit of the Lord was upon him. Re-Aylah and I followed closely behind him. Ben-Tubal and the Nephilim, however, remained behind to mollify the Watchers.

Meanwhile, Sheshi slipped out of a side door and caught up to us at the front steps of the Tower. "Take me with you, Zhayfeth," she pleaded. "I cannot stay here anymore."

I gave Father an imploring look. "No," he said, still burning with anger from his exchange with the Council and Hura.

"Why not?" I asked. "They'll kill her if she doesn't flee."

"Don't be foolish, son. This is not a stray dog you're taking in. She's a witch. And her master is our mortal enemy."

"A person can change," said Re-Aylah. "I did."

"Perhaps," said Father. "But I suspect that the forces that have a hold on her will not relinquish their claim easily."

While we were still at that impasse, Ben-Tubal emerged from the Tower. No doubt he had been taken to task for defending us, because he was seething as he passed us by. Father said to him, "I'm grateful to you for traveling all the way to Enoch-Nod and for speaking on our behalf, Your Excellency." But Ben-Tubal just glared at him and strode down the steps without answering. "I'm sorry for all the trouble I've caused you," Father called after him. Without looking back, Ben-Tubal and his attendants mounted their carriages and left the courtyard in haste. As the carriages drove away, Father added to himself, "I'm sorry that trouble has come upon everybody."

By then, the temple courtyard was filling for the midday rituals and Father turned his attention to the growing crowd. Never one who could resist an audience, he shouted to the people below, "Woe to you, Cainites! You have sold yourselves to do evil in the eyes of the Lord by your detestable sorceries. The time is soon coming when the Lord will destroy this abominable Tower and all of you along with it. Tremble with fear because all Enoch-Nod—indeed all the world—is about to be swallowed up in doom. Repent now for your days are numbered! And when the time comes, the only sanctuary from destruction will be the ark in Nephil!"

As Father descended the steps, I motioned for Sheshi to follow us. Occupied as he was proclaiming his warning, Father made no further protest about her. Every step of the way, he repeatedly warned the people about their impending doom, his booming voice resounding off the buildings of the central district. As we advanced, the people made way because Father was hot with conviction. Surely they had never heard anyone condemn their leaders or their way of life like that before. The city was thrown into pandemonium, and I marvel to this day that we were not torn to pieces in the riot. But block by block, and then through the great encampment of tents surrounding the city, we continued unmolested. All the while, Father never stopped warning them to flee from the coming wrath of God. When at last we left the masses behind and reached the ridge that overlooked the abominable city, Father turned and shook the dust of it from his feet.

As much as we would have liked to put more miles between the city and ourselves before we stopped for the night, it was clear that Sheshi could go no further. During the fearful march through the angry mob, Sheshi had grown increasingly ill. Her face appeared ashen and her gait became like that of a sleepwalker. Several times she had stumbled and would have fallen if Re-Aylah and I had not steadied her between us. Just before sunset, we spotted an abandoned stone quarry not far from the road and we decided to pass the night there. Before we even pitched camp, we unrolled Father's mat for Sheshi to lay down on. Instantly, she was asleep—if sleep you could call it—for there was no peace in it. She moaned frequently and shivered, though the night was not cool. We built a fire to warm her out of some old scraps of wood that had once been used as hoists and covered her with Father's blanket—the only one we had managed to make it out of the city with.

Our small fire did little to restrain the encroaching shadows, which threatened to be dark indeed beneath the quarry walls. By the time we had eaten a little, that threat had been fully realized. We huddled glumly around the tiny flames wishing we had more wood, but it was too late to venture out and look for more. Despite our close proximity to each other, Father avoided looking me in the eye and I tried not to speculate about what that meant.

Suddenly, Sheshi sat bolt upright and whispered, "He is here!"

We looked and there was Hura, solitary and menacing at the edge of the firelight. We had not heard him approach. "Why have you kidnapped my daughter, after all we have done for you?" he said.

"I think you know that's not true," said Father, his voice steady and measured. "She came with us of her own free will."

"Nonsense," said Hura, his response directed not to us, but to his daughter. "Sheshi would never abandon her father and her home, would you my dear child?" But Sheshi just hid her face from him.

"Can't you see how frightened she is?" said Re-Aylah, while trying to comfort Sheshi. "She begged us to take her because she fears for her life."

"That's perfectly understandable," Hura said, his voice suddenly less scolding and more compassionate. "Being misled and rejected by this troublemaker has been quite an ordeal for you. No wonder you're not thinking clearly. But I can protect you. And I can ease your suffering. All will be forgiven if you return home with me now."

From somewhere within herself, however, Sheshi mustered her resolve. She looked up and said, "No, Father. I'm not going back." I have little doubt that it was the first time in her life that she had ever told him "no."

Hura moved closer and I could see that the expression he bore was more than that of a concerned father. It was a look of desperate ferocity like I had seen in the eyes of the animals trapped at the compound. "Come now, you don't mean that," he said, the soothing tones in his voice sounding very strained. "That is only your illness talking. But I know what you need." Sheshi's eyes went wide with recognition as he held out to her a vial, not unlike the one I had seen her drink from before. "Yeesss, you know that you want this—you need this. That is why you are sick."

With trembling hands, Sheshi reached out and took the vial from her father. "That's a good girl," said Hura. "Drink up and you'll feel better."

Hot with anger, I started toward Hura, but Father's hand restrained me. "You can't defeat an enemy like this with violence—it will only strengthen his hand," Father said quietly. "Sheshi must make her own decision—you can't force her to reform her ways."

Eyes fixed on her father, Sheshi raised the vial to her lips.

"Don't do it," Re-Aylah whispered to her. "Whatever that is can't be good if this is what it does to you."

Sheshi hesitated, torn over what to do. Hura nodded reassuringly and said, "It is the only way, my child."

Still, Sheshi did not drink. Slowly, she lowered her shaking hand and said, "I will not do it."

"Do I need to remind you of the consequences?" said Hura sternly. "You cannot just walk away from the priesthood. You know the penalty! I will not be able to stop them."

"I know the penalty," said Sheshi. She turned the vial upside-down and poured the contents on the ground.

Hura watched, horrified. For a moment, he was just a father whose daughter had turned against him. And for that moment, I almost felt sorry for him. Then the warmth of paternal compassion faded, and turned not angry, but cold. It was an expression that could only be countenanced by the very proud who have been much abased. "So be it," he said with frightening finality.

"And what about you, Hura?" asked Father. "Perhaps it is not too late for you to turn aside from the path you have chosen as well."

"Save your breath, prophet. I am not a weak-willed girl you can brainwash into believing your myths. You are the ones who have chosen foolishly. My master holds dominion over this world and your underestimation of his power will be your undoing."

Then Hura turned to me and said, "At the risk of offending the High Council and my own master, I freed you from the dungeon and from certain death in the pit because I saw potential in you. You could have been a powerful priest in the Cult of the Morningstar. Apostates are always stronger servants of the master than those who never believed. That's why we recruit them whenever we can. I could have overlooked the fact that you didn't want to stay—not all of the Morningstar's servants dwell in Enoch-Nod. But you weren't content with freedom and chose to repay my kindness by turning my daughter against me and against her lord. So when she suffers, you will know in your heart that you were to blame. And mark my words, this is not the end of it. I will be avenged!"

The fire suddenly flared up so that we were temporarily blinded. When we could see again, Hura was gone.

"I'm not an apostate," I said to myself as I stared at the place he had been standing. "I'm not." But that did little to dispel the doubts that troubled my mind. Having that observation made by someone who was so obviously an expert on the subject was most unsettling. All I had to do was look at my father to be reminded that my faith was not what it should have been. And I had recent vivid memories of a lake of fire to recall as I contemplated what the likely outcome of my doubting would be. From *that* pit, there would be no escape.

Sheshi's sobs startled me out of that morbid reverie. She sat with her head buried between her knees while we all tried to console her. None of us dared to inquire about the "penalty" of which Hura had spoken; it sounded too awful to contemplate.

When at length Sheshi's crying subsided, she drifted back into an uneasy sleep and we laid her down on the mat. Soon, however, her eyes opened again, though she did not seem to see or respond to anything—at least, not in this world. But somewhere, in the eye of her mind or her soul, something terrible was happening. She bore an expression of open-mouthed horror that was frightening to behold. Her extremities began to twitch, followed by full body spasms alternating with complete rigidity. Between seizures, we caught fragments of her thoughts, though her words seemed to emanate from some great distance. "Watchers ... trapped—nowhere to hide ... falling into darkness... so hot ... the pain ... I am undone!"

"Do something!" I said to Father.

"What do you want me to do?" Father snapped. "I told you her masters would not give her up. I'm just a man. This is beyond me."

"Won't you even try?"

I didn't know what I was asking; if I had, I don't think I could have asked it of him—not even to save the life of my dear friend. He looked at me gravely and slowly exhaled. Then he pointed his finger at me and commanded, "Pray!"

He got down on his knees, laid himself across her bosom to bosom, and cradled her head in the crook of his elbow. Immediately, she began drawing strength from him and relaxed a little. A struggle ensued that was beyond my understanding as Father contended with forces for which mortal man is no match. Demon-kind do not relinquish their victims willingly; the only choices they offer to humankind are servitude and oblivion. But somehow, the spirit of my father stood with Sheshi's spirit and together they resisted the onslaught. I tried to pray, but couldn't concentrate as my attention continually returned to the invisible battle that raged before me. Soon Father was writhing in pain like he was being skewered with red-hot knives and crying out, "No ... no ... no ..."

Re-Aylah turned to me in fear and said, "We're going to lose both of them."

"Father, come back," I said in panic. "Can you hear me? Come back!"

If he heard me, he did not respond, nor did he loosen his grip. The very ground beneath us began to shake. Rocks dislodged from the quarry walls and crashed down alarmingly close to where we knelt. One shattered stone rolled across the campfire with great force, scattering sparks everywhere. At that moment, Father shouted out in a loud voice, "In the name of the Living God, you shall not have her!"

An unearthly wail that came from nowhere and everywhere at once went up from that place. Suddenly, everything became deathly still.

I laid my hand on Father's shoulder, not sure if he was even alive. "Are you all right?"

He looked up slowly, blood trickling from his left nostril onto his beard. He nodded his head and said, "She is free." He laid her head gently down and rolled over on his back, exhausted.

I found a cloth in Father's pack and had him hold it under his nose with his head tilted back. I couldn't help thinking as I tended him that he looked very vulnerable laying there. He had always been as strong a man as I ever knew (excluding men of exceptional size like the Nephilim) and the hardest working. Even at six hundred, he could still best me in a test of pure strength. But there was no denying that the constant adversity he had faced in his life had worn him down and it showed then like I'd never noticed it before. Realizing that my father was mortal after all was an unpleasant shock, though I know I wasn't the first or last man to experience that unsettling fact. Considering everything he had been through, I couldn't help but wonder if he might be reaching the end of his endurance.

While I was still worrying over Father, Re-Aylah said, "Jay, you'd better come here—now."

Sheshi had opened her eyes and with great effort, was trying to speak. Even though I bent down close, I could barely hear her as she said, "I am finally at peace. Do not mourn for me when I'm gone, Zhayfeth."

"Mourn?" I said, for my mind at first refused to comprehend her words.

"My spirit is untethered," said Sheshi. "I go now to seek the true enlightenment of which you have told me."

"Don't speak that way," I said. "Father says you're free from the dominion of the Watchers. You'll be all right now."

Sheshi continued as though she had not heard me. "You must yet endure times of great trouble—though not alone. I have foreseen it."

When she had exchanged a knowing look with Re-Aylah, her hand reached heavenward and she said, "I see the lights."

Then her arm fell lifeless to the ground.

ELEVEN

"Oh, no! Is she …?" I started, but couldn't bring myself to say the word.

Re-Aylah touched Sheshi's neck and said, "I don't feel a pulse."

"What's all this?" said Father, rolling over on his side.

"It's Sheshi," I said.

"I think she's … dead," said Re-Aylah.

"Dead?" said Father. He sat up and shook his head. "But I thought … I'm very sorry."

We sat in disbelief for a few moments, not knowing what to say. "It doesn't make sense," I said at last. "If Sheshi repented, why did she have to die?"

Father paused for a moment before answering. "I can't answer that. I'm not even certain myself about what she just went through, much less able to explain it. In fact, I really don't recall any of it. It's strange, but there's a space in my mind where the memory should be, but I suppose mortal minds weren't made to hold such thoughts. Maybe being wrenched free of the demons was just too much for her—not to mention that cursed poison she was addicted to. And she did seem like a delicate … say, I think you are mistaken. There is yet life in her!"

"You're right," said Re-Aylah excitedly. "She's breathing again."

"But I could have sworn …" I took her hand and said, "Sheshi, can you hear me?"

When Sheshi opened her eyes, I said. "We thought you had left us."

"I did," she said weakly. "For one glorious moment—I wish I could remember it. But it was not my time after all, it seems. I was sent back for a reason."

"What is it?" I asked.

"I do not think I will know until the time comes."

"Well, I'm glad you are back with us again," I said.

"We all are," said Re-Aylah.

Sheshi turned to Father and said, "Thank you for risking your life to save me."

"The Lord was the one who saved you," said Father. "I just stayed with you while he accomplished it, though that in itself was a sore test. And well deserved on my part—I might add—for giving up on you too soon back in Enoch-Nod. I am truly sorry about that."

"I do not blame you for not trusting me," said Sheshi.

"I'm glad that Jayfeth and Re-Aylah did. I promise not to give up on anyone again, no matter how little hope for their reformation I might have. Now we should all try to get some sleep. We have a long, difficult journey ahead of us and I am anxious to get to the end of it because I am missing my wife terribly."

Sheshi closed her eyes and fell asleep—a natural one this time—and Father's sonorous breathing soon indicated that he had followed his own advice. After all that had happened, however, I did not find it so easy, even though I had slept little in days. Apparently, Re-Aylah didn't either. We were laying on opposite sides of the campfire, as close to the dying embers as we dared for warmth, because neither of us had more than the clothes we were wearing to cover ourselves with. I thought I caught her looking at me across the fire, but she looked away before I could be sure. I turned my back to her and tried not to torture myself by wishing she were on my side of the fire. Eventually, I fell into a fitful sleep, troubled by the occasional scuttling sound of some small animal moving through the loose stones. I worried that it might be a rat—and even more that it might be *the* rat.

Mercifully, the sun rose at last. And while I felt little rested after sleeping on a bed of rock, at least the daylight afforded us an opportunity to move on from that forlorn place. Father and Sheshi were somewhat improved, though only able to go at a slow pace. Still, any pace at all was an improvement as long as we were moving away from Enoch-Nod.

As we walked along that morning, I could tell that Re-Aylah's mind was troubled. Finally, she said, "There's something I need to tell you all— something that bothered me all night. It might not mean anything, but somehow it seems better to say it by the light of day. Something about Sheshi's father seems familiar to me. I've been thinking that I've him seen before."

"But you've never been to Enoch-Nod until now," I said.

"True," said Re-Aylah. "But that doesn't mean that he hasn't been to Cush. Or perhaps I met him on some other journey."

"He does travel frequently," Sheshi offered. "Sometimes he is gone for several weeks or even months at a time."

"What's really bothering me is that I can't recall where or when," said Re-Aylah.

"Maybe he was in different guise," said Father.

"What about the …" I said, touching my forehead.

"The serpent?" said Re-Aylah. "That's a good point. I don't know how I could have forgotten that."

"He often hides it under a turban or other covering," said Sheshi. "He speaks of the importance of blending in with the natives when he is abroad."

"There you have it," said Re-Aylah.

"We believe you, Re-Aylah," said Father.

"Anything is possible in these strange times," I said. "But let's hope our paths do not cross again. I have a feeling, though, that I won't be that fortunate. Sorry, Sheshi."

"I understand," said Sheshi. "But say, rather, that you would not have your paths cross again until he has had a change of heart."

"Agreed," said Father. "There is always hope."

The trek home was not without the usual hardships of Nod. But our previous travels and experiences had hardened us to them somewhat. Compared to what we had already been through, the journey seemed relatively uneventful.

Not so for Sheshi. Practically everything we encountered was outside of her previous experience, having been kept, as she was, wholly unaware of the plight of her people. She was cut to the heart whenever she witnessed some new misery or came across a scene that reminded her of how completely she had been deceived. Even after several days, when Father was fully recovered, Sheshi continued to look ill and would tremble frequently for no apparent reason. Father said it was her body's memory of the poison it had become addicted to, and that undoubtedly contributed to her condition. But I think there was more to it than that. By nature and training, she was a person of such delicate sensitivity that she seemed to feel the slightest perturbation in someone else's mood. Thus, with little practice in how to brace herself or shut it out, witnessing suffering on such a scale simply overwhelmed her psyche. I say this in retrospect, because I didn't want to admit to myself at the time that it might have been beyond her capabilities to make the transition to an unsheltered world.

When at last we crossed the Gihon and our feet once again touched the soil of Cush, our eyes drank in the loveliness of all things green and beautiful. And when we felt the embrace of our loved ones long separated from us, our joy was very great indeed.

Our gladness, however, was tempered by the sobering business at hand. Father gathered the family together and said, "How long do you estimate until the ark is finished, Ham?"

"We've been making excellent progress, as you can see," said Ham. "At this rate, I think we could be done in two years."

"We do not have two years," said Father gravely. "I don't know if we even have one. Things in Enoch-Nod are far worse than I feared. What is being planned there must not be allowed to come to pass."

"But the judgment will not come before the ark is finished, will it?" said Ham.

"A day of judgment has been appointed and cannot be delayed," said Father. "It is up to us to be ready."

We took Father's words to heart and worked harder than ever on the ark. Laboring from dawn until late each night, we paused only for quick meals. Even so, I did not begrudge the toil. Although I had often in my life resented such work, my recent experiences had given me a renewed appreciation for the simple pleasure of working with my hands.

Father and Mother took Sheshi into their tent where Re-Aylah, who had become like a sister to her, was continuing to stay. Sheshi eagerly assisted Mother in her daily cooking and work routine. As long as she stayed busy, Sheshi appeared content, if very quiet, and her health did gradually improve to a certain extent. Still, it was also clear that some lingering sadness was haunting her. After a couple of days, I asked Re-Aylah over lunch how she thought Sheshi was doing.

"I wish I could say that I thought she was doing well," said Re-Aylah.

"It's only been a short while since we got back," I said. "It will take some time to learn our ways.

"Oh, it's not that," said Re-Aylah, "though I'm amazed that she doesn't know things about daily life that we learned by the time we could walk. But Mara has taken her under her wing and you know how patient she is. Then I suppose she had to be patient with all you men to contend with."

"Thanks a lot."

"Honestly, I think Mara is delighted to have someone to mother."

"I know what you mean," I said. "She should have had many grandchildren by now if not for the curse. I'm glad that Sheshi can help fill the void for her."

"It makes you wonder what happened to her own mother."

"They have very strange customs about that among the well-born in Nod," I said.

"Strange?" said Re-Aylah. "Sinister is more like it. No wonder things are in such a state there. A child needs her mother."

"I'm really sorry you don't get on with your own."

"That's thoughtful of you to say," said Re-Aylah and the expression of sorrow on her face gave no doubt that she meant it. "Things weren't always bad, though. We were happy once, until things began to come between us. Anyway, it has made me resolve to be a better mother to my own children … if I ever decide to marry."

That turn of conversation made me uncomfortable, so I tried to steer us back to the original subject by saying, "Well, Sheshi is exceptionally bright and there is no finer teacher than my mother."

"I have no doubt that she can learn the tasks," said Re-Aylah. "But there's more to it than that. I don't think she feels like she's fitting in. Everything she has encountered since she left Enoch-Nod is completely outside of her experience."

"New experiences can be good, don't you think?" I asked, grasping for some hope that all would turn out well, in spite of the evidence to the contrary.

"They can be—if you survive them," said Re-Aylah. "And if that's all she had to contend with, she might eventually learn to cope. But it's more complicated than that, I think. I've seen how her shoulders sag in her unguarded moments and heard her late at night quietly crying herself to sleep. I have little doubt that she is tormented by a terrible sense of guilt about leaving her father. Believe me, I know how that feels."

"So, what do you recommend?"

"I wish I knew. But I'm really worried about what she might do."

Although I tried to downplay them, Re-Aylah's concerns about Sheshi confirmed my own. I had little time to do much about it, though, with all the preparations that had to be made in such a short time. In fact, I was a little surprised that when the Sabbath came, we continued to observe it. I said, "If the need to finish is so urgent, why are we resting today?"

"The Lord has set aside this day for rest," said Father. "I will not violate the Sabbath to speed up the work."

"Even if it's the Lord's work?"

"The Lord's work must be done the Lord's way," he said, as he always did on that subject.

After our morning devotions, I climbed to the roof of the ark to sit by myself for awhile. As I relaxed and stared at the hills far away to the west, I began to realize how tired my body really was. Father was right. We did need the rest. I had forgotten how good it felt to do nothing for awhile.

While I was thus in repose, Re-Aylah sat down beside me and said, "Your thoughts are far away today."

"I was thinking about when I was a boy, roaming over those hills without a care," I mused. "But like Ben-Tubal says, trouble has followed me ever since. Sometimes, I wish I could go back and leave all these worries behind."

"I have felt that way at times, too," said Re-Aylah sympathetically. "But even if we could go back, I'm not so sure we'd find everything as we'd want it to be, because we wouldn't be seeing it through the eyes of children."

"I suppose you're right. We probably remember the past more fondly than we actually experienced it."

"Maybe it's really not the past we want, but the eyes of a child."

"You're very profound."

"How perceptive of you to notice," she said.

I laughed and said, "So tell me, Profound One, is it possible to trade old eyes for young ones?"

"That depends on whether you're willing to change your outlook," she said. "Children don't spend much time longing for the past or worrying about the future."

"Then you're saying we should live for the moment."

"If you think about it, that's all we really have," said Re-Aylah. "The past is gone and the future is uncertain, so 'now' is the only time we *can* live. Don't you think we ought to make the most of it?"

"Yes, we should."

She nodded and said, more to herself than to me, "Then today is the day."

"The day for what?"

"A wedding," she said and turned to me. "I mean *our* wedding."

"Our wedding? Did I miss something?"

She looked down again and said in a shy voice that I was quite unaccustomed to hearing from her, "That is, if you haven't changed your mind about me."

When I realized that she was completely in earnest, I was dumfounded. "I don't know what to say!"

"Maybe that's for best," she teased. "You wouldn't want to say something that might make me change my mind again."

"No, I don't want to take any chances," I said, as my astonishment turned to elation.

"So why don't you just kiss me instead?"

A few minutes later, we found Father and Mother sitting together in the camp and told them the happy news.

"For a long time, we have hoped and prayed for this," said Father, beaming. "As soon as the ark is completed—"

"We would like to marry today," said Re-Aylah.

Father shook his head and said, "I'm afraid we cannot spare the time for your bridal month."

"And it takes much planning for a big ceremony," said Mother.

"I don't care about a big ceremony," said Re-Aylah. "And my bridal month can wait. I have delayed this for too many years and Jay has been patient with me long enough."

"I just don't know …" said Father.

"Please," said Re-Aylah. "Since my own father disowned me, you have been my kinsman protector these many years. Be now my father."

Father thought for a moment and grinned. "How can I refuse—daughter!"

We assembled the family out in front of the ark—Father and Mother, Shem and Ohlibah, and Ham and Jirah—along with Sheshi. Re-Aylah and I faced each other and clasped hands. I said, "I pledge to you my whole heart, which you know very well you have held in your hands since we were children. I will always love you. I will always be faithful. I will always protect you no matter what the cost. Most of all, I will always honor and respect you for who you are and never try to make you conform to my idea of who you ought to be. So help me God."

Then Re-Aylah said, "You, my love, have waited patiently for this day, though it was in your power to compel it sooner, keeping yourself pure even in the face of overwhelming temptation. In this, you have demonstrated a depth of love for me that is far beyond what any words could express. How can I but love you in return? You have traveled around the world, crossed the desolate wasteland, and risked your life to save mine. In this, you have demonstrated that you value my life even above your own. How can I feel otherwise than safe with you by my side? And you, above all others I have ever known, have come to respect me as equal. In this, you have shown that you value me for who I am. How can I but honor you in return? Therefore, I give myself to you wholeheartedly and unreservedly for all the days of my life."

Then Father said, "Let it be as both of you have pledged in the sight of God. May the Lord bless your union."

A feast was hastily prepared. I enjoyed it immensely, though I have little recollection of what I ate. Even amid all the trouble we faced, my joy was such that I could have eaten grass that day and been quite content, for surely the proverb is true, "Happiness is the most delicious of seasonings." And ever afterward we loved each other, like Re-Aylah had said, as if "now" was all we had. With doom looming over our tomorrows, we strove to make the most of all our todays.

TWELVE

Three months after our wedding, Jirah returned from Nephil one evening with news we had all been dreading. "A decree has been issued summoning people from all the lands to a great festival here in Nephil. The Sons of the Gods will be choosing wives for themselves from among the people. A great wedding feast is being planned, the likes of which the world has never seen."

"This is it," I said, thinking out loud. "This is how they're going to recruit the women they need for their diabolical plan."

"How soon?" asked Father.

"Six months from now," said Jirah.

"Six months!" said Ham. "That's not enough time—even if we already had all the parts we'll need."

"It sounds like we don't have any choice," said Father. "Here's what we'll have to do. We'll put all our efforts into the preparations that absolutely have to be completed by then—like gathering food for ourselves and the livestock and making the ark seaworthy. We can finish everything inside as time allows—even if it's after we're already underway. Jirah, do you think you can persuade His Excellency to provide us pitch to coat the ark inside and out?"

"How much do you need?" she asked.

"Ten thousand gallons," said Father.

"Ten thousand!" said Jirah.

"Nine thousand seven hundred thirty-eight, actually—if that difference is helpful," said Father.

"That will not be easy to come by—even if he is disposed to help," she said. "He is still not completely over the incident in Enoch-Nod. But I will try."

"Good," said Father. "And as soon as the exterior of the ark has been entirely covered with pitch, we should dismantle the towers and scaffolding."

"Why?" asked Ham. "We have a lot of work invested in building them."

"There's nothing to be gained by preserving them now if they're going to be destroyed soon anyway. And it would prevent any possibility of them being used against us. If there's trouble, we'd be better off with only the side entrance to defend."

"Do you think it will come to violence?" asked Re-Aylah.

"I wouldn't be surprised," said Jirah. "The decree came directly from Enoch-Nod."

"What's the significance of that?" I asked.

"Don't you see?" said Jirah. "His Excellency is the governor of this land. The edict should have been made through him. The fact that this news bypassed him is an ominous sign. There is much speculation in the palace about what it all means. Even some of His Excellency's strongest supporters are beginning to distance themselves from him."

"I hope he has not lost standing on our account because of that episode in Enoch-Nod," said Father.

"This was coming anyway," said Jirah. "I think deep down, he has known for a long time that this day was inevitable. But he will not go quietly, I assure you of that."

Ben-Tubal did agree to provide the pitch we requested, even though it was difficult to obtain because no pine trees grew in the vicinity from which the resin could be extracted and cooked. But it always seemed he was willing to go to extreme lengths to win my father's favor. The pitch did not come all at once, but in shipments of a few hundred gallons each over many days. That did not matter, however, because the new shipments always arrived before we ran out, and we had plenty to keep us busy in the interim. We heated the pitch in large vats and applied the coating liberally to the entire outer surface and inside the exterior walls and floor, filling every crack. When it cooled, it dried to a hard, black finish that was waterproof. The ark was not the only thing we covered; our bodies were soon splattered with the sticky stuff that did not wash off with water. The worst was crawling underneath the ark between the foundation beams upon which it was resting. Shem, Re-Aylah and I had to lie on our backs and work directly above us. No matter how much care we took, we couldn't keep it from dripping onto our faces and hair. Ham kept us supplied with the heated pitch and gave us no end of grief over our appearance, calling us everything he could think of that was black or speckled. The air did not circulate well underneath and the pungent aroma was overpowering. So I was very glad to crawl out one afternoon and say, "I'm glad that's finished."

"Not quite yet," said Father. "We still have to cover the places where the ark is resting on the support beams."

"And how do you propose to lift it?" I asked. "You're strong, but you're not that strong!"

"I've been thinking about that," said Ham. "The ark is so massive that it can't be lifted all at once even with our powerful hoists. However, if we put them all first on one corner and then another, I'm hoping that the gopherwood will flex enough to lift a portion at a time."

"Sounds risky," said Shem. "If a hoist slips while we're painting, someone could get his arm crushed."

"Or her arm," Re-Aylah corrected.

"No one's going to be under there while it's lifted," said Father. "We'll hitch the oxen to the support beams and as soon as the weight is off, we'll drag them forward a couple of feet—just enough to expose the uncoated places."

It took all the next day to move the towers into position and secure the ropes. On the day following, we started early. Father manned the rope for one tower, Ham the second, Re-Aylah and I the third and Shem and our burro Naysa the fourth. Muscles straining, we hauled on the ropes with all our might. The ropes sighed and the towers creaked, but the ark didn't budge, even with all our force focused on one corner.

"We're almost there," said Father. "We just need a few more pulleys."

"Yes, but we haven't got any," said Ham. "We have more ordered for the door, but parts have been hard to come by ever since you stirred the pot in Enoch-Nod."

"More counterweight then?" said Father.

"I'm afraid to," said Ham, grimacing. "I put on as much as I dared. It would be risky to add more."

"We'll have to settle for more hands then," said Father. "Why don't you and Shem go get your wives."

"I don't think—" Ham started.

"Don't think," said Father. "Just go get them. Jayfeth, rub some oil on the underbelly next to the beams. That should make them slide easier."

Ohlibah willingly took her place beside Shem and Sheshi gladly stood with Re-Aylah and me, even though she was hardly bigger around than the rope. Jirah, however, stood to one side and pouted, even though I had little doubt that she was at least as strong as I was.

We started pulling again and made it a little further than we did before, but still not quite far enough. Then Mother took hold of the rope next to Father and said, "Let me have a try at it."

"You'll hurt yourself, woman," said Father.

"I haven't taken care of you all these years and raised three boys for nothing," said Mother. "We'll see which one of us is able to get out of bed first in the morning."

"Come on, then," said Father. "And Jirah, you can help too."

"Why don't you let me ask His Excellency," she said. "We could have fifty men here to help in half an hour."

"I haven't resorted to forced labor yet," said Father. "And I don't intend to now."

"You don't seem to mind forcing me—even though I'm not accustomed to such work."

Then we heard a petite voice say, "Will you be still for once and do as you're told? We're all sick of your complaining." We realized with amazement that it was Ohlibah. It was the first time I had ever heard her say anything of the sort. In fact, we hardly ever heard her say much at all, being as quiet and unassuming a person as I ever knew. But on that occasion, she expressed the feelings of everyone—with the possible exception of Ham, who knew he would catch an earful over it. Re-Aylah and I looked at each other and tried to suppress snickers as Jirah went purple in the face and took her place beside Ham.

When we all put our shoulders to it, I felt the rope move slightly. "We're gaining on it," said Father. "Again."

We heaved again and another inch was ours. "One more time," said Father. And when we pulled again, a small crack opened between the ark and support beam.

"Haw!" Father shouted to the oxen and they lunged forward, dragging the beam with them. When they had gone about three feet, the uncoated area was completely exposed. "That's good," said Father. We relaxed our grip and cheered.

"Now, we just have to do that twenty-nine more times," said Ham. "And thirty on the other side."

"Don't remind us," I said.

Once we knew what we were doing, we made the best time we could and moved five more beams that day. The chief slowdown was the amount of time it took to advance the towers and ropes along the side of the ark. The next day, Ham didn't exactly withdraw his objection to adding more counter-weight. But it is fair to say that his protests hardly sounded heartfelt and none of us had to wonder why. Whatever the risk, the additional counter-weight made the rope-pulling easier so that the women (excepting Re-Aylah) were no longer needed. Still, it was a slow process that consumed several days—precious days, it seemed, with the festival and the predicted doom looming ever nearer.

After a week, we reached the north end of the side facing Nephil, so that the beams were all laying at slight angles. We moved the towers to the west side to begin working our way southward to straighten the opposite ends. On the first pull of the morning, we set up as before. But when we proceeded to haul on the rope, we heard the snap of timber breaking.

We saw with horror that the tower that Father had been pulling on was collapsing.

"Look out!" cried Shem, but he was too far away to do anything about it. Just in time, though, Re-Aylah lunged and knocked Father out of the way as the hoist assembly crashed to the ground beside them.

"Are you all right?" we all said at once, rushing to where Father and Re-Aylah lay only a few feet from the nearest pulley.

Re-Aylah sat up and nodded as I hugged her. "Yes, but easy on the shoulder."

Father sat up more slowly and shook his head to clear it. "I'm all right," he said, groaning as he gingerly touched his ribs. "Although I don't think I'll be sleeping on my right side for awhile."

"I'm sorry," said Re-Aylah. "There was no time to be gentle."

"Oh, I'm not complaining. If you didn't have such quick reflexes, I'd have more to contend with right now than sore ribs." He sighed and added, "I'm getting too old for this and too slow. Maybe I should stay in the camp from now on and tend the cooking pot before someone gets hurt on my account."

"Nonsense," said Re-Aylah, patting his arm. "You're still as strong as any Nephilim—and twice as handsome."

"I should have had many daughters to flatter me like you do," said Father, forcing a smile. "But I'm afraid my strength has overmatched my head in this case. Ham warned me against adding more counterweight and I'll admit he was right."

"Before Ham says 'I told you so,' you'd better look at this," said Shem, picking up a board from the rubble.

Ham inspected the board and said, "I'm not backing off of my warning. But Shem's right. This board was sawn half in two before it broke. And there's another one over there. It's like—"

"Like someone wanted this to happen," said Shem. "I'd say someone is very disappointed right now that one or two of us aren't lying beneath that pile of rubble."

"You think someone was trying to murder us?" said Re-Aylah. "Well, whoever it was very nearly succeeded. And since it would have looked like an accident, no one would have ever been brought to justice for the crime."

"But who would do such a thing?" I asked.

"It could have been anyone," said Shem.

"Or anyone's father," muttered Ham.

"What's that supposed to mean?" said Re-Aylah.

"Well, it's no secret how your father feels about us," said Ham. "And the Cainite's father too, for that matter."

"Her name is Sheshi," I said.

"And while you're making lists of fathers to suspect, you can add your wife's," said Re-Aylah.

"There's no cause for—" said Ham.

"Enough," said Father. "We all know there's no shortage of people who might have reason to oppose us. But let's not start making wild accusations without any evidence. Matters are drawing to a close and things are likely to get more dangerous even than this. It's natural to be apprehensive, but we can't allow our fear to drive wedges between us."

"Wedges?" mused Ham. "Now there's an idea." But none of us knew what he was talking about at the time.

That day, we folded our tents and moved inside the ark to the rooms we had been preparing on the upper deck. We also began taking turns watching at night, which was the last thing any of us felt like doing after a hard day's work. Jirah told us that Ben-Tubal became angry when he heard about the incident and subsequently ordered his own guards to increase their patrol of the area surrounding the city. Even with all those extra precautions, we still felt vulnerable after that and each day our anxiety grew.

Thirteen

Repairing the damaged tower would have taken days that we could ill afford to spare. More importantly, it seemed ill-advised to use that method again once its susceptibility to sabotage had been exposed. So, Father and Ham had a long debate about how to proceed after that. Eventually, they came up with a plan to drive wedges between the beams and the ark using levers and jacks to relieve the stress. This was even more laborious and time-consuming than lifting it with the towers, but slowly they inched forward.

Meanwhile, Father set the rest of us to gathering grain for ourselves and the animals. We put the scythes to good use and the honed blades made quick work of the ripening grain which grew in abundance on the Nephil Plain. In a few weeks, we had cut many acres to the north of the ark. We placed the cut stalks in piles to cure out in the fields before we separated the heads from the stubble, which we planned to bundle and store for fodder and bedding.

Even looking out over so great a supply, my calculations kept coming up far short of what I thought we needed. That only added to other upsetting thoughts that had been nagging at me for some time. Finally, I had to ask about it. "The number of animals in the world is way beyond counting. I know the ark is huge and we will have a very large supply of food when we bring the harvest into the granaries. But how will we house and feed even those in this part of the Gihon Valley, much less those from the lands beyond?"

"Only two of each kind will be saved—a male and a female," said Father. "And seven of those that are domesticated, ceremonial or birds."

"So few?" I said, alarmed. "What about the rest?"

The look on Father's face indicated that this troubled him as well. "I don't know, Jayfeth. I'm only obeying God's commands. They are his creatures. He will do with them as he sees fit."

"If that's all that are going to be saved, why are they wearing themselves out cutting so much grain when we have other more pressing tasks?" said Ham. "They already have enough cut to last for many days. And being finished with the gathering would make life more tranquil for me, if you know what I mean."

"I do know what you mean, but it will be more than a matter of days we have to prepare for," said Father. "We need to stock up for at least a year—maybe longer."

"But why can't we just go out and gather more as the need arises?" asked Ham.

"You don't understand," said Father. "There won't be anything left to gather."

"Nothing?" said Ham.

"Nothing," said Father.

As soon as Father walked away Ham rolled his eyes and said, "He's always such a doomsayer. Surely it won't be as bad as all that."

"What do you know," I said, "You've never missed a single meal in your life, though it wouldn't have done you any harm to miss one occasionally."

"Maybe not," said Ham. "But what's that got to do with anything?"

"If you've never been to Havilah or even Nod, it's no wonder you have difficulty comprehending Father's words. But I've been there and I can tell you that it leaves an indelible impression upon you. If all the world is going to be like those barren places … well, if he says stock up, we'd better stock up."

Late one night when I was on watch, Re-Aylah came and walked with me as I patrolled around the perimeter of the ark. I said, "Shouldn't you be in bed?"

"I couldn't sleep without you," she said. "So I thought you might like some company."

"You really should be resting while you can. But I won't lie to you. I really am glad you're here. It gets lonely wandering around in the dark. And honestly, a little scary too."

"I know what you mean. Ever since that tower collapsed, it's been easy to imagine some new menace everywhere I look. I guess that's why I couldn't sleep tonight, even though I'm exhausted. I couldn't shake off the feeling that something bad was about to happen."

We made our way around the north end of the ark. As we turned the corner toward the west, I said, "That wasn't your imagination—look!"

Twenty or thirty men were rushing over the riverbank carrying torches and setting fire to all the grain we had left standing in piles. "Wake the others, quickly!"

Re-Aylah was off like a gazelle to raise the alarm. Meanwhile, I advanced a few paces yelling at the men to stop, but to no avail. They took no notice of me and made quick work of the cured grain. There were many men and the shocks were widely scattered so I didn't know what else to do. And that's how the others found me a few moments later.

"What are you standing there for?" said Ham as hundreds of small fires lit up the plain.

"One man against thirty?" I said. "What did you want me to do?"

"Jayfeth's right," said Father. "I won't come to blows over something like this. And they'd be long gone by the time we could get to them anyway."

"Couldn't he at least have tried to start extinguishing the fires?" said Ham.

"The dry grain burns so quickly that we couldn't carry water from the river fast enough to save the hundredth part," said Shem.

"All right," said Ham. "Maybe there was nothing he could do. But what I want to know is, why does disaster always seem to strike on Jay's watch?"

"It is not Zhayfeth," said Sheshi. "It is the influence of the omen. Look, you no longer need a telescope to see it."

She pointed and there was the comet, now clearly visible to the naked eye, even with the fires burning brightly.

"Whether the omen itself actually exerts the influence is a debatable matter," said Father. "But there is no doubt that we are living in evil times."

"Evil times indeed," said a sinister voice behind us.

"It is the Saur-El of the Tower Guard," said Sheshi in a frightened voice. And indeed it was, along with a dozen of his henchmen.

"You don't sound very upset by either evil times or our misfortune," I said.

"And you don't sound very grateful for the clemency that was shown you in Enoch-Nod," said the Saur-El.

"I remember your hospitality," I grumbled, as the memories of beatings came back to me.

"Those who invite misfortune should not be surprised when it visits," said the Saur-El. "But as for evil times, that's why I have been sent to Nephil."

"To bring them?"

Saur-El laughed derisively. "No, to deal with them. I'm here to assess the security situation and ensure that everything is in readiness for the festival. But if this lawlessness is any indication, I have my work cut out for me. But do not worry, I will offer the assistance of my own security forces to His Excellency. I'm sure he will not refuse. Oh, and by the way, I have a message for you, Priestess. It's from your father."

"What is it?" Sheshi answered apprehensively.

"He told me to tell you that he is coming soon." With that, Saur-El turned his back on us and headed back toward the main gate with his men.

"They're just trying to scare you," I said.

"And doing a job of it, too," said Mother, hugging Sheshi. "She's shaking all over. I'd better get her back to bed."

"We may as well all go back to bed," said Father. "No point in keeping watch now. The damage is done."

"I won't rest very easy as long as *that* man is in the valley," I said.

"I thought you were exaggerating," said Shem. "But your description of him didn't do him justice. I never met a man that I sensed was so filled with cruelty before."

"That might be the answer to who did this," said Father. "It would be just like Enoch-Nod to deliberately start trouble and then conveniently show up to deal with it."

"His Excellency is too proud to accept their help," said Jirah.

"He may not have any choice," said Father.

The shocks of grain had been quickly consumed. All that remained were hundreds of red-glowing eyes. A smoke that was at once both sweet and sharp hung thickly over the plain.

"Where are we going to get all the grain we need now?" I asked as we surveyed the aftermath. "There are no other fields close by and it will take much time to haul it over a distance."

"Time we don't have," added Ham.

"I don't know," said Father. "The Lord will provide a solution."

One day soon after that, we saw a great caravan with many men and wagons approaching from the north. As they drew nearer, we recognized them as our kinsmen from Tabor Spring, six of whom were bearing on their shoulders a litter carrying the Ancient One. As the men set the litter down, Father greeted Methuselah warmly and said, "I have long hoped that you would come. There is plenty of room on the ark for you and your whole clan. You have arrived just in time."

With great effort, the Ancient One rose to his feet and said, "No, my son. I am soon going on a journey that will require no earthly vessel to bear me to my destination. But before death closes my eyes, I wanted to see the ark for myself and to bring you this offering of grain and provisions." With a sweep of his hand, he indicated the wagons still rolling in from the north.

"All this!" exclaimed Father, looking at the great quantity of supplies.

"The Lord has blessed me," said Methuselah. "And now I want to bless you. When you live as long as I have lived, you can accumulate much and I don't expect I will have further need of such things. From the looks of this fire-scorched plain, you could use it."

"Indeed we can."

"That much, at least, I can do for you, even if I have no real power anymore. Alas, that has fallen to others and I cannot say I think it is for the better as far as our tribe is concerned. But let us speak no more of that now. First, show me all that you have accomplished here."

They spent the rest of the day looking over the whole ark, though all the rest of his kin kept their distance from us except for unloading the wagons, pitching their tents about half a mile to the north. The Ancient One could only shuffle in small steps and had to be helped up the ramps, which was hardly to be wondered at considering his astounding age.

That night, Methuselah dined with us. After we had eaten, he said, "The Council of Elders will be convening here in a few days."

"Here?" said Father. "I don't believe they've ever met in Nephil before. And now is not even the time of convocation. This must be an extraordinary occasion."

"Extraordinary, yes," said Methuselah. "But little to be wondered at. The Sethites have ignored the great upheaval in the east for too long. I fear it is long since too late to change the outcome, but we must decide at last how we are going to respond."

"What do you think the Council will do?" asked Father.

"That is just the point—what can they do?" said Methuselah. "Anyway, I can no longer control or predict the younger members," said Methuselah. "They have a new chief elder now—or hadn't you heard that Irad has succeeded Hublis the Dananite?" Everyone was silent for a moment as that realization sunk in. "I see that this is news to you—and not good news."

"As you know, my brother and I have never been able to see eye to eye on things," said Father. "And the years and circumstances have not lessened our differences."

"That is a gracious way to say it," said Methuselah. "I know much and suspect even more. Irad has always been driven by ambition for this position. Now that he has achieved it, though, he finds himself in a very difficult situation. It is hard to say which way things will turn."

At that point, Re-Aylah got up and excused herself. I could see she was upset, so I followed her up to our room and said, "I know it's still hard for you."

"Being chief elder was all my father ever seemed to want," said Re-Aylah. "And my mother always wanted it for him as well."

"He has his wish now. I hope he finds it to his liking."

"I'm ashamed to say that there was a time when it was my wish for him, too—and not just for his sake. All that power and prestige used to have a very heady appeal for me. But now it just makes me ill."

I didn't know that Father had followed us until I heard him behind us saying, "He's still your father."

"And he's still your brother," Re-Aylah was quick to reply.

"Yes, you are quite right in saying that. So, I will be careful with the advice I give because I know I have to apply it to myself as well. It's a bitter thing when someone you love hurts you. Nevertheless, the Lord would have us continue to love him anyway."

"It's too hard," said Re-Aylah. "I can never forget that look on his face."

"Maybe he regrets the look he saw on *your* face," said Father. "Maybe we can all find it in our hearts to forgive each other."

"Even after all he has done?"

"Even after all he has done," said Father. "He wasn't always this hard-hearted. In better days when the world was younger ... Someday, I will tell you stories. But for now, let me say that we never know but what our love for him will help change his heart."

Re-Aylah thought about it for a moment and said, "I will try. I can't make any promises, but I will try."

We didn't see much of the Ancient One over the next several weeks, nor of his clan once they had unloaded all of his gifts to us into our storage holds. Meanwhile, we finished coating the ark with pitch, inside and out. Since we had no further use for the towers or the scaffolding, we dismantled them. Father had calculated to the exact board how much more lumber we would need to finish the interior and made us throw the excess in the river. It seemed like a waste, but he insisted that the danger of it being used against us outweighed any further benefit it might provide.

Ever since its earliest days, Nephil had always been a bustling city. But during that last phase of construction on the ark, the level of activity grew frenzied as the festival neared. The masses overflowed the city and spilled out into tents on the plain—not unlike the encampments we had seen in Nod. None of the people ventured too near the ark, however, as if we had some aura of superstition about us. The crowds included one visitor of whose coming we had been warned and whose arrival we dreaded—namely, the High Priest of the Morningstar. And so it was that one evening at supper, we were saddened, but not entirely taken by surprise, to hear Sheshi say, "My father has arrived in Nephil. I am going to him tonight."

"But why?" I asked. "Is it something we've done?"

"No," said Sheshi. "You have all showed me great kindness and tried to make me feel welcome. But it's clear to me that I don't fit in here."

Mother was very distraught and said, "Won't you give it more time? Or tell us what else we may do for you?"

"It's not that at all," said Sheshi. "You have been a mother to me and taught me your ways. But the only man I have ever loved has married another. Will you bear more sons that I may have a husband also?"

At this, I felt a stab of guilt. The last thing I had wanted to do was to hurt her. And even though I had to be true to my own heart, knowing that I had wounded her deeply was a hard burden to bear.

"But that is not the principal reason I am leaving," Sheshi continued. "If my own pain was all I had to contend with, I might be persuaded to stay. Yet I have others to consider in this decision. Will the suffering of my people be eased by my taking refuge here? My position is such—I mean, *was* such—that I might help them in some way. If I stay here, will their cries ever stop piercing my heart? I cannot shut out their voices." She closed her eyes and shook her head.

"I'm afraid we have no easy answers for you," said Father. "These perilous times are fraught with difficult choices and you have to do what seems best to you. But I can't let you leave without telling you that I have grave reservations about your departure. The Lord has promised me that all who take shelter in the ark will be protected. If you go, you'll be removing yourself from the refuge he has provided.

"I can't explain how I know," said Sheshi. "But perishing in the judgment will not be my fate."

"I believe you *do* know," said Father. "You've been given a measure of the gift of seeing. But you have to understand that the nature of the gift is such that it can sometimes be bound up with our own actions. You're acting on an insight into the future. And that can be dangerous, because your actions may very well be bringing about the outcome you have foreseen. Yet if you turned aside from the course you have chosen, things might be different."

"And what about your father," I said. "He has shown what kind of man he is and what he represents. You've come so far. I hate to see you turn back now."

"You are right," said Sheshi. "I have come too far to turn back now. But I want to help others who have fallen."

"It takes a strong hand to lift someone up without being pulled down," said Father. "Especially if he doesn't want to be helped."

"Nevertheless, my place is at his side," said Sheshi. "Goodbye for now, but not forever. I foresee that we will see each other again before the end."

Thus, there was nothing we could do to dissuade her. And despite her assurances that our paths would cross again, our parting was painful—especially for those of us who loved her most deeply.

Fourteen

s the elders of the other clans arrived for their council, the number of Sethite tents to the north of us swelled, though they kept themselves separated from us and from the peoples who were camping under the shadows of the wall. Of their deliberations, we heard little news. I know Father was hoping that they would seek his advice, but secretly I doubted that they would.

Then one day Father was summoned to their camp, though it turned out that it wasn't to seek his opinion. Out of curiosity, I invited myself to go along. Outside of Methuselah's tent, Irad met us. It was the first time I had seen him since Re-Aylah and I announced our engagement. The intervening years had taken a toll on him and he appeared to have aged considerably since then. I hoped that with those gray hairs had come an added measure of wisdom.

"Greetings, Brother," said Father. "I understand congratulations are in order."

The other men standing nearby looked at Irad, waiting for his reaction. He merely nodded toward the tent and said, "His time is at hand. He has been asking for you."

I followed Father into the tent and found the Ancient One propped up on his mat, unable to sit up by himself. "Is that you, Noah?" he said weakly. "My eyes have grown dim."

"I'm here, Father Methuselah, along with my firstborn."

"Good. First, I want to warn you. The elders have reached a decision. They have agreed to throw in their lot with Enoch-Nod."

"I was afraid of that," said Father. "They've been inching that direction for years. Still, it grieves me to hear that they've taken this final step."

"The final step will be the fatal one," said Methuselah. "They were strongly influenced by the one they call Ghurabbi. He is one you should beware of."

"Thank you for the warning. I will be vigilant."

"I have something else to say to you in parting. I realize that the years have not been easy for you. But I want you to know that I am proud of you, and you, too …"

He pointed his twig of a finger at me and I said, "Jayfeth."

"Yes, yes, Jayfeth. Well, if you live to have as many descendents as I do, you won't remember their names half as well."

"No, Father Methuselah. I'm sure I won't."

"Now what was I saying? Oh, yes. I wanted to tell you that this ark is the greatest project that has ever been built by the hand of man—or ever will be. Some will be bigger and many more beautiful. But never has so great a work been accomplished by so few. And never for such an important purpose. Your handiwork will bear the very fate of mankind as its cargo. And your name and your deeds will never be forgotten."

"I have sought to do all that the Lord has commanded me," said Father modestly.

"Yes," said Methuselah. "And with little time to spare. The fulfillment of the prophecy draws near."

"Then you still hold to the interpretation?"

"I believe it more strongly now than the day I first uttered it. See how everything has come together at this moment in time?"

"Yes, we could not even begin to foresee it then," said Father.

"But the Lord did. And here we are at the very end of the age."

"Yet even now, with so little time remaining, no one takes the message seriously."

"Do not think that your efforts have been in vain," said Methuselah, his voice barely above a whisper. "God will preserve a remnant through you."

This was the last thing he said. He peacefully breathed his last and his spirit departed to its eternal rest.

Father Methuselah had lived longer than any man who had ever come before him—nine hundred sixty-nine years in all. On account of his great longevity, he was venerated throughout the land by all people, not just his kindred. Even in an age noted for the long lives of its patriarchs, Methuselah was exceptional. Everyone was amazed that a man could live so long.

As word of Methuselah's death spread, people came from miles around.

They laid him to rest on the following day on a heather-topped hillock about a mile west of Nephil, just off the Gihon Road. Those in attendance at his funeral numbered in the thousands, including no small number of Nephilim and Nodites. Even Ben-Tubal himself came, as did Merib.

Since it was grudgingly acknowledged that Methuselah favored my father, our family was accorded a position near the front of the crowd, though Father was not asked to speak. Many dignitaries did, however, including Ben-Tubal, who promised to erect a monument there in Methuselah's honor. The last and most honored eulogy was reserved for Irad as chief elder of the Sethites. He spoke words which were commended by all as a fitting final tribute to the Ancient One.

The ceremony concluded, but the most enduring legacy of Father Methuselah's life had been neglected by all the other speakers. Father, however, was unwilling to let the moment pass without saying the things he felt needed to be said. Before the crowd began to disperse, he called out in a loud voice, "Many years ago, the Lord spoke to the forefathers of the Sethites and said, 'My spirit shall not always strive with man. The number of his years shall be one hundred twenty.' The sign of the coming doom was given in the form of a prophecy concerning Father Methuselah—that the disaster would not come in his lifetime. Listen to me my kinsmen and all you who come from far off. The years since the oracle was made number one hundred twenty. The Ancient One, of whom the oracle was spoken, lives no more. With his last breath, he reaffirmed his belief that doom is at hand. Humble yourselves before God and take refuge in the ark or you will all be destroyed!"

Someone in the crowd shouted, "Show some respect for the dead!"

"He's right," said Irad indignantly as the crowd began making its way back toward Nephil. "This is a solemn occasion. Why do you have to defile it with such inappropriate comments?"

Plucking up her courage Re-Aylah said, "Noah is not defiling his memory, Father. He's honoring it because the Ancient One believed this, too. That's why his last wish was to come here and see the means by which God will save us."

"You have no right to address me as 'Father,'" said Irad. "That relationship was severed a long time ago when you chose to disgrace our family."

"I do not repent the decision I made," said Re-Aylah. "But I do regret the pain it caused you. I would take that back if I could. All I can do now is to say that I still love you in spite of your harsh reaction. And to ask you for your forgiveness for doing what I was compelled to do."

"Forgive?" said Irad. "Do you think all wrongs can be so simply erased? I will never forgive you and I will never forget."

"Listen to yourself, Irad," Father admonished. "How did your heart become so hard? You'd better pray that God doesn't judge you by your own words."

"Who are you to lecture me?" said Irad. "But then you've always thought you were better than everyone else. Well, I have news for you. I'm the Chief Elder now. I'm the one that people listen to—not you."

"You're right, they do listen to you," said Father. "So why don't you use your influence to warn the people? If for once you would heed the word of the Lord, you could save a lot of people—including yourself."

"The word of the Lord," said Irad, his voice dripping with derision. "It always gets back to that, doesn't it? 'Listen to me—I'm a prophet. God talks to me and nobody else, so you'd better do what I say!'"

As Irad spoke those words, an insight came to me and I understood him in a way that I never had before. It seemed to me that in him I saw a pitiful picture of myself—or at least what I had the potential to become, if I allowed myself to be consumed with envy for the gift I did not possess. The thought sickened me.

I was brought back to the moment by Fehud saying, "Are we going to stand here all day? I'm hungry."

"This is important, Fehud," said Re-Aylah. "Why don't you listen with your heart instead of your stomach?"

Fehud responded with a loud yawn. "What about you, Mother?" pleaded Re-Aylah. "Or you Sirah? Won't any of you listen? This may be your last chance."

"Fehud speaks for us all," said Irad. "We are long bored of hearing about these delusions. It's pointless to reason with a madman or his followers and I won't waste any more time or breath on it. I have more pressing business to attend to."

As Re-Aylah sadly watched her family leave, I put my arm around her and said, "I'm sorry they wouldn't listen."

"I'm not even angry anymore," said Re-Aylah with a sigh. "I feel … pity."

"You have grown much through all this," said Father. "Your wounds are healing."

"What about his?" I asked, with a keen personal interest in the answer. "Are Irad's wounds incurable?"

"No," said Father. "I refuse to believe that anyone is incapable of change, because with the Lord, anything is possible. Now Re-Aylah, why don't you and the others head on back as well. Jayfeth, you can stay with me. It looks like Ben-Tubal and Merib want to have a private word with us."

Ben-Tubal had been standing to one side with Merib during our exchange with Irad, anxiously waiting to speak to Father. I thought it very telling that he did not have his usual crowd of sycophants milling about with him.

"What about you, Your Excellency," said Father. "Do you think like my brother that these are the ravings of a madman?"

Ben-Tubal answered, "I have taken you under my protection. I have provided for your needs—whatever you have asked of me. I have honored you before my people. I have even given you my daughter in marriage to your son. Yet when I defended you before the High Council of the Watch, you chose to humiliate me. I have asked myself over and over why this is so. And yes, madness has crossed my mind."

"You know that I meant no disrespect toward you," said Father.

"I know that," said Ben-Tubal. "I have ruled over a vast territory and people too numerous to count. But you are unlike any of them. Many years ago, in the counsels that led to our coming to Cush, the rumor of you first reached my ears. It was said that the Sethites would be like sheep before us. The only complication they foresaw was a prophet of the Highlands named Noah. My curiosity was aroused because they seemed concerned out of all proportion to the threat. I asked myself, what could one man do against so mighty a force—a lone holy man in a remote area? And when I came to Cush I found the people just like I expected them to be and it was easy to do as we pleased. But everywhere I went, they talked about the same holy man. They said he was blameless and upright, but touched with a madness for his god. I wondered what it was about you that made people so widely dispersed talk about you. I knew then that I had to meet you and judge for myself. And lo, you sought me out. But I did not find you as I expected—not a wild-eyed fanatic. Nor was your speech that of a raving lunatic, although even you would have to admit that some of the things you say strike others as implausible."

"I do admit it," said Father. "And they would be implausible if they didn't come from God, who has the power to bring them about."

"And what a vision he has given you! And what boldness to build it at my doorstep. If it had only been a tenth of its size, I would have insisted that it be dismantled and taken somewhere else, for it is ungainly to look at. But the scale of it so inspired me that I could not help myself but let it proceed. How often have I marveled at it from the tower of my palace, fascinated by your force of will that kept the project moving forward all these years in spite of every obstacle that you encountered. And that is what has impressed me more than anything else about you. The chief of your people—your very own brother—cannot dissuade you. You have held steadfastly to your convictions in the face of overwhelming opposition—even to the point of violence and expulsion from your tribe—without wavering or showing a hint of malice or retribution toward those who persecute you. You even stood before the High Council of the Watch and fearlessly opposed them to their faces—a feat that no one else has ever accomplished or even attempted, I assure you. For all these reasons, I have respected you more than any man I have ever known. You and I are not like other men. We stand apart, stand above the rest. Even now, I would make you the third highest ruler of my domain, behind myself and Merib, if you would swear allegiance to me."

"I am honored, Your Excellency," said Father. "And in turn, I would say that I have found much in you that I deeply admire. You are like one who stepped out of the elder days before the race of men was lessened. It is little wonder that you have so dominated our age. However, even if I was not so urgently pressed by the Lord's business, I would have to decline your offer because I cannot serve your masters."

"You do not speak it, but I hear the accusation implied," said Ben-Tubal. "Before you judge me too harshly, though, I would say a word in my own defense. The Watchers bred me and trained me. Thus, I was in their service before I knew my right hand from my left, so I can hardly be blamed for that."

"No, but it has been a long time since you and I reached the age of accountability," said Father. "And surely you must take responsibility for your governorship under their appointment."

"If I had defied them openly, they would only have installed another, undoubtedly crueler leader in my place," said Ben-Tubal. "But I was endowed with a measure of wisdom that opened my eyes to the growing menace. So by accepting the opportunity that was thrust upon me, I have been able to protect the interests of humanity to a degree. I have done what I could to mitigate the suffering of the Nodites. And it was by my counsel and skill in diplomacy that I prevented Cush from being conquered by force.

Otherwise, the Sethites would have been destroyed long ago, instead of the beneficial alliance we enjoy now. And if I occasionally had to employ the skills of unsavory characters like Baldag, it was only because I found myself confronted with ill choices and deemed the evil I could manipulate the lesser. Compared to what it might have been, my reign has been a peaceful one."

"Peaceful, yes," said Father. "But at what cost?"

"Too great, perhaps. And for all my efforts, I fear that I have only postponed the day of reckoning." He paused for a moment then continued in a low voice. "I think you know that the Watchers are preparing to reveal themselves at the festival and assume power openly."

"I suspected this, yes."

"And when that happens, they won't need me anymore, so I must act quickly. I have a plan to meet their challenge. If you will join me in my effort, I believe we can unite the people and drive the usurpers out of our world."

Father shook his head. "Your plan—whatever it is—is not God's plan."

"That's why I need your help, Noah. I'm asking you to intercede with your god to help me defeat the Watchers."

"The Watchers *will* be defeated," said Father. "But it won't be by your hand."

"Your plan is better?" said Ben-Tubal. "All I see is unending labor on your ark."

"But the ark is the only hope we have. When the judgment comes—"

"Yes, yes. I've heard all that before. But I'm no carpenter. This is a desperate situation. I've seen with my own eyes what they do to people. We must take action to defend ourselves, or the human race as we know it will be annihilated."

"Listen to me, Ben-Tubal," said Father with great earnestness. "The wrath of God will be poured out on the earth in a very few days. I plead with you to be on the ark when it comes."

Ben-Tubal sighed and shook his head. "I'm afraid that you will have to go your way and I will have to go mine."

"Wait," said Father as Ben-Tubal turned to go. "If we can't be partners, at least let us part as friends."

Father extended his hand. Ben-Tubal hesitated a moment, then took father's hand in his. "Yes, friends," he said. "And in what after times may be, when destiny has done with the demands it has made upon us ... well, we shall see."

FIFTEEN

The passing of the Ancient One was the sign that confirmed for Father that the fulfillment of the times was imminent. On the day after the funeral, he took me aside and said, "The time has come to begin loading the animals onto the ark. Because of your gift, the honor of calling them should fall to you."

"But I don't know—" I started to say.

Father waved off my objection and said, "Nothing's ever easy for you, I know. But don't make it harder than it needs to be. When it comes to the will of the Lord, it's better to just obey."

So, I climbed through the hatch to the roof of the ark and shouted all around, "Creatures of the earth, God has chosen certain ones among you to be saved in this ark from the coming destruction. In the name of the Lord, I bid you now to come."

Some of the people in the nearby camps looked at me and shook their heads. I have to admit that I felt more than a little silly as I looked at Father and shrugged. He nodded, indicating that the duty had been discharged to his satisfaction. To my amazement, by the time that I climbed down, two small rabbits had already appeared below the ramp—from where I do not know.

I carried the rabbits inside to a hutch on the upper deck, beginning what seemed like an endless procession in numbers so great that we all had to stop everything else we were doing to keep up with them all. The great diversity of life was astounding—from alpacas to zebras and everything in between. It was all I could do to keep from getting distracted by all the unusual creatures I had never seen before. Shem, who had a knack for such things, took charge of organizing and directing the loading, assigning the stalls and recording their occupants with his characteristic skill. We penned the largest animals on the lowest deck, with the medium sized in the middle and the smallest on top opposite where our rooms were. One end we had left open for an aviary.

It didn't take long before the whole place was bustling and we had quite a struggle to keep order through it all.

That first afternoon as I carried a small squirrel up the ramp, I remarked to Father. "I wasn't expecting them to be so young. Some are barely weaned."

"It's not surprising if you think about it," said Father. "The immature animals will take up less room and require less food. They also have all of their breeding years ahead of them when this is over."

The animals coming to the ark were not the only ones we saw. At first, there were singles and small groups, but oddly their numbers grew until there were whole herds moving up from the Lower Gihon Valley. And with so many people beginning to stream into Nephil for the festival, it seemed that every living thing in the world was on the move. We were so busy, however, that we did not have time to give much thought to the implications of this great migration.

By the time we got all the animals settled and fed, it made for a very short night. And though we rose early, more animals were already waiting at the foot of the ramp by the time we awoke and the second day continued like the first.

About mid-morning, I looked out and saw a familiar silver shape approaching. "Re-Aylah, look!" I shouted. "It's Moonbeam."

"You remember us, don't you girl?" said Re-Aylah as Moonbeam nuzzled our legs. "Where do you suppose her master is?"

I shook my head and said, "I fear that the Priest of Melchi is no longer among the living. Remember his parting words?"

"Sadly, yes. But Moonbeam is not alone. See!"

A ball of silver fur was wobbling unsteadily through the grass toward us, yipping for his mother.

"So, you found a mate after all," I said. "And a fine one he must be judging by your pup. Come here, boy."

The four of us rolled on the grass for several minutes and the reunion was indeed a happy one until I heard Shem calling, "Hey, you two. You can't play all day. We're getting a backlog here."

"I'm afraid Shem's right," I said. "Come with me, Moonbeam. "I'll make sure he assigns you one of our best stalls."

I started up the ramp, but Moonbeam didn't follow. I realized then that she had no intention of coming aboard the ark. I said to her, "Am I not right in saying you have no master now? Why don't you stay with us?"

But Moonbeam only barked, "Master."

"Even I understood that," said Re-Aylah.

"See, I told you that you could learn to communicate with animals if you spend time with them."

"It helps that I've heard it before. The last time she really was going to her master. But where could she be going now?"

"It makes you wonder, doesn't it?" I said.

Moonbeam nuzzled her pup one last time and started away. The pup tried to follow her, but she turned and barked for him to stay. Then she ran swiftly up the river valley and did not look back again. The pup whimpered pitifully, but he didn't try to follow her. I felt so sorry for him that I let him follow me around for the rest of the day. Everywhere I tried to walk he was constantly under my feet, but I didn't have the heart to put him in his pen yet.

The next day, we saw more and more animals passing by Nephil in such great numbers that it was impossible to ignore. I noticed that my little burro Naysa kept looking nervously at them. "Don't worry," I said to reassure him. "You'll be safe with us."

Naysa hung his head and didn't reply. In all his years with us, I had never seen him act that way. I looked up and thought about the great westward migration. With a sinking feeling, I realized what was troubling him so. "You're supposed to go, aren't you."

He raised and lowered his head.

"Then what keeps you here?" But I knew the answer. We were all he had ever known. He had served us loyally for my whole life and I had loved him as a dear friend. It was clear, though, that he heard a different call now.

"You have been a faithful servant and trustworthy friend," I said. "But now I release you from our service and bid you to follow the call. Farewell, wherever you go."

I stood aside and Naysa took a few steps, then stopped to look back. "Go on," I said, trying to put on a brave face. He turned again trotted westward, then broke into a full gallop. I did not see him again.

When the gathering was only a week away, the Lord spoke to Father and said, "The wickedness of man has filled the earth and I am grieved that I have made him. In seven days, I will bring a great and terrible flood of waters over the face of the whole earth and put an end to the abominations that are being practiced. But you have found favor in my eyes and have done all that I commanded. You and your family will go into the ark and be saved from the coming destruction."

As Father related the message, we all sat dismayed at the revelation that we were so close to the end of the world as we knew it. Finally, Father said, "I know this is difficult, but we have to accept it. It's not like we haven't been preparing for this for a long time. Everyone has been working hard and nearly everything is ready."

"What about the door?" said Ham.

"I think we have to face the fact that the parts we ordered aren't going to come in time," said Father. "So we'll have to use what we have."

"I've told you ten times, the pulleys we salvaged from the tower won't work for that door," said Ham. "They're too big in diameter. That's why I ordered the others."

I made the mistake of asking, "What difference does it make?"

"Not that you would understand," Ham replied, "but that door weighs six tons. If you put too much stress on the guides, they'll snap. Then the whole thing will crash to the ground and break into pieces. And I don't think you can bail water fast enough to keep a boat afloat with a thirty-foot hole in its side."

"I agree that it would have been better with the smaller pulleys," said Father. "But it's too late now. We'll have to make these work. I'm sure we'll find a way."

Late that night as I lay staring into the darkness, Re-Aylah leaned over and said softly, "I can tell by the sound of your breathing that you're not asleep, though it's long past time that you should have been."

"I'm sorry I woke you," I said. "Go back to sleep."

"Not until you tell me what's wrong."

"It would be faster to tell what *isn't* wrong—you and me, together. See, the list of what's right is very short. Everything else in the world, though, is going very badly."

"I know how you feel," said Re-Aylah. "That's why I'm awake to know that you're awake. It's bothering me, too."

"You know, it's very strange," I said. "I've lived my whole life in the shadow of this prophecy. Even in times of doubt, deep down it always rang true for me. But today, when Father said 'seven days,' the realization of it suddenly hit me in a new way. It's not a prophecy about the future anymore.

It's a present reality. God really is going to destroy the world. And now that the time has come, the thought of it terrifies me."

"All of us are frightened, if there's any consolation in knowing that you're not alone in feeling this way. But we have to trust the Lord to see us through this."

"You sound like someone else we both know."

"He is a rock," said Re-Aylah. "You and I both know we'll never have faith like that. It's easy to just let his faith carry us all. But sometimes I think we rely on him too much and he pays a price for it. Something tells me, though, that this may be a time when we have to look to our own faith rather than his."

"You're right, of course," I said. "I just wish there was some other way."

"Some other way besides God's way?"

"Not if you put it like that. It's just that I can't shake this awful feeling of dread. I wish it were all over with."

"I do too, Love," she said as we held each other close. "I do too."

The next day, Father sent Jirah into Nephil to inform her father and brother about God's final warning and plead with them to join us on the ark. She returned that evening in great distress. "His Excellency and my brother are implementing their conspiracy against the Watchers. Merib left heading west just before nightfall in the hope that all attention will be focused on preparations for the festival and that he will not be missed."

"West?" I said. "Why would he be heading toward the Highlands?"

"I do not know for certain because they are being very secretive with the Tower Guards everywhere," said Jirah. "But I did hear them talking about following the river to its source."

"I don't like the sound of *that*," said Father. "The land there is forbidden."

"Please do something," said Jirah. "If he is missed, they will know something is afoot. And if the land at the river's source is forbidden, he must be prevented from entering. Either way, his life is in jeopardy."

Father looked down and said nothing.

"You are going to go after him, aren't you?" said Jirah.

An awkward moment of silence followed. Before I even realized what I was doing, I spoke up and said, "I'll go."

"Haven't you heard what Father has been saying?" said Shem. "The time is almost at hand. Merib has made his choice and cast his lot with his father.

I know it sounds harsh, but people have to bear the consequences of their decisions. If you go chasing after him, you could perish along with him."

Jirah appealed to Ham with her eyes, and he spoke up. "Yes, brother, we are all well aware of that. But we still have five safe days left, haven't we? Merib couldn't have gotten far yet. If Jay leaves now, he could be back in plenty of time. I'd—uh—go myself, but ... well ... I'm needed here."

"And I'm expendable," I said.

"That's not what I meant," said Ham. "If you want to stay here and work on the door rigging in my place, that's fine. If we don't figure out a way to get that door shut when the time comes, this will be a very short trip."

"What if something happens to Jay while he's out looking for Merib?" asked Shem. "A lot can go wrong along the way."

Everyone turned to Father to see what he would say. But it was not an easy decision for him and he had difficulty making up his mind. At last, he said, "Go, though I perceive it will be to no avail. But he is your friend, and you will always regret it if you don't try. Come back in three days, or four at the latest. Whatever you do, do not press the time or any unforeseen delay could be disastrous. Everyone must be on board by sundown on the fifth day from now. Anytime after that ... well, I shouldn't have to remind you of the consequences."

"I'll go with you," said Re-Aylah, and I knew better than to argue with her. "I know a shortcut."

We left hastily and made our way running along the Gihon Road. The half-moon at our backs lit the way, so that we had no trouble seeing. Yet it seemed strangely dark.

"I know what it is," said Re-Aylah when we had slowed to a walk for a bit. "Where is the omen tonight?"

"That's a good question," I said. "The comet has been burning so brightly the past few weeks that all the other stars have looked pale by comparison. I wonder why it would have suddenly disappeared."

"Do you think that it's good or bad that it's gone?"

"It's hard to say. I know the Watchers didn't like it. But honestly, I can't say I did either. It had a very ominous appearance. I wouldn't be sorry to see it go away."

"I know what you mean," said Re-Aylah. "Still, I would like to know what happened to it."

That was all the thought we gave it at the time, for other matters soon pressed upon us. Little did we know, however, that the same question was at that very moment perplexing the Watchers—or how desperate their uncertainty might make them.

SIXTEEN

Re-Aylah and I reasoned that Merib would have taken the Upper Trail to avoid being seen by the east-faring festival throngs. Our plan was to follow the Gihon Road to the Great Bend in the river in the hope of getting ahead of him and then take Re-Aylah's shortcut through the woods to cut him off. We traveled all night and made good time—better than we did during the following day, tired as we were and because the caravans we met made us feel as though we were swimming upstream against the current, so to speak. By early afternoon, we reached the bend and veered off the road to the north. An hour later, we intersected the upper path, having saved several hours by choosing speed over stealth. A quick survey of the path, however, indicated recent footprints—large ones made by a very tall man—and they were already growing cold.

"He's already been here," I said, dejected. "And longer ago than I would have thought."

"What should we do?" asked Re-Aylah. "He's moving so fast that it's not going to be easy to overtake him."

"I don't suppose you would turn back if I asked you."

"Not unless you're coming with me."

"Are you up for another run then?"

"Try to keep up," she said and took off down the path.

We held to a grueling pace all the rest of the afternoon, pausing only infrequently to look for signs before halting for the night, which seemed to the weary all too short before dawn broke. At first light, we were off again, alternating between running and walking with only three brief rests all day. When dusk fell, I was so foot-weary that I hardly remember laying down before I fell asleep. The next morning, getting started was not so easy and we had gone some distance before we got the stiffness worked out. At midday, we rested and ate a little. By then, we were well up into the Highlands and the hardwoods were beginning to give way to conifers. That familiar pine forest scent brought back memories of better days. I savored every breath until I noticed that Re-Aylah was looking at me. I said, "I know what you're thinking."

"It's the third day and we are a long way from Nephil," she said.

"These tracks are fresh. We've gained on him. I hate to give up now when we're so close."

"We're not even sure that they're his. If we keep on, there's no way we're going to make it back in time, even if we catch him. We've got to turn back."

I thought about it for a moment and said, "You're right, I know, though Jirah will take it ill—assuming we're not too late ourselves. Even if we push at least this hard on the return journey, we'll be cutting it close and we're starting out already tired. Still, I wish I could have tried just one more time to persuade him."

Suddenly, from the rocks below, we heard a surprised voice say, "It's you."

"Merib!" I said as he emerged from behind a rock and showed himself.

"I thought I heard someone following me," he said as he joined us. "So I circled back to see who it was. I thought ... well, I am relieved to see that it is you. What brings you so far from home?"

"This *is* my home—or at least it was at one time," I said. "But the reason we're here is that we're looking for you. What takes you so far from yours?"

"Have you changed your mind about our plan?"

"No, we haven't changed our minds," I said.

"We don't even know what your plan is," said Re-Aylah.

Merib hesitated, pursing his lips much like I had often seen his father do. So I added, "You can tell us. After all, we did come all this way out of concern for your safety. And Jirah is beside herself with worry."

"We've had to be very careful," said Merib. "The ones who can be trusted now are few. And even from them the Watchers have ways of finding things out."

"They do have frightening powers," I said.

"Powers, yes," said Merib. "That's why I'm making this quest—in the hope that we can balance the scales."

"And how do you propose to do that?" I asked.

"You know the legend. At the source of the great rivers are two trees, one bearing the fruit of life and the other knowledge. If we eat this fruit, we can attain ultimate wisdom and immortality, so that the Watchers will no longer have the advantage over men. Then we can reclaim our world from the usurpers."

"I don't think it will work that way," I said. "Eating from the forbidden tree was what allowed evil to enter the world in the first place. You cannot set things right by committing a second wrong. And besides, you are forgetting that the entrance itself is guarded by a Spirit Being. That is no legend—Ham has seen him. He is not in league with the Watchers of Enoch-Nod, but he will not suffer any to enter the Eastern Gate."

"I know that, too," said Merib. "But our diviners have foreseen an opportunity that we cannot afford to miss—the Guardian is being recalled."

"That's strange," I said. "I wonder what that means?"

"I don't know," said Merib. "But I have to try. Ben-Tubal is ruler over all this land. For my whole life I have trained, believing that when the time came, the office would fall to me. But if the Watchers have their way, not only will I not be ruler, they will make slaves of us all. Not me. I will not be a slave to them or anyone else. I will not give up my right to rule without a fight!"

"You still don't understand, do you? There's not going to be any fight. And the Watchers are not going to prevail. Something terrible is going to happen on the third day from now. And if you're not on the ark when it comes ..."

Merib was silent for a moment. Then he put his hand on my shoulder—a gesture of intimate friendship for him—and said, "Then you'd better hurry back to your ark. Goodbye, my brother."

I didn't know what else to do, so I gripped his forearm with my hand and said, "Farewell, brother."

"Take care of him," he said to Re-Aylah. "He is ever in need of it."

Without another word he was running down the pathway at great speed and quickly disappeared from sight. Re-Aylah leaned her head on my shoulder and said, "I am sorry."

"No time to grieve for him now," I said, trying to shake off my great sadness at his departure. "We'd better heed our own advice and hurry back. We have no time to spare."

That far up the Gihon, we were not far from where the upper path rejoined the main road. We cut through the woods a mile or two, leaping and bounding down the slope between the trees and rocks, until we came to the road. It had been many years since either of us had traveled that way and it was strange to see how deserted it was. By then, most of the camps had been abandoned for years. The few that weren't long deserted were empty then because of the festival. We both knew that area like the inside of our own room and it filled us with a strange sense of melancholy to walk mile after mile without seeing anyone at all.

"It feels like we're the only ones left in the world," said Re-Aylah as the shadows lengthened and faded into darkness.

"Soon, we might really be," I said.

"I can't get my mind to envision what that would be like," said Re-Aylah.

"It's beyond comprehension, isn't it?" I said. "But maybe something will happen and God will relent at the last minute."

"Maybe," she said. "But I don't think we should count on it. We'd better keep pushing ahead."

We traveled onward into the night at the fastest pace we could maintain, denying the weariness that tugged at our legs. Knowing that we had spent too much time looking for Merib, we didn't dare to stop and rest for the night that far from Nephil. We were fully aware of the great distance we had to cover in the two safe days we had left to us and had no illusions that we wouldn't need every minute of them.

In the middle of the night, we slowed instinctively, knowing what lay ahead. "You don't think any of your clan remained behind, do you" I asked.

"I saw most of them at Father Methuselah's funeral," said Re-Aylah. "Still, it would not be unlike my father to leave some behind to guard his camp."

"Would you prefer to go around?"

"We'll lose time stumbling around in the dark if we leave the road," said Re-Aylah. And I can't imagine any encounter with my family that would be worse than the ones I've already had. Besides, if anyone is there, they deserve the same last chance as the others."

We approached cautiously, but everything seemed deserted and the cooking fire appeared to be several days cold. We were just turning to go, when a voice behind us gave us a terrible fright. "A little late for an evening stroll, isn't it?"

"Hura!" I said. He was sitting on a rock not far from the road. We must have passed only a few feet from him without knowing it.

"What would you be doing so far from the refuge of your ark at this late hour?" he said, but both of us knew better than to divulge anything. "I wonder. It wouldn't have anything to do with treason, would it?"

"We don't know what you're talking about," I said, though probably not very convincingly. His next words, however, made clear that it wouldn't have made any difference anyway.

"Come, now," he said. "Why deny it? We know all about Ben-Tubal's petty scheming. We know *everything*."

Indeed, it seemed that they did and I found it very unsettling. It's hard to outmaneuver an opponent who knows your every move. "So what are you doing here?" I finally managed to say for lack of anything better to come to mind.

"Surely you're not surprised to see me," said Hura. "After all, we have some unfinished business."

"We don't need to defend ourselves to you," said Re-Aylah. "Let's just get out of here, Jay."

"Ah, yes," said Hura. "Running away is your solution to most problems, isn't it?"

"You don't even know me," said Re-Aylah. "So you can't know how I solve my problems."

"Oh, but I do know you," said Hura. "Don't you remember the night your father and I arranged for you to marry Baldag? We sat right over there, as I recall."

Re-Aylah and I stood there shocked for a moment as the implications of that sank in. "I told you he looked familiar," said Re-Aylah. "But the reason I couldn't place him was because he was passing himself off as the elder of a distant clan."

"I am an elder of your tribe," said Hura. "I have been for many years. And a very convenient way to influence the Council it has proved to be."

"You are Ghurabbi!" she exclaimed, finally making the connection.

"So it was you that the Ancient One warned us about," I said. "Little wonder that you would be the one behind the trouble that's been brewing among the Sethites all these years."

"I don't know how he contrived this deception, but if that was him …" said Re-Aylah, her voice trailing away as she thought.

"It's all coming back now, isn't it?" said Hura. "I've visited this camp many times over the years."

"Like the night you persuaded my father to burn Noah's lumber!" said Re-Aylah.

"So that's how Irad knew we were away from home!" I said, my anger flaring. "That cost us fifteen years of work!"

"Yes," said Hura. "Arson is such crude work. I leave it for rougher hands than mine, so that I may devote my personal attention to … more subtle arts. With Irad's ambition, it wasn't difficult to manipulate him to do certain things in order to win the favor of the Council. He was so jealous of his brother, half the time he thought they were his own ideas. We didn't even understand the purpose of the ark back then. We only opposed it because the Terrible One commanded it. But Noah has proved very stubborn in this pursuit. And now we know why—unfortunately for you."

Precious minutes were slipping away and we had a long way to go, so I said, "You have Sheshi back. What is it that you want from us?"

"Just one small thing," said Hura. "To make sure you do not board the ark."

I recall hearing a twang like the snap of a string from some unseen mechanism and instantly I felt a sting in my neck. I barely had a moment to pluck out a small dart before my arms went limp at my sides. As my knees buckled, Re-Aylah lunged to catch me. Another dart twanged and she crumpled and fell beside me.

Hura began binding our hands and feet as I lay there helpless as an infant, unable to offer the least resistance. "It seems your father may have been right about the impending catastrophe after all," Hura said as he worked. "The Watchers are in great agitation because they fear they may have misread the timing of the omen, so we can't take any chances. But fortunately, the schemes of the Terrible One are transparent to my master. And all the more so when he involves weak and ignorant people like your family. The solution to this threat is simple, regardless of when it comes. All we have to do to prevent the catastrophe is to keep anyone from boarding the ark. The Terrible One will not leave himself without a remnant among men for his amusement. And it will take time to raise up more hapless followers like you out of the rabble. By then, other plans will have time to unfold."

"Dislodging my father from the ark might not be as easy as you think," I said through thick lips. "Then what of your plan?"

By then, we were both securely tied. Hura leaned down close to my face. In the moonlight, the serpent on his forehead seemed poised to strike. "At least I will have the satisfaction of thinking about you two all alone and vulnerable here when the catastrophe strikes. That's right. This little potion won't kill you—just immobilize you for awhile. As much as I would like to kill you myself, there are certain considerations that restrain me at the moment. But it would be quite ironic if you died at the hand of the one you claim to serve. And it would serve you right for apostasy. But look at the bright side, it would be a more humane way to die than a slow death by thirst and starvation, which I think is the more likely possibility. Your father also has certain weaknesses which are not difficult to exploit. I am confident that the ark will be quite deserted when the time comes."

Hura mounted a horse hidden in a nearby thicket and galloped away east at great speed. As the sound faded into stillness, I lay there unable to move at all—and bound securely even if I could have moved.

Re-Aylah had fared even worse than I did. Out of the corner of my eye, I could see her laying unconscious beside me, the dart still protruding from her shoulder. Every beat of her heart pumped a little more poison into her deathly still body. But there was nothing I could do about it—nothing to do at all but count down the hours until the end of the world.

SEVENTEEN

The poison-induced drowsiness must have overtaken me. The next thing I remember was hearing movement in the bushes across the road and up the hill from where we were laying. As the rustling grew more distinct in the pre-dawn stillness, there was no mistaking that whatever was making that sound was moving toward us.

With some effort, I managed to call out weakly, "Is somebody there?" But there was no answer.

Except for where it lingered in my hands and feet due to the tightness of my bonds, the numbness in my limbs was fading. I managed to turn my head enough to scan the hillside and thought I could see a tigress moving in and out of the shadows. Many thoughts went through my mind as it approached, and most of them were not pleasant. But when it was close enough that I could get a good look at it, I saw that it was not a tigress at all, but a woman crawling on all fours.

With the way things had been going, I wasn't sure that I liked that any better. But having no other options at the time, I thought I should make the most of the opportunity. "Can you help us?" I ventured. "We've been drugged and bound."

Still no answer was offered. The woman paused for a moment and rose up on her knees. In the waxing glow of dawn, I could see that her whole body was covered with what looked more like thick paint than clothing, including dark stripes that had put me in mind of a tigress. And there was something more—something vaguely familiar about her face.

When she was only a few feet away, she stopped again, tilted her head and looked at me. I tried to see behind the heavily-caked paint on her face and searched my recollection.

"Minnah?" I asked, wondering if this creature could possibly be the woman I had known all my life. "Or should I say Ell-Esa?" At some level, she appeared to recognize at least one of the names. But the response was not what I would have expected. Her eyes were devoid of any human spark. The association with the Watchers seemed to have robbed her of that. Or maybe it was the fact that she had denied those human attributes for so long in the affair of Giblith and Baldag that she had forfeited the capacity to use them. Whatever the case, she looked, instead, more like a highly intelligent animal. And I suppose, in a very real sense, that is what she had become.

"Have you escaped from your master?" I asked.

Minnah nodded slowly.

"But you followed him here?" Then I added, more to myself than to her, "I guess that's part of the curse. You want to get away, but you can't."

Minnah made no reply. In retrospect, I guessed that through Hura she had been under the influence of Enoch-Nod long before she ever went to dwell there. And although it in no way excused her actions, the realization did help to reaffirm the compassion I had always felt for this love-crossed woman whose passion got twisted into something evil. She was just the kind of victim that the enemies of God delighted to exploit to their own purposes.

"Can you untie me?" I said, leaning over to indicate that my hands and feet were bound. Apparently, she understood what I was asking, because she was behind me in a moment, loosening the ropes. When my hands were freed, I reached out to thank her, but she shrank from my touch. "I'm sorry. Don't be scared. I won't hurt you."

But if some vestige of obligation lingering in her heart had caused her to seek amends for the wrongs she had done me, she now deemed them fulfilled. A new caprice took hold of whatever mind she had left. In a moment, she was up on her feet, jumping from rock to rock. "Come back," I called. "Please. We can help you."

My pleas did not avail; she never looked back. A stark realization came to me—that the presence of the Others offered only two choices to mankind. The first was resistance. As futile as that might seem in the face of such overwhelming strength, it was the only alternative that preserved our humanity. The other, more frightening alternative was demonization— frightening because the nature of the contact was such that any level of cooperation with them robbed people of those essential qualities that made them human. What remained was human in form, but not in nature. As I watched Minnah disappear in the first rays of dawn, I shuddered to think that I might be witnessing the future of the human race.

I turned my attention to Re-Aylah. Rather clumsily, I managed to pluck the dart from her shoulder. Even as numb as my fingers still were, I could tell that her skin felt hot to the touch.

"Re-Aylah, can you hear me?" I said, patting her face. "Wake up, Sunshine." But she did not respond.

After I untied my legs, I rose to my feet with great exertion, collapsed, then stood again. In my condition, I didn't think I could carry Re-Aylah to the river, so I stumbled around the tents until I found a blanket. Rolling her onto it, I dragged her as gently as I could down the slope, hoping that the Gihon would have a therapeutic effect upon her wound.

When we reached the edge of the river, I scooped up a palmful of water and sprinkled a few drops on her face. Encouraged to see her stir a little, I soaked a corner of the blanket and patted her face and arms with the wet cloth. After a few moments, she scrunched up her nose and opened her eyes.

"I can't move," she mumbled through thick lips.

"It will pass in a little while," I assured her and held her close. "Just lie still."

"No time," she said. "Leave me. Save yourself."

"Shhhh ... don't talk that way. I'm not going anywhere without you. Where would I ever find someone else who would put up with me like you do?"

"I bear the burden as well as I can," she said and almost managed a smile.

Encouraged to see her spirit returning, I said, "You have suffered the burden nobly. And we've traveled a very long road to come all the way back to the place where I first confessed my love to you. It was right over there, remember? And if it comes right down to it, I would rather die here with you than to get on the ark without you."

Re-Aylah shut her eyes again, spilling tears down her cheek. As I wiped them away, she whispered, "I love you."

I applied a poultice to Re-Aylah's shoulder to relieve the swelling and draw out what I could of the poison. I held her there in my arms as the hours passed. Save for the faint sound of the flowing water, the silence was nearly complete—no people, no animals, not even any insects. Except for the two of us, the whole world seemed deserted.

As the hours slipped away, Re-Aylah slowly regained the feeling in her limbs. By mid-morning she was able to stand up and walk, though slowly at first. We started eastward, arms around each other for support, at the best pace we could maintain—which was 'nowhere near what we needed to make up lost time. All my calculations had counted on avoiding delays and making better time on the return journey using the main road. The poison had left us both feeling weak and queasy—especially Re-Aylah. Every time we tried to pick up the pace, she got nauseous. So, instead of making up time, we fell further and further behind. Still, we plodded along as best we could, though we had no real expectation of making it back to the ark in time. When night fell, we could go no further and collapsed by the side of the road.

In the middle of the night, I awoke and gently shook Re-Aylah. "How are you feeling?"

"Terrible," she said. "But that's an improvement over yesterday."

"It's nearly fifty miles from here. And you know what happens tomorrow."

"We'll never make it."

"I know," I said. "But the question is, 'Are we going to try?'"

"Maybe we should just find a pleasant place to sit by the river and wait for the end to come. If it's our last day on earth, why not just enjoy it?"

"I could pick strawberries while you cook a pot of soup. I could do with a good meal."

"Afterward, I'll sing you a love song recounting the heroic deeds of my lover," said Re-Aylah. "And you can write a poem extolling the virtues of your beloved."

"We'll drift off to sleep in each other's arms and simply never wake up," I said.

"And that would be as happy a last day as we could ask for," said Re-Aylah.

We both sighed and wished it could be so.

"We're going on, aren't we," said Re-Aylah at last.

"Has being with me ever been easy?"

"The easy way has never been our lot, I'm afraid. Let's be off, then. But if, by providence, the sun rises on us again tomorrow, I will not forget that you have promised me strawberries and a poem."

"Which I will deliver in eager anticipation of soup and a song," I said. "You will make the song sound impressive, won't you?"

"Generations to come will venerate you on account of it—if there are more generations."

And so we talked to pass the hours and miles as we made our way down the road in the moonlight. When dawn came and we no longer had to be quite so careful picking our way along the deteriorating road, we increased our pace to a grueling, mile-eating run. By mid-morning, though, we were both weary and our pace began to lag. We no longer had breath to spare for conversation, so we encouraged each other with our eyes and by touch. When we couldn't run any more, we walked. We did not dare to stop even briefly for fear that we would not be able to get going again. By noon, we had covered barely half the distance and both of us knew we couldn't continue much longer. Exhaustion pushed us to the edge of despair. With each mile, it became more of a struggle to put one foot in front of the other.

The will to live must be bound up with the life force itself, because all living creatures I have observed appear to possess a generous measure of it. But man, it seems, was endowed with a double portion, for I have seen a man go on in dire circumstances when an animal would lay down and die. Indeed, it is upon the will that death makes its first assault. The will, until it is vanquished through extremes of pain or suffering or weariness, somehow keeps death at bay, because death rarely comes to the unwilling. Thus, it was that will to live that kept us trudging onward beyond the end of our strength.

Even willpower has its limits, however, and we were nearing the end of ours. Re-Aylah was practically unconscious on her feet and I was little better off when the silence was broken by a far distant sound. As we listened, we heard a horse-drawn carriage approaching. I briefly contemplated hiding, just to make sure that the approaching driver was not unfriendly. But we were too tired to make the effort to get off the road and knew full well that even if its driver were hostile, it wouldn't hasten our demise by more than a few hours anyway. To my everlasting relief and astonishment, though, it was Shem in the driver's seat.

"We should have known that our family wouldn't give up on us," I exclaimed to Re-Aylah.

"Praise God, I've found you!" he shouted as he pulled to a stop. In a moment, he was off the carriage that had been provided courtesy of Ben-Tubal. "Father is frantic that you have not returned," he said as we leaned on him. In fact, his embrace was just about all that was still holding us up.

"You know the Nephilim are as swift as eagles," I said, trying to catch my breath. "It wasn't easy to overtake him."

"Then you found Merib?"

"Yes, but he would not be dissuaded."

"Just as I feared," said Shem. "The hearts of those who persist in unbelief grow ever harder."

"And how are things back at Nephil?" I asked.

"Bad and growing worse by the hour. The decadence is beyond description and the festival doesn't even officially begin until sundown. Well, you will see it for yourself soon enough. We'd better be going, though, or we won't reach Nephil by nightfall. And after that, the end could come at any moment."

"You don't have to convince me," I said. "That very thought has been on my mind for many scores of miles."

"There is one hopeful bit of news to report," said Shem, as we helped Re-Aylah into the carriage. "Irad sent word to Father this morning that he wanted to talk with him."

That perked up Re-Aylah as much as anything could have. She said, "Do you think it's possible that he wants reconciliation?"

"That was Father's hope," said Shem. "He was just going to meet with Irad as I left."

"Things are looking up," I said as I climbed in the back beside her. "Maybe everything will turn out all right after all."

That was the last thing I clearly remembered. I closed my eyes and for several hours I drifted in and out of sleep. Shem drove the horses hard for the rest of the afternoon and we made good progress on the deserted road. By the time I fully awoke, I was pleased to see how far we'd come. I let Re-Aylah go on sleeping while I climbed up front with Shem and caught him up on all that had transpired.

The shadows had begun to lengthen when Shem said, "We won't be able to drive much farther. Close to Nephil, the road will be choked with travelers and the whole plain is thick with tents and people. We'll make better time and attract less attention by abandoning the carriage and traveling the rest of the way on foot."

About four miles west of Nephil, Shem pulled off the road. The horses had been growing increasingly restless as if they knew that something was about to happen. Shem unhitched them and let them go free. Immediately, they headed back up the Gihon Road and were quickly lost to sight.

I kissed Re-Aylah on the cheek and whispered, "It's time to wake up. We're almost there."

Re-Aylah opened her eyes slowly and said, "I've been having the most bizarre dream."

"How could your dreams be any stranger than the times we live in?" I said.

"You're right, it's hard to tell the difference these days," said Re-Aylah. "Did you say we're almost home?"

"Yes, but we'll have to walk the rest of the way."

Without the horses and carriage drowning out all other sounds, we were quickly aware of the noise of revelry echoing up the river valley. A quarter hour later, we rounded a bend and could see the top of the ark rising above the plain and the spires of Nephil beyond. But between our destination and us lay a crowd of people such as had never been assembled in one place before. The encampment stretched all the way to the burial mound of Methuselah and to the north as far as my eyes could see. As the last rays of sunset faded, we entered the time long foretold. From that moment on, doom could strike at any moment.

Eighteen

The opportunity to marry into the power and privilege of the Sons of the Gods proved to have very strong appeal—not to mention the threat of death hanging over any who chose to defy the order to attend. Many women were even said to be abandoning their husbands for a chance to escape the desperate poverty in which most were living.

We stuck close together for fear of becoming separated in the crowd. As we entered the throng, we observed that the great majority were already heavily intoxicated, mixing their libations with the blood of animals slaughtered at makeshift altars and eating the flesh raw. Things even more shameful than that were being practiced as well of which I will not speak. It was frightening to see the depths of degradation to which the world had sunk. All the while, we kept looking to the sky, dreading to see the first sign of disaster.

The crowd was still superstitious of coming within a hundred yards of the ark. After what seemed like hours of zigzagging the last two miles through the tumult, we reached the open circle around the structure and breathed a sigh of relief. When we looked inside, though, we found to our dismay only the frightened animals. Our family was gone.

"Where could they be?" I wondered out loud. "Father was emphatic that everyone be on board before sunset and it's hours after that now."

"Do you suppose he received a new revelation?" said Shem.

"There's no sign of a struggle," said Re-Aylah. "He wouldn't have willingly left the ark unless ..." She stopped in mid-sentence as a terrible suspicion came to her.

"No," I said, sensing her thought. "I know relations are strained between our families, but I don't think Irad would go that far."

"But remember what you told me that Hura said about exploiting your father's weaknesses," said Re-Aylah. "What is the greatest of these, if it is not his soft heart?"

"Once they had him, the others would put up no resistance out of fear for his safety," said Shem.

"That would be a new low—even for Irad," I said, "especially considering the lateness of the hour."

"He probably just wanted Noah out of the way for awhile so he wouldn't embarrass him at the festival," said Re-Aylah. "You know how he hates to lose face. Besides, you're forgetting that he doesn't believe all that anyway."

"Maybe deep down he does believe it," said Shem. "Or at least he doesn't want to take any chances. So he bought into Hura's strategy of keeping us off the ark."

"Even if this is true, what can we do about it?" I said. "The three of us can't fight the whole tribe and rescue them by force. We don't even know where to start looking for them."

"Maybe Ben-Tubal will help us," said Re-Aylah.

"If he still can," said Shem.

We all knew Shem had a point. But since none of us had any better ideas, we headed for the palace—but not without grave misgivings. After going so long with the single-minded purpose of getting back to the safety of the ark, it was with no small amount of apprehension that we stepped off it again, knowing that doom could strike at any time.

The dark night closed in around us as we made our way across the open space that lay between the ark and the mob surrounding the city. And there we were met with a darkness of a different sort, a depravity so profound that to witness it was oppressive to the spirit. The degradation of the Havilah mining camps and the drunken revelry I had witnessed in Enoch-Nod were but a faint foreshadowing of the unbridled orgy underway in Nephil—so wanton, so craven, so revolting that I will not endeavor to describe it.

We linked hands, with Re-Aylah between us, as we passed through—as much to encourage each other as it was to prevent us from becoming separated. Ignoring all the offers to join in the dissipation, we hurried as quickly as we could and tried to attract the least amount of attention possible. Before we had gone a hundred yards, some cad with a blood-smeared face made a grab for Re-Aylah, but I shoved him down in a drunken heap before he got his hands on her (which I am confident was more humane than what she would have done to him).

It took well over an hour and much seeking back and forth for a way through before we reached the main gate. Inside the city, though, the boulevards were impassable because of the crowds. Fortunately, we were well acquainted with the side streets and made reasonably good progress for some distance until we reached the courtyard where a great mass of people was gathered around a massive stone altar in the center. At the top of the platform was Hura, the High Priest of the Morningstar, and Sheshi at his side.

At a safe distance from the intense heat rising through the chimney, Hura tripped a lever that released a trap door covering a chute that dropped to the furnace. A black ram standing in the holding pen over the trap door plunged screaming to his death as the crowd roared with wild delight. As soon as the door sprang shut again, two other priests dragged a terrified she-goat into the pen to repeat the slaughter. People laughed as she hurled herself repeatedly against the bars in a vain attempt to escape.

"How horrible," said Re-Aylah. "No wonder we saw all those animals fleeing in fright. They must have rounded up thousands for this."

"So much for the bloodless sacrifices Hura bragged about," I said.

"You shouldn't be surprised if the godless go from bad to worse," said Shem. "They always do."

"But I can't believe that Sheshi would be involved with something like this," I said. "I wish we could get to her somehow and talk to her."

"Well, we can't go this way," said Shem. "It would take all night to get through that crowd—if we could at all."

"And we'd be forced to endure more of this," I said. "I don't think I could stomach it. Maybe we can sneak in the back way through the palace garden."

We backtracked to the western entrance of the long, narrow strip of the garden, one of two such arms stretching away from the palace. The gate was closed, but unguarded, and it was not difficult to climb the low wall that separated the garden from the courtyard. To our relief, we found the garden deserted and quickly made our way to the palace steps. We were not so fortunate at the entrance, however, because the guards there refused to give us admittance.

"But you don't understand," I said. "We must speak to His Excellency immediately. It's urgent."

"His Excellency is indisposed," said one of the guards. "Go away or I'll have you arrested for trespassing."

I started to argue some more when I looked up and saw the Saur-El standing nearby—and I didn't like the way he was leering at Re-Aylah. "Well, well, well, what a pleasant surprise," he said when he recognized who we were. "Do I understand that you have business here?"

I hesitated a moment, but at that point I didn't think we had much to lose. "We believe that our family has been kidnapped," I said. "We're here to seek His Excellency's help."

Saur-El paused and almost smiled. "I'll take you to see His Excellency. I'm sure he would be glad to help reunite you with your family. This way."

I wasn't so naïve as to trust Saur-El. But since he was taking us where we wanted to go and we had little prospect of getting there otherwise, we didn't have much choice but to follow him. At the end of the long, arched corridor, we came to the throne room, which was brightly lit and filled with people, though it was unusual for His Excellency to be holding court at that hour. When we entered the domed chamber, however, we saw that Ben-Tubal would not be holding court anymore—not in the land of the living. The end of his reign had come at the end of a rope, for he was hanging from the ceiling with a noose around his neck. Ben-Tubal, the greatest ruler of the age, had died a most ignoble death.

Gleeful at seeing the shock on our faces, the Saur-El then sprang his second surprise, which in its own way, was just as bad, by saying, "May I present to you His Excellency Irad, son of Lamech, the new governor of the realm."

There sat Irad on the throne, having in the end far surpassed his lifelong ambition of being merely the Chief Elder of the Sethites. And in seeing him there, the full extent of our peril was revealed. Not only would we not be receiving any help from the governor, we had unwittingly begged admittance into the new stronghold of our enemies.

I had little doubt, though, that Irad's reign would be short-lived. For besides being seated on the throne with the heavily bejeweled scepter in his lap, he gave little appearance of being in charge of anything, including his own wits.

Scarcely able to believe my eyes, I said, "What have you done, Irad!"

"I—I," stammered Irad. "There were certain ... steps—necessary steps ..."

"Father, how could you?" said Re-Aylah in anguish.

Irad rose from his seat and gestured as if he were rehearsing the points of a speech. "The good of the people," he began. "Security is paramount ... An end of tyranny ..."

"Brilliant," said Saur-El sarcastically. "He'll make an outstanding governor, don't you think?"

Although Irad gradually moved closer to us, he didn't really seem to be speaking to us. With an endless string of rationalizations, he babbled on, "Return to prosperity ... Peace will be ours ... No need to fear ... A new order ..."

That was a dark moment indeed and I found that I could no longer suppress an awful doubt. It was one that had lurked undispelled in the back of my mind since I was a youth, though I feared to give it credence, and had grown worse as the times grew more evil. What if nothing happened after all? What if the scoffers had been right all along and my father was merely deluded? What if we had spent our lives in vain preparing for a disaster that would never come? And what if, worst of all, there was no way to stop the dominion of the Watchers?

"You don't look pleased," said the Saur-El in mock surprise. "You wanted to see His Excellency and now you've seen him. Oh yes, I remember. You also asked to be reunited with your family. And now it's time to accomplish that as well. And just in time, too. You will be part of the main attraction tonight." He turned to the guards and said, "Take them to the altar—except for you." Saur-El took hold of Re-Aylah's arm and added, "You can come with me. A beautiful flower like you deserves my special attention."

"Let go of me," said Re-Aylah, trying to wrench free of his grip.

"Get your hands off her!" I shouted and started toward him, but the guards restrained me from doing all that I intended to do.

"Please let me go with my husband," Re-Aylah pleaded. "I would rather die with him than be defiled by you."

"You want to die?" said Saur-El. "Oh, I have every intention of granting your wish. But there are ways of killing you that will bring me more pleasure than watching you be incinerated."

I've never been a violent man, but the thought of that sadist harming one hair on her head filled me with such rage that I struggled wildly to free myself and get my hands on him. But I never got the chance. Saur-El had mocked the babbling governor and turned his back on him at his own peril. For if there was anything that Irad could not tolerate, it was being humiliated. And if that weren't enough, his tormentor's unmasked intentions toward his daughter apparently re-kindled some last spark of fatherly concern. I didn't even see the blow come crashing down on Saur-

El's head—only that his eyes went suddenly wide. He toppled forward and as he fell face downward on the marble floor, I could see that Irad had struck him so hard with the scepter that some of the jewels had broken off and embedded in the back of the Saur-El's skull, sparkling in their new setting of liquid crimson.

This turn of events also caught the other guards completely by surprise. But in a moment they reacted, and Irad fell only a few feet away from Saur-El.

Re-Aylah rushed to her father's side as his life ebbed quickly away from a half dozen spear wounds. Looking up, he gasped, "I never meant for things to go this far. I'm sorry." And then he died.

NINETEEN

At that point, the guards seemed unsure what to do. A few wore the uniform of the Tower Guard, but most were holdovers from Ben-Tubal's palace servants, whose duties had always been mostly ceremonial. I suspected that most of them were as dismayed as we were about what had happened to their governor and had only been forced into the service of the new leaders through fear and intimidation. Among those who didn't seem to have their hearts in what they were doing, I recognized Dayak, the man who had helped me when Baldag kidnapped Re-Aylah.

Before we could use their hesitation or my acquaintance with Dayak to our advantage, however, the Watchers Semjaza and Azazel emerged from what used to be Ben-Tubal's private chamber. Semjaza was in a different body than when I had last seen him, but the air of authority in his unhuman expression and voice left no doubt who was speaking. "What's all this commotion? We left orders that we were not to be disturbed."

When Semjaza saw what had happened and recognized us he said, "The priest told us that he had dealt with this situation, but once again I see he has not. Why were we not informed?"

The guards all looked very uncomfortable at this question until finally one of the Tower Guards spoke up and said, "The Saur-El was handling the matter personally, Your Celestial Majesty. Apparently, he did not want to disturb your deliberations."

"What do you think we are deliberating about?" said Azazel.

"Their minds are limited," said Semjaza. "They do not understand that matters hang in a very delicate balance."

"Which we have only made more precarious by delaying what we should have done long ago," said Azazel.

"Killing the untouchable prematurely would have had consequences of its own," said Semjaza.

"But surely we cannot wait any longer," said Azazel.

"No, if there is a possibility that we miscalculated the omen, we have no choice but to act now," said Semjaza. "It is very fortuitous that they have come here instead of their sanctuary. Otherwise, carelessness could have proved to be our undoing. The Saur-El has paid for his lapse of judgment. And the Priest might be next if he isn't more diligent." Then he turned to the guard who had spoken and said, "You are Saur-El of the Tower Guard now. See that these prisoners are taken to the others and disposed of at once. Secure this area and get these bodies out of here. Understood?"

"Yes, Celestial Majesty," said the new Saur-El. His hardened visage made it hard to tell if he was pleased or alarmed by his promotion.

"Come, Azazel," said Semjaza. "Let us return to the Council and continue seeking the location and meaning of the omen as well as we may in this place. I am beginning to wonder if it was wise to leave the Tower of the Watch."

As soon as they were gone, the new Saur-El said, "All right, you heard the orders. Dayak, your squad will transport the prisoners to the holding room and inform the priests that the whole lot is to be dispatched at once. Guard them closely, because it'll be your life for theirs if anyone escapes. The rest of you, get this hall in order. The Sons of the Gods are in no mood to tolerate sloppiness!"

"We have to go," I said, gently lifting Re-Aylah from where she was still kneeling over the body of her father.

Surrounded by a squad of twenty spear-bearing men, we were escorted across the portico that led from the palace to the temple. I thought it ironic that the same path we had once trod to Father's triumphal speech on our first visit to Nephil was the same that now led to our impending execution.

Curiously enough, I noticed that Dayak, walking behind us, bore an expression that bordered on terror. I said quietly over my shoulder, "Judging by your face, I would have thought that you were on the opposite end of that spear."

"What do you expect from a man going to his death?" said Dayak.

"I thought we were the ones who were going to be killed," I said.

"No harm befalls you because you have a powerful magic," said Dayak. "Even the Watchers are worried. Doom awaits all who oppose you. And now mine is hanging over my head."

"I don't hold this against you, if that makes you feel any better," I said.

"If you're so concerned, why don't you help us instead?" suggested Shem.

"That would mean certain death as well," said Dayak, looking around at his fellow guards. "I'm doomed either way."

"A man is not doomed by fate, but by the choices he makes," said Shem. "Change your choices and you can change your destiny."

"And do it soon," I added. "One way or the other, time is running out."

Another guard spoke up and said to Dayak, "You shouldn't be talking that way with the prisoners. It might get reported and then you really will be in a fix."

We reached the side door of the temple and in an anteroom found our family, shaken but as yet unharmed. In fact, Father managed a smile as he said, "I am relieved to see that you all have made it back safely."

"I wouldn't exactly call this safe," I said. "They're getting ready to kill us because they think that by keeping us off the ark, they will prevent doom from falling on them. That's why Irad ..."

Then I remembered that Father did not yet know about his brother. "You do not need to say it," he said. "I see it in your faces."

"He died trying to save me," said Re-Aylah.

"There is some comfort in that," said Father. "And when time allows, we will mourn for him. But as for our enemies, they have underestimated the power of the Lord. He has a way of bringing their schemes down on their own heads."

The priests of the Morningstar cult led us down an idol-lined corridor, with Dayak's squad following closely behind. When Father saw the eagle he had carved long ago for Ben-Tubal sitting on one of the pedestals, he knocked it to the floor in disgust as he passed by.

"That'll cost you," said one of the guards.

"Leave him alone," said Dayak. "It was his to do with as he sees fit."

Emerging through the front entrance of the temple, we could see that the area between the temple and the altar was roped off from the crowds to provide a staging area for the sacrifices. Through this we were led and then up the ramp to the platform on top of the altar. The priests made us stand over the trap door, while Dayak and his men prevented any possibility of escape down the ramp. When the mob below realized that the next victims were going to be human instead of animal, it broke into a new crescendo of frenzy—and all the more seeing that it was the exasperating prophet.

As we stood there trapped and awaiting our execution, we could feel the intense heat rising up through the opening in the center, even though it was some fifteen feet away. On the opposite side of the chimney were Hura and

Sheshi. I wished that I could see Sheshi's eyes, to know if she had truly fallen back into the evil way. But she kept her head down and was too far away for me to get a good look at her.

Hura held in his hand a rope tied to the lever, giving him access to the mechanism while he moved about the platform. He took several steps toward us to make himself heard above the din of the crowd and the roar of the furnace. "Well, how convenient," he said, the madness in his face distorted by the shimmering heat. "I don't know how you contrived your escape, apostate. But now I'll have the pleasure of watching all of you die at once."

The crowd below began chanting, "Burn! Burn! Burn!"

"What do you think? Should I give them what they want?" said Hura, hoping that we would beg for mercy.

But he got no such satisfaction from us. In the face of what looked like certain death, we all felt a strange sense of peace. We gripped each other's hands and were not afraid.

"What we think is that you should renounce your master and plead for mercy from Almighty God," said Father. "This is your last chance!"

This was not the reaction Hura had been hoping for and he was greatly displeased to see that we were not cowering with fear. His hand lifted the rope, slowly and dramatically, and I braced myself for what was coming next. But before Hura could dispatch us into the furnace, Sheshi flew at him from behind. She hit him squarely in the back with all her force and the momentum carried them dangerously close to the top of the chimney. Hura yanked on the rope, either to stop himself or to take us down with him as his final act of wickedness—or perhaps both. But the rope was slack, apparently cut or untied by Sheshi when no one was watching. With one last effort, she twisted and pulled him after her into the flames.

"Sheshi!" I cried, but it was too late. They were gone in a blaze of white hot sparks. The stunned crowd gasped and fell silent.

"This is what she foresaw on the night she left Enoch-Nod," said Re-Aylah. "This is why she came back."

"She bought our lives with her own," said Father. "But if her sacrifice is not to be in vain, we should get back to the ark at once."

As we fumbled to get the gate open, the three other priests on the platform inexplicably leaped after the High Priest into the furnace—a symptom of madness or demon-possession, I suppose. Their screams nearly curdled our blood to hear them, but there was nothing we could do to prevent it.

When the gate opened, we turned to face Dayak. He hesitated for a moment before his fears completely unmanned him. He dropped his spear and fled down the ramp screaming, "We're all going to die! We're all going to die!"

Seeing all this must have unnerved the other guards as well, and they shrank back from us like they were seeing ghosts. We simply walked past them unhindered, like they weren't even there.

When we reached the bottom of the ramp, Father said, "Stay together." That command was unnecessary, however, for none of us would have dared to allow ourselves to become separated if it could be helped. We started forward, with Father in the lead and the rest of us following closely behind him. The crowd drew back in apprehension and murmured as we passed, "Stand back … Don't let them touch you—you'll be cursed … If you look them in the eye, you will die … Let the Watchers deal with them."

Thus we strode through the middle of the courtyard. And if our progress was not rapid, it was steady, and no one laid a hand on us. When we reached the other side, we found the boulevard running to the main gate relatively deserted. The night's debauchery had run its course and most of those outside of the hardcore courtyard revelers were sleeping off the effects of their dissipation.

By the time we reached the gate, the first rays of the last dawn were breaking over the eastern horizon. It was a normal sunrise just like any other, with nothing unusual to indicate that the end of the world was at hand.

TWENTY

The first object on the plain that the sunlight fell upon, because it was the tallest, was the ark. But between the gate and our goal lay a sea of stupefied bodies strewn across the plain in lewd, shameless repose. Before we started across, though, Shem received a vision. "I see Eden before me," he said. "And from Eden, a causeway spanning to a window in the heavens."

"I know that place!" I said. "I was there."

"The sentient animals are departing this world in vast numbers by way of the bridge," Shem continued. "I see Naysa and the behemoths."

"Departing?" said Ham. "Where could they possibly be going?"

"Their destination is closed to me," said Shem. "I cannot see beyond the window. Now the scene is changing. I see the East Gate. And look! There is Merib rushing across the valley. He means to force his way through the gate."

Jirah gasped and clapped her hand over her mouth. "Well, go on, Shem," said Ham. "Go on!"

A look of shock came over Shem's face and we could see that something was terribly wrong. "What is it?" I said. "Did something happen to Merib?"

"No. He is standing there bewildered."

"At what?"

"Paradise. It's ... it's gone."

"You mean you've lost the vision?" I asked.

"No," said Shem, shaking his head. "Paradise is no more. It has rolled up like a scroll and vanished from the face of the earth."

"What does that mean?" I said.

Shem answered gravely, "It means that the judgment is about to start."

Father hadn't waited to be told what it meant—he already knew. Before any of us realized what he was doing, he was running from camp to camp, trying to rouse the people.

Meanwhile, we heard a commotion behind us coming from the heart of the city. "I'd say that the Watchers have found out that we've escaped," said Ham. "And judging by the sound, they're not very happy about it."

"Come on, brothers," I shouted. "Let's get Father now, even if we have to carry him. Everyone else get to the ark as fast as you can."

"Repent!" Father screamed as he frantically leaped from person to person, pleading at the top of his voice. "Flee to the ark now! Doom is at hand! There will be no more delay!" Wherever he went, the people recoiled as if he had thrust a burning firebrand in their faces. But his pleas did little more than arouse them from their stupor, because their hardened hearts were too full of wickedness to lie idle for long. They rejected his final warning—just as they rejected all the others—and soon resumed their revelry with such reckless abandon that it seemed as if all previous indulgences had only whetted their appetites.

While we were still trying to catch up with Father, we heard another voice above his, emanating from the top of the main gate. I recognized it instantly as Semjaza's. By what craft or devilry he could make himself heard over the din, I do not know, but his voice seemed to carry over the whole Plain of Nephil. "People of the earth, listen to me!"

A hush fell over the crowd and Semjaza continued, "You have been summoned here today to usher in a new age—an age when you will have no more need of governors and no more need of laws. The gods themselves have come down from the heavens to dwell among you, to intermarry with you and teach you the way to live. Behold your gods!"

The Sons of the Gods stepped forward to the front of the wall, some two hundred of them in regal array—an awesome spectacle in the morning sun.

"You are our gods," the people chanted. "You are our gods."

Semjaza raised his arms to quiet the crowd and said, "This very day we will take wives from among you. They shall bear our offspring who will be gods like us. We will teach you our ways and your bliss will know no limits. Side by side, we will worship what we make together."

They brought forth a yearling bull calf—the same one, I presume, that was born when I was in the labyrinth of Enoch-Nod. Its hide was like polished gold, dazzling like a statue. But it was not a statue. It was, rather, a living thing, a grotesque monstrosity intended to usher in an epoch of abominations that could not be allowed to come to pass. Fire glowed from inside its eyes and mouth. And when it bellowed, like many horns blowing, the awestruck people prostrated themselves before the beast and worshiped it.

When Father paused to look, we took the opportunity to seize him. He resisted and we made little headway at first. But his fury was waning and Ham was a bull of a man in the peak of his strength. Step by step, we pulled and pushed and wrestled him toward the ark.

"The Sons of the Gods have been among you for long ages, watching over you for your good," Semjaza began again. "We have seen your misery. The ground is cursed and no longer yields its bounty for you. Your wombs are barren and the laughter of children is no longer heard in your villages. You labor from dawn until dusk and only by wearisome toil are you able to eke out the most meager living. Don't you think you have suffered long enough under the curse of the unjust god and his prophet Noah?"

At this, there were murmurs of assent from the crowd.

"Are you tired of enduring hunger and hardship while others prosper at your expense?"

This time, the people shouted in unison, "Yes!"

"Wouldn't you prefer to live in peace and happiness where food is plentiful and grack flows in rivers?"

"Yes!"

"Then hear this," said Semjaza. "One obstacle alone lays between you and a new golden age—the prophet of doom, the madman Noah. He is the High Prophet of the Terrible One who is plotting your destruction. Your freedom and your very lives depend on this: *If he or any of his offspring lives this day, you will all perish.*"

It was frightening to see how easily the Watcher manipulated the weak-minded mob to turn on us, even though it was common knowledge that the real oppression emanated from Enoch-Nod. But somehow the overwhelming force of Semjaza's mind made them suddenly see us as the cause of all their afflictions and they began screaming for our blood, "Kill them. Rid the earth of them! There they are!"

By then, we were climbing up the ramp of the ark. Father, crushed in spirit, was offering no further resistance. He practically collapsed in Mother's arms, spent from his exertion.

Over the noise of the frenzied crowd, I yelled, "Let's get that door shut now!" That order was unnecessary, though, because Shem and Ham were already at the ropes.

"Easy now," shouted Ham as we began hauling up the door. "A steady pull—don't panic. We've only got one shot at this."

With the mob rushing toward us, we put our backs into it and the door lifted off the ground. The critical point came at about eight feet when we heard a heartbreaking snap. The left guide pulley had broken loose. Ham sprawled backward as his rope went slack, but Shem and I were jerked forward as the door fell to the ground with a great thud.

"Well, that does it!" exclaimed Ham. "I told you all that this wouldn't work. We're finished now."

The menacing crowd had temporarily scattered, startled by the falling door. As they regrouped and began to advance again, Shem lifted his hands and eyes upward. "Lord, your servants have labored long and done all that you have commanded," he said. "See now our plight and rescue us from the hands of our enemies!"

The door began to rise—without anyone touching it. We stood back and watched in awe as the hand of the Lord himself shut us in. The portal slammed tight with jarring finality. All lots had been cast; the opportunity for the masses to escape destruction had passed.

I will confess that I was relieved and elated to be protected from the mob that was bent on killing us—until I looked at my father's face. Seeing that no one had heeded his decades of warnings dealt him a devastating blow. Mother, Re-Aylah and Ohlibah coaxed him like a sleepwalker up the ramps to his room where he fell facedown and wailed. Mother stayed by his side, but he refused to be comforted.

Meanwhile the mob outside was organizing itself against us. We could hear them testing the door as Ham, Shem and I hoisted two horizontal reinforcement beams against the door into slots that had been prepared for that purpose. I know that what the Lord had sealed, no one could have opened, but it made me feel better to have it in place anyway.

Since the lower and middle levels of the ark were completely blind, we climbed the ramps to the upper deck and looked through the narrow window slits to see what was happening. Shem stood next to me and Re-Aylah soon joined us, while Ham tried to comfort Jirah in their room. The mob pushed against the side of the ark by the thousands until it began to rock. Those in front screamed as they were crushed by the masses surging from behind. They finally managed to lift the ark a few feet off the ground, but couldn't get enough people under it to push any higher. They didn't know that was a futile pursuit. The ark had been constructed to make tipping a virtual impossibility. It would always right itself, no matter how high the waves— or any other force—lifted it. Even with so many pushing, they would never be able to overturn it. When they lost their momentum, the ark fell down again, crushing untold numbers of people underneath.

When they realized those efforts would not avail, I heard the Watcher called Azazel shout, "Why not burn them out instead!"

The mob had to search far and wide to find fuel, because every easy-to-find stick for miles had already been consumed in their campfires. Even so, with so many looking, they found enough combustible material within a few minutes to kindle a small fire against the side of the ark.

"Father knew what he was doing when he had us dispose of the extra lumber," I said to Re-Aylah. "It's going to take a bigger fire than that to ignite the gopherwood."

"Don't underestimate the power of the Watchers," said Shem. "Remember, they can conjure strange fire if they want—probably even at a distance."

"I don't think they'll have to," said Re-Aylah, sniffing the air. "I know that smell—it's hot pitch. It won't take a supernatural fire to ignite that!"

"She's right, Shem," I said. "When that fire gets hot enough, it could set the whole ark ablaze. What are we going to do?"

"What we should always do," Shem said. "Trust in the Lord."

The words were hardly out of his mouth, when a bright light flashed overhead and a blazing ball of fire streaked across the sky from west to east. Although nobody had known, including the Watchers, where the comet had been hidden for the past week, no one had to wonder anymore. It disappeared from sight, but not before many smaller pieces broke off of the main body and scattered in every direction. The startled crowd ceased its attack and a tense silence ensued.

A few seconds later, hot drops of water, scattered in the wake of the comet, began falling from the clear sky. The people began to dance around, for they had never seen anything like rain before. "This is it?" they said, trying to laugh off their fears. "This is the disaster they tried to frighten us of? Their god is weak. He can't harm us. The Sons of the Gods will protect us. We need more fuel. Bring anything that will burn."

Then someone put an end to their demented jubilee by shouting, "Look! Enoch-Nod is on fire."

Away on the southeastern horizon we could see a column of smoke rising into the air. It must have been a colossal fire to be visible so many hundreds of miles away.

"I think the Watchers outsmarted themselves trying to calculate the meaning of the comet," said Shem. "That comet wasn't just a portent of doom. It was the doom itself—at least the start of it. The judgment has begun."

"It's only fitting that the first blow should fall upon the Tower of the Watch," I said. "And if it was indeed the Watcher's portal between the realms, I wonder if their path of escape didn't just get cut off."

"The Lord lured them out of their stronghold through their own arrogance," said Shem. "And now he will destroy them."

"Look out!" said Re-Aylah, perceiving a peril from our vantage point fifty feet above the plain that the mob on the ground below could not—the ground was moving like a wave and the force of it was practically upon us. "Brace yourselves!"

Though we grabbed the sill with both hands, we were still thrown to the floor when the earthquake hit. Like being in the belly of some monstrous beast, the timbers around us growled as the ground shifted beneath us, but the structure remained secure.

When the quake passed, we looked around and saw that while we were shaken, none of us was injured. The same could not be said for the mob below. Many were on the ground, writhing in pain, injured either by the earthquake or trampled by the frightened crowd. As they realized that their doom was upon them, panic had broken loose among the people. They ran in every direction, not knowing where to hide from the wrath of God.

In my life, there have been occasions more numerous than I care to remember when I have heard cries of pain, wails of mourning and even the gasps of death. But I swear and attest that all those sounds, pitiful and gut-wrenching as they may have been, were but infant whimpers compared to the screams of the terror-stricken when the disaster struck that day. Even after all these years, to recall that scene still chills the marrow in my bones.

The Watchers clung to the parapet, trying to restore order, though no one paid any more attention to them. But although the wall had somehow survived the first onslaught, it did not survive the second, because the comet and the earthquake had only been a prelude to the calamity yet to come. Suddenly, a great fissure opened up along the base of the wall of Nephil. Before the Watchers could react, the wall collapsed into the chasm. Their physical bodies—for which they had forsaken their heavenly realm—proved their undoing in the end. Unable to escape the prisons of the flesh in time, they found themselves subject to the same limitations as everyone else. The earth swallowed them up, so that they went down alive into the Abyss, just as the Prophet had foretold. As far as I know, they remain there still.

Fissures like that one opened up far and wide, so that the face of the land cracked like pottery that has cooled too fast. Then the fountains of the great deep burst forth through the cracks with a series of great concussions, spewing fire, water, smoke and ash thousands of feet into the air. The force of the blast created an updraft that drew in a hard wind from every direction, sucking great quantities of debris across the Plain and up blowing it aloft. By that time, we could not make ourselves heard, even by yelling, above the roar of the eruption. I was thankful, though, that the noise spared me from hearing the agonizing screams of the survivors below. The ash from the eruptions turned the azure sky to black, blotting out the light from the sun. The heavier rocks fell back to the earth with devastating results for those unfortunate enough to be in their path. Some hit the ark with such force that it made me wonder whether we would survive after all.

A brilliant light flashed inside the dirty billows of smoke, momentarily casting an eerie purplish hue upon the interior of the ark. This was followed immediately by a sound so loud that it made me jump back, for I had never heard thunder before.

Neither had I seen rain, but I saw it then. First it started lightly and was barely distinguishable from the ash. In a moment, though, the sky collapsed as if the very floodgates of the heavens had been thrown open. The water from the sky met the fire and water spewing forth from the earth with great fury. The wind suddenly shifted downward and outward across the Plain with gusts so violent that we were instantly soaked. The lightning struck ferociously, jagged fingers crackling in every corner of sky and earth. Thunder boomed over the rumble of the eruption in a building crescendo as molten rocks screamed and hissed and exploded all around us in the maelstrom.

Recoiling from the fury, we staggered backward from the wind howling through the windows. With our backs to the interior wall, Re-Aylah and I clung to each other, her head buried in my shoulder and mine in her hair, cowering in fear next to Shem and Ohlibah as the cataclysm intensified. Between gusts, I could hear Jirah screaming hysterically in her room, "Make it stop! We're all going to die!"

Just when I thought that the ark would surely be broken to splinters and us along with it, Father appeared in the doorway of his room with Mother at his side. Haggard as he looked, his presence still gave us strength and new hope. He knelt in front of us and said in a voice that boomed above the storm, "Take heart. The Lord has promised me that we will surely not die. He will deliver us from doom. Together, we will make a new world!"

His calm assurance comforted our fears. Even as he spoke the words, the wind began to abate. Wet and cold and trembling, we thanked God to be alive.

By then, we were so completely spent that it defies description. It was as if the weariness of all the years of toil and hardship descended upon us at once. Realizing that we were no longer in immediate peril, we could bear it no more and retired to our rooms while the terrific storm raged outside.

The afternoon was waning when I awoke to find the rain from the heavens prevailing over the fountains of the great deep. Pulling away from Re-Aylah, I struggled to my feet and crossed out of our room to the window. Though it did not completely quench the fire and steam spewing into the sky, the mighty deluge at least washed the air clean enough so that we could breathe a little easier. My thoughts turned, sadly, to all that lay outside of the ark. Re-Aylah followed and stood by my side. Occasionally, when the lightning happened to flash at just the right moment between the heaviest of the torrents, we could see the ruins of the city in the distance.

"It's hard to believe it's all gone," said Re-Aylah.

"Nephil was beautiful," I said. "In a way, it represented some of the best that man is capable of."

"And some of the worst," said Re-Aylah.

"True, but I will miss Ben-Tubal anyway," I said. "And no doubt Merib perished, too, all alone out there where Paradise used to be. Now it's gone, too."

"And my father and all my family," said Re-Aylah.

"Let's not forget Sheshi, either," I said. "And all the other countless souls who met their fate today—Sethites, Nephilim, Nodites and everyone else. Even though they opposed us, they were still our brothers and sisters."

"All lost in a single, terrible day," said Re-Aylah. "It's impossible to comprehend."

I shook my head and felt a sudden stab of guilt. "What I don't understand is why I was saved when everyone else was lost," I said.

"But you spent your whole life building this ark—"

"But I'm not the best of men. You know better than anyone my flaws and shortcomings and how I've struggled with my faith all my life. Why was I spared when they weren't?"

Re-Aylah turned my face toward her with her hands and said, "Don't torture yourself that way, Love. We weren't saved because we deserved it. We were just the only ones who took advantage of God's gracious provision for escape. We got on board the ark. That's all. Don't make it harder than it needs to be."

From time to time, when I am haunted with grief and guilt because I survived when everyone else perished, I think about the answer that Re-Aylah offered that day. And when I am tempted to think more highly of myself than I ought to because I did survive, I check my pride with those same words. It was a truth—as all truth seems to be—that was profound in its simplicity: We got on board the ark. I would never be a spiritual giant like my father, but in the end, I had just enough faith to do that.

Re-Aylah's arm encircled my waist and she laid her head on my shoulder as we stared out the window. The poor visibility through the storm spared us from seeing most of the carnage that we knew surrounded us. The faint glow of the clouds between lightning flashes indicated that somewhere— behind all of that fury—the sun was setting in the west as it had every evening since Creation. I took some small solace in knowing that there were still some things and some places that lay beyond the reach of all that death and destruction.

Below us, the surface of the land was already indistinguishable through the standing water. In one place, though, I could faintly make out the small rise where I used to pitch my tent. I hadn't ever given much thought to that patch of ground before. Compared to some of the other places I had seen in my life, I hadn't considered it to be particularly remarkable. But as I stared, I was suddenly overwhelmed with emotion. That humble plot would be my last glimpse of the ancient world. I hung my head and mourned for all that was lost.

EPILOGUE

And so it was that all we had known passed into oblivion, with only the eight human survivors on the ark left to keep the memories alive. These writings are but a poor reflection of the wonders of the former age and the horrors of its last days. But alas, all who might have written more eloquently perished in the Flood. In their absence, I have done my best to provide an eyewitness account of all that transpired.

What lay ahead, we did not know. Water inundated all the land and darkness shrouded the face of the deep—much like it was said to be in the beginning. A second creation was coming and it was up to this remnant to start over and establish a new world.

As this realization began to sink in, it seemed more daunting than even building the ark had been. I have not hesitated to recount the weaknesses and foibles of this family—and most especially my own. How we could accomplish such an unimagineable task I could not comprehend. Even so, in facing such an extraordinary undertaking, I drew strength from the memories of all the adversity we had already overcome and found comfort in our love for each other, our hope for a better future and our faith in the God who had saved us from doom.

www.ingramcontent.com/pod-product-compliance
Lightning Source LLC
Chambersburg PA
CBHW021336310726
48971CB00001B/147